THE LAST TRAIN FROM PARIS

JULIET GREENWOOD

Storm
PUBLISHING

Ebook ISBN: 978-1-80508-285-9
Paperback ISBN: 978-1-80508-287-3

Cover design: Eileen Carey
Cover images: iStock, Shutterstock

Published by Storm Publishing.
For further information, visit:
www.stormpublishing.co

ALSO BY JULIET GREENWOOD

The Shakespeare Sisters
The Last Train from Paris

The Girl with the Silver Clasp
The Ferryman's Daughter
The White Camelia
We That are Left
Eden's Garden

For my mother, who taught me more about war than anyone.

Et aussi pour Christophe, Anne et Gabrielle

PART 1

ONE

IRIS

Cornwall, 1964

It was always the same, whenever she came over the brow of the hill leading to St Mabon's Cove.

Iris pulled her Mini Minor into the lay-by and stepped out, drawing salt air deep into her lungs, stretching her shoulders after the long drive from London. Before her, the sea spread out in undulating blue, turning to a deeper green in patches, edged with the brief rush of white against the cliffs of the north Cornwall coast. A haze of cloud gathered towards the horizon, obscuring where water met air, strafed by rays of luminous gold. Every time she stopped here, in the moments before she burst back into the complexity of family life, she felt the calm and the beauty steal inside her, relaxing every fibre of her body.

But not today. Iris shivered in the evening breeze, reaching into the back seat for her swing coat dating from before the war, which enveloped the shortness of her favourite Mary Quant dress, covering her body to halfway down her calves. The deep blue velvet of the coat had worn thin in places, and retained hints of mothballs and old wardrobes, but had still been a prize trawl from Portobello market.

This time she could not relax. This time she was finally going to find an answer. A knot formed deep in her belly. Her mother always avoided questions about the past. As a child, Iris had hated seeing the pain in her mother's eyes when she asked – the way Mum changed the subject, leaving her feeling lost and ignored.

France, 1939.

The words burned into her brain.

Growing up, Iris had heard other adults in St Mabon's go over their memories of the war again and again, the most intensely lived six years of their lives, with the bombings, the rationing, the constant fear of invasion and the mourning for those who'd been killed. But not Mum, who'd lost everything when her home had been destroyed, and who couldn't bear to watch war films like *The Cruel Sea,* or *Odette* or even the more domestic drama of *Mrs Miniver.*

Iris's father, being American, hadn't been expected to share the memories of Cornwall at war and, not having even been a GI, remained an unexplained oddity in St Mabon's, considered unlikely to share the real wartime heroics of Hollywood stars like Jimmy Stewart and Clark Gable. Love had brought him to Cornwall, he always declared. Love of Mum. Love of Iris. That was all anyone needed to know.

But she *did* need to know. Iris pulled her coat tight around her. Now, more than ever, she needed to understand. It was why she had come a few days early while her father was still working abroad, so she could ask questions when it was just her and Mum, as it had been in her earliest memories, before Dad came to join them.

France, 1939.

The words had jumped out at her when she'd first seen her certificate of adoption. No mother, no father, no hint of who she might have been, or even an exact place of birth. It seemed such a bleak statement of her existence when she had sat in her bedsit in London, finally holding the copy in her hands.

France, 1939. She'd been born the year war was declared, in a country that, unlike Cornwall, had endured the agony of invasion, of total war. The realisation had sent her obsessively hunting for photographs of France in the nearest library. They had shown aerial views of whole towns obliterated, fields turned to mud and streams of human beings of all ages, from the hunched-over elderly to the wide-eyed bewilderment of small children. Some pushed carts, others prams laden with belongings; refugees heading into the unknown. Iris had read with increasing horror the accounts of survivors hiding in ditches when the enemy aircraft came, bullets thudding into the earth around them, life hanging by the frailest thread.

She read of children lost in the chaos of a sudden exodus, some never to be found, and the women raped, or forced to exchange sex for the faintest chance of survival. One photograph had been taken in the aftermath of an aeroplane attack, the bodies of women and children strewn across an endless roadway sending a deep chill through her veins.

Was that place of utter suffering and destruction where she'd come from? She'd always known she was adopted, but seeing Mum and Dad named on an official document had made it real. The adoption certificate was dated 1950, five years after the war had ended. But surely she had clear memories of Mum during the war? Along with Land Girls and gas masks and terror that the smallest chink of light might escape through the blackout curtains as bombers droned above them in the dark.

Mum and St Mabon's. That was how it had always been. Except, over the past months as she began her studies at the University of London, that security had begun to fall apart, allowing other images to hover at the edges of her mind. Terrifying echoes, of screams and the roar of engines, and the taste of blood in her mouth. Maybe real, maybe not, but coming ever closer. The photographs of the haunted faces of concentration-camp survivors and huddled bodies left where they had fallen had begun to cluster, ghost-like, at the edges of her dreams.

She could put it off no longer, however much Mum might wish to avoid the subject. For her own sanity – maybe even for the choices she would make for the future – she had to know the secrets in her past that no one would tell her.

'I need to know who I am,' she murmured to the softly gilded horizon as she returned to the car and set out once more along the winding lanes towards home. 'And if anyone I once loved is still alive out there somewhere. Whoever they are.'

'Mum?'

Hope Cottage was silent. The windows had been opened in the living room to let in the spring breeze, stirring the sheafs of music on the upright piano into life.

There was a stretching and a yawning from one of the armchairs near the unlit fire, followed by a large tortoiseshell cat leaping down to rub herself ingratiatingly against Iris's Doc Marten boots.

'Hello Piaf.' She bent down to tickle the cat's head, which instantly butted against her hand. 'No, I don't have any Friskies. You'll have to wait.' Piaf purred louder. 'You can live in expecta-tion. Come on, let's find her.' Bored now there was no sign of a tin opener making its appearance, Piaf abandoned her purr and led the way through the open French windows onto the grass. Despite overlooking the sea, the garden was sheltered by shrubs and trees, planted by generations of occupiers to preserve the more delicate plants, not to mention the humans, from the salt winds of summer and the wild battering of winter storms.

Spring was turning towards summer, with rampant forget-me-knots filling the borders, interspersed with the last of the primroses and the first hint of bluebells. Piaf stepped delicately through the grass, leading the way towards Mum's favourite chaise longue, its metal frame softened by cushions, a tartan travelling rug keeping her warm. A half-finished cup of tea stood on a low table next to an ornate metal biscuit tin Iris couldn't remember seeing before, decorated with art deco designs and rusting slightly at the edges.

'Mum?' she said gently. The face beneath the flickering shade from the bare branches of the Victoria plum looked so peaceful, so free from her all-too-frequent pain, that Iris hadn't the heart to disturb her.

A breeze gusted in from the sea, stirring her mother's hair cropped close around her face, dislodging a piece of paper in her hands. Iris caught it as it fell. The postcard was old, its colours faded and the edges moth-eaten, but there was no mistaking the Eiffel Tower rising up against the skyline. Despite choosing to study French for her degree, Iris had never been to Paris, but she'd seen that view a thousand times in books and photographs. Some of the pictures she'd seen in the library showed Hitler parading through the streets after Paris had been occupied; in one he posed in front of the Eiffel Tower itself. Curious, Iris turned the postcard over. There was no address, no message, no signature. Just one word, scrawled in faded pencil. She peered closer, trying to make it out.

'I'll have that back.'

'Mum!' Her mother was sitting up, watching her intently. 'I was worried it'd fall on the grass and be trodden on.'

'Well, it's safe now.' She put the postcard back in the tin. 'I wasn't expecting you until later, darling.'

'My lecture was cancelled, I managed to get away early.'

'That's good.' Her mother smiled. She looked tired, great rings around her eyes as if she'd barely slept for days. 'You're looking well, darling. London suits you.'

'I suppose it does,' Iris replied carefully, not wanting to

offend, or suggest Mum's beloved St Mabon's had become too small for her.

'Of course it does, London's a place for the young. I once thought I'd never leave.' As her mother rose to embrace her, Iris's heart clenched at the feel of the skeleton beneath the frame, but the arms that held her had regained some of their old strength. Maybe Mum was going to be all right after all, she prayed inwardly, kissing the hollowness of her cheek and breathing in the familiar scent of the Eau de Cologne from the bottle with its distinctive green and gold label that always took pride of place in the bathroom cabinet.

'I'm always glad to come home,' she said.

Mum sighed wistfully. 'It hasn't been just you and me for so long, darling, and you never know when we might get the chance again.'

'There'll be plenty of chances,' said Iris, squashing a sense of unease. Her mother was still eyeing her with intensity, as if trying to fix her face as it was now, dappled with the last of the sunlight beneath the branches, seeking to hold it within her memory forever. 'I know you never want any fuss, but I've brought a Battenberg cake. Shop bought, I'm afraid.'

Her mother laughed, eyes sparkling, the creases around them deeper than before, but animating her face with sudden delight. 'My favourite. They're always so fiddly to make. Thank you darling. Come on, let's get you settled. Your room's ready, you can settle in while I make a pot of tea.'

'Mum—'

'Don't.' Her mother turned away, folding the blanket neatly on the cushions. 'Not yet, darling. It's so good to have you back with me. But not yet.'

So she'd guessed. The moment she had known Iris needed to present a copy of her adoption certificate as part of her application for a passport, Mum must have realised the questions would come thick and fast, and she wouldn't be able to put off the answers any longer. Sadness coursed through Iris. For as long as she could remember, her mum had protected her. It was strange now to want to protect her in turn. But, for all her fierce care, Mum had let her go. It had never struck Iris before how much her mother, even more than her father, had always encouraged her to spread her wings, to defy the convention that condemned as unladylike her ambition to study foreign languages and work for the UN, promoting peace and equality throughout the world. Instead, Mum had always encouraged her to fly as high as she could go. To follow her dreams.

Guilt shot through her. How could she repay her with the hurt she could already see gathering in the tautness of her thin face? But it was already too late. It was there hanging between them; they both knew it could never be so deeply hidden again.

As they turned towards the house, Mum reached for the art deco tin, and paused. 'Perhaps you'd like to bring that in, sweetheart. In fact, why don't you put it in your room for safekeeping? It's been in the loft for so long, I'm not sure I want Dad to put it up there again.'

'Yes, of course.' The tin was light. Nothing shook or rattled in its depths.

'No jewels, I'm afraid.' Mum's smile was gentle, tinged with sadness. 'It's things of the heart that count in the end. You learn that when you've lost everything, however much you gain in the future. I was thinking you might like to take it with you when you go.'

'Yes, of course, Mum. I'd love to.'

'Good.' A shadow passed across her mother's face, a kind of longing Iris couldn't quite read.

'I can leave it here and look at it when I visit,' Iris said.

Her mum shook her head. 'It's yours. It's not mine any longer. I've kept it too long. It's time for you to take it. Bring the cushions as well, would you, darling? The tide has turned, the dew will spoil them.'

. . .

Later that night, after an evening of dancing around the questions hanging in the air, Iris washed her face and cleaned her teeth in the bathroom on the second floor, next to her parents' bedroom, before retreating upstairs to her own room beneath the eaves.

'Good night, darling,' called her mother as she made her way to bed. Always with a tumbler of water covered with a piece of embroidered linen weighed down by an edging of beads that clinked gently against the glass, book in the other hand and reading glasses in the pocket of her dressing gown.

'Good night,' Iris called back. Curiosity overcoming her, she took the biscuit tin and climbed into bed. Propping herself up against the pillows, she settled the tin on the familiar flowered pattern of her childhood quilt and opened it carefully. Inside were a series of pale envelopes, darkened at the edges with age, stacked up against each other. Some had red English stamps; old ones, before the Queen's time, adorned with the face of George VI. Others were blue stamps she didn't recognise. They rested on a piece of ivory-coloured wool, lacy with an intricate pattern, but fine enough to be warm. She'd seen something similar while admiring her friend Susan's new baby, wrapped up carefully in its new shawl. A tingling began in her toes, creeping up towards her belly. She suddenly had an unaccountable urge to run.

She shut the tin hastily, placing it on the floor out of sight, trying to remove the feeling. Around her the house settled down into its old remembered silence. The familiar smell of Lux soap flakes rose from the sheets and blankets to mingle with the richness of beeswax furniture polish. Iris opened a side window, leaning out into the dusk turning towards darkness, sending large blooms of rhododendron into shadow. The scent of bluebells mixed with an early rose hung in the air, along with a hint of newly mown grass. In the distant woods an owl called; something rustled in the undergrowth. A hedgehog trundled across the lawn in search of slugs and worms, while pipistrelle bats swooped in the night air, chasing the myriad of insects.

These were the sounds and scents of her childhood she'd almost forgotten in the new world of Carnaby Street, of pulsating music and daring, bright colours. Tonight they swept back around her, no longer reassuring but fragile, as if painted on rice paper, easily torn away.

That night, the dreams came again. She was trapped, caught and submerged in darkness, too rigid to move, the world at an impossible distance, too far, far too far to return, her ears filled with the sound of weeping.

Iris shot up in bed, gasping, reaching vainly for the light, bewildered in the darkness. It was all right. She wasn't in her bedsit in London, she was at Hope Cottage, the switch for the lamp was on the bedside table, not the wall behind the bed. Panic began to subside. On the floor below she heard the toilet flush followed by the padding of her mother's slippers back to her room, then the creak of the springs as she settled into bed.

Iris switched on her bedside lamp, dreading any return to sleep. Moving slowly so as not to disturb her mother, she reached once more for the biscuit tin. Gently, she pulled out the first envelope. It was torn and stained with water, obscuring the address. She eased out the small pieces of white paper, faded and moth-eaten at the edges and covered in close handwriting, as if as much as possible had been squeezed onto one sheet. Was this Mum? Or perhaps an unknown lover, hearts poured out to each other within the inviolable privacy of a sealed envelope? It felt excruciatingly personal, like overhearing your parents having sex. She hastily shoved the paper out of sight back into its envelope.

Down in the hallway, the clock struck the hour. As she replaced the envelope, another fell back. Her eye fell on the stamps. *Postes*, they declared. French stamps. Her heart began to beat fast, the knot in her belly tightening even closer.

Iris pulled out a slightly larger envelope, this one was filled with photographs, some black and white, others sepia. People she didn't recognise wearing old-fashioned clothes in cafés and city streets with a definite continental appearance, tables set on pavements and shutters at the windows. One showed a woman, face turned away, gazing up towards snowclad mountains. Were these her past? If so, there was no indication as to how, or why. Disappointment surged through her. Perhaps Mum had no intention of relinquishing her secrets after all.

The last photograph was smaller and more faded than the rest, blurred down one side by what looked like a water stain. Iris could make out a terraced house, a man and woman, arms linked, standing on the front step. Their clothes were even more old-fashioned, the man in a suit, the woman in a low-waisted dress. The hairs began to rise on the back of her neck. Surely they must be Mum's parents, in the house that had been obliterated, like so many, during the terror of the blitz. Like the photographs of the fleeing French refugees, it was a terrible past suddenly made real. Personal. The love, like a hundred thousand others, that had been lost amidst the cruelty of war.

Iris opened another envelope, a little gingerly this time, half dreading what she might find. But there were only postcards, the first a black and white image of St Paul's Cathedral, the second of Trafalgar Square. The third, labelled '*les petits bateaux*', showed miniature boats being floated by a crowd of children on a large circular pond in the Jardin des Tuileries.

The final postcard glowed with the vivid Technicolor of Hollywood films. Tall half-timbered buildings with shutters and tiled roofs, flowers tumbling from window boxes. The kind of timeless place found in fairy tales. 'Colmar' was printed against the blue of the sky, while in one corner a small red and yellow shield had been superimposed, the yellow stripe at the top stating 'Alsace'. She'd learnt about Alsace-Lorraine at school, the part of France forever caught on the front line with Germany, fiercely proud of its identity, but also horribly vulnerable. Just like the photographs and postcards, there was no writing to be seen and there was no sign it had ever been posted.

Iris reached into the box, searching for the faded image of the Eiffel Tower Mum had taken from her. It had fallen right to the bottom. As she pulled it out, she could see something scrawled on the back in pencil. It had not been her imagination. In the lamplight, she could make out a single word.

'Forgive.'

TWO

SABINE

Paris, 1938

Sabine Schongauer folded up the letter in her hand with a smile, placing it on the café table as she returned to her abandoned *café au lait*.

Opposite, her husband Emil was still absorbed in his own missive, dark brows pulled together in the brooding concentration that always reminded her of Gary Cooper in the American movie *A Farewell to Arms*. Even after nearly six months of marriage, that look still had the power to turn the hairs on her arms tingling with anticipation. She restrained the familiar urge to touch him, to call his attention back to her, to see the desire in his eyes as he absorbed her presence, which always prompted the afternoon to end in the ancient bed, their passionate love-making held within the heat of their tiny attic apartment.

Sabine leant back in her chair cradling her cup in her hands. She turned her attention instead to the purposeful walk of passers-by, mingled with conversations from the café tables in both French and English with a smattering of German, accompanied by the rise and fall of languages she could barely recognise. Even though she'd lived in Paris for nearly three years, she still drew in the vibrancy of the city as if it were her life blood. She couldn't imagine living without the everchanging mix of cultures of the City of Light. She had felt herself thrive as never before amongst the sense that all the world could be found here, drawn together by the capital's historic beauty and the understanding that here, all things were possible.

She knew Emil felt the same. It had been the intensity of his passion to escape the provincial expectations of his family in Colmar, in faraway Alsace on the border with Germany, that had attracted her attention on the first day of their journalism class. Even then, she'd felt it mirror her own flight from her quiet country upbringing just outside Paris, where little changed from generation to generation. It had been an instant meeting of minds, a fiery attraction of body and soul that had, within weeks, consumed them both. It had fed their ambition too, leading them both to become the leading lights of their class, predicted to have bright futures in the world of newspapers and magazines.

Around them, the little pavement café in the eighth arrondissement was beginning to fill up with afternoon customers. Many of those sipping coffee or lingering over their wine were familiar to Sabine. But with its tantalising glimpse of the Eiffel Tower and the promise of the nearby Arc de Triomphe and the Avenue des Champs-Elysées, the regulars were interspersed with tourists who flocked there every summer. The Americans at the next table were enthusing loudly over the grandeur of that morning's visit to the Château de Versailles. With her almost fluent English, Sabine followed their conversation easily, as they drank their coffee and *citron limonade* while pouring over their guidebooks and map of the Métro, arguing over the best route to the white dome of Sacré-Coeur in the eighteenth arrondissement, to explore the cobbled alleyways of bohemian Montmartre.

'England?' Emil finally looked up from his letter, eyes falling on the envelope next to Sabine. 'Who on earth's writing to you from England?'

'My friend,' replied Sabine, dragging her mind from concentrating on understanding English to return to her mother tongue. 'The one I met when I gave that talk in London last year. She has a request.'

'London? *Londres?*' A hungry look came over Emil's chiselled features, as it always did when the subject of the city of Shakespeare and Dickens arose. Victor Hugo, Dostoevsky and Kafka might be his role models, but Shakespeare and Dickens were his true idols. She had understood how much effort it had taken for him to swallow his disappointment when she'd been the one in their class selected for a month's work experience at *The London Evening Standard.* She'd been astonished when the English paper had accepted her article on the London chef Rosa Lewis, famed for her French style of cooking, who'd risen from obscurity to become the owner of the Cavendish Hotel. That single article had given her the opportunity of a lifetime to work on a real English paper.

In the end, Emil had supported her. She would be eternally grateful for his pride in this accolade of her ability to write as fluently in English as in French, with her German not far behind. More than that, it had confirmed her trust that, despite his own ambition to use journalism as a gateway into making a name for himself through newspapers and magazines, ready to launch his great novel on the world, Emil respected her wish to be more than simply a housewife.

'So?' demanded Emil. 'What does she want, this Nancy?'

'Nora,' corrected Sabine, rather sharper than she'd intended, irritated by Emil's dismissive tone. 'Her name's Nora. She's asking about chef-training courses in Paris.'

'An English girl become a chef? When English cooking is so terrible?'

'Nora works in a French restaurant, so she understands cooking.'

'Near the Ritz?' said Emil, showing an interest. 'Buckingham Palace?'

'Further out,' replied Sabine. 'Not far from Hampton Court,' she added, fairly certain Emil had no idea where Hammersmith, or even Richmond, might be. 'She changed shifts and travelled all the way into central London to hear me talk about Rosa Lewis. She has a passion.' She smiled, trying to lighten the mood that always darkened when Emil communicated with his family in Colmar. 'Perhaps there's hope for the English palate after all.'

'Hm,' grunted Emil, returning to his letter.

Sabine watched him, absorbed in his brother's words, blocking her out entirely. Sometimes, for all their closeness, she didn't understand Emil at all. There was some part of him that remained outside her grasp, even after the most intimate of moments, when their bodies had opened up completely to each other, nothing held back, nothing secret. And yet, there was something there. Perhaps even Emil himself remained unaware of its presence.

It had been his ambition that had struck her with the greatest force after their marriage, now he was no longer wooing her into spending her life inextricably entwined with his, and they were barely apart. These last weeks she'd watched him as he slept, sprawled on his back in the relaxation of the body after sex, but the tension never quite leaving the crease where his eyebrows met. Emil's ambition terrified her at times with its single-mindedness. Even more so since he'd finally permitted her to read parts of the novel he was bashing out on the typewriter perched on the table in their barest excuse for a kitchen. How do you doubt someone you love? How do you reassure him, when the sentences fail to move you, when there's a whisper in your heart, born of your own excoriating self-criticism, that his words are grandiose, self-absorbed and quite probably unpublishable?

She was being unfair, she scolded herself. He was at the start of his career, everyone has to learn, even those who are eventually recognised as geniuses. The tutors on their course agreed he was a good student and an accurate reporter. After all, wasn't that how Dickens had started out? And wasn't there so much material for truly serious fiction in an examination of the human condition? Where Dickens had thundered the evils of Chancery and the Circumlocution Office and the humiliations of the debtors' prison, Emil Schongauer was determined to expose the foolishness of the provincial world, unable to see outside its own petty concerns.

Sabine had an uneasy feeling that he might also dismiss as petty the domestic life of the female sex, if it featured at all in his work. Emil's manuscripts were filled with exclusively male acts of heroism and intellectual debate. But then who was she to judge? She was hardly a woman of the people, being the daughter of an ancient family unable to keep up with the times, now barely clinging to their land and tumbledown chateau. Besides, her formal education was minimal, supplemented only by the curiosity and love of reading that had been encouraged by Mémé, her grandmother. An intellectual she most definitely was not. Her mind blanked over at Emil's patient explanations of the ideas of Immanuel Kant, Heidegger and Nietzsche. She tried not to notice the somewhat self-satisfied expression on his face as he attempted to make good her ignorance.

'How is your brother?' asked Sabine, blocking out such treacherous thoughts. Every marriage had its drawbacks and its difficulties. They were only just getting to know each other. There was still room for them to adjust to each other. Hadn't they agreed they'd always support each other and let each other grow? She might not know much of the world, but she understood that compromise was rare in a husband, most of whom expected their wives to fit in with their lives, as if women had no inner world of their own.

'Albert says the shop is struggling more than ever,' said Emil, without looking up. 'This damned recession has hit Colmar as badly as everywhere else.' His tone was bitter. 'It means there's not much of a market for boots. So the finest boot-makers go under first before those who cut corners.'

'There must be a way—'

'Albert's already thought of it. He's talking about making high-end walking boots for the rich who go through Alsace on their way to Switzerland or the Austrian Alps. They still have money. It means investing in new equipment. Maman agrees. She always agrees with Albert, like she did with Papa when he was alive. Albert knows that.'

'I'm sure he's doing it for the best of reasons,' said Sabine. A knot twisted deep in her belly. It was all very well marrying for passion on a wing and a prayer, but the rent still had to be paid, however much they economised elsewhere, cooking the most basic of meals in their tiny kitchen. This coffee in the beating heart of Paris was the treat they gave themselves once their rent had been covered. But no more, it seemed. She'd always sensed Emil's humiliation at being dependent on his brother to make up the rent on their tiny apartment, but if Albert needed to invest to save the family business, even that might go.

'I was so close,' said Emil, biting his lips. 'I'm getting more journalism work by the day. It might not be enough now, but a few more months and I could have covered the rent until my novel is ready to be sent out to publishers.'

'Perhaps I can find a few more places that will take my arti-cles,' said Sabine, with an attempt at cheerfulness. 'And Mme Dallier from the *boulangerie* is always asking me to do extra hours. I don't mind, as long as we can survive until we're both more established and your novel is published; we can stay in Paris and make our own future.'

'I don't like the thought of you demeaning yourself serving in a shop,' said Emil.

'It won't be for long. It's what students do, remember? I thought we agreed we were the living embodiment of *La Bohème*? Without the fading away from tuberculosis, I hasten to add, as I've no intention of doing any fading!'

That made him smile. He reached across the little table to take her hand in his. 'You always do me good, Sabine. You always see the positive in everything.'

'I hope I see a way through, rather than just being naïvely optimistic,' she retorted.

'Of course.' He was still smiling at her, those dark eyes locked onto hers with such depth of meaning that her stomach fell away, the blush rising to her cheeks as her body responded, as it always did. 'A glass of good wine, I think,' he said, turning away, his own cheeks slightly flushed. He beckoned to the waiter. 'This might be the last time we can afford more than the cheapest from the market for a while. Time to savour the civilised trappings of life while we still can.'

'It'll be all right,' she said, seeing his face fall back towards brooding.

'Of course it will. And once my novel's been accepted, I'll be able to support you properly, as a husband should.'

'I like working,' she responded firmly.

'For now,' he replied, reaching for his much-depleted packet of Gitanes and equally sparse box of matches. 'I'll be a good husband, and give you everything you could possibly desire.'

I already have it. Sabine did not voice her thoughts aloud. Allow a husband his dignity, she told herself, remembering her mother's strictures on marital harmony. Emil's pride was already at its lowest ebb, without her expressing a wish to be independent of him, as if she didn't trust him to give her every-thing she needed. Despite her doubts over his novel, she was still happy to support him while he pursued his career until he could support them both, trusting in an unspoken assumption that it would then be her turn to have the space and time to pursue her own desire to be a campaigning journalist, following up on injustice and righting wrongs.

On the other hand, when Papa had been alive, Maman had always found a way to work around him while making him feel that his authority hadn't been challenged at all. She invariably acted as if any development in the farmland and vegetable patches she and Mémé had worked out between them had been his idea in the first place. Maybe Emil was right in thinking her naïve in the face of reality. If she was going to do something out of the ordinary, then she was going to have to work at it, not just expect it to fall into her lap. Like Maman, she could use the power of persistence, until, little by little, she could persuade him to at least allow her to try.

The pungent scent of his cigarette reached her, the tailwind from a passing car blowing it full in her face. Out of nowhere, her stomach heaved.

'Ah, here it comes.' Emil sat back in his chair, relaxed and confident once more that he was master of his own fate.

It couldn't be. Panic shot through Sabine as her body threatened to betray her in its uniquely female way. She'd ignored the two missed monthlies, putting it down to the stress of getting that last story in on time to the Paris newspaper where she freelanced, and working more hours than usual at the *boulangerie*. It couldn't be. It couldn't. Not now. They'd been so careful. She took the glass Emil filled for her, trying to sip the wine with a show of enthusiasm, more than glad for once that Emil knocked his first one back and was reaching for the bottle before she'd swallowed her first token mouthful. They had agreed. Not now. Not until they were ready. Even with Albert's help, it took both of them working all hours to simply survive, and heaven knows how they were going to live now.

They'd been so careful ... But not always, she acknowledged, seeing her husband's second glass emptying almost as rapidly as the first. There had been some nights, fuelled by a productive day at the typewriter and a bottle of cheap *vin rouge*, when Emil hadn't been so careful, and she'd been too lost in her own sensations to care.

'To the future,' said Emil, raising his glass in salute.

Sabine pulled herself together. It had just been a brief queasiness, and she was overtired. Besides, as her mother had warned her on the eve of her marriage, a first pregnancy doesn't always go to term, and she mustn't set her heart on something over which she had so little control. Maman would no doubt be mortified if she knew her daughter was now hoping and praying this was nothing more than her inadequate cooking of last night's fish.

One day, of her time and her choosing. But not now, not yet. Not with so much at stake.

'To the future,' she echoed quietly, ignoring the rebellion of her stomach at the sharp smell of the wine. 'And to Paris.'

THREE

NORA

London, 1938

The postmark was from Paris, the handwriting unmistakeably that of Sabine Schongauer. Nora Herridge grabbed the envelope sitting on the hallway table next to Dad's copy of *The Times* and Mum's *Stitchcraft* and the latest *My Weekly,* and shot out into in the tiny back garden of the terraced house in Turnham Green.

She read through eagerly, for once skipping over the details of her friend's life in Paris, with its descriptions of visits to the Louvre on her days off, and to see the paintings of Renoir and Cézanne in the *Musée de l'Orangerie,* or wandering in the Bois de Boulogne in the heat of the day. To her excitement, Sabine had found two courses held next year that might be suitable, both exclusively for women, with proper chefs and female-only accommodation. Nora let out a sigh of relief. Not even Dad could object. Her father had long made it clear that every man who walked the streets of London was out to wheedle Nora out of her precious virtue and disgrace the family by leaving her unwed and pregnant. She still had no idea how to persuade him to allow her to brave the seductive charms of the French male, but at least female-only accommodation, with a concierge on the door at all hours, would be a start.

The shorter and far more affordable course in French cookery was held over six weeks in Chartres, a hundred kilometres from Paris, home to a magnificent cathedral Nora had seen portrayed in books in her local library. A quick calculation told her that this was just over sixty miles. Sabine's information said it took under two hours from Paris by train. But that was still almost as far as London was from Canterbury, and that felt a long way.

The other course was based in Paris itself, not far from where Sabine and her husband were living. From Sabine's descriptions in her best English, Nora was beginning to feel she knew Paris almost as well as London. She could sense the romance of the City of Light, the pavement cafés, the world of haute couture, the galleries and museums showing the best of human civilization from as far back as Egyptian times. The allure was irresistible.

Besides, Dad would be reassured by the idea of a married woman acting as chaperone. He didn't have to know that Sabine was newly married, and only a few years older than Nora. If she told him Sabine was only in her early twenties, her father would probably imagine she was as sophisticated and sexy as Claudette Colberg in *Cleopatra* or *It Happened One Night* (which Dad considered a little too racy, and likely to give girls ideas). It would be no good trying to explain that Sabine wasn't like that at all.

When she'd braved the library near St James's Square to hear the lecture on Rosa Lewis, Nora had been expecting an ancient academic of the fearsomely intellectual variety, but Sabine had been a breath of fresh air. Nora had barely been able to take her eyes off the effortlessly elegant young woman, her grey jacket cinched in at the waist over a straight skirt revealing a touch of shin, speaking in such perfect English.

It was only halfway through the lecture that Nora had caught Sabine's eye for a second and realised she was incredibly nervous, while hiding it well. That brief exchange of emotion had given her courage to go up to her afterwards to ask more about Rosa Lewis. She had even hesitatingly attempted speaking French, acquired through the class in the local library held by Mademoiselle Duval, whose family had been refugees from the German occupation of France in the Great War.

After chatting for a while about their shared enthusiasm for a woman who'd made her own way in life, it had been only natural to exchange addresses. Sabine wished to improve her written English, Nora was eager to become fluent in French. It was, after all, the language of the kitchen and the banter flying to and fro between the higher echelons of the kitchen at *La Belle Époque* where she worked. Mind you, as her knowledge of the language had come on leaps and bounds under Mademoiselle's exacting standards, Nora was beginning to suspect that several of the chefs were not quite as familiar with *parler français* as they wished to make out. It had made her wonder about the rest of their much-vaunted expertise, particularly given their insistence on everyone else being kept firmly in their place and fired out of hand the moment they questioned anything.

If I ever run a kitchen, she told herself firmly, *the first thing I'll do is to outlaw bullying.*

She read Sabine's information on Mme Godeaux's *Cuisine Française* again, slowly this time, absorbing it carefully. A whole six months to experience Paris. A chance to learn French recipes from a real French chef, a woman too, who'd cooked for kings and presidents no less. There were still a few places left on the course starting in April the following year, although Sabine warned her they usually went fast. She had enclosed a leaflet giving instructions on how to apply, a map of the Paris Métro and a train timetable from Calais.

Nora took a deep breath. The course in Paris was terrifyingly expensive. It would take all of the small legacy left her recently by her grandmother, and the money she'd managed to save working at *La Belle Époque*, which both her parents happily assumed was earmarked for a wedding dress and furnishings for her future marital home. It was a risk. Not least revealing to Dad that she wasn't about to follow the conventional route and settle down to a life of domestic bliss. But if she wanted to be taken seriously as a chef, and to earn her own living, there was no other choice. The men she worked with might pour scorn on the idea of a woman ever becoming a renowned cook, let alone a head chef, or even running her own restaurant. But Nora was one day going to prove them wrong.

After that meeting with Sabine, Nora had been to gaze at the Cavendish, taking inspiration from the hotel Rosa Lewis had once owned, just off Piccadilly, in St James's, a short walk from Fortnum and Mason.

It wasn't that Nora had a desire to actually buy such a grand establishment, but she'd give her eye teeth to work in one as a chef. Not a tea lady or a cleaner, but a woman respected for her skills and in charge of her own future.

Nora had learnt several important lessons in the three years since starting at *La Belle Époque* as a dish washer, the day she turned sixteen. The first was that being the lowest of the low was a trap, one very difficult to escape, being expected to work all hours for little pay, shouted at by all and sundry and generally being viewed as naturally stupid. It was exhausting. She could understand why the men – who had no domestic duties to rush home to – retired to the pub after a long shift to lift their spirits with a pint or two.

All too aware that if she'd tried to join them she would have signalled herself as a loose woman, little better than the local prostitute, Nora had taken to studying instead. However worn out, however harried and bullied, and the expectations from her parents that she'd help at home, she'd managed to pick up enough from the other kitchen workers, and the books in the library, to rise from general dogsbody to the most junior of cooks.

'But if I want to rise any further,' she said to herself aloud. 'I need to be trained.'

The cooks at *La Belle Époque*, all male, saw it as beneath their dignity to show a mere slip of a girl any more than the most basic of sauces. Well, a hollandaise, however expertly made, wasn't going to get her anywhere.

Nora felt a quiver of excitement race through her from top to toe. Decision made: Mme Godeaux it would be.

'Paris,' exclaimed her mother, iron paused in her hand. 'Well I never.'

'Why travel all that way at all that expense when you can study here,' added her father, shaking out his copy of the *Daily Mirror*. 'I thought you were learning all you needed at that restaurant? Stroke of luck getting in there, you know.'

'They won't teach me anything more than the basics, Dad. I've tried. The chefs all say girls are incapable, and are only going to get married anyway, so it isn't worth it. Mme Godeaux is supposed to be the best teacher you can find. My friend in Paris has found a charity for the education of women that'll help with travel and accommodation expenses. The rest I can pay for myself. It won't cost you a thing, I promise.'

'It's too far.'

'I don't see why not,' remarked Mrs Herridge, returning to her husband's shirts. 'It's a compliment to Nora's talent that her friend thinks she could be accepted on this course, and more women are taking up professions these days. Besides, don't I always say a woman needs to know she can stand on her own two feet, even if she never actually has to.'

Mr Herridge grunted. 'I'm not sure this is the right time for a young girl to be so far away from her family.'

'There's been talk of war for years, darling, it might never happen. Surely we're not going to go through all that again, not after last time.'

'Let's hope the politicians see things like that,' he replied gloomily. 'To think we used to think that Hitler chap was a bit of a joke, with all that nonsense about a master race.'

'But that doesn't mean there'll be a war with Germany,' said Nora quickly. 'Or at least not now. Surely the sooner I go, the safer I'll be? From the timetable Sabine sent me it's only a few hours by train from Calais to Paris. The first sign of anything, and I promise I'll be back before you know it.'

'We'll see,' he grunted, returning to his paper.

The reaction was much the same from Nora's sister Pearl, who lived with her husband Fred in a small terraced house in the next street.

'Paris? Are you sure? It's such a long way,' Pearl exclaimed as she rocked her baby to sleep in the pram out in her back yard, beneath a washing line of drying sheets and the white squares of nappies. 'I thought you were happy where you were.'

'I love it,' said Nora enthusiastically. 'The moment I started there, I knew it was what I wanted to do. I've told them I want to learn more, but all they really want is someone to prepare vegetables and make a few sauces when they can't be bothered.'

In the pram, little Jonny began to wail.

'Oh, what is it now!' exclaimed Pearl despairingly, adjusting the pram hood to keep him in the shade. 'I thought he'd go off.' She rocked the pram but the sobbing failed to subside. 'He'll wake the street,' she muttered, looking towards the fence dividing her garden from that of her neighbour. 'And the old bat needs no excuse. She's always complaining. He's a baby, for goodness' sake.'

'I'll take him,' said Nora, 'I'll walk him around, that usually sends him to sleep. You finish your tea.'

'Are you sure?'

'Yes, of course.' She picked up the little bundle that smelt of soap and milkiness.

'What she really means is that I shouldn't have kept him because he's disabled,' Pearl muttered, scowling at the offending fence. 'That I should have handed him over to an asylum, or goodness knows what. She's always shouting at me that he's a half-wit, and worse. You know the kind of thing. And saying that he shouldn't be here in a respectable neighbourhood. Vile woman. I don't care what they say. It's not as if her sons are perfect. Loud and rude, that's what they are. They're always marching with Oswald Mosley's British Union of Fascists and waving that horrible flag around. No manners between them.'

Nora brushed the carefully knitted blue bonnet away from the little face with its unusually shaped eyes and strangely scratchy skin. Jonny had calmed at the sensation of movement, breaking into a broad smile. It didn't matter that he wasn't like other babies; he was still a baby, who laughed at the dance of shadows over the pram, panicked when he was hungry and crotchety when he was tired. She loathed it when people stared when they were out, especially the women who bent over the pram clucking indulgently, then turned away when they saw his face, so different from the round chubbiness of other babies, while Pearl's expression grew stonier by the minute.

'I hate people,' she'd muttered after one particularly stressful outing. 'I want to scream at them. I don't care what they think, he's just a baby. And they're quite wrong, he's not an imbecile. They don't know him.'

Nora walked and rocked, as Jonny snuffled quietly in his

shawl. Pearl was lucky, Fred had agreed they'd do the best for Jonny at home, even if he never learnt to walk or talk, and couldn't do anything for himself for the rest of his life. Fred hadn't followed the advice of the doctors and nurses, and even his own parents, who'd assumed Jonny would be sent away, out of sight, as was the normal thing for such 'unfortunates'. They'd been told children like Jonny didn't live long, but Pearl would still dedicate years and years of her life to his care. Other children would grow up and get married and have ordinary lives, while Pearl had been told that, however long he lived, Jonny would never grow up at all.

Nora walked to and fro under the rustling of the neighbouring plane tree, cradling the little body as it relaxed back towards sleep. She felt more determined than ever to take the course in Paris. She'd spent enough time with Pearl to see how her sister's life was completely absorbed in looking after her home and one baby, let alone if she had any more.

Nora wanted love and a family of her own, of course she did. But she was different from Pearl, she didn't want her life to be completely taken over by domestic responsibilities. Besides, working in a kitchen full of men with wandering hands and a fondness for boasting about last night's conquests made a girl wary. You soon acquired sharp elbows, an even sharper tongue and an absolute avoidance of dark corners. Along with a certain degree of cynicism when it came to your superiors' apparently insatiable ability to send any Greta Garbo lookalike into a frenzy of desire.

In the little yard Nora paced to and fro with the sleeping child, determination growing by the minute. Her mother, who had seen so many of her female friends lose husbands and fiancés in the Great War, and the women who'd never married due to the lack of men afterwards, had always impressed upon her that a woman couldn't rely on finding a husband to support her. The course in Paris might be her only chance to follow her ambition to become a proper chef, or at the very least to acquire the skills to support herself if she never married, instead of being stuck at home for the rest of her life as a failure, pitied by all who knew her.

Just a few months of her life. That was all. Then she would return and things would be as they'd always been. Surely, Nora told herself, it wasn't wicked to ask, just once in her life, for something so simple?

FOUR

SABINE

Paris, 1938

The day Sabine finally confessed to Emil the fact of her pregnancy, confirmed a few weeks before, she stared at her husband in dismay.

'How could you!' he exclaimed, anger, disappointment and disbelief distorting his handsome features.

'Not without you,' she retorted, her own temper rising. 'And don't you ever forget that, Emil. I'm not having you lay the blame for this on me.' Until this moment it had never crossed her mind that Emil might walk away, leave her as an encumbrance he could shake off to pursue his ambitions. From the expression on his face, the possibility seemed all too real. 'It might not be the best timing—'

'You can say that again,' he broke in. 'You know there'll be no more money coming from Albert, for a year at least. Not until he gets the boot shop back on its feet.'

'We'll manage.'

'How? Do you expect me to work day and night in a factory to pay our way?'

'No, of course not. I'm not ill, Emil. I'm not dying. I don't even have the dreaded morning sickness. I've never felt so well in my life. I'm just going to expand, that's all. Women have been doing this for centuries. I can still work at the *boulangerie*, right up until just before the baby's born. I can go home for the birth, Maman will look after me until I'm back on my feet, and my aunt will help with looking after the baby here while I work.'

His brows snapped even tighter together. 'You've discussed it with them? You discussed it with them, before you told me?'

Sabine bit her lip. She should have known better than to insult his pride like that. She couldn't explain that in her fear and her uncertainty at this unexpected change she'd needed the reassurance only her mother and her female relatives could provide. She'd needed to know she would be supported through this, whatever happened, before finally confronting the reality of this new life that would be entering theirs in just a few short months.

'Emil—' The hand she laid placatingly on his arm was shrugged off. He sat at the kitchen table, the scene of so many leisurely Sunday breakfasts, with the bells of Notre Dame echoing through the city calling the faithful to prayer, half turned away from her, blocking her out.

Sabine took a sip of her coffee, now grown cold and harsh on her tongue. The silence was unbearable. She rose to grind the remainder of the beans in the ancient cast-iron coffee grinder Maman had given her when she first left for Paris. The turning of the little handle, with its familiar resistance and the rising scent of coffee, always reminded her of home and her carefree childhood. There was an ache inside her to escape the complexities of adult life, with its conflicts and its uncertainties. How she longed to return to the world of the Chateau Saint-Céré, with its rolling fields broken only by the lazy winding of a willow-banked river that could easily have come from a painting by Cezanne or Monet.

But those days were gone. She was to be the parent now, creating an equally carefree milieu for her own child. How ironic that she'd spent so many years longing to escape to a larger, more exciting, world. It wasn't even as if the chateau was a real castle. Its ancient origins had long since been absorbed into the now-crumbling stone of a manor house, half hidden by a gnarled vine and surrounded by orchards of equally twisted lemon and apple trees and the dry rustling of an olive tree, given years ago by a distant cousin in Marseille.

Sabine finished the grinding. She pulled out the little tray to spoon the coffee into the waiting percolator and placed it onto the stove to heat, keeping her attention away from the table.

'Leave those,' said Emil as she turned her attention to the dishes in the tiny sink. She heard him rise, felt his arms around her, the warmth of his breath on the back of her neck. 'Come and sit down.'

She felt thin, stretched, caught between her longing to be held within his embrace and fierce protectiveness for the tiny new life inside her. 'I'll finish these,' she said. 'We need to leave soon if we're going to meet the others.'

'They can wait,' he replied, nuzzling gently at her ear, pulling her back towards the table. 'We see our friends most days, they can wait a few more minutes for us.'

She turned to face him. 'Emil, I can't keep this hidden for much longer. We're going to have to tell everyone at some point.'

'Of course, chérie.' He gently manoeuvred her to her chair and turned to attend to the cups and saucers as the percolator came to the boil, the familiar thump of liquid hitting the lid as the grinds were absorbed.

A touch of anxiety shot through Sabine's relief at her husband's return to his customary attentiveness and kindness. Perhaps it was that new protectiveness, such as she had never felt before, or her more recent recognition that Emil, for all he loved her, would always put his own interests first, that made her doubt him. She had a sudden horror that he was about to offer her an ultimatum, as she'd heard some men did when faced with an unwanted child. However he might try to persuade her, she wasn't about to hand over this new life inside her to an orphanage, or, even worse, take the terrible, illegal, life-endangering route that meant there would never be a child at all.

'I know it's not the best timing,' she resumed. 'But we always knew it could happen.'

'So we did.' His eyes were grave. 'I'm sorry Sabine. You were right. That was unfair of me. It's a bit of a shock, that's all.' He sat down, taking her hand in his. 'Maman will be pleased she's going to have a grandson. She always regretted Albert never marrying. She'll be so pleased.'

'I'd rather *you* were happy, Emil,' said Sabine, trying to read which way the wind was blowing. Once, not so long ago, she had felt she could understand his every thought, their minds seemed so attuned. Now she wasn't so sure.

He kissed her cheek as he rose again to attend to the percolator as the smell of freshly brewed coffee filled the little kitchen. 'Of course I am, my darling. I always said you'll make a good mother.'

'Oh?' said Sabine, who was perfectly certain he had said no such thing, but too relieved that he at least seemed to be coming round to the idea to challenge his version of their past.

'Of course.' He poured the coffee thoughtfully. 'Besides, this'll give me the push I need to finish my novel. The sooner I get it to a publisher the better. I've already got ideas for the next, and I can take on more journalism. We always said we were going to stand on our own two feet as soon as we could, and one day buy an apartment of our own. I'm on my way. Don't you see, by the time the baby arrives, we won't need Albert!'

'And I've told you I can still work,' said Sabine, taking the proffered coffee, the unease returning that Emil was already mentally ordering their life to suit his dream of his future, as if he couldn't possibly fail. 'I won't have to stop for months yet.'

'And if your family helps with the child, as they should, we'll manage,' he continued, only half hearing her. His expression brightened. 'A baby. Think of that. We'll be the first of our friends to produce offspring. We can tell them today, they're bound to be envious. I must ask Maman to send my old clockwork train. I know she put it up in the attic for when Albert had a family. Well, we can have it now.'

'Maybe,' said Sabine. Emil appeared to be already building up a vision of the perfect child, one that could be taken anywhere, that would sit quietly, to be presented as yet another of his achievements. Sabine might not know much about children, but she'd seen enough to understand the noise and the chaos surrounding a baby, let alone an inquisitive, self-willed toddler. She hoped Emil was not destined for disappointment, his ideals once more at odds with immutable reality.

She pulled herself together. On the other hand, fatherhood might be just what Emil needed to ground him. Maman always said it had been the making of Papa, who had turned from youthful restlessness to becoming a doting father for Sabine and her brother Guillaume. This unexpected addition to their lives might, after all, turn out for the best.

Over the next few months Sabine worked as many hours as she could get, trying to lay down a store of money for necessities for the baby, as well as to support the family when she was unable to work. At least she didn't need to worry about clothes or napkins. She'd always been slightly amused at the way, the moment word was out, women gathered together, fetching down clothes from their attics and busily knitting tiny coats and mittens. Now it was her turn, she'd never been so grateful for the quiet, largely unnoticed way the female of the species dealt with such things.

The prospect of losing her precious income, along with the imminent arrival of a new mouth to feed, spurred Emil to finish his book and send it to publishers. Despite the regular rejection of the manuscript over the autumn months, he was determined to retain his optimism, while Sabine did her best to hide her doubts that it would ever be published, let alone make the fortune her husband had been so confidently expecting. After all, as Emil reminded her, some works of fiction were so brilliant even the dullest publisher had to eventually recognise their genius and launch them into the world.

By Christmas, her bulge was most definitely showing. As 1939 began not even her most voluminous dresses would fit, and she was starting to waddle. For all her determination, it was clear she wouldn't be able to carry on working all hours for much longer. One frosty morning, when she'd barely been able to make the short walk, and the thought of standing on her feet was almost beyond her, she finally gave in her notice. She struggled through the next week, torn between relief that the decision was made and an ever-present fear of how they were going to manage.

Although Sabine was thankful she'd soon not have to face one more day at work, her legs and back aching and her veins throbbing, a knot inside her warned her that from now on she would be almost completely dependent on Emil.

Or maybe not completely. As well as the savings she'd set aside, she could still send articles in to the journal that had been accepting her work on a regular basis over the autumn. After her series of articles on the English chef Rosa Lewis, she'd written several more focusing on unusual and enterprising professional women. The journal might not pay much, but it was at least a start in making a name for herself as a journalist. More than that, it was work she'd surely be able to carry on with

a small child at her feet, and she could leave her baby with her
mother or aunt while she visited locations and conducted
interviews.

A nagging feeling at the back of her mind told her that she
was more than a little like Emil in not facing up to the reality of
bearing responsibility for a new life, but at least it kept her sane.
More than that, the thought of being stuck alone in the apartment all day while Emil worked no longer filled her with dread.
Instead, as her final week at work dragged on, she began to look
forward to the freedom to concentrate on building her own
reputation, and perhaps one day making a career as a journalist.

After her last day at the *boulangerie*, Sabine made her way
slowly home through the chill of January, with mist rising from
the Seine and stealing through the Parisian streets. She
lumbered her way up the stairs, the post in her hand, thankful
there was no bulge of a rejected manuscript that, since Christmas, had become a familiar prelude to Emil heading out to walk
off his frustration, only to return with the smell of Absinthe on
his breath, a bottle of cheap wine in his hand.

She placed the letters on the table, lacking the energy to
look at them, and reached for the percolator, her body craving
caffeine before she started work preparing the vegetables and
the small piece of meat she'd bought from the market.

Once she sat down, she found it hard to even think about
getting up again. How she hoped one of those letters was from a
publisher accepting Emil's manuscript, declaring it would set
the world on fire. Or at least holding out the prospect of it
selling a few copies. Then she wouldn't have to worry about
soothing Emil's wounded pride, and steering him from his
conviction that no one in the posh publishing houses would give
a working man like himself a chance, preferring the empty plati-
tudes of the comfortably middle class.

The top one, she could see from the English stamps, must be from Nora. She reached for it, worries fading as she read her friend's excitement, in rather less fluent French than usual, with whole sentences in English thrown in. Nora had been accepted on the six-month course; her father had finally been persuaded. She would be in Paris in a few months. Her course was from April to September 1939, and she couldn't wait to see Sabine again, and her baby, when it arrived.

Baby. Sabine stared out over the grey rooftops around her, towards the heart of the city. It had been Mme Gérin the midwife, sweeping in early that morning for her usual baguette and croissants after a night delivering babies, who had first put the thought in her head.

'Good grief, *ma petite*,' she'd remarked, catching sight of Sabine's painfully stretched dress. 'Are you certain you haven't got two there? These doctors know nothing. It wouldn't surprise me in the least.'

Sabine, in an effort to save money, and feeling perfectly well in herself, had not been anywhere near the medical establishment since the initial confirmation of her pregnancy. But she'd seen enough of Mme Gérin to know the elderly midwife had more expertise than most doctors when it came to births. That meant her prognosis was at least possible. A new despair coursed through her: now she was faced with the prospect of not one, but two babies. Surely not. The thought of one somehow forcing its way out of her was terrifying enough, but two would break her apart. Downstairs, the front door banged, followed by Emil's familiar footsteps making their way up towards her.

Sabine dragged herself unwillingly to her feet to pour the coffee, ready for her husband's arrival. She prayed one of the letters might be an acceptance. Let him have hope and pride, and something to distract him.

'No manuscript,' said Emil, relief in his voice as he pushed through the door. 'I told you that last publishing house sounded the most promising.'

'Yes, of course,' replied Sabine mechanically, pouring coffee, her mind too full to even attempt to match his enthusiasm.

'How was your last day?' he asked, hanging up his coat on the back of the door before kissing her.

'Tiring. I know we'll miss the money, but I'm not sure I could have done another week.'

'Now you can sit down for as long as you please,' he said, brushing loose tendrils strands of brown hair from her face. 'And once we get you to your mother, you'll be waited on hand and foot.'

Sabine laughed. 'I'm not sure idleness would suit me.'

'But you deserve to be looked after,' he said, kissing her once more.

She stood there, held in his warmth, the curve of her body against his. How she wished it could be like this always, the way it once was and the way she'd dreamed it would always be, without Emil's ambition and frustrations coming between them. Other couples managed to live in what, from the outside at least, looked like harmony, and raised children between them, dealing with whatever difficulties life threw at them. Surely they could find a way too?

'Drink your coffee,' he said, releasing her and reaching for the letters. The moment was gone; she could tell from the eagerness in his voice that his hopes had been raised that at least one envelope contained the message that would set him off on the path towards fulfilling his ambitions.

She was sinking into a relaxed dose when the silence alerted her. 'Emil?' He was sitting at the table, not moving, an opened letter in his hand. 'Emil, what is it?'

'Albert. He's dead.'

'Dead?' Her brain struggled to take it in, grief rising, not so much for her unknown brother-in-law, but for Emil. And maybe, in a flash of insight, a little for herself. 'Emil, I'm so sorry.'

'It was a train accident. Most survived. But not Albert. Why him? Of all the people there, why him?'

She rose and put her arms around him. 'I'm so sorry, so sorry.'

'How could he?' Emil pulled away, dashing the letter down on the table. 'I could have had an answer any day. But now ...'

'Now?' She scarcely dared ask, already knowing the answer.

'Maman says we're to go home immediately.'

'To Colmar?'

'Of course to Colmar. Don't you see? Now it's my turn. I only escaped because I'm the second son and Albert wanted to follow our father into the boot business. Now it's up to me.'

Her stomach lurched. 'You mean to live there? In Colmar? To leave Paris?'

'There's no other choice,' he replied.

'But Emil ...'

'There's no other choice,' he repeated loudly. 'You can't possibly understand. Women can do as they please, it's the men who are tasked with the duty of making sure a business doesn't fail. I can't leave Maman to face that alone.' He pushed aside the coffee, reaching for a half-empty bottle in the small cupboard where they stored their foodstuffs. 'I always knew it would come to this. Why on earth did Albert ever get on that cursed train?'

'Emil,' Sabine began gently, putting her hand on his arm in an effort to comfort his grief. He shook her off and filled his glass with a shaking hand.

'I'll give the landlord notice first thing in the morning. At least we have enough savings to cover the train fare and to send what we can't carry. We have no choice,' he added, as she began to protest. 'We have no choice. We are going to Colmar.'

FIVE

IRIS

Cornwall, 1964

In the early morning light, just before dawn, Iris could toss and turn in bed no longer. Dressing as quietly as she could, she slipped out of the front door, taking the path to the cliffs above St Mabon's Cove. She breathed in deeply, trying to clear her racing brain. There was a taste of salt on her skin as the waves, stirred up in the night by the strengthening wind, crashed against the entrance of the cove.

Forgive.

That single word had led to her restless night; she'd been unable to settle, the moment she began to doze off, her mind had raced with wild dreams. Most she could not remember, apart from in snatches, filled with noise and screams, waking with the taste of blood in her mouth, when there was no blood there.

She walked along the path above the cliffs, drawing in the sense of peace, the familiarity of the place that had been her whole world. As a child, she'd never been given the freedom to roam where she pleased. Mum and Dad had encouraged her in her studies and in making the most of the sea and the beach, but they'd always insisted on knowing where she was, and, when she was older, that she be back at specific times if she went out with her friends. No wonder she'd revelled in the freedom of London.

The sun was rising and St Mabon's was beginning to stir. Iris checked her watch. She'd been out longer than she'd thought and Mum would be wondering where she was. As she turned, a glint caught her eye from the direction of the harbour. The sheen of sun on glass.

Hurrying through the car park, deep in thought, she rounded the only car there, a battered Morris Minor traveller, almost bumping headlong into a young woman in jeans and a much-washed Fair Isle jumper.

'Oops, sorry. Wasn't looking where I was going.'

'That's okay,' said the woman cheerfully, continuing to place several large bags onto the back seat. 'Beautiful morning, isn't it?'

'Very,' said Iris.

'Such a lovely place. I'm sure if I lived here, I'd never want to leave.'

'It can be bleak in winter,' replied Iris, aware that the young woman seemed eager to strike up a conversation. She was conscious that Mum would be up and she hadn't left a note to say where she was going. It struck her that she'd always felt her parents' anxiety when they hadn't known exactly where she was, Mum in particular. It had taken her years to persuade them to allow her to take up her university place in London.

Of course, parents were always more anxious about girls. But all the same, she remembered envying her schoolfriends' freedom to hang out at the single bus stop on the harbour once the Milk Bar shut its doors for the night, while she was expected straight home from school, and then from college.

As she reached the path that struck across the fields to the cottage, she looked back towards the Morris Minor, still the only car in the car park. It must have arrived very early, or been there all night. The young woman was leaning against the bonnet. It was still an oddity to find a woman travelling on her own in sleepy, old-fashioned St Mabon's, where strangers stuck out like a sore thumb and always prompted curiosity. She was probably waiting for someone. On the other hand, at least one of the bags looked like it housed a telephoto lens, the kind only professionals or particularly keen amateurs could afford to use. Perhaps the young woman wanted to capture images of birdlife, or views of the sea in the early morning light.

No doubt St Mabon's gossip would tell her the stranger's every move, thought Iris with a wry grin as she resumed her journey home.

As she reached the small back gate into the garden, she found the French windows wide open and her mother in her dressing gown amongst the flower beds, a cup of tea in her hand, lost in thought. She looked thin and pale in the slanting morning sun. With her hair down, she held an air of fragility resembling a hospital patient, foreshadowing how she might look as an old woman. Iris's heart squeezed painfully again.

Her mother turned, smiling as she caught sight of her. 'Ah, there you are, darling. I wondered if you'd gone down to the beach.'

'Sorry, Mum. I should have told you where I was going.'

'Nonsense. You're a grown woman.' A strange expression passed over her mother's face. 'I have to let you go sometime.'

Iris kissed her. 'I'm not going anywhere, Mum. Come on, I'm going to cook breakfast.'

'There's really no need ...'

'Yes, there is,' returned Iris. 'You're always looking after everyone else and keeping us all in order. Well, now it's time for us to look after you. No arguments.'

'Well, just this once,' conceded her mother as Iris took her arm, gently propelling her back inside. 'Besides, it's high time I got dressed.'

As they reached the hallway, the telephone began to ring. 'I'll get that,' said her mother, shooing her in the direction of the kitchen. Iris obeyed, filling the kettle as her mother picked up the receiver.

'Yes?' Iris smiled. It was good to hear Mum's business voice again, transforming her instantly from a patient to an efficient manager. 'Yes. Yes, it is. How can I help you?'

Iris instinctively headed for the coolness of the pantry to fetch a bottle of milk, before remembering her parents had finally succumbed to the convenience of a refrigerator to keep meat and butter chilled on the hottest of days.

'Absolutely not.' As she opened the refrigerator door, Iris jumped at the controlled anger of the voice in the hallway. 'Like I told you, this is nothing to do with me, or my family. I have nothing to say.' The receiver slammed.

Iris abandoned the milk. 'Mum? Is everything all right?'

'It's nothing. Just a nuisance call. Nothing to worry about.'

'Yes, Mum,' said Iris, unconvinced. There was a touch of colour back in her mother's pale cheeks, the kind that appeared when she was angry. Or maybe frightened. Mum had always been such a strong presence in Iris's life; the kind you knew you could always turn to for solutions. She'd never relied on Iris's dad to clear gutters and she'd shocked some of their more conventional neighbours by being quite capable of wielding a saw or even a drill. Iris didn't remember seeing Mum frightened before. It was unsettling, giving her an instant urge to hug her.

But her mother had already reached the stairs, a touch of the old determination back in her step.

Breakfast was eaten out in the garden at a table set under the old Victoria plum tree, with a glimpse of the sea in the distance.

'I looked at the letters,' said Iris as she poured the tea.

'I wondered if you might.'

Iris had so many questions she didn't know where to start, but she had to start somewhere. 'Who's Karl Bernheim?'

Her mother started slightly. 'Why him?'

'Nothing in particular. I thought the name was familiar, that's all. One of the letters mentioned him. It was in French, I couldn't make it all out. Whoever wrote it didn't sign their name, they just drew a heart. They sounded worried.'

'They had every reason to be.' Her mother brushed crumbs from her hands and reached into the small leather handbag that rarely left her side. She pulled out a faded black and white photograph, worn at the edges, and placed it on the table.

Iris expected to see the image of a man in uniform or wearing the jumper of a resistance fighter. But instead the photograph showed two small babies in what looked like a large pram, one turned towards the camera, squinting in curiosity, the other turned away, face hidden.

'That's them,' said Mum, with a faintly wistful smile. 'Valérie and Violette,' she added, pronouncing them in the French way. 'They were such tiny babies. So impossibly fragile.' Her eyes filled with tears. 'They were twins, you see. All they wanted was life. Not riches, not glory, just life. Not that it matters to a man like Karl Bernheim.'

'You don't have to tell me, Mum,' said Iris quickly. 'I didn't mean to upset you.'

'That's all right, darling. You have a right to know. They're your history, all three of them, along with so many others during the war whose stories were woven with yours, for both good and for ill. I couldn't tell you before.' She shook her head. 'Don't ask me why. Not yet.'

France, 1939.

Iris felt unaccountably nervous. Whatever Mum had to tell her, she understood in a flash that it would change her life forever. But she'd started the conversation, and there was no going back.

'There were postcards of Paris in the tin,' she ventured. 'And one of Colmar, in Alsace.'

'That was where they were born. In Colmar.' Mum reached for the photograph of the two small children, as if she couldn't bear to let it go. 'I can't help wondering how many other babies were born in those first months of 1939. It's a miracle that babies survive to term at all, and then there's the birth itself, drawing those first breaths and reaching out towards the future. So many born that year had no future at all, or the most terrible of ends. The old and the very young, they're always the first to perish when war comes.'

France, 1939.

Iris swallowed. 'There was another postcard,' she began tentatively, but her mother was deep in memory, and didn't seem to hear.

'It's strange, looking back, darling. We were so innocent in those days. We never thought a war would really happen. Maybe the older people did, the ones who remembered the First World War, but not those of us who were young. We were so confident even a madman like Hitler wouldn't do anything so stupid as to risk destroying everything. We didn't know about the concentration camps, you see, and what was really happening in Germany. It was beyond imagination that human beings could be so perverted, so unspeakably cruel.'

In the hallway, the telephone began to ring.

'Leave it,' said Mum sharply. 'Let it ring. Lord save us from the ambitious, who have no idea of the lives they destroy on the way up. She can further her career somewhere else, thank you very much.'

'She?'

'Just some reporter. She thinks she's on to a story, but she has no idea.'

'A young woman down in the harbour stopped to talk to me,' said Iris. She opened her mouth to add about the professional camera lenses but thought better of it. The phone had stopped and she didn't want to disturb Mum any more than she had to. All the same, she glanced carefully around the secluded garden, in case of the glint of a camera lens catching the sun.

'That'll be her, I expect. Promise me you won't talk to her.'

'Of course not, Mum.'

Her mother gave a wry smile. 'Jeanie Dixon was the name on the card she pushed through the door. Looks like a freelancer pushing her luck. The address was in London, so she's no idea how a small community like this protects its own. She'll get nothing out of anyone here.'

'Mum ...'

'It's all right, darling.' Her mother took her hand, holding it tight. 'I'll tell you what I can. Like I said, this is your history. You have a right to know, not the likes of Miss Jeanie Dixon. It's odd, but when I was thinking about it just now, I realised that those months in 1939 were when my life really began. What a time to choose, eh?'

'Yes Mum,' said Iris as the telephone began its strident ringing once more, unanswered.

SIX

NORA

Paris, 1939

Nora left for Paris during the Easter holidays of 1939. Her father had finally agreed, and that it might as well be now, with the future so uncertain, and who knew what might happen in a year or so?

Nora decided to leave her parents still assuming she'd have Sabine to watch over her while she was there. It wasn't exactly lying: they never thought to ask, and Nora hadn't mentioned the scribbled letter telling her that Sabine was travelling to Colmar and might never return to Paris. The disappointment of not seeing her friend hit her like a blow to the stomach, but she understood that Sabine's husband needed to help his mother after his brother's death. Nora looked up Colmar on her map of France, hoping it was close enough to visit. But it was near the borders of Germany and Switzerland, five hundred kilometres away, over three hundred miles, the same distance again from London to Paris. No wonder Sabine hadn't suggested a visit: it would take days out of Nora's course, and was much too expensive, given the little money she possessed to keep her going.

Sabine had given her the address of her aunt, Marie-Thérèse, who'd agreed that Nora could turn to her in any emergency. So she really wouldn't be entirely alone amongst strangers in Paris.

Far more frightening, as far as Nora was concerned, was giving in her notice to *La Belle Époque*. Her request for a leave of absence to train in French cooking had been flatly turned down, with her employer lecturing her on the inconvenience of losing staff, what with them being so hard to come by.

Especially the good and reliable with no other choice than to live on starvation wages, thought Nora, escaping to the kitchens only to be shouted at for taking so long. For the rest of the day she wavered. Leaving was so very final. There was no guarantee she'd ever get a job in a kitchen again, or that if she annoyed her present employer he would even give her a reference.

On the other hand, she refused to relinquish her one chance of taking up her place on the course. She would take her chances, and face whatever the future might bring.

In the end it was a relief to give in her notice. A few days later she set off for Dover, waving through the train window to Mum and Dad, who'd insisted on accompanying her to the station.

As she settled into her seat, rucksack on the rack above, and watched all that was familiar flash past, her courage momentarily failed her. What on earth was she doing, a young girl on her own setting off towards an unknown city in a foreign country? But she was soon drawn into the novelty of new landscapes, and glad to be ignored by the man and woman on the opposite side of the compartment, and left alone with her thoughts.

She watched as swathes of fields between hedgerows flashed by, a church spire in the distance. A man paused on a bridge over a canal, terrier by his side, while women hung out washing in the back gardens of terraced houses, small children at their feet. All she had ever known (apart from a few brief forays into central London) had been her street in Turnham

Green and the Hammersmith Road. Now, it felt as if life was finally opening up before her, offering a host of possibilities.

By the time the train drew into Dover and the smell of the sea air enveloped everything around her, Nora's nerves were replaced by anticipation. As the boat was loaded with cars and vans, and the manoeuvring of lorries that barely seemed to fit through the opening, she joined the other foot passengers making their way on deck.

Going far?' asked a young woman about her own age, who stayed behind while the rest of her party, pickaxes and ropes attached to their rucksacks, went below to find a cup of tea.

'Paris,' said Nora a little shyly.

'Lucky you! Paris is such a beautiful city, day and night. They don't call it the City of Light for nothing, you know.' The young woman had clearly spotted that she was travelling on her own and was eyeing her with curiosity. 'Visiting friends?'

'Not exactly. I'm taking a course. To become a cook. Well, a chef.'

'A chef! That's usually men, isn't it? My goodness, you must be a brilliant cook.'

'I'm not sure.' Nora grinned. 'Well, even the most exacting chefs at work had to agree that I'm not bad. I'm hoping to become much better.'

'Good for you. We're heading off to Switzerland. I'm part of a ladies' climbing group. We're all teachers, making the most of the Easter holidays.' She grimaced. 'While we still can.' She indicated the crampons attached to her rucksack. 'It was touch and go whether we went this time. If things get more uncertain, it might have to be Scotland next year. It's beautiful, but the mountains aren't so high, and the snow isn't so good. It's climbing in the snow, right up to where the air gets thin, that's the real challenge. It always makes me feel so very alive.'

'I'm sure,' said Nora, smiling at her irrepressible enthusiasm. They turned to watch the crew squeezing in the final cars.

A particularly nervous Austin 7, hood down, filled to the gunnels with cases and passengers, was being beckoned inside. Then shouts erupted as the hold was closed, followed by the rumble of an engine from deep in the bowels of the ferry, accompanied by a swell of foamy water all around. With a crash and a bump the boat began to slide away from the dockside, making its way out of the harbour towards the wilder waters of the English Channel.

All through the crossing, Nora remained at the rail, breathing in the salt air and the sense of freedom. She'd only ever been at school, working at *La Belle Époque* or at home with Mum and Dad. She exchanged visits with friends, of course, but that was always in their homes, with parents nearby. This was the first time she'd ever done anything on her own, with no one to rely on but herself. The realisation was both terrifying and exhilarating.

As the Calais skyline began to appear, she made her way to the front of the ship, watching the coast, its long stretches of beach not so very different from photographs she'd seen of southern England. They became larger and more defined as they drew nearer until she could even make out the men on the harbour wall, waiting to secure the ferry as it arrived.

For a moment her nerves caught up with her. Suppose she couldn't find the train? Suppose she couldn't understand? She pulled herself together. People made this journey all the time. There must be others among her fellow foot passengers who were making their way to Paris. She took a deep breath, pushing away her fears, concentrating instead on the excitement bubbling up inside. This was where her adventure truly began.

As she emerged from the passport office, she was disorientated by the abrupt change into French, not to mention the noise and chaos around her.

'Going to Paris, are you?' called an English voice through the melee. She turned to see a woman with two young children clinging to her, while her husband staggered under the weight of a large suitcase.

'Yes, I am.'

'Thought you were.' The woman beamed. 'That's where we're heading, too. You stay with us, love, the train's just over there.'

'Thank you,' said Nora gratefully, tucking her passport safely away, swinging her rucksack over her shoulder and following in their wake.

The correct train safely located, Nora joined her new acquaintances in their compartment, once again watching as the countryside flew by.

'Such an adventure,' said Mrs Phillips as her children settled down to a game of I Spy with their father. 'My sister went to Paris last summer, she had such a wonderful time, we said we just had to go. Only a week, mind, it was all so expensive. But Lilly said it was worth it. I never thought I'd ever go abroad, but you have to try these things, don't you? Especially with things being so uncertain nowadays.'

'I spy with my little eye,' began the boy.

'Something beginning with "r",' put in his sister quickly.

'That was my turn!'

'Was not.'

'Anyhow, it's road. Anyone can tell that.'

There was a brief squabble as the fractious and overtired children gave vent to their irritation, much to the disapproval of a French family on the opposite side of the compartment who were clearly having their worst views of English family discipline confirmed.

'For goodness' sake,' said Mrs Phillips, turning pink round the ears. 'Pipe down, both of you. We're going back to Totnes next year at this rate.' She fished out a square of grease-proof paper, unfolding it to reveal a small pile of egg and cress sandwiches which the children seized on with glee, munching happily away, while their mother poured tea from a Thermos flask. 'We've more than enough sandwiches if you'd like one, my dear,' she said to Nora, who smiled and shook her head. The knot of excitement was twisting her belly so tight that the thought of eating anything was quite impossible.

Once they arrived in the noise and confusion of the city, Nora said goodbye to her travelling companions, who headed off towards their hotel. She took out the map Mme Godeaux's secretary had sent her along with the details of the course and followed the instructions as methodically as possible.

She lost her way a couple of times, but by retracing her steps, she got herself back on the correct route. When she knew she was near, but the actual street was nowhere to be found, she summoned up her courage to ask an elderly woman for directions.

'Mme Godeaux?' The woman nodded, gesturing towards a small side street.

'*Merci*, thank you,' said Nora, relieved she could understand the subsequent instructions to turn right and then left. Her ears were already attuning to the language and she was thankful for all that practice writing to Sabine, which meant that she was now almost fluent. Nearly there. She finally arrived in front of a tall building, easily recognisable from the brochure, which announced itself in large letters as the famed school of cuisine.

She'd done it. She'd made it safely, with only minimum help, to Paris and to Mme Godeaux's establishment. Relaxing a little, Nora drew in the smell of fumes, edged with exotic hints of olive oil and garlic, along with the distant roar of traffic, racing with even more impatient abandon than the helter-skelter around Piccadilly Circus.

Glee soared through her. She was in Paris, the city of Notre Dame and Montmartre, of the long tree-lined walk of the Champs-Elysées leading towards the Arc de Triomphe, all of it dominated by the high metal peak of the Eiffel Tower, so high it was sometimes swathed in fine wisps of cloud. Whatever happened, nothing could ever take that excitement away.

She still felt sad at the thought of not seeing Sabine, and that it might be years before they saw each other again. But she had her address in Colmar, she could still write to her, and hear about the baby when it arrived. And one day, before too long, she hoped they could meet.

Taking a deep breath, Nora rang the bell of the cookery school, and within minutes was making her way inside.

SEVEN

SABINE

Colmar, 1939

Sabine arrived in Colmar less than a week after leaving the *boulangerie*, and just days before Violette and Valérie were born.

Although it was still several weeks before she was due, the long train journey exhausted her. She manoeuvred her hugely swollen belly, squashed for most of the journey next to a suitcase that refused to fit with the other luggage in the rack above their heads. Her back ached, her ankles swelled in the heat, but most of all it was the grief that tore her apart as she was hurtled away from Paris, without even the opportunity to visit her family and say her farewells.

There was fear, too. Fear of the unknown and the new life that awaited her, horribly aware that she, and the imminent baby – or babies – would now be totally dependent on Emil and his family. It gave her an unnerving sense of helplessness, as if she'd been abruptly thrust back into being a child again.

As they reached Colmar station, she was thankful to find that Emil's telegram had got through in time for someone to be there waiting for them on the platform to help with the luggage, and there was a car to take them straight to the Schongauers' house on the outskirts of town.

'It's good to see you again,' said Emil in French, shaking the hand of a tall, sparsely built man with closely cropped fair hair sporting a brown leather jacket of somewhat military appearance.

'Condolences,' replied the newcomer, concentrating on Emil and barely appearing to notice Sabine at all. 'We always said the railways were mismanaged, and now Albert has paid the price. The management should be sued.'

'I agree,' replied Emil, 'although I expect my mother won't hear of it.' He turned to Sabine. 'We're lucky to have such a good helper. Karl Bernheim is my oldest friend, we were at school together.' He turned back to Karl. 'This is my wife, Sabine.'

'*Plaisir*,' said Karl curtly, nodding in her direction.

Even in her dazed state, Sabine recoiled instinctively at the expression in Karl's piercing blue eyes as they briefly met hers. The hostility in their depths was unmistakable. He continued to address her husband while totally ignoring her, slipping increasingly into a language that sounded more closely aligned to German than French that shut her out completely.

'We're proud of our country and our language,' remarked Karl, switching back to French as he helped her into his squat Volkswagen Beetle, spotlessly clean and highly polished. 'I expect you'll get used to hearing Alsatian being spoken.' He leant across her to place a small bag on the other side of the back seat, his arm slowly and deliberately brushing across her swollen breasts. 'Even a smart Parisienne girl like you,' he added, just too low for Emil to hear.

'I know some German,' she replied in that language. 'And Emil has been teaching me Alsatian, so I expect I'll be able to understand before too long.'

'Sabine is very clever with languages,' said Emil, forcing the large suitcase into the luggage compartment at the front of the car.

'Indeed.' Karl gave her the most perfunctory of smiles, his eyes travelling over her voluminous dress, his expression one of carefully directed distaste, gaze lingering just a little too long on every curve.

Sabine turned away, staring into the distance, trying to shut out the faint snort of satisfaction suggesting Karl considered her suitably cowed by his masculine superiority. She'd met men like him countless times before on the Métro going to and from work. Men who expressed contempt for women, while at the same time resenting that none fell to worship at their feet. When she was with Emil they were far more guarded, generally far too cowardly to insult another man's woman and risk consequences they would never face when abusing a woman on her own. But here in Colmar there was no escape. This time the perpetrator had already been introduced to her as her husband's oldest friend.

As Karl took his place at the wheel, with Emil in the passenger seat beside him, she could hear their voices fall into what was clearly a familiar rhythm. She might not be able to follow the conversation, but she sensed it was a repeat of an old one, quite likely carried on since they were barely able to walk. Emil had already taken on the hectoring tone he assumed when discussing politics with friends in their favourite pavement café. She could hear Karl seeming to defer to him, while slipping in comments of his own that had Emil nodding fervently in agreement.

Sabine clenched her fists. She'd always sworn she'd never be ignored, seen as nothing, the woman in the background, useful only for servicing others' needs. In Emil, she was fairly certain this negation of her presence was unconscious, but for Karl it was quite deliberate. Her eyes briefly met his again in the driver's mirror. She had the strongest sensation that he could read her discomfort, however much she tried to hide it, and that he was enjoying every moment.

It seemed an age until they arrived at a narrow, end-of-terrace house with gleaming white walls and neatly painted shutters, rows of window boxes waiting for the summer profusion of hot pink geraniums Emil had showed her in photographs.

'Ah, there you are.' A compact little woman with Emil's dark hair and brown eyes arrived at the door, wiping her hands on her apron. She embraced Emil tightly, while deep sobs escaped her.

'Maman,' said Emil, disengaging himself with a look of embarrassment and speaking in French. 'This is Sabine.'

'You are very welcome,' said his mother, dashing away her tears and taking Sabine's hand in hers. 'My son's wife is always welcome here. You join us at such a sad time. So very sad. Come on, we can leave the men to unload the car. You must be worn out, especially in your condition. Let's make you feel at home.'

Over the next days, Sabine did her best to settle into her new surroundings. She tried not to miss the freedom of her days in Paris and, to cope with the lack of privacy, the two of them squashed into Emil's childhood bedroom, surrounded by books on philosophy, famous Roman leaders and the art of war.

She equally did her best not to offend her mother-in-law. Claudette Schongauer had her own set ways of running the household and cooking Emil's favourite dishes. She clearly assumed that Sabine would simply fit in seamlessly to the way things had always been done.

'You'll learn, my dear,' said Claudette a few days later, speaking in French as she instructed Sabine (who'd never been

much of a cook) on how to slice onions to the correct thinness.
'And soon we'll have your little one to look after.'

The kitchen where they were preparing the evening meal
opened up into a small, white-washed courtyard at the back of
the house. Sabine could hear Emil's voice putting the world to
rights with Karl Bernheim over glasses of Pernod and red wine,
as he had every evening since their arrival.

'Well at least we won't have him around much longer,'
remarked Claudette abruptly, reaching for a fresh bottle of *vin
rouge*. 'Karl Bernheim,' she added to Sabine's enquiring glance.
'He's got a new job with his German cousin, just over the
border. Freiburg.'

'In Germany?'

'Quite.' She sniffed. 'Herr Hitler's welcome to him. He
won't be missed here.'

'I can't say I took to him,' said Sabine warily. This tiptoeing
on eggshells, trying not to say the wrong thing, was wearing her
down. She kept reminding herself the family were still grieving,
but she couldn't help but hate that feeling of being invisible.

To her relief, Claudette gave a low chuckle. 'Emil did say
you were a sharp one. Intelligent, I mean.' Her eyes returned to
the drift of men's voices from the courtyard. 'Karl's always been
a pig of a man, like his father before him.' She sighed. 'But he
and Emil were always thick as thieves, talking of revolution and
making the world a better place, so what can you do?'

'Wait for them to see sense?' said Sabine, growing a little bolder.
She was beginning to feel some kind of sympathy with her mother-
in-law. Ironic that it should be Karl Bernheim who revealed it.

Claudette laughed out loud as she drew the cork. 'Let's
hope so, my dear. Let's hope so.'

'I'll take that out to them,' offered Sabine. 'It's the least I
can do.'

'If you're sure?'

'Completely. I'm not afraid of him.'

Claudette nodded approvingly. 'Good girl. Men like that, they thrive on fear. Fear in the eyes of others they see as weaker. And especially women,' she added grimly. 'His father was reputed to do more than just beat Karl's mother black and blue. From when I was a little girl I was warned to keep clear of old M. Bernheim. I was lucky, but I know others who were not. I can't forgive them that, father or son.'

Sabine took the tray towards the freshness of the courtyard, bordered with roses in pots and a large bougainvillea.

'Purity!' The banging of a fist sent up a protesting screech from the metal table. 'That's what it's about. Purity of race, purity of mind. You should come and hear him speak, Emil. He's electrifying. The visionary of our age. He's transforming Germany. One day he'll transform the world.'

'So you say.' Through the half-open door, Sabine saw her husband watching the speaker intently, half repelled, half swept up in Karl's enthusiasm.

'Degenerates.' Karl finished his Pernod, warming to his theme. 'Jews and Gypsies and the mentally incapable. That's what's been dragging Germany down, and France too. Squashing us all, taking away our honest living.'

'But I thought we agreed he was a joke, Karl,' said Emil. 'A madman. Someone who'll never last in the seriousness of real power. Last time you told me there was talk of him being a criminal, hiring thugs to do his bidding.'

'I said no such thing.' Karl was contemptuous. 'That was all just propaganda. The old guard that just spend their time lining their own pockets while the rest of us are only just able to get by, however hard we work. They're so afraid of his vision, they spend their time blackening his name. A war hero. A man who has the people in his heart, not the generals and the bankers.' He banged the table once more with his fist. 'And England is the worst of them, with her lords and ladies living in castles while the peasants starve.'

'I thought Herr Hitler liked the English,' remarked Sabine, placing the tray on the table. 'I'm sure I've read he's expressed admiration for their empire.'

'And their literature is second to none,' said Emil, sending her a grateful half-smile, the slightly dazed look in his eyes clearing.

'Oscar Wilde!' retorted Karl, in tones of an argument won. From the corner of her eye Sabine caught the sly glance he sent her. Either he thought this reference to homosexuality went over her head, or he was trying to shock her into silence.

Sabine ignored him. She finished pouring the wine and sat down next to Emil. She wouldn't let Karl drive her away, to flounce out like some silly schoolgirl and embarrass Emil by her desertion. Besides, she wanted to hear the kind of poison he was feeding her husband's restless, discontented mind. Knowledge was power, or at least the only chance she had of fighting the influence Karl had over him, as he dragged Emil back to their youthful idealism and the days they had spent together before Paris, discussing politics in Colmar's cheaper cafés and restaurants.

'I'm not sure I could support imprisoning those who disagree with me,' said Emil, reaching for an open packet of Gauloises, sending the pungent smell of Parisian cafés and the rush of the morning Métro to hang amongst the hyacinths. 'After all, if Herr Hitler is interning communists, we might well be among them.'

'I was never a communist,' snapped Karl.

'Come off it, you were always quoting Marx. And wasn't Stalin one of your heroes? I heard you tell Albert that Stalin was inspiring you to volunteer to support the Republicans in the Spanish Civil War.'

'I didn't fight in the civil war,' said Karl. 'I was a socialist, yes, we all were, but never a communist. Never a communist.'

'As you say,' replied Emil quietly, sounding more like the rational student she'd known in Paris, always eager to see both sides of the argument, eschewing any suggestion of violence.

Sabine hastily hid her smile. She sensed Karl staring at her straight in the face, the bully's old trick of trying to intimidate anyone he considered a thorn in his side. She'd made an enemy all right, without even trying. Karl clearly loathed any woman who spoke her mind or dared to contradicted him. And she had a sense of him hating her most for any influence she might have over Emil. Her influence versus his, in ways Claudette, as a mother and a woman who deferred to male authority, could never do.

Sabine shuffled slightly in her chair to ease the ache in her back. Thank goodness for Claudette, and for knowing she wouldn't have to deal with him for much longer. Once Karl had returned to Germany, she and Emil would have a chance to rebuild their lives. And by the time of Karl's next visit she'd be more established in the household. She hoped their paths would only ever cross very briefly in future, if at all.

It was later that night that Sabine went into a long and difficult labour. Even Claudette's initial calm cracked the next day sending for the local doctor to assist at the vital moment.

Afterwards, Sabine lay dazed in the darkened room, body torn apart, unable to comprehend that she'd given birth to one baby let alone two. She'd heard them cry, one weaker than the other, but definitely both alive. A rush of fear went through her. Why hadn't they been handed to her? She struggled to clear her mind, to focus on the everyday sounds around her.

The doctor was still in the room, speaking in a low voice to Claudette.

'Possible mental incapacity with this one, I'm afraid Madame. Even if the child does survive. And in these cases, perhaps it would be as well ...'

'Thank you, *monsieur le docteur*,' Claudette replied smoothly. 'I'm sure we'll do what's best.' She waited until the doctor had taken his dignified way outside before adding, 'Pig of a man, shouldn't be allowed to practise'. She returned to lift the smaller of the sleeping bundles, holding her close, her expression as fierce as a lioness. 'You fight, little one. We aren't losing you, I swear, whatever those fools might say, my little flower, I'll make sure you live your life, if it's the last thing I do.'

EIGHT

NORA

Paris, 1939

During her first days in Paris, Nora revelled in her new existence.

Her only regret was not sharing the sights with Sabine as they'd planned. There was also a nagging worry at the back of her mind because her last letter to Colmar hadn't been answered. But, she reminded herself, it was most probably because Sabine was adjusting to her new life, and her baby was due any day now. Sabine was bound to have responsibilities she couldn't imagine, so she was silly to expect an answer so soon.

When summoned to Mme Godeaux's office on the evening she arrived, Nora found her new mentor was a tiny woman with greying hair caught in a tight bun behind her head. The severity of her expression was reflected by the darkness of her clothing: an elegantly cut skirt that skimmed her ankles, topped with what looked like a man's waistcoat and a tailored jacket.

'So, you work in a French kitchen?' was Mme Godeaux's first salvo, in precise French.

'Yes, Madame,' Nora replied in the same language. 'In

London.'

'*Londres*,' repeated Madame, with a theatrical shudder. 'The food there, I've only sampled it twice. That was quite enough. And so you think you're familiar with French cuisine?' Her tone of sarcasm was unmistakeable. 'Cooking with such experts.'

'They're not experts,' exclaimed Nora. Surely she'd already explained this in her application?

'Of this you are certain?'

'Well, no.' Nora chewed her bottom lip. She cursed herself for not expecting to be grilled on *La Belle Époque*. It took her a moment to gather her thoughts and mentally translate what she wanted to say. When she looked up, she found Madame frowning at her with more than a hint of impatience. 'I'm sure they feel they're experts,' she said at last. 'But I'm not so sure. It all feels very heavy and a bit, well, bland.' She stumbled to a halt. That sounded mean, and who was she to criticise? Mum had never considered herself more than an everyday cook, and she'd never been able to afford even the cheapest restaurants closer to the fashionable centre of the city.

Madame laughed. 'Yes, that's what I've heard. Oh, I have my sources,' she added to Nora's look of surprise. 'You're quite right. The dishes are French, but the cooking prosaically English. I see I have much to teach you.'

'That's why I want to learn,' said Nora, suddenly afraid she was about to be dismissed and told to go home.

'Of course. I can see that. It's easy to write; I needed to hear it.' She gave a wry smile. 'And that your French was as good as you claimed it to be, given the English are as terrible with their languages as they are in their kitchens. And so it is. Good. Now you join the others. We start first thing tomorrow. I can see we have no time to lose.'

Relieved to have safely passed her first test, Nora returned to the large room on the fourth floor she was to share with two dark-haired sisters from Spain. She found the fourth inhabitant, a flaxen-haired young woman, unpacking a small suitcase and placing her underclothes in a small chest of drawers set beside each bed.

'Hello,' said Nora, shyly introducing herself. Her new room-mate appeared to be older than the other girls she'd passed in the corridor on her way in, in her mid-twenties at least. She was heavily made up, a cigarette between her scarlet lips, despite Madame's prohibition on smoking indoors.

'Heidi,' the young woman replied abruptly in almost fluent French. 'Heidi Braun. And no, no relation to Eva.'

'Who?' demanded Nora, feeling ignorant and foolish.

'Eva Braun.' Heidi's lips twisted briefly. 'Well, you're not alone. Many others haven't heard of her either, here or at home in Germany.' She returned to her suitcase, back turned towards Nora. 'Along with so much else.'

It was a definite dismissal. Nora turned towards her ruck-sack, placed hastily on the neighbouring bed when she arrived. As she did so, something slipped from the quilt on Heidi's bed, fluttering unseen to the floorboards. Nora instinctively picked it up. It was a photograph of a young man with fair hair smiling out at her. A warm smile in a pleasant face. She found herself smiling in return.

'That's mine,' said Heidi, sharply.

'I was just returning it.'

Heidi took the photograph, placing it in her handbag without so much as a glance, returning to her unpacking. Nora had a distinct feeling this was one fellow student she wanted to avoid as much as possible.

'Thank you.' Nora looked round in surprise as she reached her bed. Heidi still had her back to her, but the rigidity of her stance had softened a little. 'I really don't want to lose that picture.'

'It was a pleasure,' she replied.

At this, Heidi looked up. 'You're English?'

'Yes. From London.'

'London.' A wistful expression came over Heidi's face. 'I hoped to study there once. Tower Bridge. The Houses of Parliament. Buckingham Palace.'

'I don't live near any of them, I'm afraid,' said Nora. 'Although I have seen them.'

'Why did you leave London?' asked Heidi, switching to English.

'To study here.'

Heidi considered her for a minute. 'Perhaps you should return,' she said with her earlier abruptness, resuming the placing of her belongings in the chest.

Feeling slightly pummelled for no apparent reason, Nora reached for her suitcase and felt relieved when her companion left without saying another word.

Nora soon discovered she'd been right in her estimation of the cooks of *La Belle Époque*. Over those first weeks, she began to understand just how little they knew.

Under Madame's eagle eye, as she learnt the secrets of sauces and *omelette aux fines herbes,* Nora had begun to suspect that *La Belle Époque* had as little to do with real French cuisine as fish and chips. She knew far less than the others, even Heidi, who, from her brief interjections into the conversation, had never worked in a kitchen, just her father's bakery in Nuremberg.

The other girls seemed frighteningly familiar with dishes beyond *La Belle Époque's* London clientele, such as steak tartare, duck confit and bouillabaisse, let alone the deep richness of olive oil – only available from the chemist at home – and Madame's vast array of herbs. It all made Nora feel unexpectedly provincial, and very unsophisticated.

To her dismay, her fellow students were equally familiar with *patisserie* and confections such as financier and gâteau St-Honoré. Nora gazed in awe at the displays in the shops along the nearby streets, marvelling at the jewelled rows of neatly formed macarons, interspersed with primrose-yellow *tartes au citron* and the glossy domes of raspberries topping *tartes framboise*, all set between the layered wonders of mille-feuille and opera cake. She had no idea how she was going to tackle a jaconde sponge, or a genoise, let alone achieve such miniature uniformity and perfection of fruit and icing.

At first she was overwhelmed by everything she had to learn, and by Madame's exacting standards until, finally, she achieved the correct creamy consistency with her béchamel sauce. She stood, absorbing the flavours, entranced by the revelation that something so simple could be so rich and delicious.

'Not bad,' allowed Madame, the highest praise yet. 'You learn flavours, yes?' A slightly wicked gleam appeared in her eyes. 'So, now you try the olive again.' At Nora's instinctive wrinkling of the nose at the unfamiliar fruit her fellow cooks ate with gusto, Madame laughed and gestured to her lips. 'Think. Feel it. Find out everything. Then think again.'

Not to be outdone, Nora obeyed, holding the oily sharpness in her mouth, concentrating on absorbing the flavour. It was so much more intense than the small vinegary versions used sparingly at *La Belle Époque*. Equally distant as the lemons from the market – which were large, with paler, strangely more knobbly skin – than those Mum used at home to make lemonade in the summer, but with an unfamiliar touch of sweetness amongst the sharpness that set her palate racing.

Nora stood entranced as the unfamiliar assault on her tastebuds of that first morning transformed into the deliciousness of strong sunlight, of greater warmth than she'd ever known in her life. She opened her eyes to find Madame still scrutinising her.

'Now, you are a chef,' she said quietly in English.

So that was what this was about! Nora felt dizzy as under-standing flooded over her. The new techniques and unfamiliar ingredients were simply tools to serve the alchemy of texture and taste that made the true beauty of a dish. From that moment she eagerly absorbed everything about this new world of flavours; Christmas dinner back at home seemed bland, and the finest banquet laid out for a wedding party at *La Belle Époque* greasy and heavy on the stomach. Even if she never learnt to be the finest chef, she'd been awakened to a whole new way of seeing. It was like life itself, opening up, with endless possibilities.

During their few free hours each week, Nora joined her fellow students in exploring Paris. They were guided by Manon, a small, elegantly dressed young woman who, Parisienne born and bred, was taking the course to fulfil her ambition of opening a restaurant along the banks of the Seine. Nora drank in the sights and atmosphere of the city, adoring the magical reality of places she'd only seen in books. In Notre Dame she walked in awe between the tall medieval arches of the cathedral, breathing in the soft echoes of footsteps in the vast space, accompanied by the scent of candles and incense, entranced by the light dancing between the vivid blues and reds of the rose windows. She loved it when Manon took them to the eighteenth arrondissement, racing up the steep steps and cobbled streets of bohemian Montmartre, pausing to watch the artists engrossed in painting street scenes, some catching passers-by to sketch their portraits, or attempting to capture the pale-domed elegance of Sacré-Coeur, with its view of Paris laid out below.

One day, as they returned to their lodgings after visiting the faded grandeur of the Jardin des Tuileries, Nora found a letter from Sabine. She read it eagerly, absorbing the news that her friend's babies had been born. Twin girls, Valérie and Violette. Born prematurely, but they'd survived, and Valérie, at least, was thriving. Nora paused at the next sentence, the chatter of voices around her fading into the far distance. She took her letter up to the solitude of the metal fire escape outside her room, where the more daring of her fellow students retreated for a cigarette.

She concentrated on Sabine's words. The smaller of the twins, Violette, had been born with a harelip. Nora could feel how hard it had been for her friend to write those words. Violette was surviving, she said, but only just. The deformity made it difficult for her to feed. She had so wanted to take her to the local hospital to see if anything could be done to help her. But her husband and mother-in-law were convinced nothing could be done, especially as the doctor who'd attended at the birth had suggested she may also be mentally impaired.

Nora sat in the fading heat of the day, remembering when Jonny was first born, how Dad pretended for months that nothing was wrong, as if he were ashamed of having a disabled child in the family, feeling it would reflect badly on him. Pearl had been the one to take her son to the nearest children's hospital, demanding he be treated when he developed pneumonia when only a few months old.

Nora frowned, remembering something half forgotten. She'd gone with Pearl to the hospital to offer the support her sister desperately needed. There'd been a boy there called Timmy who'd been born with a harelip, but he'd been operated on, the gash in his lip closed up. She tried to remember the half-overheard conversations between the women in the waiting room about Timmy's operation going so well, you hardly knew the gap had been there, his speech was already coming on in leaps and bounds. One day, his mother had announced proudly, you'd never know there had ever been anything amiss.

There was a treatment. But Nora had a feeling it needed to be performed when a child was very young. If there was a surgeon in London who treated harelips, then surely there was also one in Paris, perhaps even one located nearer Colmar.

On their next free day she didn't join the other students heading to the Louvre, but instead made her way on the Métro to the nearest hospital. After much toing and froing, and with the help of her trusty dictionary for more complex vocabulary, she was finally directed towards a nurse just coming off duty. Yes, the nurse confirmed, scribbling down a name in Nora's notebook, there was indeed a surgeon in Paris who dealt with that kind of thing, but she understood he was rather overwhelmed.

As the nurse handed back the pen and notepad, she paused. 'For you?'

Nora shook her head. 'For a friend. In Alsace.'

'Ah, a pity. The only other surgeons I've heard do that operation are in England. Oxford is one, I think, and one on the coast, I'm not sure where. The south, I think.'

'I can find out when I get home, if Sabine isn't able to get to the surgeon in Paris,' Nora said. She wasn't about to leave any stone unturned.

The nurse nodded and scribbled two more names. 'Such a small thing can make such a big difference to a life. *Bon courage* good luck,' she said, swinging her bag over her shoulder and wearily heading out into the streets.

Nora paused at a pavement café on her way back to the cookery school to write to Sabine telling her what she'd found out. It might be of no help, or Sabine might not be able to afford the surgery, but she'd done all she could. She'd felt the fear underlying Sabine's words, the same fear she'd once seen in her sister's eyes. She couldn't bear the thought of seeing it in anyone else's.

NINE

SABINE

Colmar, 1939

Sabine read through Nora's letter once again, her heart beating rapidly in her ears. There was hope. Her instincts had been right: there was a solution. Violette might yet thrive.

The bedroom at the back of the house was cool from the faint breeze wafting in from the half-open shutters, the only sound the steady breathing of her tiny daughters as they slept. Valérie's eyelids fluttered as she dreamt, one chubby fist opening and closing as if grasping some invisible toy. Violette frowned slightly, her serious expression clearing instantly into the blissful calm of unconsciousness. Sabine longed to lift her up and hold her and never let her go. She'd never dreamed love could go so deep into every part of her. She would do anything, fight anyone, let the life be torn from her, to keep her children safe; most of all Violette, struggling with all the strength she had to absorb the milk she needed to sustain life itself.

Down below she heard Emil telling Claudette about his day in the boot shop. A new determination went through her. She had to find a way of persuading Emil to agree to let her take

Violette to Paris. In the weeks since their birth, Emil had avoided his daughters. Not just because he considered looking after them as women's work, she recognised with sadness, but because he saw Violette's disfigurement as a reflection of his own inadequacies. Sometimes, she had a dread in her heart that her husband would rather lose Violette than see the unfinished, gaping hole of her imperfect perfection.

The next morning Sabine cleared the breakfast table and brewed coffee on the stove. It had become their morning ritual if the babies were asleep, the half hour in their day when they had some privacy.

She took the cups and placed them on the courtyard table. Above her the sky was a delicate blue, a promise of heat to come. She breathed in the clear air, enjoying the morning sounds of the street stirring, the footsteps and greetings of 'Güete Morge' between the clop of horse's hooves and the occasional roar of a motorised vehicle.

She turned with a smile as Emil emerged from the house to join her, fastening the buttons of his waistcoat. 'It's going to be a beautiful day.'

'So it is,' he replied.

'I thought I might try taking the girls out in the perambulator. The fresh air will do them good.'

'It's going to be hot,' he muttered, frowning.

'If I go early, no one will see us.'

'That's not what I meant.'

But it was. There was always some reason not to take them out. She knew they needed the air and the stimulation. They couldn't go on being confined in Emil's childhood bedroom forever and she refused to take Valérie out on her own. It would be the start of Violette's exclusion from their lives, of fulfilling the doctor's muttered warning of possible mental incapacity. On the other hand, to deprive Valérie would be equally cruel.

She sat down opposite Emil. 'I've heard from my friend in Paris.'

'Oh?' He sipped his *café au lait* with disinterest, reaching for his cigarettes.

'She tells me there's a chance Violette's lip can be repaired.' She saw him wince. 'There's a surgeon in Paris who can sew the pieces together so neatly it'll barely be noticeable after a few years.' Silence. 'Emil, she could be the same as Valérie. No one need ever know. If she can feed properly, she'll get stronger. She can be healed.'

He drew smoke deep into his lungs. 'But not the metal incapacity.'

'Nora also asked about that. She says she was told that a harelip doesn't always signify mental incapacity. But even if Violette is impaired in some way, we'll love her just the same. She might not be like other children, but she'll still be our daughter. She'll find a way through.'

He finished his coffee in one gulp and stubbed out the remains of his cigarette. 'I'll be late.'

'At least it's worth a try, surely?'

He pushed back his chair 'And who's going to pay for this?'

'I still have a few savings from my work at the *boulangerie*, and Maman ...'

'No.' Mortification suffused his face. 'I'll not have people say I can't support my own family. It's none of their concern. Your family never thought I was good enough for you in the first place.'

'That's not true!'

'You may have chosen not to see it, but it was made clear enough to me. You'll always be the girl from the castle, I'll always be the son of a bootmaker.'

Sabine gazed despairingly at her husband. 'It's not like that,

Emil, and you know it. My family want us to be happy. They want to help.'

'Then they can give us the name of this surgeon. *I'll* pay for it. The business will turn around before long. In a year or two.'

No! He wasn't going to fob her off, put his pride before everything else. This was their daughter they were discussing, a child's future, perhaps even her very survival.

'Nora also said that the earlier the procedure can be done, the greater chance of success.'

'We'll speak about it tonight.' He brushed past her without his customary kiss and strode out, boots retreating along the tiles of the hallway.

Slowly, Sabine collected the empty cups, fighting the urge to scream, to dash the amber-hued glass against the flagstones, obliterating them forever.

'I was a fool,' she muttered beneath her breath. It might have been only a few years ago but she'd been a child then, absorbed in her own world, so certain her future would be just as she planned, and nothing could stop her. The brilliance of the courtyard wavered in front of her eyes. She loved Emil, of course she did. And he loved her, despite the difficulties and responsibilities that made him impatient with her at times. But her children came first.

Frustration tugged at Sabine. In truth, the few francs she had left from her wages would barely do more than cover the train ticket to Paris. She might only have been earning a pittance before her marriage, but at least what she had was hers. She could choose not to eat and go to the theatre instead. It hadn't been a hardship, it had been her choice. When they were first married, she and Emil had pooled their resources to make ends meet. Now, Emil earned the money and Claudette controlled it, leaving her with no financial independence.

But she was not giving up so easily.

. . .

There was no opportunity to speak to Emil that evening. As Sabine had dreaded, he appeared with Karl, who'd returned from Germany for one of his periodic visits, the two having clearly paused at a café on the way back for wine and cognac.

Sabine had just got the twins off to sleep when she heard them below, their voices even louder than usual. At least the babies, who'd been restless all day, were both deep enough asleep in the cool of the evening not to wake. She sat with them for a while, watching their steady breathing, absorbing the baby smell of soap and milkiness, until Claudette called up, asking if they were drowsy yet, with more than a hint she needed assistance.

'I'll be down now,' she called. 'They've just settled.' She took one last look at them, so tiny, so impossibly fragile, with their miniature fingernails and the soft fineness of their hair, and closed the door behind her, leaving it slightly ajar so she could hear if either of them stirred.

'Like I told you,' said Karl, as she laid the table around them. 'It's a management position. Well-paid and secure. The Führer is rearming Germany, taking her pride back. It's a job for life, and there aren't many of those around in Alsace, or France, these days.'

'But Freiburg ...'

'It's not so very far away. The company has branches in Munich, maybe one day in Paris. Don't you see? I can give you a way in. Once there, you'll easily rise through the ranks like me. I can introduce you to people. Come on, Emil, there's a new world coming, anyone with any sense can feel it. This'll all be swept away. Do you really want to be left behind?'

'The boot shop,' began Emil, then stopped.

'Sell up. Papa always wanted me to continue the farm, but I refuse to be held back just because that's how things have always been done. I'm making my own life, on my own terms.' Karl knocked back his glass of Pernod. 'If you've got plenty of money, that's the way to do everything you've ever wanted, not wasting your energies on keeping some old shop going because that's what your father wanted.'

Sabine quietly refilled their glasses, using as little of the aperitif as she dared, topping it up with water, her nose wrinkling at the milkiness of the resulting liquid and the smell of aniseed. She hastily retreated, taking the bottle with her. Claudette was always careful to control the alcohol consumed in the house, giving Emil just enough to mellow his mood, but not so much that he slurred his speech or was unfit for work the next morning.

'Karl wants Emil to take a job in Germany,' she blurted out as she closed the kitchen door behind her.

'*Quelle surprise.*' Claudette continued to calmly inspect her casserole.

'You don't mind?'

'Of course I mind, and I'd rather it wasn't with Karl, but we have to be practical.'

'You mean, we have no other choice.'

'Quite.' Claudette replaced the lid and returned the pot to the oven. 'Poor Albert was the businessman, and even he could see the writing on the wall.' She sat down, a rare pause in her usual whirl of making sure all the sections of the meal came together at the same time, and took a cigarette from her apron pocket. Sabine tried not to stare. Her mother-in-law smoked as rarely as she drank, just a few token sips to keep her son company, yet now she was drawing smoke into her lungs as if it were the freshest air she'd ever tasted.

'Stops the feeling of hunger,' Claudette remarked. 'Or at least that's what we told ourselves. The last time, that is.'

'The last time?'

'The war.'

'Oh,' said Sabine, the fear that lay just beneath the surface of their lives these days rising to chill her to the core.

They paused as a cough, followed by a brief wail, came down from above. There was a faint whimper, followed by a return to silence.

'You wouldn't believe the hunger,' said Claudette, her eyes instinctively gazing up towards the sleeping children. 'You young ones are lucky, you don't know what total war means. When you're doing everything you can to survive, when you count as nothing. When the weak and the vulnerable, the old and the very young, are the first to die, and however hard you struggle, whatever you try, there's nothing you can do to stop it. Karl always filled my boys' heads with glory and the march of triumphant armies, like in a fairy tale. War's not like that, not at all, not when you live through it. No one wins.'

'Don't!' Sabine stared at her in alarm. War had always seemed something that had taken place in the distant past, before real life, modern life, began. Yet she'd been a small child when the war had ended in 1918. She hadn't thought of it like that before, that it was so close. So close. There was ice in her blood, crackling through her scalp. She had an urge to run upstairs, sweep up her sleeping children and hold them tight, take them anywhere, anywhere safe, away from the vision haunting the deep shadows in Claudette's face. Shadows she'd never understood before.

'I can't believe they're about to let it happen again.' Claudette reached for the bottle of wine she'd been using for the casserole, splashing generous amounts into glasses, pushing one towards Sabine. 'Cursed politicians, they're all the same, out for their own glory and lining their own pockets, while we're always the ones to suffer. They never think of that. That's when you realise you're nothing to them, you don't count.'

'You don't really think there'll be another war, surely?'

'I hope not. But I fear it might, what with that madman and his ridiculous fantasies. And we're right on the border here, neither one thing nor the other. I don't like the thought of Emil being in charge of making armaments, but at least, if the worst happens, he wouldn't be drafted into the army.' She drained her glass. 'And who knows which army that would be? French? German? That's what happened last time when Alsace was annexed; one day we were one thing, the next another. We were even forbidden to speak French. Not that it stopped us, of course.' She took a long drag on her cigarette, deeply drawing in the smoke as if to obliterate every sensation in her body. 'The truth is, the only way anyone truly wins a war is just to survive. Nothing more. Just live through it to build a future once the madmen have obliterated each other, as they always do. I'd do anything to make sure Emil survives.' She poured the remainder of the bottle into her glass. 'Even be civil to a boor like Karl Bernheim, if that's what it takes.'

Within weeks it was settled. Sabine went through the routine of feeding and cleaning Valérie and Violette in a daze, feeling increasingly powerless as the Schongauers negotiated with a bootmaker's in Mulhouse to take over the business.

As she held Violette, taking time to make sure she fed, fear lingered in the back of her mind. Albert's death had been so sudden, she'd not had time to think when they'd made the move from their tiny apartment in Paris to Colmar. They'd simply packed what they could carry, handed in the keys to the concierge and headed for the Gare de L'Est and the train to Colmar. They could travel light in those days, when it had just been the two of them, when the two tiny babies hadn't come into the equation, with their fragile helplessness and their need to be fed and kept warm and safe from harm.

Even when Karl returned to Freiburg and they no longer had to put up with his suffocating presence most evenings, which had increasingly felt like living through a particularly strident performance of *Götterdämmerung*, Emil felt distant, untouchable.

'I've got the job,' he announced one evening, over dinner. 'Karl was right. With his recommendation, they've chosen me over all the other applicants. Herr Zimmermann phoned me at the shop this afternoon. He sounded very eager. They want me to start next week.'

'Without even meeting you?' frowned Claudette.

'Karl's recommendation was enough. He's very highly thought of. And he's right, they need all the reliable workers they can get.'

'I just didn't think it would be so soon.'

'The sooner the better,' he answered. 'The shop will be signed over next week.'

'I thought it wasn't until next month.'

'The new owners are in a hurry. They have a contract to supply army boots, they're taking the stock and all the workers. Besides, the way things are, who knows what might happen in a month or two? Best to strike while we can.'

'No knock-down in price?' demanded Claudette suspiciously.

Emil flushed. 'Of course not, Maman. What do you take me for?'

His mother ignored his humiliation, deep in her own thoughts. 'So at least the debts will be paid. And we won't lose the house, thank the Lord.'

'We were never going to lose the house.' He frowned at her. 'Did you really think I was so useless compared to Albert that I'd forfeit everything he and Papa and Grand-père worked for?'

'I'm not blaming you. I understand times are hard.'

'I'll never live up to him is what you mean. You never expected me to. That's the only reason you let me train to be a journalist in the first place, so I'd be safely out of the way and making a fool of myself in Paris and London, where no one here would ever know.'

'That's not true, and if you really think about it, you know it. I understood your passion to be a journalist, and so did Albert. You did so well at school and worked so hard, neither of us wanted to stand in your way. It's what your father would have wished for as well.'

'I'm not likely to achieve anything now.'

Not with a wife and children to support. That's what he really meant, Sabine thought, hearing the bitterness in his voice. Across the table, she met Claudette's eyes, seeing the older woman's mouth tighten. Perhaps if it had just been Valérie ...

Later that night, as she returned from settling the twins, Sabine found the light still on and Emil sitting up in bed going through his papers.

'Everything all right?' he asked, looking up with a smile. With his spectacles on his nose he once more resembled the Emil she'd first known.

'Yes, they're both asleep. Valérie went straight off, but Violette was restless again.'

'I see.' He returned to his papers, shutting her out. Or rather, she saw with sadness, shutting out any mention of Violette. Since their disagreement about the surgeon in Paris he'd avoided the subject, always appearing to be asleep by the time she'd attended to the twins.

At first she'd tried to put it all down to the stress of dealing with the sale of the business, and had even been grateful for being able to avoid any physical intimacy. She still felt stretched so tight, her mind a whirl of new responsibilities and emotions; all she wanted to do was curl up in a ball and be left alone to sleep. Even the thought of lovemaking was beyond her. She had nothing more to give. But it wasn't just that. It was his dismissal of her wishes, him putting his own requirements before those of their daughter that created a gulf between them she wasn't sure she could overcome. She needed time, space, to think things through, to come up with a solution.

Slowly she climbed into bed beside him, feeling his warmth next to hers. On the other hand, she missed him. She missed their conversations, the squeeze of his hand, his smile when Claudette wasn't looking. One of them had to start to bridge the chasm that had opened up between them.

'Still things to sort out for the shop?'

'Yes. The last ones now.' He placed the papers on the bedside table and removed his glasses. 'I've been thinking, maybe we could have made a go of it. If we'd held out for a commission for army boots ...'

'The shop's probably too small to attract large orders like that,' she replied gently. 'But even so, is it really what you wanted to do all your life? When we were in Paris, didn't you always say it was what you were trying to escape from?'

'That's true.' He smiled at her again, settling down on the pillows, pulling the covers over them. The house was silent, just the sound of Claudette below tidying up dishes and sweeping the floor in her final ritual before bed. His hand brushed the hair from her face. 'Karl says there's a local newspaper, always looking for material. I can make a start there.'

'Then it's worked out for the best.'

'Yes.' His hand lingered across her cheek. 'I've been thinking. It's happened so fast I haven't had time to make proper arrangements. Karl has offered me a room in his house until I can find a place of my own. It's just a room. It'll be too small for all of us, and you don't know anyone there. I think it's better if you stay here until I'm properly settled. With my wages, I can easily send Maman enough to support you all.'

'You want to leave us behind?' She'd spoken more sharply than she'd intended. His tender hand paused, then moved away.

'I'm not leaving you behind. Like I said, you're better off here until I can find somewhere bigger. I'm only thinking of you. Surely you can see that?'

She was too tired to fight. Her treacherous brain couldn't even begin to express her feelings, to argue rationally with him, the sort of argument they'd once so enjoyed the more heated it became, knowing halfway through that it was a prelude to the most intense lovemaking.

'Yes,' she said sadly. Out of sight, out of mind. The truth was, he couldn't bear the thought of others seeing Violette. His failure. His lack of purity. His degeneracy. The goblin, not the tragic Valkyrie of his imagination. His hand returned, reaching towards the softness of her neck. Every part of her was rigid. This felt like ownership, not love. She closed her eyes, taking herself away from him to a quiet place deep inside herself, willing the act, that had once expressed the deepest trust and affection, to be simply over. Done with. Not a mutual expression. How could she open herself, body or soul, to a man who was so unthinkingly putting his needs before hers and their children's? His hand paused again. Instinctively, she opened her eyes. He was watching her, as if slightly puzzled, as if he'd never quite seen her properly before.

'We'll talk about this in the morning,' he muttered, turning away, as if to sleep.

On her abandoned side of the bed, Sabine curled herself up in a ball, for all the heat of the evening still unable to get warm.

She wanted to make him turn towards her, to rekindle what had once been. He wasn't made of stone. A touch, a murmured word, a welcoming softness of her body, not the tensing against him he'd felt, would be enough. Yet she lay there unmoving.

Her mind had cleared. If she left with him, she'd be in a place she didn't know. An alien place, with a hint of uncertainty. Karl would make sure she was unwelcome and she would have to live with Emil's shame of Violette. On the other hand, if she agreed to being left behind, she had a chance. Claudette might always put her son first, but she loved her grandchildren, they were part of her. There was a practical side to Claudette she could reach, whereas Emil's pride would block her out. It might be her only opportunity to get Violette to the surgeon in Paris before the threatened war broke out, putting an end to the baby's only chance.

She was almost glad when a whimper from the next room had her creeping out of bed.

She sat by the window, holding Violette's fragile body, exhausted after her desperate attempts to feed. It felt as though she was finally emerging from a fog that had enveloped her ever since they left Paris. She'd put her own life to one side to support Emil, she'd followed him when he'd unexpectedly been summoned home. She'd done it all willingly, from love. But Emil was a grown man who could fend for himself. Violette was a fragile scrap of life, one she'd fight to the ends of the earth to save. She would find a way of getting Violette to the surgeon in Paris, if it was the last thing she did.

Gently now, Sabine rocked the tiny baby in her arms until Violette's breathing deepened once more into sleep. She gazed down at her face, the faint curve of closed eyelids, darkening eyes that looked out at her so confidently, so certain she would protect her, lead her towards the days ahead. No life deserved to be thrown away, especially not this precious scrap she loved with all her being. Sabine swore to herself that whatever it took, whatever it cost her, she would make sure her daughter was safe.

Emil left for Germany as soon as the sale of the boot shop was settled.

Sabine came down to join Claudette the next morning to

find her mother-in-law sitting at the kitchen table, lost in thought.

'They've settled,' said Sabine, doing her best to sound cheerful.

'So I hear,' replied Claudette, moving slowly to retrieve the coffee bubbling on the stove, her movements stiff, like that of a much older woman.

Sabine rose to help her. 'Are you not feeling well, Maman?'

'I'm well enough.' Claudette straightened her shoulders. 'Sit down, my dear. I need to talk to you.'

She sounded ominous. Sabine braced herself for criticism of her mothering, or an instruction from Emil to persuade Sabine to place Violette in some kind of institution for the disabled. She sensed a fight ahead.

Claudette poured the coffee, pushing the second cup towards Sabine. 'You said there's a way of healing Violette.'

'Did Emil tell you?'

'No. I heard you talking. I wasn't certain I'd heard correctly, so I prised it out of him. My boys could never keep any secrets from me.'

'Oh,' said Sabine, wishing the coffee would flow straight into her bloodstream to give her energy and a sharper mind to do battle for her daughter.

'He doesn't believe it's possible,' added Claudette.

'I'm not giving up. From what my friend Nora told me, it *is* possible, and the surgeon in Paris is one of the best. But the sooner it's done, the better the outcome. It would give her a chance of a normal life.'

'But it costs a great deal.'

'I'll find a way to raise the money.'

'Yes, I'm sure you will.' Claudette's eyes rested on hers. 'Mothers will do everything they can for their children.' She was silent for a moment. Then she reached into her pocket, taking out a small wooden box which she placed in front of Sabine. 'For you.'

Sabine opened the lid, revealing an ornate pendant with a deep glow of a jewel at the centre, surrounded by a thick gold chain. 'I can't take this!'

'It was my grandmother's. She wanted it passed down through the female line.' Claudette's voice wavered slightly. 'I had a daughter once. Briefly, all too briefly. The boys never knew about her. She died before she was born.'

Sabine winced, remembering her own secret wish when she was first pregnant that her baby didn't exist. It had only been momentary: from their first kick the thought of losing the twins had torn her apart. She took her mother-in-law's hand. 'I'm so sorry. I had no idea.'

Claudette grunted. 'We never talk about such things, do we? Yet they happen all the time. A little tragedy. Just women's work. Invisible. Even the memory to be brushed aside. Well, no child should ever be brushed aside.' She nodded towards the box. 'Take it. Sell it.'

'I can't do that!'

'Yes, you can. The diamond is too valuable to wear. And besides, it's an ugly piece, made for show, not for beauty. I wanted to sell it years ago. I'm glad I didn't. For Violette, my dear. A dead lump of metal and a stone torn out of the earth; what use are they if they can't give a child a life.' She turned away. 'It's not just that. One of my cousins lives in Germany. At least he did. He visited here last year, just before he sold up and moved to Ireland. The things he said ...'

The subsequent silence was unnerving. 'Maman?'

'There are things Karl doesn't talk about. Maybe he shuts them out and doesn't even see, or doesn't care. Or maybe he approves. He's mad enough. But my cousin Heinrich talked of places where the government send those they consider "imperfect", anyone with a disability of some kind. Useless eaters, they call them. The Nazis are quite open about it. Useless eaters take the bread from the mouths of good Aryan citizens. So they're removed. You don't think about it when it's nothing to do with you. You're horrified, of course, at such barbarity. But you don't ever think it will come close.' She glanced up towards the bedroom where the twins were sleeping. 'My cousin said you just agree with them or hide your thoughts to survive, and leave if you can. And the only way a man can succeed there is to be pure, with nothing "imperfect" in their family.'

So this wasn't just about Violette. She might have known. 'You mean Emil's career would be held back if he was known to have a child with a disfigurement?'

'My poor Emil has been disappointed once, and now he has a chance for advancement, we mustn't let him be disappointed again. I worry what it might do to him.'

So this was how you made a pact with the devil. Sabine gazed at the necklace in front of her, mind working fast. Claudette was right, it was a vulgar piece, created to demonstrate a woman shackled to a rich man. The Sabine before children would have pushed it away with scorn, but she was different now. She could remain silent, hide her thoughts and pretend that her only concern was for Emil's advancement. Anything, anything Claudette wanted, so long as she could save her child.

TEN

NORA

Paris, 1939

Sabine was returning to Paris!

Nora finished her eager scanning of the letter and returned to the beginning, reading through more carefully. The chatter of her fellow students, relaxing after an intense day of Madame's instruction in their favourite pavement café a few streets away from the cookery school, faded into the distance. Sabine wrote that she'd already contacted the hospital. She was travelling within the week with the twins, and staying with her aunt while a decision was made about Violette's operation.

Nora sensed the new optimism in her friend's words and prayed she hadn't given her false hope. But the surgeon had agreed to see Violette, she reminded herself, and Timmy, the little boy she'd seen in the hospital with Jonny, had been treated successfully. She was being silly, it was going to be all right.

'Good news?' said Manon.

'I hope so,' replied Nora, folding up the letter and meeting her fellow student's gaze with a smile.

'We could do with that,' said Manon gloomily.

Nora eyed her. Manon's conversation had grown more despondent of late, as she resisted pressure from her family to leave in the first week of August, to go with her mother and aunts to their summer home in the Swiss Alps. From the way they were packing, Manon had declared, they were planning to stay there until things settled down again, leaving her father behind in the capital.

Despite her determination to make the most of the course to hone her skills, Nora had become increasingly aware of the sense of unease that now lingered beneath every conversation. Every day more refugees seemed to be arriving in Paris from Germany and, following its takeover by the Nazi regime, from Czechoslovakia as well. The talk in the cafés as August approached had begun to be peppered with the inevitability of a war with Germany.

Even Mum's last letter from home had hinted at things in Europe looking more uncertain, and that perhaps Nora should think of leaving early, just in case anything happened. Nora had answered in vague terms. It was only a few more weeks until the course ended, and the students had reached the point where they were beginning to put everything they had learned together in Madame's restaurant.

The noise and the rush of getting dishes out on time, let alone to Madame's exacting standards, was both terrifying and exhilarating. It was an opportunity she might never be given again, and Nora was determined to make the most of it. Besides, talking to her fellow students, who were equally frustrated at the lack of opportunities to follow their passion unless it was under the direction of a father or a brother, had given Nora some new ideas. Manon had plans to open her own restaurant in the shadow of the Eiffel Tower, on her own terms, avoiding the male-dominated world of haute cuisine. Of course, Manon, with her wealthy family and a large inheritance from her late mother, could manage such a thing, even in Paris.

On the other hand, there had to be other ways, even if you didn't have such advantages. Someone somewhere must be prepared to take on a female chef. If she could prove herself to Madame, and show she could deal with the responsibility of serving real customers, she'd be able to ask the famous chef for a recommendation to accompany the certificate she'd be given at the end of the course. Not many applicants to kitchens in England would have such training, let alone the experience. It would make her stand out from the crowd. Every day she was there improved her chances of overcoming the disadvantages of being a woman in a man's world, and escaping the drudgery and wandering hands of places such as *La Belle Époque*.

I don't know why she's here at all,' continued Manon with a sniff. 'There must be plenty of cooking schools for the oblig-atory domestic mädchen of the Third Reich. And Herr Hitler is supposed to be a vegetarian, so if she's hoping to cook for him she's out of luck.'

'Not all Germans are National Socialists,' put in Nathalie, whose brother had recently opened a restaurant in Metz, closer to Germany.

'Well, Papa says all Germans are arrogant,' said Manon loftily.

'The rich are the same the world over,' retorted Nathalie.

'Did you see that?' put in Renata, the younger of the sisters from Barcelona, gesturing with her head to a woman passing on the opposite side of the street. 'That jacket is so beautiful. So elegant.' She nodded towards Nora. 'Like the Duchess.'

'Duchess?'

'Of Windsor. It was in a photograph.'

'Oh,' said Nora blankly. She'd only vaguely been aware of the scandal of Wallis Simpson, and that, for some vaguely scan-dalous reason, it was impossible for her to become queen. Mum disapproved of her because she was a divorcee, and always refused to discuss the matter. Now, Nora found, her fellow students seemed to think she was an expert.

'It's a Schiaparelli,' remarked Heidi, her eyes following the woman as she swept down the street. 'The Italians are so very stylish, don't you think?'

Nora sent her a grateful smile, which was returned with just the slightest nod of acknowledgement as their companions flew into defence of the superiority of French-born designers like Chanel and Bruyère, forgetting the intricacies of the British royal family.

'I don't care much for couture,' said Heidi, falling into step beside Nora as the now-fortified little group made its way back towards their lodgings. 'A fancy coat can only cover, not change, what's underneath.'

'I suppose so,' said Nora, who'd seen plenty of expensive evening coats at *La Belle Époque* but hadn't quite been able to put her feelings about more than one of them into such blunt words. 'I don't live in a very elegant part of London, I'm afraid.'

'Far better,' replied Heidi with a grunt and switching from her customary French to English, which had taken on an increasingly American twang. 'To be invisible. Far away from the centre. That is the best, sometimes.' The bright red of her lipstick tightened into a thin line. 'Maybe all the times.' Before Nora could reply she'd walked ahead, striding into the distance.

Sabine arrived in Paris a few days later, just as August began. The intense heat, heat that Nora had never felt before, was already building in the city, inescapable even in the shade.

After giving Sabine time to recover from the journey, and to take Violette for her first appointment at the hospital, Nora followed her friend's directions to Marie-Thérèse's apartment.

'You look well,' said Sabine as she opened the door,

speaking quietly so as not to wake the twins. 'Paris clearly suits you.'

Nora returned her embrace, automatically kissing her on both cheeks in the French manner as if she'd never done anything else. 'I love it,' she replied. 'I've never felt so alive. I've found what I want to do with my life, I'm so glad I came. I can never thank you enough for finding out about the course and giving me the courage to take the risk.'

'My pleasure,' said Sabine with a slightly sad smile. 'And you've more than repaid me. You heard there was an operation that could help Violette and you found out more information from the hospital when I didn't have the means to do it myself.'

'I'm glad I could help,' said Nora.

'I don't know what I would have done without you.' Sabine sounded tired and strained. Nora noticed the thinning of the face, sharpening her wide cheekbones and making her eyes seem larger than ever. She couldn't help thinking that while she'd thrived and grown stronger during the challenges of her course, Sabine had become more fragile. She was no longer the invincible student journalist Nora had met only a few years earlier, but now a mother with the weight of the world on her shoulders.

She followed Sabine into a tall room, its shutters drawn against the heat, sending shadows across the polished wooden floor. Delicate curtains that appeared to be of white gauze stirred in the breeze, like pale ghosts in the darkness.

While Sabine brewed coffee in the tiny kitchen they chatted in low voices, catching up with the details of each other's lives.

'I've loved having your letters,' said Nora. 'I feel I know you so well, even though we've only really met once before.'

'I feel the same,' replied Sabine. 'It's good to have a friend.' She sounded slightly forlorn. 'There are things I tell my mother, and things I don't.'

'I know what you mean,' said Nora ruefully. 'There's plenty I won't be saying to Mum when I get home. Oh, I don't mean about men,' she added hastily at Sabine's expression. 'I haven't had time to even think about romance. It might have been months, but it feels such a short time. I want to learn everything I can.'

In the next room a brief cry signalled that the babies were waking from their nap.

'I really hoped they'd sleep longer,' said Sabine, 'so we'd have more time to talk.'

'I'm sure we'll have plenty of time, and I'd love to meet them.'

A second hiccup echoed the first cry, which was now growing stronger. Nora followed Sabine into the little bedroom, where Valérie and Violette were beginning to wriggle in their bassinet.

'They're so tiny!' she exclaimed. 'I remember Jonny when he was this age, but I'd forgotten they're so small.' She smiled at Valérie, who stared at her from her mother's arms as she was picked up, a puzzled expression on her face as she attempted to focus on the newcomer. 'Shall I get Violette?'

'If you're sure.'

'Positive.' Nora reached in for the second baby, so much lighter and frailer looking than her sister.

'She has difficulty feeding,' said Sabine, sounding defensive.

'But she's alert,' said Nora. The blue eyes focused on her face, trying to make her out, inspecting her with great solemnity.

'Yes she is. She has such a will to live. You can feel it. But I sometimes feel she's too small for such a serious operation.'

'She's survived this far,' said Nora firmly, remembering Pearl's doubts. 'You said the doctor's convinced she's strong enough. My sister felt that about her baby, too. I think maybe you feel more protective when they're a little different from other children?'

'Yes, that's true.' Sabine sighed. 'To be truthful, I never really thought about having babies, at least not for years yet. Now here I am with two.'

'They're healthy and happy, so you must be doing something right.'

Sabine laughed, the tense lines of her face easing. 'I'm glad you're here, Nora, it's good to have a friend. I wish I was staying longer in Paris. Violette's operation is scheduled for the first week in September. Marie-Thérèse is being very patient and is happy to look after Valérie when I go to the hospital, but I know it's an imposition on her free time. I'm sure she misses taking *tisane*, and conversation and attending performances at the *Opéra*. So we're going to stay with my family for a few weeks. My mother and grandmother can't wait to see the babies and at least there's more space there and it'll be a bit cooler than Paris. My brother is picking me up this weekend.'

'Oh, I see,' said Nora, trying not to sound disappointed she'd be seeing so little of Sabine after all.

Sabine adjusted Valérie's cardigan with her free hand. 'It's only a short distance away. Perhaps you'd like to join us? You're welcome to stay the weekend, and Guillaume will run you back in time for your course on Monday morning.'

'I'd love to,' said Nora enthusiastically. 'If you're sure. I'd love to meet your family. And, do you know, I've realised I've only really seen cafés and tourist sights since I've been here. I haven't been inside a real French home.'

Sabine laughed. 'You might regret it once my mother and grandmother get their hands on you. They can be quite alarming.'

'No one can be alarming after Mme Godeaux,' replied Nora, smiling down at Violette who was propped up in her arms, solemnly watching them both as if following every twist of the conversation, one fist tightly clutching the nearest thumb. 'She's a bright little thing.'

'They said at the hospital there's no sign of any mental impairment,' replied Sabine. 'Once she's had the operation it'll be almost impossible to tell there was ever a problem. I can always say it was an accident, a fall, that left the scar, and no one will know.'

There was a moment's silence. Neither of them had broached the subject of the war, and the unsettling rumours coming out of Germany. Nora was all too aware of talk of parents there so desperately afraid for the future they were putting their children onto trains. She couldn't imagine sending a son or daughter alone to another country, knowing they might never see them again, or even hear what happened to them. She felt certain from her friend's closed expression that she'd heard the same. After all, Sabine had trained as a journalist. She couldn't shut her ears to rumour, even if she wanted to.

How simple my life is, thought Nora. She couldn't imagine being Pearl, constantly harassed by her neighbour's disapproval of keeping a child who wasn't considered perfect. She dreaded to think how Sabine felt, with a daughter about to undergo a serious operation as war loomed on the horizon, while her husband was living and working in a country that might soon be the enemy.

She pushed the thought away, concentrating on being practical. That night she'd ask permission from Madame for a few days away, arguing that it was a chance for her to see real French cooking in a domestic environment. She felt certain Manon or Nathalie could be persuaded to swop shifts; she'd offer to work extra hours, if need be. She was already looking forward to meeting Sabine's family and seeing where she'd grown up; a proper part of France, not just an Englishwoman visiting the tourist sights. And sadly, given the unsettled times, it might be her only chance.

ELEVEN

SABINE

Paris, 1939

Sabine watched Nora with a smile as she set off towards her lodgings, weaving through the pedestrians with confidence as if she'd lived in Paris all her life.

It had been good to have company that afternoon rather than being alone in the apartment doing her best to keep two small babies clean and fed and entertained. Thank goodness they were still at an age when they spent much of the time sleeping. She couldn't imagine trying to cook and clean with the demands of two small bodies hurtling around her feet.

How she'd missed conversation too, especially with someone of her own age. The Nora she had come to know in their letters felt older and more assured than the young girl she'd first met in London. It was easy to see that being pushed to the edges of her ability on her cookery course was doing wonders for her confidence.

Sabine couldn't help feeling sad at how much she herself had changed since she'd last been in Paris. She was no longer the young student journalist, ready to take on the world, but a mother whose every hour, and every thought, was taken up with keeping her babies alive. Had the future she'd once dreamed for herself gone forever? Collecting knitting patterns for babies' magazines was hardly going to set the world alight.

She could understand all too well Emil's disappointment at the dashing of his dreams of becoming a renowned journalist, then a world-famous novelist. His novel had been rejected by every publisher he'd sent it to; several had been dismissive of its quality. Even before he'd left for Germany, she'd suspected he no longer told her when the familiar thud of the manuscript came through the door, or of any accompanying comments. Taking the position in Freiburg, for all his talk of submitting articles to the local newspaper, had been an admission of defeat, both as a businessman and a great author.

He hadn't written to her since he left. She sometimes wondered if Claudette might not have forwarded his letters. She might not even have posted Sabine's letter telling him she was taking Violette to the surgeon in Paris.

It felt horribly like the parting of the ways she admitted to herself as she finely sliced rose-tinted onions the way Claudette had taught her. She placed the onions with some fat tomatoes from the market already waiting in a bowl to complete Marie-Thérèse's favourite *salade de tomates,* which was to go with the *omelette aux fines herbes* planned for their evening meal.

Exhausted by the afternoon's visitor, the twins snuffled together in their bassinet. Even Violette was drowsy with milk and the afternoon heat. Sabine wanted nothing more than to curl up beside them and sleep, but Marie-Thérèse would be back from her job at the pharmacy any minute. Sabine mixed in the olive oil and vinegar along with chopped coriander, keeping half back to sprinkle on top at the last minute.

Placing the salad on one side, she reached for the ancient terracotta butter bell. Next came the eggs in their round wire basket. Finally, she lifted the omelette pan from its hook and placed it ready on the little stove, just as footsteps announced her aunt's return.

'How was your English friend?' asked Marie-Thérèse, as they sipped *thé au citron* on the tiny balcony overlooking the roofs of Paris, the Eiffel Tower in the distance.

'Enjoying her course. I think it'll be the making of her.'

'Good,' replied Marie-Thérèse, poking absently at her slice of lemon. 'And she's leaving soon?'

'The second week of September. Just after Violette's operation.'

Marie-Thérèse, who never took sugar, dropped several cubes into her tea. 'You could go with her, you know.'

Sabine stared at her. 'You mean, to England?'

'Of course. Weren't you planning to work in London? That's why you took all those English classes, wasn't it?'

'But that was to be with Emil.'

'So? Must you do everything with Emil?'

'Marie-Thérèse!' To Sabine's shock she found her aunt had tears in her eyes. 'Marie-Thérèse, what is it?'

'I've heard people talking about it at the pharmacy. I couldn't believe it, but it's true. The Nazis are quite open about it. They're putting away anyone they consider imperfect. It's all very logical. There's not enough bread to go round after the economy was ruined by reparations after the last war, so only those who are of use are to be kept alive. They say it's done humanely. The obscenity of such a belief.'

'Don't,' said Sabine, heart banging hard in her chest, the bitterness of the lemon harsh against the tannin of the tea. 'It's just a deformity, it can be healed.'

'All the same, I do worry Violette might be seen as not worthy of life.'

'This isn't Germany, Aunt.'

'Not yet. But the talk is that Hitler is about to sign a pact with Russia. That will leave the Nazi regime free to invade

Poland. If that happens, England will declare war, and so will France. The Germans didn't take Paris in the last war, I hope they won't in this. But if they do ... She paused as Valérie sneezed in the room next door, followed by a small waking cry. Fortunately she was too sleepy to remain alert, a half-hearted gurgle being followed by a return to quiet. 'You might be safer in England.'

'Among people I don't know?'

'You know Nora.'

'But her family aren't rich.' She caught her aunt's sceptical look. 'Truly, Marie-Thérèse. I know how much Nora had to save to afford this course, and she still needed money left to her by her grandmother. She'll have nothing when she goes back, she'll have to work every hour she can, like her mother and father. How can I expect her to support me and two babies? I can't work at the moment. If I'm with Maman while they're little I'm relying on family, ties of blood. I won't be imposing on strangers.'

'At least think about it.' Marie-Thérèse finished her tea and reached for a bottle of wine, filling their two glasses.

'What about you?'

'I'll stay. For now.' She downed her glass of wine with unusual speed and immediately refilled it. 'I have no dependants. I can leave at a moment's notice if need be. I'm not staying if the German army are at the gates, I've heard too much of what the Nazis do to their own people. From the sound of things, if they find out I was once a member of the Communist Party, however much I reject it now, I'll be finished. I'm not waiting around to be hauled off to one of their vile camps. I worked as a cleaner when I first came to Paris while training to be a pharmacist. I can do it again if I have to.'

'I'm not doing anything to risk Violette's operation,' said Sabine, taking a small sip of her own wine, fearing that only half a glass might send her into a heavy sleep when she needed to be alert during the night to tend to her daughters at a moment's notice.

'Yes, of course. I didn't mean that.' Marie-Thérèse smiled at her reassuringly, but the expression didn't reach her eyes. 'I mean once Violette is recovered enough to travel such a long distance. It might not happen for months. Even a year or two. Hopefully never.'

'Let's hope so,' said Sabine, as a wail from the next room told her that Violette was awake and hungry again.

'Try not to worry about it,' said Marie-Thérèse, squeezing her hand as she rose. 'I couldn't in all conscience not say anything, that's all. Go and see to Violette. You leave the omelettes to me.'

Sabine sat by the window as her aunt beat up the eggs and evening light bathed the roofs in gold, doing her best to encourage Violette's desperate attempts to feed. She wished with all her heart that Emil were here, that they could face the future, whatever it might bring, together. But Emil was far away and she couldn't help asking herself if he might, deep in his heart, wish that his 'imperfect' daughter would vanish, be spirited away as if she'd never existed, leaving only Valérie's perfection behind.

TWELVE

NORA

Paris, 1939

Towards the end of August, Nora took the train with Sabine and the twins to a small village station just outside Paris. They were collected by Sabine's brother Guillaume, a shy, taciturn young man with a shock of brown hair, who arrived in an ancient Fiat that rattled its way through country lanes to the iron gates of the chateau.

A little to Nora's disappointment, Chateau Saint-Céré was not the Gothic-towered palace of her dreams, but more like a large mansion house, with a steep slate roof and sharp little turreted windows on the top floor. But she was thankful to step out of the late August heat into spacious rooms filled with capacious wooden furniture that gave off the aroma of beeswax.

Lunch was an informal affair set out on a large trestle table beneath the shade of an apple orchard, sunlight flickering between the ripening fruit above their heads.

'*Cidre*. Cider,' Guillaume explained to Nora.

'You make cider?' she returned.

'*Oui.* Yes. And brandy. Very good brandy.'

'Very strong, you mean,' said Sabine. 'Don't let him give you any.'

'I wouldn't do such a thing,' he retorted, blushing violently. 'Not all French men are like that.'

'I'm sure they're not,' replied Nora, feeling his embarrassment. He was several years younger than his sister, polite and rather awkward. She watched him being gently teased by his family, the banter often too fast around the table for her to follow every word.

'Don't worry about my brother. He thinks English girls are very sophisticated,' said Sabine, as her uncle embarked on a heated conversation with several of the older men from the village who helped him manage the castle's extensive farmland. 'He's only seen photographs of the aristocracy in London. He thinks you all live like that. In a palace or a castle, with afternoon tea at the Ritz.'

Nora tried not to laugh. 'I certainly don't. I'm as ordinary as can be.'

'Bloody Germans. *Boches.*' At the far end of the table a fist was banged, sending the wine bottles rattling.

'It still might not happen,' said Sabine's mother, Mme Lavigne, filling up her brother's glass. 'The world might come to its senses.'

'No? So they invade Austria and no one turns a hair. Hitler talks about *Lebensraum* and a new empire and people think he's joking? And Chamberlain believes the Munich Agreement will keep him off our backs. I wish he was right. Dear God, I wish he was right. None of us want to go through the senseless stupidity of war again. We remember too much about the last one.'

'Heaven help us,' muttered Mme Lavigne. 'Will human beings never learn?'

'Memories fade,' remarked Mémé, Sabine's grandmother,

who was sitting at the foot of the table. She was a sturdy woman with greying hair, her flower-patterned apron enveloping a black dress that almost reached her ankles. 'For us, it remains a horror. But the young don't know. They think it won't ever happen again.'

'Surely not,' said Sabine, looking up from the family's ancient perambulator where the twins were sleeping in the heat. Nora could see the strained pallor of her face. 'Surely the politicians must find a way to avoid it.'

'And deal with a madman?' said Mémé. 'My cousin in Munich has taken his family to Australia.'

'Australia!' Sabine stared. 'But, Mémé, they don't speak English.'

'They'll learn. They saw the writing on the wall with *Kristallnacht*. It doesn't seem to matter that Magda's only half Jewish and has been a Catholic all her life. They weren't willing to take the risk.'

'You didn't tell me that, Maman,' exclaimed Mme Lavigne.

'I didn't want to worry you, Joelle, my dear. Besides, you barely know them. We haven't seen them for years. I remember playing here with Wilhelm when we were children. They used to visit us here every summer. It didn't matter if you were French or German in those days. He was a good friend. Now, I don't expect we'll ever see them again. Another piece of my life gone forever. The Germans took everything from us when they came last time. They didn't care whether we starved or died. We were nothing. They could do as they pleased, the bastards. I don't want to live through that again.'

'You won't, Maman, it'll be all right, you'll see.'

Nora swallowed. She was forgotten as the older members of the family sank into memories.

At home in London her father rarely talked of his experiences in the army during the last war, but she'd heard her mother reminiscing with Mrs Phillips from next door, of seeing the Zeppelins looming overhead, monsters against the night sky. They talked of the firebombing, the poor people who lost their homes or their lives. But they'd also talked of the bravery of the firefighters heading towards the devastation, of the collections for those who'd been bombed out, the charities working tirelessly to find them new homes and take them to hospital where their injuries could be treated.

Even the snippets reaching her from around the table in the orchard of Chateau Saint-Céré told her it had been a different experience entirely being occupied by an enemy army. Some of the occupiers had been decent, others brutal, but they generally viewed conquered citizens as not even human beings. In London, Mum and Dad had at least remained within the structure of an ordered society, and a government knowing that one day it would have to face a reckoning at the ballot box.

Nora felt the chill of winter creep into the late summer richness of the well-stocked table, with the quiet hum of bees and the scratch of chickens under the apple trees.

'That husband of yours had better come home soon, before he finds himself on the wrong side,' announced Mémé with a scornful sniff.

'I expect Emil will be back in Alsace soon,' said Sabine quietly. 'He's doing his best to support us.'

'Help himself, more like,' snorted Mémé under her breath.

'They don't usually talk like that,' said Sabine later while her mother looked after the twins, leaving the friends to walk through the meadows in the cool of the evening. 'Uncle Davide and the farmhands are always talking politics, but not like that. They must think an invasion really could happen. Perhaps you should go back to London. If you left now, you'd know you'd definitely get home.'

'I'm not leaving yet!' exclaimed Nora. 'It's only a few more weeks, I'm learning so much here, I want to stay until the very end.'

'At least the hospital has moved Violette's operation forward to the first week in September. I pray that nothing happens until it's over and she's well enough to leave.'

Nora gazed at Sabine's face, not so many years older than her but already lined with anxiety, not only about the possibility of war, but also that Violette's operation might go wrong, that she might not survive at all. Nora longed to be able to ease her friend's fears. At least she only had herself to take care of. That alone made her feel she could face anything.

'I hope I can come back to France to visit you again,' she said wistfully. 'And one day you can visit me in London.'

'I'd like that very much,' said Sabine. 'Before we were married, Emil wanted to live in London. To be a great writer, like Charles Dickens.'

'Then you'll have to come. Both of you, and the twins. You can stay if there's a war. You'll be safe in London.' She wasn't sure how she could ever manage to fulfil her rash promise. She could just imagine Dad's face if she suggested foreigners stayed with them while they found a home of their own.

Nora pulled herself together. A war wasn't going to happen, she told herself firmly. It was all fear. It was just talk, as it had been for months, even years. Violette would come safely through her operation and recuperate at the chateau. Then Sabine would return to Colmar, and Nora to London. Nothing was going to happen.

Nora loved every minute of her weekend at the chateau with Sabine's family. She enjoyed the noise and the chaos of so many generations inhabiting one house, and the hours spent on an ancient quilt, spread out on the lawns in front of the castle, entertaining the twins.

Guillaume, true to his word, drove her back to Mme Godeaux's restaurant on Monday morning in time to start her shift. That evening, she staggered back to her lodgings exhausted by the weekend and the demands of preparing for lunch service, followed by the evening meal.

She made her way wearily upstairs, more than ready to collapse into bed. Not looking where she was going, she almost crashed into Heidi who was standing on the landing, cigarette in one hand, blowing smoke out of an open window.

'Sorry,' exclaimed Nora. 'I thought everyone was downstairs.'

'No matter.' Heidi didn't turn from the window. Nora hesitated, torn between the demands of sleep and appearing impolite. Heidi took a long drag of her cigarette. 'They're leaving.'

'Leaving?'

Heidi gestured with her head. 'Renata and Sofia. There was a telephone call this morning. They packed their bags immediately after breakfast. Their family has sent the chauffeur to take them home.'

Nora joined her at the window. Down below, in the gathering dark, their former roommates were handing their suitcases to a burly man in a smart uniform, an array of gilded buttons down the front.

'But there's only a few days left of the course.'

'Renata said their mother didn't want to risk the borders being closed. It is a long way to Barcelona.' Down below, the sisters were hurried into the back seat of the large Daimler, which immediately set off at speed. 'Manon's father is sending her to the family's summer home in Chamonix. She told us once he works for the government, so he must know there could be an invasion any day. I wouldn't be surprised if Madame shuts down the course in the next few days and goes to stay with her sister in America.' She breathed out a long line of smoke. 'You should go too.'

Nora steadied herself. It struck her how low and earnest the conversation had seemed amongst their fellow students as she'd passed the sitting room, with the same undercurrent of unease she'd sensed at the chateau.

She glanced at Heidi, noticing a small sheet of writing paper crumpled in her hand. If there was a war, Heidi was the enemy. Her brain failed to take in the enormity. Heidi was just like herself. She liked her, for all her prickly ways. She wasn't monstrous, or alien. Nora swallowed. Heidi had mentioned her brothers. Did that mean they'd be enemy soldiers?

'Will you go home too?' she asked tentatively.

'My mother tells me I am to take the next train to Nuremberg.' Heidi's cigarette was almost finished. She lit a new one from the embers, drawing the smoke deep into her lungs. 'It is what is expected.'

'I'm sure they want to keep you safe.'

Heidi grunted. 'The American salesman I sometimes meet is going home. He wishes me to go with him on the boat. He says he will marry me once we arrive at New York.'

Even Nora knew better than that one; every warning hackle on her neck was rising. 'Heidi ...'

'I know, I know. I'm not a fool. He only wishes to make his voyage less tedious. What happens afterwards ... I have never been on a liner,' she added, sucking in more smoke as if her life depended on it.

Nora felt like a child again, the world around her beyond her comprehension. 'Wouldn't you be better going home?'

'Home.' There was silence again. 'My mother is pleased,' she said, her tone bitter. 'My father has finally found a husband for me. A friend. A very important friend. SS-Gruppenführer Schneider. His wife is dead, he has a son in the Luftwaffe, but also three much younger children. He needs a new wife so he can look like a real man before war breaks out all around Europe.'

'But if you don't want to ...'

'Then I am also dead,' said Heidi, bleakly. 'Don't you see? That is why they sent me here. I persuaded them I wanted to learn to be the best of cooks so I could be a good wife and an excellent hostess. At least that got me out of Germany. But now I can be a proper Aryan, with my blonde hair and blue eyes. I will be the perfect Nazi Party *hausfrau* to keep them safe, too. Because the Nazis can do anything. Anything.'

'Surely there has to be some other way?'

'I believed that once, too.' Heidi turned towards her, the carefully controlled arranging of her features gone, a dark agony in her eyes Nora had never seen before in any human being, not even amongst the grief at her grandmother's funeral. A deep chill shot through her. 'You should go. Get home. Believe me, you don't want to be here when they arrive. We were innocent, we didn't understand.'

Something fell into place. 'The young man in the photograph?'

Heidi nodded. 'Hans was a student at the university. I was in love with him, we believed in the same things. All I did was help him and some friends hand out a few leaflets. But you mustn't question the party. The local Nazi officials said the students were communists. They weren't. All they wanted – all we all wanted – was a free press. My father knows people in the party, he got me away. He was so pleased when he told me Hans had died in one of those vile camps they have for communists and Jews and anyone who disagrees with them. It was like a warning to me not to be so stupid again. He didn't care that he killed my heart as well.'

Nora stared at her in horror. The talk of war around her had always been speculation, but this was real. This wasn't even the distant past, this was now. Her mind wouldn't take it in, and yet she knew in every cell in her body that what her fellow student was telling her was the brutal truth.

'Heidi, you can't go back!'

Heidi drew on her cigarette again. Nora could see her hands were shaking. 'At least if I travel to America I have a chance at a new life.'

'You could come with me to London.'

'And what do I do in London?' Her smile was bleak. 'You have a kind heart, Nora. But I have no money, no way of living.'

'You could translate, maybe? One of my aunts used to translate messages from German and French into English for the War Office during the last war.'

'My brothers are all in the *Wehrmacht*. How can I fight against them? If I can get to America I can start a new life. Away from all this. I can put up with the price for a few weeks. A few months, even.' Her smile was bitter. 'Thank goodness my father had no idea I know how to make sure I don't become pregnant.'

Nora grasped her arm, feeling hopeless, out of her depth, but desperate to help, to alleviate such utter despair. 'There has to be another way.'

'In times like these, people survive the best they can,' returned Heidi. 'At home, the price of survival is silence. If I marry Schneider, that will mean shutting my eyes to everything, not saying anything. I'll just be the little wife in the party-approved dress. His youngest son is already a member of the *Hitlerjugend*. They even encourage them to betray their own mothers. I would rather be dead.' She stubbed out her cigarette, carefully returning the remains to a packet of Lucky Strikes. 'You should leave too. First thing tomorrow. Before it's too late.' She pulled her arm away. 'Thank you,' she said, her blue eyes resting on Nora's face. 'You reminded me that there is good, and kindness. I will remember.'

Nora hesitated, longing to be able to do something, say something that would make things right again. But Heidi's back was turned again, shutting her out.

Heidi was not an enemy, just an ordinary person caught up in something out of her control. Would that happen in France, too? Nora's mind filled again with the memories of Sabine's family, the horror of being occupied by an enemy capable of inflicting such suffering on its own people, let alone an alien population. She thought of Sabine trying to keep her babies safe, of Violette about to undergo a delicate operation that would need weeks, if not months, of careful nursing. What would happen if there really was an invasion?

Head whirling, Nora stepped into the bedroom. The beds normally occupied by Renata and Sofia were turned neatly down. Only the absence of their clothes was a reminder they wouldn't be returning for the morning's lesson. It took a moment to realise Heidi's belongings had also vanished.

There was a clip of heels on the staircase. Nora reached her window in time to see Heidi, suitcase in hand, arrive on the pavement. A few minutes later a bright red convertible Cadillac drew up. A young man in casual slacks and a jacket jumped out, taking Heidi's case and placing it in the boot before helping her inside and climbing into the driver's seat. Then they were gone, speeding into the streets of Paris.

Nora reached down to grab her rucksack, pulling under-clothes from the chest of drawers next to her bed. Her over-whelming instinct was to get home, to be amongst the familiar, surrounded by the protection of those who loved her, where she belonged. Darkness was beginning to fall. Not even the urgency of getting home made her want to risk the unsettling energy of a city at night. She would leave first thing in the morning. There were only a few days left of the course. Madame would understand.

Nora stopped. She couldn't just leave. Not without seeing Sabine. She couldn't abandon her now that Violette's operation was only days away, especially when she'd promised to go with Sabine to the hospital and wait with her there until the operation was over. Sabine and her family had welcomed her into their lives with such warmth, she could at least do her best to make sure they were safe.

She couldn't leave, not yet.

THIRTEEN

SABINE

Paris, 1939

On the morning of September 3rd Sabine was thankful from the bottom of her heart that Nora was accompanying her to the hospital. She couldn't help feeling terrified, despite the doctors' reassurances, that Violette might be too fragile to survive the anaesthetic, let alone the delicate procedure to mend her hare-lip. She'd barely slept the previous night, her heart torn apart at the thought of her daughter's fear and pain, with no way of explaining to her what was happening, that it would transform her life for the better.

Nora joined them at the apartment at first light, face pale, a rucksack on her back. 'So many of the students have left, the rest of the course has been cancelled,' she explained. 'Mme Godeaux insists I catch the train to Calais tonight.'

'Then you should go now,' said Sabine anxiously.

'Sabine is right,' said Marie-Thérèse, appearing from the bedroom with Valérie in her arms. 'I can go with her to the hospital.'

Nora shook her head. 'You're looking after Valérie, she'll be calmer here rather than at the hospital. Besides, I'm not leaving until we know Violette is safe.'

Sabine hugged her tightly, fighting back her tears. She kissed Valérie, who clearly sensed something was amiss and was wriggling in her aunt's arms. They hurried down to the street where Marie-Thérèse's Citroën was parked. Nora held Violette tight as Sabine drove her aunt's car through the empty streets of the capital, arriving at the hospital well before time.

As Nora opened the door of the hospital for her, Sabine's courage failed her. 'Supposing I'm wrong. What if this isn't the best for her? What if it's only her appearance that I'm afraid of?'

'You're doing it for Violette,' said Nora firmly. 'The doctors all agreed this is her best chance of leading a normal life, of not being stared at all the time.'

'Yes.' Sabine returned the pressure of her friend's hand. 'Yes, you're right. I still wish you'd left, but I can't help being glad you're here.'

'I'll be here all the while Violette's having her operation,' replied Nora. 'I'm not going anywhere.'

Sabine took a deep breath and smiled down at Violette's alert face, her eyes trying to focus on the strange surroundings. Yes, of course Nora was right. This was for the best. She was doing it for the best. The sooner this was over, the sooner Violette could begin her recovery and the sooner they could return to the Chateau Saint-Céré for her to recuperate.

It was only as she began to walk through the hospital corridors, the quiet as unnatural as the empty streets of Paris, that a new anxiety began to enter her heart. The sight of a nurse hurrying towards her, face white as a sheet but with an expression of steely determination, only confirmed her fears.

'Madame Schongauer, I'm so very sorry, but we can't perform the operation today. The surgeons have all been called away.'

'I'll wait.'

'I'm sorry, but with things as they are, there's no guarantee the operation can be completed, or that the child will have time to heal if war's declared today and the Germans invade, or, heaven forbid, start firebombing the city. It's such a delicate operation. The surgeon said he'd refer her to the doctor in Oxford, that might be safer. I believe you have the address ...'

Sabine stared at her. 'But how can I get there? It's impossible.'

The nurse was already being called away. 'I'm very sorry.'

Sabine didn't wait to hear any more but rushed back through the hospital to Nora, Violette now wailing in protest at the strangeness of it all.

'They're saying war may be declared within hours,' Sabine exclaimed. 'They're getting ready in case there's an invasion. I'll drive you to the station. You can't wait any longer.'

'With Violette like this?' Nora reached for the now hysterical little bundle. 'You need to get back to Valérie. I'll hold Violette while you drive. It's all right Sabine, I know my way around Paris, I can find my own way to the station.'

Sabine hesitated, but it was clear Violette was far too distressed to settle. She nodded and led the way back to the car, while Nora followed with Violette wriggling in her arms.

They reached the apartment to find Marie-Thérèse equally agitated.

'Thank goodness you're back. I was afraid the operation would be postponed. One of my colleagues at the pharmacy called by just now, she's heading to Marseille to stay with her brother. She said the British government have given Hitler an ultimatum not to invade Poland. If the invasion goes ahead, Chamberlain will declare war, that means France too. She said there are rumours of German tanks already waiting on the border, and parachutists could be heading to Paris the moment war is declared.'

'You'd better leave,' said Sabine, turning to Nora. 'I can still take you to the station.' She could see Nora hesitating.

'You could come with me, Sabine. You said the doctors here would refer Violette to the surgeon in Oxford.'

Sabine shook her head. 'How? What would I do? And I can't leave my family. But *you* should go.'

Before Nora could answer there was a squeal of brakes on the street outside.

'It's Guillaume,' said Marie-Thérèse, peering through the shutters. 'You'll be safer in the countryside, more out of the way.'

'Maman sent me to fetch you,' said Guillaume as he reached them. 'She was sure the operation would be cancelled. The army is being mobilised, they're afraid the Germans will attack at any moment. All the borders are closing. I'll get you home, Sabine, you don't want to be trapped in Paris. If it's surrounded there'll be no way out.'

'Go,' said Marie-Thérèse. 'I'm staying here. 'But you three should go.'

'I'm only leaving if we take Nora to the station on the way,' said Sabine, hastily cramming piles of clean napkins and baby clothes into a shoulder bag. 'If the borders are closing,' she added as Nora began to protest, 'the next train could be the last from Paris to make sure you get to Calais to catch a ferry over the channel. I'd never forgive myself if you were trapped here, so far from your family.'

There was no time to argue. Within minutes Nora had helped Sabine carry the twins down the stairs and scrambled into the back of Guillaume's Fiat. With a final embrace, Sabine left Marie-Thérèse standing at the entrance of the apartment, a lone figure on the deserted street.

Guillaume drove in tense silence. Sabine steadied the twins

in their bassinet on the back seat, both worn out by the strangeness of the morning and soothed by the motion of the car.

Unlike the calm of the dawn journey to the hospital, the streets of Paris were crowded with pedestrians and vehicles, all clearly eager to leave. As they approached the station Sabine saw men and women, young and old, hurrying towards the same destination, some with suitcases, others with small children. Dogs trotted by on leads, cats meowed piteously from baskets. One woman held on tightly to a bowl filled with goldfish. The air of calm was fragile, as if about to break into panic at any moment. The thought of Nora coping alone amongst such chaos set Sabine's stomach churning.

'Maybe it'll be safer if you come back with us to the chateau,' she said.

Nora shook her head. 'It's better if I get home.'

'If they close the Channel to civilians, no one will be able to cross,' said Guillaume, edging as close as he could to the station. 'There's already talk of Polish ships being destroyed.' He pulled up next to the pavement. 'This may be your final chance to get back to England, Nora.'

'Then I have to take it.' Nora jumped out of the passenger seat and embraced Sabine, taking a final look at the sleeping babies.

'Take care,' called Sabine, torn between her own hopelessness and fear for her friend heading off into uncertainty.

'I'll write to the chateau,' said Nora. 'As soon as I get to the other side. I'll let you know I'm safe.'

Sabine watched as Nora slung her rucksack over one shoulder and hurried to join the tide of humanity streaming towards the station.

'It's her best chance to reach safety,' Guillaume reassured her, eyes following Nora's slight form as she wove this way and that through the crowd.

'Yes.' Sabine barely heard him. She gazed down at her

daughters curled up tightly together, still fast asleep. Every story she'd ever heard from her mother and Mémé about the last war was turning her blood to ice. When the invaders came, when they'd cruelly ripped away everything that sustained life, it had been the old and the very young who died first. She would fight to her last breath to protect her children from such a fate.

In the bassinette, Violette stirred, disturbed by the stilling of the Fiat's movement, the noise of urgent voices outside, turning to reveal the harelip that, at this very moment, should have been already closed under the skilled hands of the surgeon, so that, even if not fully healed, might have been passed off as a child-hood injury, or the result of a fall.

Now, it never would be. Or at least not in time to keep Violette safe. *Useless eaters. Unworthy of life.* Every word of Karl Bernheim's barbaric, utterly obscene view of the world rushed into Sabine's mind. It was a view that had already killed many hundreds – perhaps thousands – of the sick and the vulnerable, along with anyone who simply didn't conform to his twisted view of perfection. She could feel their agony, their terror, each and every one of them, as they were ripped from their families and those who loved them, the heartlessness of their treatment as the inevitable end approached, their loneli-ness, their fear the last thing they'd ever feel.

With a terrible clarity Sabine felt certain that Emil would use his authority to protect her and Valérie. But he would be the first to send Violette out of the way, terrified, abandoned, with no one to reach out to her in her final, agonised, moments, no loving arms holding her as she died.

'They're letting Nora through, thank goodness.' Guillaume crunched the car's ancient gears, preparing to set off. Soon they'd be speeding through the streets, the decision made.

'Wait.' Sabine met her brother's eyes, seeing her despair reflected in his. 'Quick, take Valérie.' He took the child without a word. Grabbing everything she could fit into the vacated space in the bassinet, Sabine grasped the handles and raced after Nora.

Chaos reigned on the crowded platform of the Gare du Nord, everyone desperate to get on the next train to the coast. Families saying goodbye. Young men saying farewell to mothers and sisters as they put them on the train to safety before heading off to join the defence of their city, their country, everything they'd ever known.

The rush and the noise overwhelmed her, but she kept Nora in sight as she headed for the train, which was ready to depart. She could hear the clash of metal as doors were closed in preparation.

'Nora!'

In the clamour Nora didn't hear. She was alerted by a young man preventing the doors closing by pushing a heavy suitcase through them, followed by the guard's annoyed tones.

'Madame, madame! If you please. *S'il vous plaît. Ce n'est pas possible—*'

'Sabine!' Nora finally turned. 'Come on up. She's with me,' she added loudly to the indignant guard. '*Avec moi. Elle est avec moi.*'

The guard gestured impatiently.

Sabine shook her head, holding the bassinet towards her friend. 'Take her.'

For a moment Nora stared, meaning beyond her, followed instantly by a look of dawning horror. 'I can't. Sabine, I can't take her from you.'

'Please. Please Nora, take her with you.' Sabine held up the bassinet, the baby inside now stirring from the noise and movement, the cloth and bottles replacing the familiar warmth of her twin's body, distress clear on her marred face. 'Please.' She thrust an envelope into Nora's outstretched hand. 'For the surgeon. In Oxford. It's her only chance.'

'*Madame* ...' The guard was losing his temper.

'Please, Nora.' Her desperation seared through the agony surrounding them. 'Give my child a chance. If she stays here she'll die for sure. You know that the Nazis will kill her if they invade.'

Nora's expression changed to steely certainty. When she reached for the bassinet the guard handed it up to the young man, who lifted it past her and inside the train.

The door slammed shut, followed by shouts and the shrieks of whistles as the wheels began to turn.

'Sabine!' called Nora through the open window. 'I'll keep her safe, I swear. I'll do everything. I'll write as soon as we get to England, I'll let you know we're safe.'

Sabine watched as the train made its way out of the station. Her heart, her mind, were breaking, shattering into a thousand pieces. It was only when the last carriage finally vanished out of sight that she was able to tear her eyes away.

'Madame?' The guard was watching her, all impatience gone. She realised hers was only one of many agonised partings he'd witnessed, and there'd be many more to come. 'Thank you,' she whispered, as his face blurred with her tears.

'You have someone?'

'Yes.' She did her best to smile, trying to reassure him, to ease his own pain. It was the least she could do. Then she turned and pushed her way through the crowds still pouring in, towards Guillaume's car, to where Valérie was waiting.

PART 2

FOURTEEN

IRIS

Cornwall, 1964

Iris pushed her way through the garden gate at the back of Hope Cottage, out onto the cliffs above St Mabon's Cove.

Her head was filled with the story Mum had begun to tell. The two young women caught up in the beginning of a terrible war, drawn together by the ambition of a female chef. With the help of the postcards and photographs, she felt she'd actually lived their lives in Paris, building their friendship and doing their best for two fragile baby girls.

Mum had just stopped at the point in the story when war broke out. Her usually clear voice had faltered, as if accessing memories too hard to bear. Iris had left her dozing in her armchair with a cup of her favourite tea – black with a slice of lemon – and the tin of letters.

Iris breathed the clean air deep into her lungs. The names she'd seen in the letters were beginning to take the shape of real people. Nora and Sabine, Maman and Mémé, and little Valérie and Violette, whose lives had barely begun. There were other names too, ones she didn't want to think about.

She wished Dad were back. She longed more than ever for his enveloping, reassuring presence. But Dad was in Paris, once more a witness in a trial, as he had been in Nuremberg just after the war. Iris had never been encouraged to question her father in any depth about his work, and neither he nor her mother ever discussed it in her hearing. All she knew was that he helped to bring the perpetrators of war crimes and genocide to justice. Often after his trips abroad gathering evidence he came home with his face drawn and a darkness in his eyes that generally took several weeks to dispel. Mum had once told her that he'd seen more of the wickedness of this world than anyone would wish to know.

That was where Mum had stopped, mid-sentence, gazing down at the single letter containing the name Karl Bernheim, as if she couldn't bear to go any further.

'You're Iris, aren't you?' With a start, Iris swung round to find the young woman from the car park smiling at her, camera bag slung over one shoulder.

'Then you must be Jeanie Dixon, the journalist who's been phoning the house,' Iris retorted. 'Mum told you we have nothing to say. She's not been well. Just leave her alone.'

'I don't want to disturb your mum,' said the young woman. 'Just a few questions.'

'No,' Iris snapped.

'Oh, come on. Aren't you curious?'

'Curious?'

'About Emil Schongauer.'

'Who?' Iris blinked at her. Schongauer. That had been the name on one of the envelopes. Sabine Schongauer. But no Emil. None of the letters she'd seen had mentioned an Emil Schongauer.

'It was all over the papers,' said Jeanie Dixon. 'Surely your family must have told you something?'

'I've no idea what you're talking about. Like Mum told you, you're barking up the wrong tree.'

'Okay.' Jeanie smiled again, an ingratiating kind of smile. 'How about Karl Bernheim? They must have told you about him.'

'Never heard of him,' said Iris, doing her best to sound indifferent.

'Come off it,' said Jeanie, openly incredulous. '*His* name's *definitely* been in all the papers. Aren't you curious how a man like that managed to escape justice for so long, and why he's resurfaced now?'

'I don't know what you're talking about,' said Iris, turning back towards the garden. 'Now leave us alone. Like Mum told you, this is nothing to do with us.' As she reached the gate, Iris heard Jeanie call after her.

'He killed a woman, you know?' Despite herself, Iris turned back. The journalist was standing on the cliff path, watching her. 'Fancy travelling all the way to France from South America, risking discovery and arrest, just to murder a poor defenceless woman in cold blood. Bernheim must have had a powerful motive, don't you think?'

There was no answer to that. Iris stepped into the garden, pulling the sturdy wooden gate closed and turning the key, before leaning back against it breathing hard.

'A very powerful motive,' called Jeanie behind her.

Iris was shaking. She tried to steady herself. She was trembling all over. From somewhere far away, memories stirred. She was caught in that feeling that paralysed her whenever her nightmares came. Being held tight, too tight, voices and a strange metallic clanging echoing around her. Then silence. That was the most frightening thing of all, the silence, just the rapid beating of a heart vibrating through her. Not the reassuring rhythm of Mum's heart that had soothed her throughout her childhood when she'd been scared or in pain. This was a different kind of beat: the raggedness of sheer terror.

Iris closed her eyes, shutting out Jeanie who continued throwing questions after her. She breathed slowly and deeply, calming herself. When she opened her eyes, all she could hear was the distant pull of the waves on St Mabon's beach. She could make out Mum through the living-room window sitting upright in her chair, the biscuit tin on her lap, going through the letters, pausing now and again to pull one out to read.

Karl Bernheim. There was something about that name that brought up a tightening in her chest. Karl Bernheim and Emil Schongauer, and somewhere – recently if Jeanie was to be believed – a woman had been murdered.

Mum looked up, seeing her through the window, beckoning her to return. Iris took a deep breath and went to join her.

FIFTEEN

NORA

Paris, 1939

'Thank you, *merci*,' said Nora, turning from the train window where she'd watched Sabine until she'd vanished into the swelling crowd at the Gare du Nord. Still dazed, she took the bassinet from the young man who'd helped her.

'Baby is yours?' he said in an accent she didn't recognise.

'I ...' she began as Violette started to cry. Nora saw his indulgent smile fade, a look of pity mingled with distaste taking over his face. 'Yes. Yes she is,' she said firmly, sweeping Violette up into her arms.

The young man nodded towards her, embarrassed. '*Madame*,' he murmured, sitting down on his suitcase and picking up a newspaper.

Nora ignored him, shushing Violette's distressed screams as best she could. Thank goodness she could see a baby's bottle sticking out from a small bag inside the bassinet. Still stunned to find herself in charge of such a fragile creature, she could only hope that Sabine had placed enough necessities in there to get them through the next hours. If only she knew more about babies!

She pulled herself together. She'd often helped with the twins since Sabine had arrived in Paris, she reminded herself. And before that she'd fed Jonny from a bottle, and changed his napkin whenever Pearl had her hands full, terrified she'd stick the outsized pin through the towelling and pierce his delicate skin.

She freed one hand long enough to stuff the envelope containing the information about the surgeon in Oxford securely inside her brassiere as the train jolted out of Paris and began to pick up speed.

There was a commotion in the carriage next to her. The door slid open allowing a middle-aged man to emerge.

'It's all right,' said Nora hastily as he motioned for her to take his seat. 'Really.' Undeterred, he picked up the bassinet and ushered her inside to join several mothers with young children, squashed up tightly together.

'Silence,' he remarked in English, gesturing to his ears with a wry grin. 'Very good.'

'Thank you. *Merci*,' she managed, blinking away tears at his thoughtfulness. Distracted by the movement of the door and the sound of chatter from inside the compartment, Violette's panic subsided long enough to allow an elderly woman to place the bassinet on the crowded rack above her head, handing Nora the smaller bag containing several bottles and napkins. The woman's eyes were red-rimmed from weeping, but as she sat down she placed a small boy on her lap and calmly read from a children's book.

Nora retrieved the baby's bottle, warming it as best she could inside her coat, against her body. Violette's eyes rested on her, at first puzzled, then breaking into a wide-gapped toothless grin. Nora smiled back, as reassuringly as she could. The responsibility for this little scrap of life was already overwhelming her. On the journey out it had just been her, confident she could deal with anything, that if the worst came to the worst, she could at least run. Now, like Sabine, like the women all around her, she held the burden of other lives to keep safe, to put before her own.

As the train rattled on towards the coast, she silently thanked the man who'd given up his seat for her. The journey was tortuous, the train regularly shunted to let trains pass filled with troops mobilised for an invasion that might begin at any moment. She watched their faces, most no older than herself, some excited, some nervous, as the prospect of putting their training into practice began to sink in.

They looked like schoolboys, like children, she thought, as one particularly elderly train creaked slowly past. Were they really about to face tanks and mortar fire and the lethal explosions she'd seen in newsreels from the last war? She'd seen the utter annihilation of life in a blasted landscape, lone figures trudging between stumps of trees in a desert of mud, with the same fascinated horror she'd viewed Boris Karloff in *The Bride of Frankenstein* and *The Mummy*. Scenes from another world, scarcely more believable than ancient Egyptian priests coming back to life.

But this was real. Vividly, desperately real. How many of these young faces had watched those same newsreels, those same horror movies, secure in the hope that the world had moved on, had become more civilised? And how many of their mothers, sweethearts and sisters were now waking up to the same reality? The thought turned her cold inside.

She looked up at the woman opposite, still reading to keep her children distracted, tears running silently down her face. She must be thinking about her own husband, being sent towards horror, towards death. The world was about to be broken apart, never to be the same again. Was that happening at home, too? Pearl's husband was a reservist. He would surely have been called up. She thought of all the boys and men she'd ever known, the jobs they loved or hated, their dreams of home and family.

She held Violette tight as she slept. In this terrifying new world all she could do was fight for the survival of this tiny creature that had been entrusted to her care. She could see all around her how war changed priorities in an instant. Her ambitions, her dreams, were pushed aside. All that mattered for now was survival.

The journey towards the coast was painfully slow. At each station Nora glimpsed crowds overwhelming the platforms, surging towards the train. With so few trains leaving, people were crammed into every inch of corridor and even stood between the seats in the compartments. Try as she might, Nora could not shut out the sounds of families saying goodbye. She could hear in the agony of their voices the knowledge they might never see each other again, that their lives might never be the same.

More stations, more desperate people. They passed small villages and fields, the harvest in full swing or already completed. Snatches of life continuing as if disaster wasn't hurtling towards them. But what else could you do but carry on?

By the time they reached the coast everyone was weary and thankful to leave the train. The night ferry was ready to depart. To her relief, they were urged impatiently towards the boat with the minimum of checks. Nora slipped through, thankful for the cursory glance at her British passport. At least being a young woman with a child marked her out as an unlikely spy or saboteur.

The boat was crowded, bodies taking up every spare inch, huddled into every corner. This time she didn't dare stay on deck to brave the night air and the spray, but allowed herself to be hurried down below by the surge of the crowd. All the seats had already been taken but she managed to find a bit of space and propped herself against a wall, the bassinet beside her.

'It's all right, there's enough room,' said a young English-woman around her own age wearing an elegant fur coat and heels, who stepped over Nora and took the remaining space next to her. 'There's no need to move your baby, honestly. There's no need.' She settled down in the narrow gap, pulling her fur around her. 'You were on the Paris train, weren't you?'

'Yes, we were.'

'I thought I saw you get off. You were in the carriage just ahead of me. I could only find space in a corridor. There was no room to sit down most of the way. My feet are killing me.' She pulled a pale Hermès suitcase next to her, slightly battered at the edges and covered with labels from Milan, New York and Greece. 'Vile journey. Wish I'd stayed.' She grimaced. 'But then I don't expect there'll be much call for haute couture for ages. It was the chance of a lifetime working in Paris, I never thought I'd be back in Birmingham so soon. I worked so hard for that. All my life. Is that selfish, to think like that, when so many people are being killed already, and young men are being sent off to kill each other?'

'I feel the same, it's only natural.'

'The trouble is, you only have one life. All I wanted was to follow a dream. I don't care about big ideas. I wanted something so simple. Like Tosca, all I lived for was my art and for love. I didn't ask to be dragged into this.'

'I'm sure you'll be able to return to your work one day,' said Nora reassuringly.

The woman smiled. 'You're right. One day this'll be over. I'll find something. I expect there'll be plenty of work sewing parachutes.' She pulled her coat more tightly around her. 'I don't want to be invaded, like those poor people back in France.

Some of the women I lodged with told me what happened last time. So barbaric.'

Deep below, the engines churned as the ferry prepared to set off. Footsteps clanged around them on metal staircases, voices echoed above.

'At least we got on the boat,' remarked a woman on the other side of Nora. 'They said this could be the last civilian ferry to leave. If that train had been delayed a little longer ...' She shuddered. 'It doesn't bear thinking about. We're the lucky ones. At least we'll get home.'

Around them passengers continued to settle in every available space, weary but relieved. Even the children were subdued as they played in the spaces in between. Rocked by the gentle sway of the ferry and exhausted by the emotions of the day, Nora felt her eyes close and her head begin to nod as she drifted into sleep.

Something was wrong. Nora's eyes shot open. The ferry was in almost total darkness. Instinctively she placed her hand in the bassinet. It was empty.

'Violette—'

'Sssssh,' hissed a woman next to her.

'The baby—'

'She's safe. She's here.' Nora turned in relief towards the woman in the fur coat. 'I didn't like to disturb you. You looked as if you needed the sleep.'

'Thank you.' Nora took the little bundle in the gloom, dizzy with relief.

'Poor little creature. What a terrible thing. Isn't there anything ...?'

'I'm taking her for an operation,' whispered Nora.

'I'm so glad something can be done. She's a pretty little thing, if it wasn't for, well, you know.'

'Be quiet will you,' came a voice, further away this time. 'The captain said not to make a sound. D'you want to get us all killed?'

Nora held Violette tight, becoming aware of the deep silence around her. An eerie, unnatural silence, broken only by the distant slap of waves against the side. No radio, no engines. In a boat crammed to the brim with passengers and crew, not a single voice could be heard.

A bitter taste lingered in her mouth. Had the engines broken down while she slept? There was a helplessness about the sway of the boat; it didn't feel like a ferry ploughing through the sea towards the shore.

'They stopped just now,' whispered the woman in the fur coat. 'They told us to switch off any radios and to be as quiet as we can. Even the children. We're being tracked by a German submarine, heaven help us. Any sound they can pick up, and—'

'Shhhhh!'

Violette began to whimper. There was only a little milk left. Nora reached inside her bag, feeling her way until her fingers closed around the bottle. Let it last, she prayed to herself while Violette sucked hungrily. *Please let it last.*

It felt as if hours passed as they remained in silence and darkness. Milk gone, Violette began to wail. Nora hushed her as best she could, enfolding her inside her coat and giving her a little finger to suck, desperation rising inside her. Why hadn't she changed the baby's napkin before she drifted off to sleep? Or at least tried to find her more milk? Inside her coat she felt her little legs kick, the wailing, for all her shushing and rocking, turning to hiccups then sobs of distress.

'Please be quiet, please be quiet,' she whispered. But Violette was striving for life the only way she knew how. Fierce and loud inside her tiny, fragile body. Nora could feel the baby's passionate will to live, to survive; she knew nothing of the craft trailing them, perhaps deciding at that very moment to snuff them out without a second thought.

She felt movement next to her. Something was being passed. Nora's hand closed round a baby's bottle.

'Thank you,' she murmured. She found Violette's mouth. The cries subsided into panicky sucking, followed by a cough and a short wail as she nearly choked in her desperation to feed. Nora removed the bottle until Violette caught her breath again, replacing it gently as she began to wriggle. This time the sucking was calmer, more contented, as her stomach was filled. Nora could do nothing about the soiled napkin for now, just hope the milk calmed Violette enough to send her back to sleep.

Nora held the bottle in position, feeling the life being willed into the little body, while all around them lay the dark silence of waiting, children's voices, children's crying, instantly hushed. Everyone waiting. She could feel the heart next to hers, now calming, but still beating strongly. She felt each breath going into her own body. Each breath that might be the last. She braced herself. Braced for the flash of explosion, for the chill water closing over their heads, until all life was gone. It could be now. Any minute.

Around her the ferry creaked, rocked helplessly in the waves. In the darkness Nora waited, like all those around her, in the silence, held between life and death. Waiting.

SIXTEEN

SABINE

France, 1939

Sabine held Valérie tight against her while Guillaume manoeuvred the Fiat away from the increasing chaos surrounding the Gare du Nord and headed back to the chateau.

As they reached the familiar countryside just outside Paris, the meadows of her childhood, bejewelled with flowers, stretched as they always had done in the heat. A flash of blue appeared between a line of spindly trees where a small river wound its way between the villages.

In her arms, Valérie grizzled, hiccupping into sobs every now and again.

'She's just tired,' Guillaume reassured her, easing between the wrought iron gates, heading up towards the pale stone of the house.

'I expect so,' Sabine replied. But it was more than that. She felt it in the restlessness of her little daughter, the fits of crying that would not be comforted by milk or rocking. She could feel the emptiness of the box she'd furnished into a makeshift bed to replace the bassinet. Valérie had twisted and turned when she'd placed her inside, trying to settle against the mirror image of herself that had always been next to her, the heartbeat familiar from their first moments in the womb. Sabine wished she could explain. Tell Valérie that she missed the tiny body too, that the emptiness was a deep pain running down her own arms and resting in her heart.

It was the right thing to do, she told herself, yet again. The only thing to do. Yet how could she have sent her child so far away with the country poised on the edge of war? Supposing they hadn't got through to Calais? Supposing the German army had already invaded and were preventing trains from reaching the coast?

It would be all right, she told herself, over and over again. She had done what she had to do. It would be all right.

'You take Valérie straight upstairs,' said Guillaume as he halted the Fiat in front of the main door. 'I'll explain about Violette to Maman. You just concentrate on Valérie.'

Sabine didn't protest, hurrying Valérie up to her room. With the baby fed and settled, finally drifting into sleep, worn out from the strangeness of the day, Sabine returned downstairs to face Maman.

'I had no choice,' she said before her mother could open her mouth.

'And what did Emil think? Didn't he have any say in this decision of yours?'

'How could I ask him? He's in Germany.'

'He was here just now. He drove on to Paris to find you.'

Sabine stared at her. 'Emil was here? Impossible. He's in Freiburg.'

'His mother told him you'd taken the twins to Paris. He said he'd come to take you to safety, as it was clear war was about to break out. He must have driven non-stop, it's nearly five hundred kilometres from here to Colmar, and he was planning to drive back immediately. You must have just missed each other. Don't worry, Marie-Thérèse will tell him Guillaume has brought you home. He'll be back before long.'

'Yes,' said Sabine. She should have been joyful at the prospect of having her husband at her side again, but she couldn't help feel unease stirring, deep in her heart.

All that day, Sabine did her best to busy herself, helping Maman collect and store the last of the apples. No one discussed the war, but it remained there, beneath everything they did.

Emil returned from his fruitless journey to Paris late in the evening. He looked pale and weary, his smart suit crumpled. But even in his exhaustion she could see the change in him from the moment he appeared in front of the chateau in a large black Mercedes, the highly expensive kind favoured by Hitler himself. Since she'd last seen him, Emil had undeniably acquired the air of a prosperous businessman. His suit was of the finest quality and he'd filled out from the nervy young man who had spent hours discussing literature in cafés and lecture halls. The first hint of a middle-aged jowl softened the once clean line of his jaw. In the few short months he'd been apart from her and lodging with Karl in Germany, he'd already become a stranger.

'You were probably wise to leave Paris,' he said later that night after they'd retreated to Sabine's room. 'And to send Violette away with the Englishwoman to have her operation. She'll be out of the way there.' He watched Valérie closely as Sabine prepared her for bed. 'Although if you'd stayed in Paris, we could have left by now and be halfway back to Colmar. We'll leave first thing tomorrow.'

Sabine eyed him, trying to make out this new Emil, straining to find a glimpse of the man she'd once known. 'And Violette? I need to know they've arrived safely in England.

What if there are no more ferries and they have to turn back to Paris?'

'We leave tomorrow,' he repeated, as if she hadn't spoken. It was almost, she thought, with a stab to the heart, as if he was relieved he didn't have to deal with the imperfection at the heart of his family.

'Return to Colmar you mean?' said Sabine.

'Of course not. Far too dangerous. I have an aunt in Switzerland, near Lauterbrunnen. I'm taking my mother there while the war's on, as Switzerland's bound to remain neutral. I'm taking you to join her. She'll look after you. You'll be safe.'

Valérie, who'd been fractious for most of the evening, had finally fallen asleep with weariness. Sabine placed her gently in the ancient cradle that had been Papa's, and had once, long ago, rocked first her, then Guillaume, to sleep.

'And you?'

'I'll return to Freiburg. There are plenty of opportunities, the business is growing. France is finished. It's a new world now. There's so much energy, so much purpose.' He leant forward, a gleam of eagerness he'd never shown towards the Schongauers' boot-making business in his eyes. 'There's a new world order coming. Once things settle down again, life will be prosperous. People are generally stupid; they prefer to cling to the old ways. They have no idealism. But they'll see sense. This'll be over before long, then a new way of life can be built. The kind of life we deserve.'

'I thought we were happy as we were. You said you wanted to pursue your journalism. And now we have our family.'

'The world is a bigger place than you can ever imagine,' he said dismissively.

'I'm not a child, Emil. You know better than to treat me like one.'

His face briefly darkened in irritation but soon softened; he returned briefly to the Emil she remembered from their courtship and those first few months of their marriage.

'I only want what's best for us, Sabine.' He drew her closer, pushing a stray lock of dark hair away from her face. 'I've a position in the local party, it's a chance to make us rich, don't you see?'

She instinctively recoiled from him as his hand strayed towards the neckline of her dress. 'You've joined the National Socialists? You used to say the Nazis spouted nonsense.'

His irritation was back. 'I'm being realistic. Not everyone who becomes a member is one of their stupid fanatics. You need to be a member to get on. That's what I'm doing. I'm tired of working all hours for no reward. I'm doing this for us.'

'Yes,' she murmured. Doubt crept into her mind. Maybe he was right, and she was simply being naïve. After all, they'd watched several of their fellow students, with less talent but the right connections, being awarded the sort of positions at newspapers Emil could only dream of. No longer in a position to contribute to the family finances, who was she to judge if he chose to play the game to advance their prospects?

He smiled, kissing her gently. 'I'll always look after you, you know. I promised I would, and I always will.'

Her body softened against his, in the old way she remembered from Paris, as she returned his kiss. She had missed this intimacy, she had missed him. Since he'd been working in Germany, she missed the hotly contested conversations they'd had when they lived in Paris. She had so often longed for his presence, the warmth of his body next to hers in the night, of being able to share this new and bewildering world of being a parent.

She berated herself for being so single minded about seeing the surgeon; she had forgotten how much he was a part of her. Now the world was so uncertain, everything felt doubly precious. Even in her distress at the Garde du Nord as she handed Violette to Nora, she had been aware of wives and daughters saying goodbye to men already being mobilised to fight, knowing they might never see them again. Claudette's words came back to her with renewed force: at least his job in an ammunitions factory meant he wouldn't be called on to fight. And yes, it might be for Germany, for the enemy, but if not him it'd be someone else. At least he'd be safe.

Sabine slipped inside the covers, curling up to his warmth, the solidness of him, the familiarity of every curve of his body, the memories of their passionate confrontations in their tiny Paris flat under the eaves.

'We'll need to start first thing tomorrow,' he murmured gruffly, turning away. 'My mother will be expecting us, we'll stop at Colmar on the way.'

Hurt shot through her. She'd been so certain he'd missed her too. Had she changed so much from the girl he'd courted and married? She gazed at the shape of his back, his body acting as a barrier between them. Once, a single touch and his hands would have slipped over her breasts, fumbling clumsily with the buttons of her blouse in his haste to reach skin on skin. Now there was nothing. Not even the comfort of intimacy, the memories of this bed, where they'd made love so often, giggling like children under the covers at the need to be quiet amongst the echoing timbers of the silent house, which had lent an additional frisson to the weight of their breathing against each other, their care not to creak or rock the betraying springs of the ancient bed.

She wasn't going to leave it like that. Not when they might never see each other again. She needed to have some sign, some reassurance.

'Emil ...'

He didn't move. She could feel from his breathing and the rigidity of his shoulders that he was still awake. He was deliberately shutting himself away from her.

A single sign. A few words, a squeeze of the hand. A kiss. That was all she wanted. And to share her worries. Besides, surely he would want to know more about Nora and why she'd sent his daughter out into the unknown, in the care of a young woman he'd never even met.

'Emil,' she tried again, her hand resting on his shoulder. At the anxiety of her tone he stirred, finally turning towards her. From the cradle, a wail began, threatening to grow louder in distress and disturb the house. Sabine was at her daughter's side in an instant, holding her against her, shushing her with the warmth and the steady heartbeat Valérie had felt all her life.

She shouldn't have sent Violette away. Sabine curled into the chair, rocking her daughter against her as the panicked sobbing began to calm. They could have gone to Switzerland together and waited out the war there. If Nora got through to England it could be years before they were able to meet. She'd been so focused on Violette as the most vulnerable of the twins that she'd forgotten about Valérie. She rocked her, fighting back her own tears. She'd deprived her children of each other. Wasn't that unbearably cruel?

She leant back in the chair, trying to calm herself. Valérie, who'd been sinking into an exhausted doze, stirred again at the change in the rhythm of her heart. Sabine concentrated on relaxing her arms, calming her breathing. Emil's jacket was slung over the back of the chair and she leant against the roughness of the wool, breathing in his familiar scent.

In an instant, the world stilled.

'Hush, hush,' she whispered to Valérie. 'It's all right, it's all right.'

Except it would never be all right. Never again. On the bed, Emil's breathing had deepened into sleep. Around her the night-time settling of the house made its familiar rustlings. It was all so normal. As it had always been. Surely it was her imagination?

She leant back against the jacket again. It was still there, the unfamiliar scent. Not the cloying sweetness of cheap perfume but the sharp edge of the highly expensive variety. Not one she could place, but the kind she'd occasionally dabbed on her wrist in a department store in Paris, wrinkling her nose and shaking her head, claiming that it was not quite her, while promising herself that one day, when she was rich and successful, she would buy an entire bottle and wear it every day.

She shut her eyes, rocking Valérie gently. Emil's expensive suit had been selected with care. That had been the difference in him. She should have seen it immediately and understood its meaning. For as long as she'd known him he'd been careless of his clothes, too eager to be the Pulitzer Prize-winning journalist or the towering novelist to take much notice. It was part of his badge. Even in Colmar he'd resisted his mother's attempts to make him wear his brother's suits, all newly cleaned and pressed. He'd continued to wear his faded linen jacket, so creased it was beyond even Claudette's ironing skills. Sabine had assumed he was dressed smartly because of his new responsibilities.

She swallowed. This was a new Emil, one she knew nothing about. In her mind's eye she could see her, the woman whose perfume lingered on her husband's clothing. Sophisticated, elegant. Rich. Fair haired and blue-eyed, in contrast to her own dark colouring. The perfect Aryan. One of the party elite. Of course. She would be one of the elite. One of Karl's carefully selected circle, calculated to ensure advancement. Karl, who from the moment they'd met had openly displayed his contempt for her, while being just a little too aware of her body. She could just imagine his spiteful satisfaction if Emil did indeed have a mistress.

Her eyes flew open. In the darkness she strove to make out the features of her sleeping daughter. She remembered with sudden vividness the way Emil had gazed down at Valérie just now. He'd never done that when Violette had lain next to her in the cradle. There had been an intensity about his look she'd assumed to be him simply taking in the changes the weeks had wrought on her, but remembering it now sent a chill through her blood. The soft, white-blonde curls that had grown into a halo around the rosy-cheeked face with its tiny button nose and clear blue eyes. The perfect little Aryan.

At the chateau she was surrounded by her family. But the moment she stepped into the car with Emil, she would have no choice. He would be in charge of her fate. He might have softened to her just now, her physical proximity stirring memories of their early days together, just as it had with her. But how long would that last? Hadn't he confessed that everything he now did was for his own advancement?

She saw herself as his party colleagues might see her, conscious that, despite that brief kiss between them just now, he would now see her through their eyes. She was all too conscious of the softened outline of her figure that had failed to snap obediently back to its previous slightness. She acknowledged the leaking breasts, the chestnut curls carelessly tied back from her face, her undisguised disinterest in clothes or cooking. Not the kind of wife an ambitious man would want to see at his side. She had a horrible feeling she was being taken to Switzerland to be shuffled out of sight, left in the care of Claudette, who'd do anything to ensure her son's happiness.

More than that, a suspicion lodged in her mind that, whatever his original intentions, she might find Valérie wrenched from her care. For who could possibly deny Valérie the advantages Emil's position could bestow? Besides, if he continued to rise through the ranks of Nazi officialdom, he might well end up at the heart of the Third Reich, about to become the most powerful empire in the world. Wasn't she being selfish by putting her own feelings first and depriving her child of opportunities and wealth beyond her wildest dreams?

. . .

Sabine slid out of bed early the next morning before Emil woke, taking a sleeping Valérie downstairs so as not to disturb him. Her mind was dazed by a night spent wakeful, lying rigid, thoughts racing this way and that, undecided what to do for the best.

Around her the house was stirring with the familiar end-of-summer routine of harvesting and preparing for winter. She sat in the cobbled courtyard rocking Valérie in the ancient perambulator, drinking coffee to try and clear her frazzled mind. The sounds and scents were those of her childhood, the safe world that had surrounded her. Summer days of playing amongst the meadows with her friends from the village and swimming in the river. It still held the feeling of eternal safety, as if war was a terrible nightmare that couldn't be real.

She missed Violette with every fibre of her being. It had been the right thing to do, she reminded herself. It had been the right thing to do. If they'd caught the night ferry they'd be in England now, heading for Nora's family in London.

Through the door of the courtyard, she could see the fields swathed in early morning mist. Was that what Nora was seeing, similar fields in a strange land as the train passed through? The south of England was not so very different from France. The buildings were different in style of course, but it was a rich farming landscape, dotted by villages and church spires. She couldn't rest until she'd heard from Nora that they were safe.

Sabine looked up as Guillaume came out into the fragile warmth to join her.

'You're leaving this morning, I hear,' he remarked. His voice was even but she could sense his disapproval. Guillaume had seen the change in Emil too, and was worried for her, which only added to her frayed nerves.

'So it seems,' she replied.

He handed her a fresh cup of coffee. 'You'll be safe in Switzerland. Heaven knows what will happen here. At least you'll be safe, and Violette will be safe in England.'

'Yes,' she murmured.

The mood over a hurried breakfast was subdued. Emil spoke little, clearly tired and irritable from the frustrations of the previous day, too important to make small talk with the ill-dressed inhabitants of the faded manor house, and impatient to return to his own world.

'The sooner we leave the better,' he said, as Sabine forced herself to be practical, packing a suitcase and collecting together everything Valérie would need for the journey.

'That's true enough,' grunted Mémé, returning from the *boulangerie*, her shopping bag bristling with the crispness of fresh baguettes. 'War is no respecter of life. There's a rumour in the village that a civilian ship was sunk last night, torpedoed by a German submarine.'

The pile of newly laundered baby's napkins fell from Sabine's hands. 'Where was that?'

'Somewhere near Great Britain. The talk is that the boat contained hundreds of refugees, children too, heaven help them.'

'It doesn't mean it was in the English Channel,' said Guillaume quickly, helping Sabine to collect the cloth squares and fold them into her shoulder bag where they could easily be found.

'That's true,' she replied, trying her best to quell her anxieties, and thankful Guillaume had been vague about Violette's destination to both Maman and Mémé. Her own fear about her daughter was hard enough to bear, without having to deal with her family's.

'We need to go,' said Emil, sounding impatient, as Maman packed bread and cheese into a wicker picnic basket, while Guillaume, arms filled with an ancient Moses basket as a replacement for the bassinet, headed out towards the car. 'Surely you have everything you need; anything else we can easily purchase when we get to Switzerland. Like I told you, I don't have to worry about money anymore.'

Sabine stopped in her tracks. At the tone of her husband's voice, all doubt finally fell away. She had sent one child towards an unknown fate. She was not risking losing another. How can you entrust your whole life, and that of your child, to someone when all trust is gone?

'I'm staying here,' she said firmly, letting her shoulder bag fall to the floor. 'And Valérie is staying with me.'

'For goodness' sake, woman.' His mood instantly darkened. So he was already a man who wouldn't tolerate being crossed in any way. This only strengthened Sabine's resolve.

'I'm trying to do what's best for our daughters, Emil. Both our daughters. I don't want Valérie anywhere near a vile regime like the Third Reich, whatever its material advantages. And I need to tell you more about Violette and where Nora is taking her to have her operation, and what might have happened to them. I only sent her away because the surgeon in Paris assured me he's one of the best—'

'Do as you please, I'm not wasting any more time.' He pushed her roughly, snatching Valérie as she stumbled to her knees. She scrambled instantly to her feet, but he was already striding through the courtyard, heading for the car, a screaming Valérie in his arms.

'Emil!' She ran after him. She'd say anything, do anything. 'Give her back, please. She needs me.' She reached him as he opened the door to the Mercedes, grasping desperately at his sleeve. 'Fine, let me come with you. You need someone to look after Valérie on the journey. Don't take her like this, please Emil. She's only a baby. You don't even have milk for her.'

He shook her off and shoved Valérie onto the front passenger seat, taking his place behind the steering wheel. He pushed down the locks on both front doors and reached for the ignition.

'Where are my keys?' he demanded angrily.

'Emil, please. You're frightening Valérie. We can talk about this.'

'My keys,' he said again, impatiently. 'I might have known you'd play a trick like this. Where have you put them?'

'I haven't put them anywhere. Open the doors. Please, Emil. I'm coming with you.'

'In that case, you can keep them, much good they'll do you.' He scrabbled underneath his seat. 'You didn't think about the spare.'

An engine roared as a tractor stopped in front of the entrance, blocking the only exit. Emil cursed, still bending to locate the spare key. In a flash Sabine shot round to the passenger side. The back door was unlocked, thank goodness. She yanked it open and reached in, sweeping Valérie out and safely into her arms before he could turn and see what she was doing.

The tractor engine was stilled as Guillaume jumped out. 'I thought you might be up to something,' he remarked coldly.

'Get out of my way, you oaf,' snapped Emil, stepping out of the car, his face puce. 'This is none of your business.'

'Maybe not. But Sabine always does the best for her children, whatever it might cost her. I respect that. I rather think you should too.' He threw a bunch of keys at Emil's feet. 'It doesn't matter to me that you look down on us. Sabine loves you, and that's good enough for me. For all of us here.' He looked pointedly towards Sabine. 'It's up to you what you wish to do. We can wait for as long as you need.'

Sabine took a deep breath. 'I'm staying here. I'm not going anywhere.'

'Then I think we should respect that.' Guillaume turned on his heel to remove the tractor.

There was a moment's silence. What was there to say?

'You haven't heard the last of this,' said Emil, returning to the driving seat. 'And you won't always have that farmhand of a brother to protect you,' he added, speeding off towards the main road.

SEVENTEEN

NORA

London, 1939

On the silent ferry it felt to Nora as if they'd waited for hours, a lifetime, in the dark, with just the distant slap of waves against the hull. Finally, the engines rumbled back into life. Nora began to breathe again, still not quite daring to hope, as the sway of the boat steadied and they were propelled forwards again through the waves, towards safety.

Around her the murmur of conversation grew. All speech was hushed, even when the captain announced the immediate danger had passed and they'd soon be docking. There were no celebrations, no joy. Just relief that they'd survived this far, tempered with the unspoken anxiety that many more submarines were out there. The only way to keep any kind of sanity until they reached solid ground was not to think at all.

In the chaos of boats arriving in Dover with their distraught and terrified passengers, Nora was able to pass through customs with a cursory glance at her passport. Pausing only to buy milk for Violette, and post a hastily scribbled note to Sabine, she caught the next train to London.

This was not the return she'd planned, or dreamt of. Clutching the bassinet tightly and ignoring the nerves twisting her stomach, she tried not to think too far ahead. The only way to face the next few hours was to take them one moment at a time.

When she finally reached the terrace in Turnham Green, her mother opened the door. 'Nora! Thank heavens. We've been beside ourselves.' Her eyes fell on the unmistakeable shape of the baby's basket. 'Oh my Lord.'

With Violette fed and finally asleep in her bedroom, Nora hastily washed her face and went downstairs to face the music.

The atmosphere in the living room was, to say the least, tense.

'You can't just come home with a baby,' said Dad.

'I don't understand,' said Mum, handing her a cup of tea. 'The child was just handed to you by your friend? At a train station of all places?'

Nora tried her best to remain calm. 'They were expecting the German army to arrive any minute,' she explained, trying to quell the heat rising through her. 'You can't possibly believe she's mine?'

'Of course not,' said Mum quickly.

'Although you have to see how it looks,' said Dad.

'People gossip,' added Mum, looking embarrassed.

Nora felt something snap. 'I couldn't just leave her!' she cried. 'Other children have been sent over as refugees, like the *Kindertransport* that's getting Jewish children away from the Nazis. Surely people will understand?'

Her parents looked at each other, obviously shocked that their well-mannered daughter was behaving like this. 'We'll talk about it tomorrow,' said Mum eventually, trying her best to change the subject. 'You look exhausted, darling. And we were so worried, especially when we heard about the *Athenia* being sunk by a submarine, with all those poor souls on their way to safety in America drowned.'

'A boat was lost?' exclaimed Nora, shuddering. Thank goodness she'd had the presence of mind to send a message to the chateau, although she could only hope the French postal system was still working and it would soon get through. If Sabine heard about the *Athenia* she'd be worried out of her mind.

'They were saying at the Post Office that hundreds were drowned,' said her mother. 'They must have been desperate to escape.' Mrs Herridge glanced at her husband. 'The poor mother must have been just as desperate, letting her young child go like that.'

'I heard stories in France of what the Nazis do to children with a deformity or any disability, Mum,' replied Nora. 'I was told they have a policy to just eliminate them as a waste of resources. I couldn't leave a baby to die like that, not when I could give her a chance.'

Her mother turned pale. 'Oh my Lord,' she gasped, eyes instinctively turning towards the photograph of Pearl holding Jonny against her as a tiny baby, wrapped in a shawl.

Nora swallowed. Her parents knew all too well what it was to have a child marked out as different, lesser, unworthy of love and care. She'd seen their pain as Pearl had been shunned and condemned as foolish for keeping Jonny rather than hiding him away. Pearl would spend her life caring for her son and she was lucky to have a supportive husband capable of earning the money to maintain them. Nora was on her own.

'But how do you think you're going to look after her?' her father jumped in, not willing to let the subject drop. 'We'll support you the best we can, sweetheart, but we can't afford to support you *and* a child, and your mother has enough to do without minding a baby.'

'I'm not expecting her to,' answered Nora.

'You can hardly return to working at a restaurant,' he said, frowning. 'So how do you expect to pay for your keep?'

'I ...' Nora faltered. The full enormity of what she'd taken on hit her straight between the eyes. 'I've no idea,' she confessed, fighting back sudden tears.

'Take no notice of your dad,' said her mother a little later as they all prepared for bed, bringing Nora a hot water bottle for comfort, despite the warmth of the evening. 'He'll come round. He saw all too well what happened to those poor people in France during the last war. He's just a bit shocked, that's all, and he worries about what you've taken on. He understands that you couldn't leave the poor little thing.' She peered down into the bassinet where Violette was beginning to grizzle. 'Poor little mite. What a thing to be born with.'

'An operation can make sure it heals,' Nora explained. 'But she needs it done as soon as possible.'

Her mother picked up the baby. 'Such a little creature. She barely weighs a thing.'

'It's not just the way she looks, it means she can't feed properly.'

'And this operation, it'll cure that?'

'Yes. If it's successful, it'll mean she can start leading a normal life.'

'And not be stared at.'

'Like Jonny, you mean.'

'People can be so very thoughtless.' Mrs Herridge looked down at Violette's face. 'Dear little creature. She must be missing her sister. Let's hope we can find a way of getting them back together again.'

The next morning Nora wrote to the surgeon in Oxford, hoping that Sabine's message would also get through. Dad might not have been happy but he made no further comment.

At least being home she had her mother's help in knowing what to do. Mum even fetched down baby clothes that had been carefully put away in the attic long ago. There were some pale pink cardigans she'd knitted that were too obviously for a girl to be given to Jonny, along with crocheted romper suits.

'Oh my goodness,' said Pearl, arriving a little later with clothes Jonny had grown out of and a small pile of much-washed napkins. 'I couldn't believe it when Mum said you'd returned with a little French baby.' She left their mother to fuss over her grandson and smiled at Violette who was cradled in the crook of Nora's arm, taking things in with her bright eyes. 'She's tiny, poor thing. Mum said she's a twin.'

'Yes, her sister's still in France.'

Pearl's eyes filled with tears. 'Her mother must have been desperate. I can't imagine how it must have felt to let her go.'

Nora felt the little bundle stir against her. Already she couldn't bear the thought of letting her out of her sight, or of any harm coming to her. How on earth must Sabine be feeling?

Over the next weeks, as she waited for a reply from the surgeon, Nora adjusted slowly to her new life. Word had quickly gone round the neighbourhood, but she braved the stares and the whispers as she pushed Violette in the ancient perambulator Mum had borrowed from a neighbour, her own having gone to Pearl.

'I never thought babies could take over so completely,' she said to Mum, who gave a wry chuckle.

'Babies are wonderful, but only if you can give them a good life. There's no time for anything else when they're so little, unless you're lucky enough to have someone to help you look after them, and to support you. I've seen so many young women's lives ruined by some sweet-talking boy who can just walk away and not face the consequences.'

'Dad's right, though,' said Nora. 'I can't rely on you for support. I need to find a way of earning a living.'

'Time enough for that,' said her mother kindly. 'You just concentrate on building that little thing up, and let's hope she can have her operation before long. Then we can work out what to do.'

Nora and her mother hadn't always seen eye to eye, but right now Nora wondered what she'd ever do without her. 'Yes,' she said, doing her best to sound cheerful. 'Hopefully I'll have some good news to share with Sabine soon.'

EIGHTEEN

SABINE

France, 1939

When the postcard from Nora arrived telling her they'd reached Dover arrived at the Chateau, Sabine clutched it tightly, legs shaking with relief. She stood in the cool of the kitchen, amongst the streams of sunlight stealing through the half-closed shutters, reading it over and over again.

'Well?' demanded her mother, knife poised above the onions and garlic she was peeling for tonight's stew.

'They're alive. They weren't on the *Athenia*. They must have reached London by now.'

'Thank goodness.' Maman put down the knife, reaching for her handkerchief and blowing her nose.

'I should never have sent her away.' Sabine paced the cool of the kitchen, berating herself as she had done every day since watching that train leave Paris with Nora and Violette on board. Only yesterday a letter from the hospital had arrived to inform her that, with things returning to normal, Violette's operation had been rescheduled for the following week. She could have had the operation in Paris, after all.

'You weren't to know,' said Maman. 'You did what you thought was for the best. It was all you could do.'

'But how am I ever going to get her home again?' Sabine asked in despair. Life might have returned to a semblance of normality, but she was all too aware that in the larger world borders were closing and submarines were patrolling the waters, while battles for control of territory could spill over into France at any moment.

But Violette could still have had her operation. Sabine could not forgive herself for the panic that had sent her fragile daughter away. After the wave of terror following the declaration of war, there had been no invasion. No tanks rolling across the countryside, no enemy soldiers, no parachutists. There had been a mass movement of people away from the cities and the borders but life was already settling down, with many of the displaced gradually returning home. Even Paris, Marie-Thérèse had told them in her most recent letter, was back to a semblance of its usual life, apart from the refugees pouring in from Germany.

Several houses in the village still lay empty, entire families having left to stay with relatives further south, abandoning their vegetable gardens to the summer heat. The Garniers, owners of the largest vineyard for kilometres around, had remained in their summer home in Monaco, even after the manager left in charge had decamped with his wife and children to join his sister in America.

'Nora looked like a sensible girl to me,' put in Mémé, clattering down the stairs with a basket of laundry in her arms. 'She'll get Violette to that doctor in Oxford, you'll see. And Violette knows her, it's not like sending her away amongst total strangers. War always means the world gets turned upside down. We have to do what we can.'

'But Violette's so young. She needs me. She'll be frightened and in pain,' said Sabine. 'And supposing she doesn't survive?

Supposing something goes wrong, or she doesn't come round from the anaesthetic?'

'The surgeons here wouldn't have agreed to operate if they didn't think Violette was strong enough,' replied Maman. 'You took the best care of her, my dear, and made sure she fed as well as she could. You've given her the best chance. I'm afraid all we can do is pray she survives.'

'And this damned war is settled soon,' added Mémé. 'You know where she is; once the borders open up again you can go and fetch her. Once Guillaume is back, he'll take you.'

Silence fell in the little kitchen. Guillaume had left only the day before to join up as a volunteer to keep France safe. Many of the other men in the village had also gone, leaving a strange quiet across the countryside.

'Let's hope it's soon,' said Sabine. Her eyes returned to the postcard, reassuring herself of its existence, that it wasn't a figment of her own wishful imagination. While things remained calm and the postal service still worked, she still had a way of knowing how Violette was faring, when her operation was to take place and if it proved successful.

She looked up as a car rumbled past on the main road, hastening to the window in an attempt to see the vehicles passing between the trees.

'Just more refugees heading south,' said Mémé. 'There's been a stream of them all morning. Not everyone's convinced the danger's over.'

'No,' said Sabine, stomach churning. It couldn't be Emil. He must be safely back in Germany by now, busy overseeing the manufacturing of armaments, following his ambition to climb up through the Nazi Party to the position of power and influence he'd always craved. He'd soon forget about her, and Valérie. He wasn't coming back. It wasn't worth his while, and especially not the risk of being caught in enemy territory should an invasion begin.

She swallowed. Maybe he thought all he had to do was wait, confident that Germany's industrial might would quickly over-power France, as it had Czechoslovakia and Poland. If he returned as a conqueror he'd be able to do anything he pleased.

In the bedroom above, Valérie, who'd remained restless since Violette had been wrenched from her side, set up a wail.

There was nothing she could do, Sabine told herself as she headed upstairs, stashing the precious postcard deep in her pocket, like a talisman promising all would be well. Apart from keep her daughter safe and help Maman and Mémé as much as possible on the farm to ensure they had enough precious supplies for the winter and seeds for next year, whatever else might happen. All they could do was survive.

NINETEEN

NORA

London, 1939

Nora had never been so relieved to find a letter from Sabine on the doormat of the house in Turnham Green. She tore it open, hastily scanning through her friend's words. At least now she was certain Sabine had reached the safety of the Chateau Saint-Céré and she knew Violette was safe.

It was strange to think they could still exchange letters, as if life was still normal and there were no mines and submarines surrounding the coastline and armies preparing for the battles that almost certainly lay ahead. As if they could still simply just catch a train to meet up with each other within hours.

It seemed the atmosphere in France was much the same as in England, the initial evacuation of children from the cities being followed by a drift back with little sign of the feared bombing. If it hadn't been for the appearance of yet more Anderson shelters sunk into back gardens, along with the expansion of vegetable patches, she could have imagined there was no war at all. You couldn't miss it on the BBC Home Service of course, or in the newspapers Dad increasingly shook his head over on a daily basis. Then there were always the barrage balloons hanging over the city, ready to hamper any attack from the air.

With a sigh of relief, Nora turned her attention to the rest of the post. She instantly spotted an Oxford postmark.

'Well?' said her mother, looking up from ironing Dad's shirts and catching the expression on Nora's face. 'That doesn't look like a letter containing good news.'

'It's from the surgeon,' said Nora. 'He says he's been sent the details from Paris, but he isn't able to do the operation.'

Mrs Herridge placed the iron back in front of the fire to heat up again. 'I'm sorry, darling. Your father was afraid this might happen.'

Nora returned to the typed letter. 'But he says there's a surgeon in a hospital in Exeter who's agreed to perform it instead. Exeter. That's down south, isn't it?'

'In Devon,' her mother nodded, 'right on the south coast.'

'I'm going,' Nora said adamantly.

'But it's such a long way!' her mother exclaimed.

'You know it's important.'

'And you don't know anyone down there,' Mrs Herridge continued, more calmly this time. 'Look, your father and I have agreed to help all we can, but we can't afford to pay for a hotel until Violette's strong enough to come home.'

'I'll find somewhere,' said Nora firmly. 'If it has to be Exeter, I'll find somewhere there I can work and look after Violette at the same time. I'm strong and healthy, there has to be something I can do.'

Later that night, as Violette finally settled down to sleep, she heard a quiet knock on the bedroom door. Nora smiled up at her mother, who handed her a cup of tea and sat down on the other bed in the room.

'I've been thinking about what you said, darling. You're quite certain the surgeon in Exeter has agreed to operate?'

'That's what he says. So long as he thinks she's strong enough.'

'Then you have to take her.' Her mother put a hand on her shoulder. 'Heaven knows how long this war will last, so the sooner the better. I just don't like the thought of you being down there in Devon on your own so far from us.'

'It'll only be for a short while, Mum,' Nora said, trying not to let her anxieties show.

'Then go,' Mum said firmly. 'Don't listen to what your dad says. I've got some savings from my housekeeping that'll help with the train fare and a couple of months' rent.'

Nora was about to protest but her mother put up her hand to stop her. 'I'd like to do something for you both.' She hugged Nora tightly. 'I can't do anything for all those poor babies in occupied Europe, but I can help this one, and I won't take no for an answer.'

A few months later, on a frosty morning as 1939 drew to a close, Nora stepped off the train in Exeter. Her rucksack was once more on her back, leaving her hands free to attend to Violette in her bassinette. She was tired from the long journey from London, trying to keep her little charge comfortable and enter-tained whilst crammed among soldiers on leave and families leaving the cities for the countryside.

Fortunately, her instructions to her lodgings were clear, a short bus ride taking them to the small private hospital on the outskirts of the city. With the help of Dr Yearsley's secretary, she'd found lodgings with the widow of one of the hospital porters who took in paying guests to make ends meet.

Mrs Williams was a middle-aged woman of generous proportions. She opened the door in a cross-over apron of pale cotton, sprigged with tiny blue forget-me-knots, a matching turban corralling her greying hair.

'Nice to meet you, my dear,' she said cheerfully. 'The room's all ready.' She peered down at Violette, who was watching her with a frown. 'So this is the little one, bless her. She'll be right as rain. Mr Yearsley is a marvel with the kiddies, he had my George's tonsils out so you wouldn't know he'd ever had any.' Her face clouded momentarily. 'Of course he's in the army now, but still, it can't be helped.'

'Thank you,' said Nora, slightly overwhelmed by her landlady's energy, but grateful that she appeared completely unfazed by Violette's appearance.

'That's all right, dear.' Mrs Williams took the bassinet, lifting it inside. 'Mrs Herridge, wasn't it?'

Nora's heart sank. But Violette was growing restless, a sure sign she was hungry and about to scream the place down, and she was too tired to lie.

'Miss.'

'Yes, I thought that's what you said.' She coughed. 'If you don't mind me saying so, I'd use Mrs. Makes it easier. You know what people are like.'

'She's not my child,' said Nora.

'So I gathered,' said Mrs Williams, with the air of one likely to know all there was to know about the comings and goings at the hospital. 'Poor little thing. Refugee, isn't she?'

'Yes,' said Nora, relieved that she didn't have to explain.

'Good for you. And I hope you know you're a lucky little girl,' she added loudly to Violette, who'd drawn in her breath as a prelude to an outraged howl. Instantly distracted by this salvo, she gave a small hiccup instead, then smiled uncertainly. 'I'd still use Mrs when you're out and about,' said Mrs Williams, beaming indulgently at the little face. 'You don't have a ring by any chance, do you?'

Nora suppressed a giggle at this instant ordering of her life, however kindly meant. 'I'm afraid I don't.'

'I'll find you one.'

'Please, you don't have to. I'll buy one.'

'Nonsense. My Gwen had a thing about finery before she got married and made me a grandmother. All cheap stuff of course, but there must be something there that'll do.' She grunted. 'It's not easy being a young woman on your own, I remember it well. If men think you've a child out of wedlock they assume you're easy; if they think you're already taken, they're more likely to leave you alone.'

Nora laughed, any irritation flying out of the window. She had a feeling that once Mrs Williams got up a head of steam there was no stopping her. Besides, she could see the sense. The soldiers on the train, naturally assuming her to be a respectable married wife and mother, had treated her with a deference she'd never experienced as a single woman. Acquiring an imaginary protector definitely had its advantages.

'Mrs it will be from now on,' she said.

The next few days passed in a blur of the disinfectant aroma of whitewashed hospital corridors that clung to Nora's hair and clothes and left a bitter taste at the back of her mouth. Mr Yearsley turned out to be unexpectedly young, in his early thirties at most, but his hands were gentle as he examined Violette, distracting her with the ease of one practised in dealing with children. Nora appreciated his willingness to explain the procedure without sounding patronising.

'Things are changing all the time,' he said at the final consultation before he was due to operate. 'We're learning so much more. New techniques, new ways of having the best functional and aesthetic outcome. It's very satisfying knowing that something so simple can transform a life.'

'I'm sure it is,' said Nora, who was beginning to panic inside. She trusted him, of course she did, but even with the greatest of skill things could go wrong. She had a sudden urge to sweep Violette up and rush her away.

'She'll come through it,' he said, as if sensing her doubts. 'She's strong and healthy, and I can see she's a determined little soul. It's only natural to worry.' He grimaced. 'Sometimes the responsibility can feel harder when it's not your own child.'

'I just wish her mother was here,' said Nora.

'I think she is, in you,' he replied gently. He gave her hand a reassuring squeeze, turning away tactfully as she wiped away the unexpected tears and blew her nose. As she stood up to leave, he was back to his professional persona once more. 'Try not to worry. Your little Violette will come through this. And I'll do my best so that one day you'll look back and wonder if it ever happened at all.'

PART 3

TWENTY

IRIS

Cornwall, 1964

Mum was too tired to finish the story that day. Iris sensed the next part would be even more difficult for her to tell, and didn't press her. A child facing an operation must be frightening enough, even without a war on the continent.

The first year of the war, Iris remembered from history lessons at school, had been known as the Phoney War, when nothing much seemed to happen. It was only afterwards that the bombing raids on the major towns, the blitz, brought the war to civilians. She had seen for herself the bomb sites in London, gaps between houses where buildings had been obliterated, now playgrounds for children until the rubble could be cleared away and the destroyed dwellings replaced.

She couldn't imagine living through something like that, let alone what happened on the continent, with whole countries reduced to rubble and the obscene cruelty of the holocaust. They didn't know much about that in England during the war, Mum had told her once, only rumours and snippets. It was only after the war that the full horror was revealed.

For the rest of the day they cooked together in a leisurely manner. Mum and Dad had put in a modern kitchen and bath-room when Hope Cottage had been connected to the mains. Iris always found it odd to think of a world without electricity. She vaguely remembered the glow of the kerosene lamp, still used in in the periodic blackouts in St Mabon's when wind brought down the electricity lines. But she couldn't imagine a world without light. St Mabon's had been completely plunged into darkness during the war, Mum had told her, blackout curtains keeping out any chink of light that might draw the attention of enemy bombers. There were even fines for people who were careless.

By the evening Mum was too tired to do any more than chat quietly, ready for an early night. They followed the familiar routine of watching the BBC News on the television Iris remembered being bought, with great anticipation, in honour of the Queen's coronation in 1953. So many of the neighbours had crowded in to watch that day, it had been difficult for them to see the black and white images on that little screen within its large wooden box. It felt reassuring to return to the memories of childhood, but Iris couldn't quite escape the feeling of tension between the calm. A sense of part of her life ending, never to be quite the same again.

After a night of uneasy dreams, Iris rose early. It was a bright, cloudless morning with a slight chill in the air that sent the dew on the grass sparkling and the sea gleaming in turquoise brilliance. She pushed her way through the garden gate and onto the fields, instinctively looking towards the car park in St Mabon's for any sign of Jeanie Dixon's car.

'She's gone,' a voice said. Iris turned with a smile towards a familiar figure walking towards her from the direction of Maltby Abbey. Miss Maltby frequently came this way, even after Mum and Dad had earned enough between them to buy Hope Cottage and turn it into a comfortable modern home. She was a familiar sight, this elderly woman with white hair swept up in a bun behind her head, striding across the cliff in wide-fitting trousers and a man's jacket before the guests at the hotel began to rise.

'Hello, Aunt Winnie,' said Iris.

'Good morning, my dear,' said Miss Maltby, kissing her affectionately, her rather severe face lit up with an indulgent smile that would have left her London suppliers, and any official from the local council, open-mouthed in astonishment. The inhabitants of St Mabon's were well aware that their lady of the manor was all hard shell on the outside and soft as butter on the inside, but weren't about to tell anyone else. She was a good landlord, and her hotel brought much-needed custom to the harbour. Besides, heaven help anyone who tried to pity her, or take advantage of her having been a spinster all her life.

'Who's gone?' Iris prompted her.

'The Dixon girl. Blasted journalists. They were just the same when I was a debutante being presented at court. George V, not Queen Victoria,' she added tartly. 'I didn't quite come out of the ark, whatever you youngsters might think.'

Iris, who knew the soft-as-butter side, grinned. 'I wouldn't suggest it for a minute, Aunt Winnie. Are you sure she's gone?'

'Oh, absolutely.' A mischievous look, known only to those Miss Maltby trusted enough to let down her usual guard, appeared. 'I still know people in London, you know. I told her I had dinner with Lord Thomson, who owns *The Times*, only the other day, and things could become awkward for her if she didn't make herself scarce. That seemed to do the trick.'

'Aunt Winnie!' exclaimed Iris, laughing.

'Well, she didn't need to know twenty or thirty others were there as well. And I would have done it, my dear. It wasn't all bluff.' Miss Maltby patted Iris's arm affectionately. 'You and your mum and dad are the nearest thing I have to a family, and a family always protects its own.' She straightened her shoulders.

'It's good to see your mum getting stronger. You tell her that replacement chef is reasonable, and will do for now, but I'll be expecting her back before the summer season begins in earnest.'

'Yes, Aunt Winnie,' said Iris, meekly.

Miss Maltby paused before making her way back to the Abbey. 'And don't worry about the likes of Jeanie Dixon, my dear. Ambition without a heart has led many a man or woman astray. That doesn't mean the rest of us have to dance to their tune. Give my regards to your mother. She's a good woman who always did what was best for you. And that, in the end, is what counts.'

Iris stood for a few minutes watching the determined little figure making its no-nonsense way back to wrestle the challenges of the day into obedience. As she returned through the gate, she found Mum standing in the garden.

'Was that Miss Maltby, darling?'

'Yes. She sends her regards and what I think she was saying is that she misses you.'

Mum chuckled. 'I can't wait to put this behind me and get strong enough to get back in that kitchen, my dear. The adrenalin does me good.'

'And she's sent that journalist away, with menaces.'

'Thank goodness for that.' The crease between Mum's brows eased. There was more colour in her cheeks this morning, as if her body was finally beginning to heal from her operation. 'I'm not sure I have the energy yet to deal with the likes of Jeanie Dixon.'

Silence fell in the little garden, broken only by the sound of a delivery van making its way down to St Mabon's, and the eternal sighing of the waves.

Iris could see her mother bracing herself for what came next. 'Come on, I'll make you a coffee,' she said.

'Thank you, darling, I could do with one.'

'Mum, you don't have to go on.'

'Yes, I do. More than you can imagine. So much happened once the war really began, with the blitz here and what happened on the continent. Thank goodness none of us could have imagined any of it. I sometimes think that it was only afterwards, when it was all over, that we could let it properly sink in. And even then, it often felt too terrible. "We that are young,"' she quoted, half under her breath.

Iris blinked. She'd studied *King Lear* for her English A level and still knew by heart the despairing final line, spoken as peace is restored: 'The oldest hath borne most: we that are young, Shall never see so much, nor live so long'.

With a rising sense of anxiety, she followed her mother inside the house.

TWENTY-ONE

SABINE

France, 1940

All through that spring of 1940 Sabine waited anxiously for Nora's letters, painfully aware that each one might be the last. They both knew the strange sense of normality in England and France could vanish at any moment. If – when – the war began in earnest, the postal service was bound to be disrupted, and if the Germans invaded France ... Sabine pushed the thought to the back of her mind.

Like the women, the old men and the children left behind in the village while their men went to defend France's borders, Sabine knew there was nothing she could do. She could only hope a conquering army was prevented from ever crashing its way through the meadows and the ripening cornfields surrounding the Chateau Saint-Céré, and that peace would come soon. Meanwhile, the only way to keep sane was to shut out any thoughts of what might take place should the worst happen.

Nora's first letter reassured her that Violette had come

safely through her operation. Sabine fled with the envelope before Maman spotted it, sitting by the stream where she'd played as a child. She read Nora's words over and over again, consumed with relief that Violette was alive, every fibre of her body racked with longing to hold her, to comfort her as only a mother could.

Violette is in the best place. She scolded herself for being so selfish. Nora told her that the surgeon was highly regarded for his skill and was pleased how well the procedure had gone. The nurses were all kind and gentle and let her stay by Violette's bedside as long as she wanted. It was now just a matter of time and seeing how well the tiny body healed.

Sabine realised there were things Nora was tactfully omitting, but she couldn't blame her. When she'd taken Violette to the hospital in Paris, the doctors had warned Sabine of the possible complications, the potential for infection, that follow-up procedures might be necessary. Nora also wasn't reminding her that Violette's hospital was near the southern coast of England, the part nearest the continent, so one of the first places to be taken if the Germans invaded.

To Sabine's relief, each subsequent letter from Nora reassured her there were no complications as Violette gradually recovered. Her ability to mouth sounds was already improving. She made sure she spoke to Violette both in French and English; the way children picked up languages so easily meant she'd become fluent in both.

As early summer arrived, Sabine began to relax a little. Violette was now well enough for Nora to take her out into the fresh air. On the other hand, Sabine sensed that more practical problems were looming. Guillaume had, through his army contacts, managed to send enough money to Nora to cover her lodgings and necessities while Violette was recuperating, but that might soon come to an end.

They were so close, and yet so far! In normal times Violette's hospital would be only a day's journey by boat and train, but now it felt a world away.

Nora's next letter told her that Violette was well enough to make the journey back to London. She read it in the little court-yard while Maman fed Valérie in the kitchen. There was a small photograph amongst the pages, taken at a studio near the hospital. Sabine seized it eagerly. Her heart twisted as she saw how much Violette had changed. It wasn't just her lip. She was propped up against a cushion, frowning solemnly at the camera, no longer a tiny baby but a small child.

She'd missed all those changes in her, the little day-to-day developments that she'd seen in Valérie. She looked down at her face, so very like her sister's, but at the same time one she no longer really knew, and felt her heart break. She hastily turned her attention to the rest of the letter. Nora was arranging to stay with her sister Pearl, who would share looking after Violette with their mother while Nora was at work.

With persistence, and the fact that so many men had been called up, Nora had finally managed to get her old job back at *La Belle Époque*. Sabine winced. Not as a chef, as Nora had once dreamed, but a lowly preparer of vegetables in a restaurant hit hard by the introduction of rationing.

For all Nora's cheerfulness – it was within walking distance of her sister's home and she would be working fewer hours than before – Sabine understood how much her friend must have put her ambitions aside to support Violette. Hopefully it wouldn't be for long, Nora added, and it would keep her hand in for when the war ended.

Sabine returned to the kitchen, pausing to kiss Valérie, beaming face adorned with the remains of mashed-up potato and carrots, now happily chewing on the remainder of the breakfast baguette.

'Mémé thinks we should consider leaving while the trains are still running,' said Maman as Sabine prepared a pot of fresh *tisane*, made with mint from the garden.

'Where would we go?' asked Sabine, wiping Valérie's face clean with a damp cloth, despite her twisting and wriggling and screwing up her face at the intrusion.

'South, to the interior. That's where the refugees all seem to be heading. Mémé says there are resettlement grants for those who wish to move further away from the cities and the German border.'

'There you are, all done,' said Sabine to Valérie, placing a fresh piece of baguette in her tiny fist. The protests subsided as her mouth closed around the crust, sucking contentedly. 'And what do *you* think, Maman?'

'That we should stay. See what happens. We've worked so hard to keep the farm going and making sure we'll have enough supplies for the winter. We're amongst friends here. We can support each other. If we take the train, who knows where we might end up?' She looked towards Valérie. 'And a child is so vulnerable. Even if we have money, how can we be certain we'll be able to buy enough food to keep her properly fed?'

Sabine hesitated, unsure of what to do for the best. Then she looked towards Valérie, now wriggling, impatient to get down from her high chair and explore the expanding horizons of her world. Sabine had sent one child into the unknown. How could she even think of doing the same with Valérie?

'Then we will stay,' she said.

After that, there were no more letters from Nora. Within weeks, the invasion they had all dreaded, and hoped would never happen, began.

For a while the papers talked of French victories, of the

German army being heavily defeated, briefly sparking hope that the conflict would pass them by. But as June wore on, more refugees began to appear, carrying or pushing pitifully few belongings, heading south towards Corrèze in the Massif Central where refugee camps had been set up, and there was at least some prospect of food and shelter.

'I really think we should reconsider and go to Corrèze,' said Mémé one evening, returning from taking food to a woman they had found pushing a perambulator containing all her worldly goods, her small children with rucksacks on their backs walking alongside, and who were now sheltering in one of the barns for the night. 'Mme Devault was talking just now of more evacuations and the German army advancing. Several of the other refugees have said the same. That doesn't sound like the picture the papers are painting.'

'There's the harvest soon, we can't abandon that,' replied Maman nervously. 'What will Guillaume say when he comes home on leave? If we don't get the harvest in, we'll be ruined.'

'We may have no choice,' retorted Mémé. 'Most of the rich families have already left for their holiday homes, not just the Garniers. You remember what happened last time war came here?'

Maman shuddered. 'How could I forget? The first soldiers to arrive were quite reasonable, but the others were out of control. They took everything, and God help you if you were a young woman.'

'Then I think Mémé is right and we should leave,' said Sabine, fear bubbling up in the depths of her stomach. 'If that's what the refugees are saying, I trust them more than the newspapers.'

'I'm not leaving,' said Maman stubbornly. 'Guillaume's due home any day. He'll know what to do, he'll advise us. I've waited so long to see him, if we leave now he won't know where we are.'

Mémé pursed her lips but did not pursue to the argument. Sabine shot upstairs to Valérie, who was becoming restless at the unfamiliar sound of children's voices from the barn, along with the nervous barking of Mme Devault's fox terrier. In the dusk, she could make out yet more families arriving, settling down on the lawns, too weary and defeated to go any further.

As she returned downstairs, to the sound of Maman and Mémé in heated argument, the squeal of brakes in the courtyard stopped her in her tracks.

'That must be Guillaume,' exclaimed Maman. 'Thank goodness.'

'It's not his car, it's far too smart,' said Mémé, flinging open the shutters.

Not Emil, please not Emil ... Sabine peered from behind her grandmother, taking in the sleek shape and the luggage piled on the roof. The back door opened and a woman jumped out.

'Why, it's Marie-Thérèse,' exclaimed Sabine, hurrying out into the courtyard, followed by her mother and grandmother.

'What are you doing here at this time of night?' Maman stared in astonishment at her sister. 'Darling, what is it? Won't you and your friends come inside?'

Marie-Thérèse shook her head. 'You have to leave, Joelle. Now. You, Sabine and Mémé. This minute. Don't wait any longer. The Germans are approaching. We only just got out of Paris. You can hear the guns and the city's being bombed. The panic was dreadful, even worse than last time. I was lucky the Verniers saw me and found room in their car for me.'

'At least stay the night,' said Maman, trying to stay calm.

'We can't, and you mustn't wait either or it'll be too late. I begged them to take the detour to warn you all, but we can't stay, not for one minute. It's too risky. There are so many refugees on the roads, it's almost impossible to move, and there's already talk of the Luftwaffe bombing refugees in case there are

French soldiers amongst them. If you don't leave now, you may lose the chance. Promise me you won't wait.'

Sabine looked towards the car and saw two young girls in the back. The nearest was watching them, her face a pale blur in the gloom, her arms clutching a small lapdog, a bow adorning the fur of its forehead.

'Don't worry, we'll leave straight away,' she said firmly, turning to meet her grandmother's eyes.

'I need to go,' said Marie-Thérèse, glancing back towards the car, its engine already revving impatiently. 'They're heading to Biarritz, but I will find you. One day, when this is over, I will find you.' Embracing them all, she ran back to the car, which set off immediately at speed, hurtling into the dusk.

'If Paris is being bombed we'll never get on a train,' said Mémé, 'if they're even still running. Besides, they're an obvious target for the Germans. We'll take the cart.'

'The cart?' exclaimed Maman.

'There's no need to look so horrified, chérie. We took the wagon when we escaped last time. This is no time for pride. At least it's a more serviceable cart this time. Anyway, Mme Devault told me that cars are running out of fuel, especially if they aren't carrying spare cans of petrol with them. At least we won't have that problem with the horses. There are a few hay bales left, we can put those in and they'll be able to keep going as long as we can find grass and water.'

In the distance came a low drone of aeroplanes high in the night sky, lumbering ominously in the direction of Paris.

'I'll help you pack, Maman,' said Sabine, feeling the unnatural calm of a true emergency going through her, her mind as clear as could be.

'And don't forget winter coats,' called Mémé, already heading towards the stables.

'Winter?' Maman sounded close to tears.

'The nights can be chilly,' said Sabine gently. 'I'm sure that's all she means.' As she steered her mother inside, she glanced up at the shadow outlining the familiar façade of the chateau. For as long as she remembered, the Chateau Saint-Céré had been a reassuring presence, a solid background to her life. She'd assumed it would always be there, eternal in its faded glory. Now they were leaving it behind. Who knew if any of them would ever return?

TWENTY-TWO

NORA

London, 1940

Nora was making preparations for the return to London when the rumours that France had been invaded began.

'Violette is most decidedly better off here,' said Mr Yearsley when Nora took her for a final check-up. 'She's doing really well.' He smiled at Violette's face that was already filling out with a baby's chubbiness. 'I can see I don't need to ask if she's feeding better now she's healing.'

'I think she's making up for lost time,' said Nora. 'She loves her bottle, and she's so much more contented. She's sleeping much better too.'

'Excellent. That's just what we like to hear.' He carefully inspected Violette's mouth. *Poor little thing*, thought Nora, seeing her little charge submit to this indignity without protest. She was so used to hospitals and being prodded and peered at. She couldn't wait to get her into a more homely environment where she could just be an ordinary child.

'That's all as it should be.' Mr Yearsley smiled broadly. 'I'm happy to release her. Just keep an eye on her, Mrs Herridge, especially when she starts teething. If you give me the name of your doctor, I'll send the details to him as well.' He eyed her closely. 'I take it you're not going back to London, what with all the uncertainty?'

'I'm not sure,' said Nora. 'My mum says several of the neighbours who returned home after being evacuated last year have headed off to family in the countryside again for fear of bombing.'

'Probably wise,' he replied. 'If you can manage it, I'd recommend you do that too. Violette's doing remarkably well, but there's still a long way to go. Peace and quiet is what she needs. What you both need, my dear. The mind often takes as long, if not longer, to heal than the body, and you've been closer to war than any of us here would want to be. You need to look after yourself as well, for Violette's sake, as well as your own.'

Nora walked out of the hospital deep in thought.

Mr Yearsley had hit a nerve. Mum had told her that if France fell, she worried it'd be their turn next. She said she'd been trying in vain to persuade Pearl to be evacuated, but Nora's sister was afraid of what people in the country might think.

While if you found a nice place in the countryside, darling, we might be able to persuade her to bring Jonny to join you, her mum had written.

Nora hesitated, torn between missing Mum and Dad, who she knew could never be persuaded to leave London, and the tantalising thought of not having to return to skivvying at *La Belle Époque*. Despite the unease that underlay everything these days, she felt a sense of freedom at the thought that if she found the right place, she could persuade Pearl and Jonny to join them. Instead of sharing the childcare between them in London, they could do it in Devon, where so many had been evacuated from London and the other big cities. It was the only way she was ever going to be able to support herself.

To Nora's frustration, her room at Mrs Williams' was only booked until the end of the week. There being no time like the present, Nora instantly began scouring the newspapers for any post that might look promising. Over the following days she pushed Violette as far Mrs Williams' ancient perambulator would go, viewing the cards placed in local post-office windows. She asked at shops and guesthouses, even answering an advertisement for a cleaner at a large hotel. But with a child in tow, even the respectability offered by the ring on her wedding finger failed to prevent an instant dismissal without even the most cursory of interviews.

By the last day of her stay in Exeter, Nora had all but given up hope of finding anything in time. Even with the money Guillaume had forwarded to her, and living as frugally as possible, her savings were almost depleted. She still had enough to get home to London, but if she tried to find another room to stay on for even a few days, that too would be gone.

She said her thanks and goodbyes at the hospital and pushed Violette towards the station to buy the ticket to London. She chose the long way, passing several rows of shops and two post offices. At the first post office she saw a card seeking a delivery boy (bicycle provided); at the second, a housekeeper at one of the guesthouses she'd already tried.

'It looks like London it will have to be,' she said to Violette, who was wide awake and watching the shadows of the awning in front of the grocer's shop next door. Nora bent down to retrieve Violette's much-loved lion, known as Lionie, knitted for her by Mrs Williams from odds and ends of wool, its slightly mottled appearance set off by bright pink loops for its mane.

As she did so, her eye was caught by another postcard, this time in the shop window. The scotch tape holding it to the glass had come loose, leaving it hanging at an angle. Nora tilted her head to make out the lettering.

Help Wanted.

It didn't specify what kind of help. Probably a gardener or a handyman, she thought gloomily. Applications were to be sent to Miss Winifred Maltby, Maltby Abbey, St. Mabon's Cove, St Ives, Cornwall. A woman might be more sympathetic. On the other hand, her title suggested she was unmarried, so she may well be an elderly spinster who hated the sight and sound of children. And, in any case, it was too late. She could hardly get an application to St Ives and back again by tomorrow morning. That was when the number caught her eye. Nora squinted at the bottom row. St Mabon's 2-1-4. Miss Maltby had a telephone.

Taking a deep breath she searched in her purse for all the coins she could find before positioning the pram outside the nearest telephone box, ready to make the call that, for better or worse, would change her life.

TWENTY-THREE

SABINE

France, 1940

How do you pack a life in a few minutes? How do you pack for survival, for as long as you might need it? Sabine's brain froze at the enormity of the task. She could see from the pallor of her mother's face that she felt the same.

First things first.

'We need papers,' she said. 'All our papers. Then any money, and anything valuable we can sell if we need to.'

'Yes, of course.'

With her mother sorting through her belongings, Sabine collected everything she could for herself and Valérie, focusing on being practical. She packed her daughter's clothes, along with blankets and coats, taking them downstairs while Valérie watched her from the safety of her high chair with solemn eyes, too absorbed in the strange goings-on to protest.

'We're going on an adventure,' Sabine told her cheerfully, placing Poupée, the battered rag doll Valérie always clutched tightly for reassurance, in her daughter's arms. 'With the horses.

You like the horses, don't you?' Valérie nodded. 'And Poupée is coming with us.'

She took her suitcase and her mother's down to the hallway, keeping Valérie busy with a piece of bread while she and Maman sorted out as much food as they could carry.

'We need things that won't perish and don't need much cooking,' said Maman, her voice steady now she was dealing with practicalities. 'Bread, fruit, cheese and that small ham.' She sighed. 'All our stores, everything to get us through the winter, the crops in the fields, and the animals. All that work, for nothing.'

'You never know, the Germans might not get this far; we might be back before too long,' said Sabine, kissing her.

'They'll take everything,' said Maman bleakly.

'Don't think about it,' said Mémé, clattering down the staircase with her suitcase and an armful of fur coats. 'Just think of the practicalities. I should have thrown these out long ago, some are my mother's, the ones she took with her the last time we had to run. They might be moth-eaten and old fashioned, but I'm not leaving them for some *Boche* officer to take for his mistress to strut about in. They'll still keep us warm.'

After a hasty last cup of coffee – none of them had the stomach to eat any of the hard-won provisions they were about to abandon – Mémé hitched up the horses to the cart. Mme Lavigne climbed up at the front next to Mémé, while Sabine placed Valérie amongst the hay bales and suitcases, made her as comfortable as possible with quilts and fur coats and clambered in next to her.

As the cart rumbled down the driveway, sunlight crept through the vines and the apple orchard, the scenes of Sabine's childhood. At the entrance they paused and looked back, one last time, at the house, its blue shutters closed up, the peaceful fields green and golden in the summer haze.

'Heaven knows what state this'll be in if we ever return,'

said her mother. 'Last time we came back to find nothing left. They'd taken the very portraits off the walls. Everything of value had gone. Even the timbers had been broken up for firewood. We started again from nothing and built all this.'

'But at least we survived, Joelle,' said Mémé. 'And we will survive again.'

Sabine adjusted Valérie in her arms. It felt so final. Fear surged through her. Despite her struggles in her first years in Paris, before she met Emil, she'd never been homeless, not knowing where she was going to sleep that night or where her next meal might come from. She'd always worked hard to at least earn enough money for bread; she'd always had friends to offer her a bed if she couldn't pay the rent. And there'd always been the chateau, the place of last resort. Even if she had to swallow her pride, she'd always known it was there, something she'd never be without. And in those days there was no child to think about.

The sight of enemy planes heading towards the capital had finally made up any wavering minds. Many other families were also leaving, some in battered cars and motorised vans, others in carts much like their own, bedding and belongings piled high between small children. Others pushed perambulators or hand-carts, the young and the old clutching whatever they could.

As they passed the train station, they found it crowded with desperate women and children jostling to board any train that might take them south towards the Spanish border. With so many of the men staying behind to continue essential work and protect the towns and villages from looting, Sabine tried to shut out the desperate goodbyes of families torn apart, knowing they might never see each other again. The sense of unease that had lurked just beneath the surface all those months since the declaration of war had finally erupted into fear. This was real.

She held Valérie tight. Her little daughter's life had only just begun. She dreaded to think what might happen to her.

When she'd been a student in Paris she would have died for freedom, for her ideals, her beliefs. She'd dreamed of travelling the world, exposing wrongs, risking her life for justice. Now when she looked down into that trusting little face, all that idealism seemed a long way off. Meaningless. Nothing was worth risking the lives of those she loved. Let the great wide world fight over ideals. She just wanted to survive.

She transferred her gaze to the fields stretching out in their summer glory, the crops almost ready to be harvested, the villages and farmhouses clustered around the local *église*, as the cart reached the main road and joined the long trail of humanity heading south.

TWENTY-FOUR

NORA

Cornwall, 1940

In Exeter, Nora finished her brief telephone conversation with Miss Maltby and replaced the receiver.

'What do you think?' she asked Violette as she pushed her way through the heavy door of the telephone box. Violette chewed in a considering sort of way at the knitted front paw of Lionie the Lion.

Strange how the trajectory of her whole life could change in the ten minutes before she was due to phone back to accept or refuse the offer of a job at Maltby Abbey. Nora eased the pram into a children's playground just beyond the row of shops, where mothers chatted together holding babies on swings, while their older children played on slides and roundabouts. Deep in thought, she pushed the pram around the small pond, where ducks and moorhens splashed in the shallows.

Miss Maltby had sounded neither particularly young nor old. Her clipped tones had definitely belonged to a privileged woman accustomed to servants doing her every bidding. On the other hand, her replies to Nora's questions had lacked the imperious assumption of superiority Nora had heard amongst the wealthier clientele of *La Belle Époque*, always the most forward when complaining about the sauce being too thin or the Bordeaux insufficiently aged.

Miss Maltby had turned over the land surrounding her ancestral home to growing vegetables for the harbour and the neighbouring villages. With Land Girls arriving from all over the country to do the work of the absent men, she was looking for a general housekeeper, hopefully an older woman with a husband too old to be called up who was prepared to carry out repairs around the house. All of which had felt a bit pointless, until Nora mentioned being a cook.

'Cook?' Miss Maltby's voice had instantly sharpened into decided interest. 'What kind of a cook?'

'I've worked as an undercook in a restaurant in London, and I recently trained as a chef in Paris.'

'But you *can* cook.'

Nora had grinned at this dismissal of haute cuisine. 'I can make dishes with anything, and for as many people as you like.'

'Can you now? Well, then. I rather think we need to talk.'

Having completed a brief circuit of the pond, Nora took a seat on a bench near the mothers, pushing the pram to and fro to sooth Violette while she weighed up the possibilities. She had to be sure. If she headed to Cornwall she wouldn't have enough money left to return to London. She'd be committing herself to staying there for a while, at least. Of course, the decision might be out of her hands. Miss Maltby had said she'd need to think about things when Nora confessed to the complication of Violette. On the other hand, she had sounded desperate.

Maltby Abbey, St Mabon's, Cornwall. A place of peace and quiet, out in the countryside, dedicated to the production of food for the war effort.

'What am I thinking of?' she exclaimed aloud. An abbey that sounded more like a stately home, or scrubbing potatoes at

La Belle Époque, which might not even survive the stringencies of rationing. She'd be a fool not to take the chance. Miss Maltby had mentioned being on the coast. That would mean beaches and fresh air. Just the sort of place where she might be able to persuade Pearl to join her, perhaps even Mum as well.

Taking a deep breath, she headed back towards the telephone box.

The following afternoon Nora stepped down from the bus lumbering its way towards Mabon's Cove, Violette in her arms, and looked up at the crumbling mansion rising from the fields. Doubt gripped her whether she'd made the right decision after all. It looked dilapidated, unloved. A place forgotten by time.

But the bus was already pulling away, its passengers eyeing the stranger with curiosity as they made their way to the hamlets and harbours along the north Cornwall coast. There was nothing for it. She headed for a stile at the side of the road, which the bus driver had pointed out as the shortest route to Maltby Abbey by foot.

As she reached the brow of the hill, she paused. 'Oh my Lord,' she exclaimed. Violette turned to scrutinise her expression. 'I didn't expect that,' said Nora, smiling down at her reassuringly. 'It's beautiful.'

In the fleeting scurry of sunlight between rain, a clear view of the sea opened out, the little harbour in the cove below and the long sweep of cliffs heading into the distance on either side. She breathed the salt air deeply, clearing her lungs.

'Looks like there's a beach down there,' she said to Violette, who eyed her wisely. 'I must have some time off, Miss Maltby can't expect me to work day and night. We'll go down and explore the first chance we get.'

The rain was threatening again, sweeping towards them across the sea like a dark curtain, leaving a line in the green water, and Violette felt heavy in her arms. Nora clambered over the stile and set off across the meadows towards the house.

They reached a brick wall that looked as if it had once formed part of a stable block. A large wooden door hung open, allowing Nora to step into a cobbled yard.

'Oh, hello.' A young woman shelling peas under cover of an awning stretched between two empty stables looked up from her bowl. 'You must be the new cook. Miss Maltby's in the fields, teaching the others how to scythe. They'll be back in a bit. Mrs Herridge, isn't it?'

'That's right.'

The young woman beamed. 'I'm Linda. Thank goodness you're here. None of us can boil an egg, if you're lucky enough to find one, and Miss Maltby's no better. I should warn you, the ingredients are all swedes and potatoes.'

'I'm sure I can manage those,' said Nora with a grin.

Linda smiled indulgently at Violette, who was fascinated by the cartoon ducks on her scarf, which had been twisted up like a turban to keep her fair hair in place.

'What a sweet little girl. Miss Maltby said you were bringing your daughter.' Her eyes rested on the half-healed scar on Violette's lip. 'Oh my Lord, are you evacuees? There haven't been any bombings have there? They keep on talking about it.'

'Just an accident,' replied Nora.

'Poor little mite.' A wistful look came over the girl's face. 'May I hold her? I'm used to babies. We've got three at home, if you count my sister Vi's little boy. Funny, I never thought I'd miss the little tykes.' She placed Violette on her hip with a practised air, allowing her to continue her inspection of the ducks. 'What's her name?'

'Violette.'

'That's a pretty name. I had an aunt called Violet, she was

kind to me.' She beamed at Violette. 'A pretty name for a pretty girl.'

Nora opened her mouth to correct her but was halted by a giggling rush of young women in dungarees in various states of sunburn, followed by a tall, middle-aged woman in trousers and shirt, her dark hair tied back in a red headscarf.

'Ah, you must be Mrs Herridge,' she said, adding her basket of pea pods to a half-shelled mound. 'Good grief, I'd no idea your child was quite so young.'

Nora's heart sank. 'She's a little small for her age.'

'Yes, yes, of course, you did tell me.' Miss Maltby shook her head. 'You'd better come with me. And bring the child with you, my Land Girls have enough to do feeding the local population without having to look after stray infants.'

Nora collected Violette who was watching the new arrivals with curiosity rather than alarm. Poor little mite. So much of her short life had been taken up with hospitals and discomfort; she wouldn't have blamed her if she'd started screaming at the sight of yet more young women who might be about to whisk her away.

'She's quite independent,' said Nora as she was ushered into Miss Maltby's office. 'She's still in napkins of course, but I can easily deal with those.'

'Never did have much time for infants,' stated Miss Maltby. 'Too much mess and noise. Still, beggars can't be choosers.' Nora's fists curled instinctively into fists.

In Nora's arms Violette paused in her solemn inspection of the walls of files, interspersed with glass domes containing a stuffed fox and an owl glowering fiercely on its perch, stoats dressed in top hats and a rather moth-eaten parrot, and turned her gaze towards Miss Maltby, breaking into a wide smile.

'She's a well-behaved little thing,' muttered Miss Maltby grudgingly, not quite able to prevent her own lips curling in response. 'Well, I'm prepared to see how we get on. Miss

Helsom from the village has proved an excellent childminder and her daughter Milly an equally accomplished children's nurse.' She sniffed. 'No good trying to explain to the men that children don't just look after themselves, and it's damned hard work making sure they don't kill themselves with anything to hand. They have no idea. No idea at all.'

'No, Miss Maltby,' said Nora, suppressing a relieved grin. Violette chortled in sympathy.

Miss Maltby straightened. 'Now then. We use first names here. When you're dealing with muck and sweat all day the formalities sound a little foolish. I will call you Nora and you shall call me Winnie. The other girls will introduce themselves.'

'Yes, miss,' said Nora, who couldn't imagine anyone daring to address upright and forthright Miss Maltby in such an informal manner.

'Now, I shall show you the kitchens.' Miss Maltby led the way through the corridor to the back of the house, to a large room lined with shelves stacked high with plates and pans, and a stone sink. Apart from a shiny new Aga cooker at one end, it looked as if nothing had been changed since Victorian times.

'Mrs Teague left them in a bit of a state I'm afraid, poor woman. She wasn't to know she was about to have a seizure. She's recovering with her daughter in the village, who's given me her recipe book to pass on, with the necessary adjustments to take into account the constraints of rationing and what we can grow in the Abbey grounds. An awful lot of carrots, I should warn you.' She gave the faintest of shudders. 'And if I don't see another cabbage in my life, I won't be sorry. Although I'm well aware of how lucky we and how those in the towns would kill for all our greens. The local Women's Institute run a very effective soup kitchen for the poorer families and they really rely on us for ingredients.'

'Yes, M— Winnie.'

'Mrs Teague says she'll soon be well enough to give you

more recipes if you need them. They're designed to make use of what we grow, and preserve what we can for the winter months, especially now butter and bacon are rationed. She has plenty of recipes for preserving fruits without the need for sugar. The vegetables can be stored and pickled. We make our own vinegar from the cider so there'll be no shortage there. There's honey from the hives – thank goodness we kept those up since the last war – and we've planted sugar beet in one of the fields. At least we're more prepared for the start of *this* war. We'll make sure no one in the villages or the harbours is reduced to starvation, especially the children.'

'I've finished the shelling,' said Linda, arriving with a mound of bright green peas in a blue enamelled colander. 'Annabel's bringing potatoes. I'd better warn you Mary Anne is a vegetarian, of all things, Mrs Herridge. It used to drive Mrs Teague mad.'

'I'm sure I'll manage something,' said Nora with a smile.

'As long as it's not just mashed potato again, everyone will fall at your feet. Come on, I'll show you your room.'

Nora followed her up stone stairs to a corridor under the eaves, in what had clearly once been the servants' quarters. Rooms either side contained clusters of single beds, their metal posts hung with cardigans, skirts and blouses to keep them as crease-free as possible. Clearly Miss Maltby's volunteers had no intention of leading a nun-like existence.

Her own room was at the end of the corridor, with a single bed and a cot for Violette.

'I know it's small, but we thought it'd be better, with a child and all,' said Linda. 'This way, no one will disturb her. We just need to put up the blackout curtains and you'll be settled in.'

'It's perfect, thank you,' said Nora. The tiny casement window under the eaves had been opened to air the room. Below her, she could see rich fields rolling down to the glittering sea, roofs and the masts of fishing boats resting in the harbour. It looked so peaceful, so eternal, the war seemed far away. She craned her neck to take in the coastline, adjusting Violette on her hip. She could make out the road winding up from St Mabon's. Just below the brow of the hill, a whitewashed cottage caught a sudden burst of sun, shining brightly within the surrounding greenery.

Pearl would love this. Nora felt calm wash over her with the distant cry of seagulls and the rhythmic crash of waves on the pillars of rock surrounding St Mabon's Cove. Whatever Miss Maltby expected, she was going to make this work, and on her first afternoon off she intended to start exploring. There had to be a cottage nearby that she and Pearl could share. A cottage with a garden, where they could grow vegetables, and Jonny and Violette could play. Even with paying for a childminder for Violette, she'd worked out her wages would allow her to save enough within months to pay the rail fare to London and return with Pearl. She drew in the sea air. The sooner the better, with talk all around her of the capital being bombed before too long.

TWENTY-FIVE

SABINE

France, 1940

The first night after leaving Chateau Saint-Céré Sabine and her family camped amongst a cluster of trees at the side of the road. At least with the cart they'd been able to pack enough food for a few days, along with a kettle and pans, and bedding to keep them warm. Sabine huddled next to Valérie, unable to do more than doze, roused every few minutes by coughing or the cry of a child from the little groups of fellow travellers camped all around, or the rustle of some passing creature in the undergrowth.

Over the next days and nights they made slow progress. Mémé was right about taking the cart. They regularly passed cars and vans abandoned at the side of the road, some with luggage still strapped to their roofs. There was no sign of Marie-Thérèse. Sabine hoped her family had had the foresight to take petrol with them, and they were now well on their way to Biarritz.

Several times they passed the shells of vehicles burnt out beyond all recognition, surrounded by perambulators and wheelbarrows, twisted out of shape by bombs and gunfire. Sabine learnt not to look too closely into the shadows under the trees as they passed, and to shut her mind to the sweet, cloying stench of death. Mémé kept alert as they lumbered slowly onwards, watching for any sign of movement in the skies, of any hint of enemy planes in the distance.

They were now in unfamiliar territory, further south than even Mémé had travelled, swept along with the tide of refugees past Orléans, heading for Limoges. Like the little group that had formed around them, they were tired, worn out from lack of sleep and the relentless onward journey, with so far still to go. Sabine did her best to keep Valérie clean and fed, but she could feel the dust ingrained in her own skin, the grubbiness of her clothes and that she stank of sweat and a lack of soap. The food they'd brought with them wouldn't last longer than a few more days, and drinking water was in short supply.

As the sun began to soften into the glow of evening, the group of refugees ahead of them veered off into a field at the side of the road, where an old barn offered at least some protection from the elements.

'Perhaps we should press on,' said Mémé, pulling up the horses. 'There's still a few hours of daylight left. It looks as if there's a village up ahead, we might be able to buy some milk for Valérie, or at least some bread.'

Sabine slid from the cart and reached for Valérie, who was grumpy from the endless jolting of the wheels and the heat of the day.

'Can't we join them in the barn instead?' she pleaded. 'It looks like there's a stream on the far side, and with so many of us arriving all at once, I think anything they have to give us in the village will be gone, and anywhere to sleep will be taken. We might have more of a chance if we wait until morning.'

Valérie snuffled into her shoulder, her face hot and damp as tears began to flow.

'It's been a long day,' agreed Maman. 'A few more hours won't make that much difference, and at least we know there's grass and water here for the horses.'

Mémé hesitated. Around them, the group traveling just behind were overtaking the cart, heading towards the comparative safety of the village. A small girl with a mass of golden curls leading a rough-haired puppy of vaguely spaniel heritage at the end of a pink ribbon waved cheerfully, before running to catch up with her family, distracting Valérie long enough to prevent her busting into full-scale screams.

'Very well,' Mémé said at last. 'We should have enough bread and cheese for tonight, but we're going to have to start searching for more provisions tomorrow.'

The barn, though dilapidated, was still fairly sturdy, and the small stream was enough for them to wash their dusty faces and for Sabine to clean Valérie's soiled napkins, hanging them on the side of the cart to dry. The Rubins, an elderly man and wife, collected fallen branches and old timbers to light a fire to boil water. The scrapings of several families' tea leaves were pressed into service, and even a pot of coffee was set bubbling in the embers, before the fire was extinguished as light faded for fear of attracting attention.

A few of the families chose to sleep in the barn, but most camped outside. They'd heard too many stories of buildings being bombed in the night.

Sabine finally settled Valérie down next to the cart and curled up next to her mother to finish the remains of her tea. On the other side of the embers she saw the brief flare of a match, followed by the glow of a cigarette.

'Marcel, do you want the enemy planes to know we're here you fool?' hissed a woman's voice.

'It's a match.' Marcel sounded no more than a boy, sixteen at the most.

'And they have machine guns. Have you forgotten how they

strafed the road when we were leaving Blois? Do you want to get us all killed?'

'No, Maman,' he muttered.

'It'll be light soon enough,' said his mother, softening. 'I know it's not easy. We're all on edge, and no wonder. At least save it until then.'

The next morning, Sabine rose in the chill of the dawn, amongst subdued coughing and the trampling of undergrowth as others nearby tried to find some measure of privacy to relieve themselves. There was still a little milk for Valérie, bought earlier in the day from a farm and kept fresh overnight in the stream. They eked out the pat of butter, leaving the bread, bought at a village several days before and now dry, and the last few jars of last year's jam, which would keep for longer in the heat.

Around them, families were making their own breakfasts, some meagre, many with nothing at all. The women with two young girls next to them packed their rucksacks wearily, ready to take to the road again.

'We can't,' whispered Maman.

'We're in this together,' said Mémé. 'Or we're all lost. Our travelling companions are sharing what they have. We must do the same.' She took one of the remaining loaves to the women, who fell on it with the eagerness of those who hadn't eaten properly for weeks.

Sabine helped Mémé harness the horses while her mother took care of Valérie.

'You need to know how to do this, Sabine. In case anything happens to me.'

'We won't leave you.'

'Yes you will. If I get ill or can't go any further, you must leave me behind and carry on. It's the only way to survive. You must think of your child. Of both your children. You must survive, or they will not.'

'I won't leave you,' said Sabine firmly.

Mémé kissed her. 'You're a good girl, my dear. Time to get on our way.' Sabine held Valérie as she walked with her mother beside the cart, directing Mémé under the underhanging branches and out towards the road, avoiding a large boulder they must have narrowly missed in the dark.

'It's clear,' called Sabine, stepping out onto the road, closing her eyes briefly to savour the warmth of the sun on her face, blissful after the chill of the night. Valérie burbled with delight in her arms at the dance of shadows across the open space as the nearby branches swayed.

'Look out!' For a moment, the words didn't sink in. Sabine's eyes shot open, blinded by sunlight. Something whizzed past, striking the trees behind. There was a roar of engines above. Screams erupted, sending the refugees scrambling for the cover of the trees, as an aeroplane, strafing the road with bullets, swept towards them.

TWENTY-SIX

NORA

Cornwall, 1940

Over the next weeks, Nora quickly settled into life at Maltby Abbey.

The house itself was a great rambling place of endless corridors panelled with wood darkened with age and polish. The rooms were vast, with portraits of Maltby ancestors stretching back through the ages to Tudor times staring down from the walls. Little was left of the grandeur of the original abbey, apart from a great arched window at one end of the dining room. And although several framed photographs showed every corner crammed with furniture and ornaments at the height of its Victorian splendour, much of it had been removed when the house was used as a convalescent hospital during the last war.

Nora rather liked the sparseness of the rooms. It gave a practical air to the place that fitted Miss Maltby's no-nonsense approach to life, and felt oddly reassuring. Even as she grappled with the ancient range and the somewhat temperamental electric cooker, Nora sensed a feeling of calm about the place. It was almost as if its original purpose for study and contemplation had never quite been dispersed by Henry VIII's Dissolution of the Monasteries, when the building had first been handed over to the Maltby family.

Miss Maltby, as she heard from the volunteers working in the grounds, had inherited the family estate following the death of her only brother in the Great War.

'Lost her fiancé, too,' said Linda one afternoon, as the workers paused for cups of tea and cake that Nora had sweetened with bottled cherries from the larder. 'Worked as a nurse out in France saving other women's sweethearts, but didn't have a chance to save her own, poor woman. No wonder she turned the meadows over to growing vegetables. That's what they did last time, you see.'

'So you all volunteered?' asked Nora, curious at the motley collection of young women housed in the servants' quarters and one of the barns.

'As soon as war was declared,' said Alice, who looked no more than seventeen, retying her jaunty paisley-pattern headscarf around her fair curls. 'Best chance I had of getting out of Birmingham and cleaning grates and scrubbing floors for a bunch of toffs who didn't even know I existed. I know Miss Maltby's a toff, but she's all right.'

'It isn't all tennis and getting dressed up for tea, you know,' retorted Annabel, whose clipped accent and expensive clothes suggested she came from a similar class to Miss Maltby. She grinned. 'I fled the moment my mother started measuring me up for my debutante dress. She still hasn't forgiven me for preferring to dig potatoes to being presented at court. But Miss Maltby comes from one of the oldest families in Cornwall, so there's nothing she can do about it.'

The little group paused to look up as they heard the familiar rumble of a Spitfire heading for the RAF airfield further up the coast at St Eval.

'I hate this war,' said Linda vehemently. 'My Bill's a pilot,' she explained to Nora. 'Well, training to be one. Funny, you think your life will go on as you expect, and you'll get married and have kids and nothing will change, not really. Then it does, and there's nothing you can do about it.'

There was a moment's silence. Then Linda blew her nose in a defiant manner and finished her tea. 'Delicious cake, Nora. You're a definite improvement. I'm not ready to half-starve for the war effort just yet,' she said.

'Me neither,' said Annabel with a shudder. 'I was always being told if I ate too much I'd end up getting hefty and no man would look at me twice.'

'Hefty?' Alice snorted. 'There's scarcely anything to you.'

'Hardly any muscle, you mean.' Annabel finished her own tea and stood up. 'Well, I intend to remedy that as soon as possible.' She glanced slyly at Alice. 'At least it might improve my tennis arm, being a toff and all.'

'Idiot,' returned Alice. The two walked back towards the lines of cabbages and broccoli they were weeding, still teasing each other, followed by Linda.

Nora watched them with a twinge of envy. She'd felt the same when she'd seen them slipping away to the Dolphin pub in St Mabon's, returning giggling with the headiness of freedom from the prying eyes of family and neighbours as much as the unaccustomed alcohol. Miss Maltby threatened to ship any girl found in the village without permission back home on the first train out, but generally turned a blind eye. With brothers and sweethearts out in the fighting, and the ever-present fear of what might happen next, they all needed to let off steam. No threats would stop any of them grabbing life while they still could.

But there was nothing she could do about it. Nora took the tray with the empty teapot and cups back towards the house, pausing at the day nursery set up in a disused stable block. Miss Maltby, who was a great believer in the benefits of fresh air, had ordered a patch of garden to be enclosed for the children to play in at every opportunity. Nora watched Violette amongst several other babies on a blanket set out in the shade cast by a large rhododendron, still clinging to the last of its crimson blooms. Nora could see she was grumpy and listless, clinging to Lionie, mane now almost bald from so much hugging. The nagging worry that had been at the back of her mind for the past few days returned.

'How does she seem today?' she asked Milly the nursery nurse, who came to greet her.

'Much the same,' replied Milly. 'She's not really joining in with the others like she usually does and she was a bit hot after her nap. But I wouldn't worry too much. She's probably teething.'

'I expect so,' said Nora, trying to remember what Pearl had said about Jonny. If only she'd listened more closely!

The worry remained as she added potatoes and greens to the mutton and dried beans and carrots for the evening's stew. Violette had been healthy since her operation, growing stronger and catching up in size with babies of the same age. But these last few days something hadn't been quite right. She couldn't put her finger on it, and maybe it was just her being over cautious, but she'd been spending so much time with her she'd become attuned to the little girl's every mood.

Her anxiety didn't ease when, the meal finally prepared, she went to fetch Violette and found her hot and fractious, turning her face away as she tried to spoon mashed-up stew into her mouth. She even shook her head at a strawberry, sobbing inconsolably into her lion toy.

After a restless night for them both, Violette was no better the following morning. It probably was teething, Nora told herself, wishing she knew more about babies. She'd never bothered to listen when Mum and Pearl discussed their illnesses and the washing of their napkins. How on earth did mothers with small children manage to cook and keep a house clean? Let alone the ones who went out to work to supplement the family income and then came back to deal with it all again. There were times when she longed for her freedom, to slip out with the others to the pub and forget everything for a few hours. On the other hand, whenever she thought of Sabine finally arriving to retrieve her daughter, her heart squeezed tight.

The worry remained even after breakfast. Mr Yearsley had promised to send Violette's details to Dr Evans in St Mabon's. She'd been so busy getting used to her new life at Maltby Abbey that she'd not had time to go down to the harbour to check if it had arrived.

As the morning wore on, Nora's anxiety grew. When Violette was no better that afternoon, she carried her the short walk down the zigzag path from the Abbey to St Mabon's, hoping that Dr Evans would agree to see her.

Her luck was in. He'd just returned from visiting a patient and the only person in the waiting room was a fair-haired young man, one leg stretched out, walking stick at his side.

'I'm in no hurry,' he said good-humouredly as the doctor's wife, who acted as receptionist and nurse, spoke briefly to her husband before telling Nora she could go in after him. 'Teach me to fall off a roof. Let the kiddie go first.'

Nora thanked him as Mrs Evans ushered her in.

Dr Evans was middle-aged and slightly rotund, his dark hair greying at the temples. 'Ah, this is the little girl I was told about,' he said. Violette stopped her grizzling, fascinated by the bushiness of his eyebrows. He smiled. 'Mr Yearsley is an excellent surgeon. He said she was a bright little thing, with no sign of any mental impairment.'

'None,' said Nora. 'She's usually very healthy and happy. I think she's teething. Mr Yearsley did warn me she might have a few problems, but hopefully only minor. It's just that she seems in so much distress.'

'Let's have a look.' He gently inspected Violette's gums before reaching for his stethoscope. She wriggled on Nora's lap. 'It's all right. Here, you have a listen.' Nora held the earpieces in place over Violette's ears as the doctor pressed the stethoscope against his shirt. Suddenly she was all attention, listening closely, whimpering slightly when he removed the stethoscope to press it against her own chest.

'There you are you see, little one,' he said gently. 'Nothing frightening.' He brushed her hot cheeks with a gentle hand. 'I understand from Mr Yearsley she's an identical twin?'

'Yes.'

'Such an interesting phenomenon,' he remarked as he inspected Violette. 'There's so much we still don't know about them. I've treated a few identical twins in my time. It still amazes me, the way they always throw up surprises. The strangest ones are those that have been raised in different households but follow such similar paths, quite unknowingly. I've been trained to follow the sciences, yet at times it does make you think there may be more things on heaven and earth ...' He cleared his throat, as if embarrassed at such irrational musings. 'She has a slight fever, Mrs Herridge, but nothing I'd be worried about at this stage. I suspect you're right and it's her teeth coming through.' He inspected Violette's gums again, as the baby watched him as if mesmerised. 'I can't see anything obvious, but you were right to bring her down. Probably best I keep an eye on her. I don't know much about harelips, but I'll telephone Mr Yearsley later and keep him up to date, unless we find we need to take her back.'

'For another operation, you mean?'

'Hopefully not. And it wouldn't be anywhere near as intrusive as the original procedure. See how she goes. If she gets any worse, or you're worried about anything, however trivial, bring her down.'

'Thank you,' said Nora, feeling her whole body relax with relief.

'Good, good. Not easy with a small child to look after.' He patted Violette's cheek with the indulgent smile of a father who adored his own offspring, no matter how loud or grubby. 'There'll be no charge.'

'I have the money,' said Nora proudly.

'I know you work hard, my dear. But having seen the correspondence from the hospital in Paris along with Mr Yearsley's reports, it's the least I can do. Let's say it's my contribution to the war effort. That was an extraordinarily brave thing to do, saving another woman's child.'

'I couldn't abandon them,' muttered Nora, concentrating hard on buttoning Violette back into her cardigan, feeling herself breaking inside. Even here, in the relative calm and safety of rural Cornwall, they were all keeping their emotions in check. With the unknown around the corner, it often felt the only way to keep sane.

'But still, quite a thing to take on.' He coughed. 'I understand from Mr Yearsley that "Mrs" Herridge is a fiction and there's no husband to support you.'

'That's right,' said Nora, frowning at him, a new anxiety flickering up inside. A doctor was a man of standing and authority in the community. Did he have the power to take Violette away from her and hand her to a more "respectable" family? 'We manage,' she continued. 'And my sister's coming from London with her little boy as soon as we can make the arrangements. Her husband's in the army,' she added for good measure.

Dr Evans's face cleared. 'Excellent. I'm glad to hear you'll soon have support.' He bent to scribble on the pad next to him, as if testing out his pen. 'I don't wish to concern you, my dear, but from what I hear from friends in the War Office in London, things are looking bad out there. For the civilians as well as the army. There are reports of whole populations trying to get to territory still controlled by the French.' He looked up to meet her eyes. 'Many of them, I'm afraid to say, are not likely to survive. I don't want to alarm you, my dear, but I feel it's only my duty to warn you that you may have to face the fact that you'll always have to take responsibility for this child.'

'I've thought of that,' said Nora.

'Good, good. I'm sure you have. And as long as you're certain.' He cleared his throat. 'I'm just mindful that you're a young woman with your whole life ahead of you. One day you might want to marry and have a family of your own. To be blunt, not all men are willing to take on a stranger's child.'

'I'll take my chances,' she answered. A huge wave of protectiveness swept through her towards this scrap of life left in her charge; its intensity took her breath away.

Dr Evans nodded. 'Just so long as you're aware of what you might be facing for the rest of your life.'

TWENTY-SEVEN

SABINE

France, 1940

The light returned slowly. Every part of her ached. Sabine forced her eyes open, her battered mind trying to grasp where she might be. She was lying under trees, the ripple of sunlight over her face. From nearby came the sound of subdued sobbing.

Valérie. It was back in an instant. Standing on the roadway, Valérie in her arms, the aeroplane with its bullets screaming towards them. Sabine turned her head, trying to see. Figures were clustered either side of her, lying flat on the grass under the trees, making themselves as invisible as possible. On the harsh sun of the open road just a few metres away lay a tiny bundle of clothing, lavender-flowered dress ripped to almost nothing.

Valérie. She heard herself croak as she tried to speak.

'Sabine, thank goodness.' It was her mother, warm arms around her. 'We thought we'd lost you.'

'Valérie ...'

'She's here. She's safe. Young Marcel here pulled you both

to safety.' Her voice wavered. 'We were so sure we'd lost you both.'

Sabine pushed herself upright. Her head throbbed violently and she was bruised all over, but there was no sharp pain, no bleeding. Valérie was watching her solemnly from Mémé's arms, too shocked, too frightened to even cry. Sabine reached for her, holding her tight. Only when she felt the rapid beat of her little heart against hers did she really believe her child was alive.

It was the doll. Her eyes cleared. The bundle of rags on the roadway torn by bullets was Valérie's rag doll Poupée. Valérie turned her hot, damp face into the soft comfort of Sabine's chest, whimpering.

'It's all right, darling, you're safe. We're safe.'

She must be going mad. The pungency of Gitanes cigarettes hung in the air, bringing with it the laughter and chatter of Paris cafés, the sunny elegance of tables set under awnings, of passionate arguments over coffee and *pain au chocolat* about the rival pavilions at the *Exposition Internationale des Arts et Techniques*, or Picasso's *Guernica* that had shocked them all with its brutality.

Not shocked enough, she thought, mind as sharp as the rays of sun. It was as if she'd just woken up, as if her life before this had just been a dream. All those conversations had been just playing at a conscience, from the comfort of a secure home and a warm bed. Horror at a distance, to be mulled over, with an edge of dread that it might just happen, but not real, not really. Almost, but not quite, envious of the reporters who were there to shock the world, to be part of the great turn of history. Almost, but not quite, envious of Emil, who'd sworn he'd become a war journalist, heroically reporting on the great movements of the world.

But that was playing at it. Not like this. Not the squalid, dreadful reality of lives snuffed out in an instant. For what? For the amusement of some boy with a machine, seeing human lives as little more than dots to be mown down. Or a deliberate policy of obliteration, following up the bombs and fires that had turned the horizon red. This wasn't theoretical. This was warm, beating life. She would never look at *Guernica*, or any image of war and suffering, in the same way again.

Something hard and solid settled deep in her belly. A determination. A fire that would never be extinguished. This moment that should have broken her, could have ended her, had instead become a beginning, her purpose in life, just as much as caring for her children and keeping her family safe.

She pushed the thought to one side. For now, she had no time for the luxury of thinking of the future, of taking her place to bear witness to the women and children and the civilians' experience of war. One day, however long it took, she would show how they were not simply a mass of victims, but individual lives, each heroic and indomitable in their own way.

'Thank you,' she said to the young lad, finally allowed to finish the cigarette that had been snatched from him the previous night. His mother was crouched next to him winding a makeshift bandage of torn cloth around his arm, the jaunty yellow print of sunflowers already turning crimson. Guilt shot through her. 'You're hurt.'

'It's nothing,' he muttered, blushing violently.

'Just a graze, thank goodness,' his mother said. 'The bleeding will clean it. Just nicked the skin. The bullet missed anything vital. Like that stubborn head of his,' she added proudly.

'Quick thinking,' said Maman. 'If Marcel hadn't pulled you both under the trees ... well, it doesn't bear thinking about.'

'Thank you. Thank you for saving our lives.'

Marcel grinned lopsidedly, trying to keep his dignity but clearly overwhelmed by this abrupt elevation to hero. He drew deep on his cigarette, hand shaking violently. Not even his mother objected when the elderly man on the grass next to them took a packet from his own pocket, removed the one remaining cigarette, lit it and handed it to the boy without a word.

'Bastards,' remarked another woman next to him, brushing down a coat that must once have been the height of Parisian fashion. 'May they rot in hell, the lot of them.'

'At least no one was hurt,' said Mémé.

'Only by luck,' said the woman. 'If we'd reached the road a few minutes earlier ... Well, who knows ...'

There was a moment's silence. Everyone in the little group, even the children, knew exactly what would have happened. What might still happen should the planes return.

Mémé led the horses onto the road as they nervously set off again, keeping close to the side, ready to throw themselves in the grass at the first sign of a dark shadow in the sky. Sabine made room for Marcel, who, despite his proud protests, was clearly still too shocked and bleeding too heavily to walk, and they set off again.

It was only as she looked back that she saw Valérie's beloved Poupée lying on the road forgotten, shredded beyond repair.

A short time later the group in front came to an abrupt halt.

'What is it?' demanded Sabine.

'Oh dear God,' whispered Maman.

'Distract the children while we pass,' said Mémé, speaking in English so the younger members of the party wouldn't understand. 'Those ahead of us. They weren't so lucky.'

They moved off slowly, avoiding obstacles at the side of the road. As they passed, Sabine chatted as easily as she could to the children. From the corner of her eye she caught sight of broken prams lying between fallen heaps of clothing. As they drew level with the burnt-out remains of a car, she began to make out the forms beneath the mounds of coats and blankets, left where they'd fallen.

On the far side Mémé pulled the cart under the shadow of some trees and jumped down to see if she could help. Sabine left the children with Maman and ran after her.

'There's nothing we can do,' said M. Rubin, the elderly man who'd given Marcel his last cigarette. 'The survivors must have already left. We can't even bury them.'

'We can at least check,' said Mémé firmly.

They went from bundle to bundle, trying to find any sign of life. Sabine did her best to shut her mind to what she was seeing; from her companions' closed faces she could see they were doing the same. The old. The young. The families. A baby's toy, a tiny shoe. In the rising heat of the day, flies were already beginning to gather.

'We can at least get them into the undergrowth,' said one of the men. As he helped Marcel drag an elderly couple under the cover of the trees, a woman passed, holding the small bundle of what once had been a baby, cradling it tenderly, folding the white of the delicately worked shawl streaked with red over its motionless scrap of humanity.

Sabine fought down the sickness rising from her empty stomach.

'You should go,' said Mémé.

'Not until we all can,' she replied. 'The sooner this is done, the safer we'll all be.' If they'd ever be safe, when this could happen at any moment.

Marcel passed her, face white as a sheet, only just reaching the nearest tree before throwing up everything left inside him. M. Rubin patted him gently on one arm. 'We're all the same, my lad. Come on, let's get this finished.'

Sabine steeled herself and moved towards the bodies of a family who'd fallen together, the mother still holding a small boy's hand, a girl in a heap next to them, her fine golden hair stirred by a sudden swirl of breeze. Sabine reached for her outstretched hand. In the cooling flesh of the wrist, there was no need to feel for any pulse.

'She's gone,' muttered M. Rubin gruffly. 'Fucking bastards. They're only children.'

A woman had already lifted the boy in her arms, while her husband pulled the mother to the side, before reaching for the body of the little girl.

Something moved.

'Wait!' exclaimed Sabine.

The man had seen it too. He bent over the child. 'Impossible.' The movement came again. He jumped back, cursing. 'Bloody dogs.' He aimed a kick towards a small creature appearing from under the girl's skirts. 'Get off with you.'

'Don't,' said Sabine as a small spaniel-type puppy shot out, the pink ribbon the little girl had been holding in her hand just last night still tied around its neck. It crouched against the motionless figure of its mistress. 'Poor thing.' The dog was shivering violently, a small puddle spreading around it in the dust. 'It's only a baby.'

'It better not bite me,' the man growled, voice cracking, the emotions of the morning finally breaking through. 'We can't wait all day.'

The puppy pressed itself against the dead girl, as if trying to disappear underneath her again.

'I'll take it,' said Sabine. She reached down and swept up the quivering body, holding it against her as she returned to the cart.

Maman looked up as she approached. 'For goodness' sake! We can't pick up every stray dog.'

'She's very young, she must have only just left her mother,' said Sabine. The girl must have been carrying her when the bullets struck. This was the small body in her arms, the one she had held onto as the plane came towards them. In those final moments of terror, this had been the living warmth the girl had felt, keeping the smallest and the vulnerable safe. The only safety the little creature whimpering in her arms knew.

She could feel the little heartbeat as the dog's nose snuffled into the hollow under her chin, as if sensing its life was held in the balance, pressing against its sole hope of survival. All life was precious. Infinitely precious. In the end, it was all any of them had. Inside, Sabine could feel herself beginning to fall apart.

'But darling ...'

'If we leave her, she'll die.'

'There's been enough of that,' said Mémé, her face grim. 'Go on, put the poor little creature in the cart with the rest. One more won't make any difference. We need to go.'

Maman relented, rejoining Mémé at the front as Sabine clambered into the back. Valérie eyed their four-legged guest curiously.

'Don't put it on the coats,' said Maman. 'Just think of the mess.'

'Animals don't mess their beds,' said Mémé. 'You should know that, Joelle. They're sophisticated like that.'

All the same ... Remembering the puddle in the dust, Sabine fished out a piece of cotton sheeting to put under the puppy, placing her next to Valérie where she could keep an eye on them both.

'Come on up,' she said to Marcel, who was closing the back of the cart.

He shook his head, his face grey, eyes haunted. 'I'd rather walk.'

'He'll be all right,' said M. Rubin. 'Needs a bit of time, if you see what I mean. I'll keep an eye on him, make sure he catches up if he starts flagging.'

They set off again, the cart trundling slowly between the refugees on foot. The sun was rising through the trees, sending warmth in streaks of light between the shadows. The little group trudged silently, even the children lost in their own thoughts.

Valérie settled down amongst the coats, drowsy after the emotions of the morning. When Sabine turned back, the puppy had crawled closer, its little body next to her, falling asleep in the warmth.

Valérie mumbled.

'Poupée. Yes, that's Poupée,' said Sabine as her daughter snuggled closer to the puppy, one arm flung across it as it had once done around her abandoned rag doll. Within minutes the two were dozing, snuffling together, two small creatures finding solace in each other's warmth, the beat of each other's heart.

Valérie's face had lost its frown, relaxing completely, as if she'd found the steady rhythm of another life she'd been seeking ever since Nora had taken Violette on their own desperate journey towards survival. The heartbeat Valérie must have felt every day, every night, from her first stirrings within the womb.

Sabine fought down an urge to weep uncontrollably. None of them could afford to feel. That would come later. For now, they needed every last morsel of energy to survive. Grief, anger, madness, they'd have to wait.

A shadow crossed the sun.

'It's only a cloud,' called Mémé. An audible relief rippled through the little group. Not a plane. Not this time. For now they had survived. They were already a little closer to safety, wherever that might be.

Sabine gently touched the soft white-gold haze of Valérie's hair. Somewhere out there Violette must be sleeping, safe in an unknown place, in an unknown building. But safe. Grief gripped her. Would she ever see her daughter again?

Slowly, the little group moved onwards in silence, every sinew braced for the first sound of danger, for the screech of bullets, the screams and the agony that would end everything.

All they could do was hope. Sabine scanned the unfamiliar landscape around her for any sign of danger. Slowly, methodically, the refugees trudged onwards, knowing each moment might be their last, every step taking them further from homes and lives gone forever. Each of them numb with exhaustion and the shutting down of feelings. All of them heading into the unknown.

TWENTY-EIGHT

NORA

Cornwall, 1940

Nora emerged from Dr Evans's surgery into the heat of the afternoon, Violette heavy in her arms. She was weary from lack of sleep and slightly light-headed, having been too anxious about her little charge to eat anything all day. She glanced at the steep path up the hill to the Abbey, which might as well have been the snowy peak of Everest.

'I need a cup of tea first,' she said ruefully to Violette. 'Or a lift,' she added, as a single-decker bus lumbered past, heading for the harbour. Hurrying as fast as she could in its wake, she caught up with it at the bus stop.

'Maltby Abbey?' said an elderly woman at the back of the queue, wicker basket filled to the brim with shopping. 'Yes, this is the right one. Won't get you right to the door, lovely, but there's a stop just before the top. Take the path through the kissing gate, and it's only a few minutes' walk.'

'Thank you,' said Nora, relieved at the thought of not having to attempt the hill.

'You're Mrs Herridge the new cook aren't you?' said the woman, smiling at Violette, who was feeling drowsy after the excitement of the day.

'Yes, I am,' replied Nora.

The woman chuckled. 'Don't look so surprised, dear. Everyone knows everyone in St Mabon's, and their business too. Husband in the army, I take it?'

'Yes,' said Nora without batting an eyelid. How her supposed husband extricated himself from the army when the war was over was a problem for the future. Meanwhile, she had a distinct feeling her new acquaintance would pass that snippet of information in every market and along every bus route within several miles of St Mabon's. Everyone at Maltby Abbey must have assumed this as the explanation for her solo state, but had been too polite to ask. In the outside world not everyone was so tactful. At least this might mean never having to answer the question again.

'It's a good place,' said the woman, picking up Lionie, who'd dropped from Violette's relaxing grasp, and handing the much-loved toy to Nora. 'We look after our own, Mrs Herridge. I'm sure you and your daughter will be very happy here, whatever the future brings.'

'Thank you,' said Nora, resisting a sudden urge to burst into tears at her kindness.

She was the last passenger to board, finding a whole seat thoughtfully left for her at the front, despite the bus being filled to the brim with passengers and shopping bags. She sat with Violette in her arms, who was soon fast asleep with the warmth and motion of the bus as it made its way between alleyways and houses before roaring slowly up the road towards the top of the cliffs.

Around her, conversations flowed. The price of fish, the impossibility of getting any kind of handyman to mend gutters these days and whether the rumours might be true of a Nazi submarine out in the bay. Several women behind her expressed outrage that Mrs Allernby's shop on the front had run out of several items on the ration. A blinking nuisance when she was your designated grocer! They'd have to make a return trip tomorrow, when Mrs Allernby had promised she'd at least have some sugar.

Nora smiled to herself, feeling part of the close-knit every-dayness of the community around her. She was nodding off herself when the straining of the engine began to slow.

'Yours is the next stop, dear,' said the woman behind her, tapping her on the shoulder as the bus came to a halt.

Nora waved to the elderly woman as the bus went on its way. Just ahead she could make out the kissing gate and beyond it a clearly defined path heading towards the Abbey; one of the male passengers was already striding along, heading in its direction.

She was about to follow when the white walls of a low-built cottage set a little back from the road caught her eye.

'That's the one we can see from the window at the Abbey,' she said to Violette, who didn't stir. Nora placed the sleeping child over one shoulder, and carefully stashed Lionie deep in her coat pocket. She then headed for a waist-high wooden gate leading through an overgrown privet hedge that appeared some-what scorched in places by the salt air.

Hope Cottage announced the sign on the gate. There was no evidence of habitation. The paint on the front door was peeling, the windowpanes strewn with cobwebs. Intrigued, Nora stepped inside, following a weed-choked path with a wilderness of grass and wildflowers on either side. The garden must have once been loved. She could make out mature apple trees and fuchsias, interspersed with beds of roses in shades of pink and crimson. The yellow blooms of a climbing rose smothered a wall on the far side, setting off a clump of bearded irises, their shaded hues of purple caught in rays of sunlight spilling through the trees.

Entranced, she almost missed the movement inside the house. It was inhabited after all. Mortified, she headed back towards the gate, just as the front door was pulled open.

'Can I help you?' demanded a woman, placing a moth-eaten carpet bag on the path.

'I was just admiring the garden,' she mumbled, feeling herself blushing furiously.

'It is beautiful, isn't it,' said the woman sadly. 'It's a pity it's been left to go to rack and ruin since my dad died, but Mum couldn't cope with it after he'd gone, not with her knees.'

'It's still lovely,' said Nora.

'So it is. Of course, I'd love to keep it on. It's where I grew up, you see. It was always such a happy home. I'd move back and live with Mum quick as a flash, but my husband's work is in Truro, and my boys' too. And now my daughter's expecting – well, it's quite impossible. So it looks like Mum will be coming to live with us once she's out of hospital if she finds she can't manage on her own, now her heart's so bad. Miss Maltby's being very understanding, but she can't keep it empty forever.'

'Is the cottage part of the Abbey?' said Nora, trying not to sound too interested, or show that her heart had suddenly leapt.

'Always has been,' said the woman. 'The family have sold off plenty of the workers' cottages over the years, but not this one. In my heart I was hoping they never would. Or that we'd grow rich,' she added wryly.

Nora said her goodbyes and headed back to Maltby Abbey, arriving with just enough time to start preparing the evening meal, not even the heat rising from the fish pie quite able to banish the vision of Hope Cottage from her mind.

· · ·

When Nora collected Violette from the crèche once the dishes had been cleared away and the table set for breakfast for the following morning, the baby seemed much calmer. Milly reported that she'd slept for most of the evening and the fever appeared to have gone.

Exhausted by the conflicting emotions of the day, Nora was thankful that Violette was soon ready to go back to sleep in her cot, Lionie clutched against her. Before closing the blackout curtains and switching on the light to get ready for bed, Nora sat for a while by the open casement window, listening to the distant sound of waves breaking against the cliffs.

It still felt slightly unnerving looking out on a landscape completely devoid of light for fear of attracting enemy attention. A giggle, quickly suppressed, followed by the crashing of bodies through the undergrowth, informed her that Alice and Annabel, who'd formed an unlikely partnership in crime, were returning, most probably from the pub. She grinned to herself as a window below creaking stealthily open was followed by the clattering of not entirely steady footsteps attempting to be silent on the stairs. Another giggle and low curse as one of them stumbled, and they headed for the little sitting room, where Nora was well aware a bottle of brandy was secreted.

She turned back to the open window, with its summer scent of mown grass mingling with the saltiness of sea air, while bats darted here and there on their nightly search for insects. It was strange how St Mabon's already felt like home, and how she seemed to have been accepted as part of its lifeblood.

If Mrs Dawson, the woman she'd met at Hope Cottage, did take her mother home and the property came up for rent, it would be the perfect place for Pearl and Jonny to join her. She'd mention it to Miss Maltby in the morning in case anyone else might step in. Of course Mrs Dawson's mother might yet return, or her daughter might find a way to stay with her. It would take time. But it was at least a possibility, and she could start working towards it now.

Nora pulled the heavy blackout curtains across and switched on the bedside lamp. In its glow she could see Violette, fast asleep, breathing quietly, at peace with the world.

Dr Evans was right. She had to face the fact that Sabine might not survive. She might already be dead. She knew that the lack of letters was due to communication lines being cut, but all the same, it was the first time she'd been without Sabine telling her what she was thinking, and feeling her somehow close by.

She looked again at Violette. If they were going to live in St Mabon's, perhaps for the rest of their lives, they were going to need to fit in and not stand out in any way. Her own way of fitting in to expectations was wearing a ring and becoming 'Mrs'. But Violette's French name would always stand out. The Land Girls could never get their tongues around the French, calling her a garbled variation of Violet. That would do for now, but one day Violette would start school. The worst thing a child could do, she recognised with a wince, was to stand out as different in any way. Which meant she needed an English name. It would be safer too, in the event that – heaven forbid – there was an invasion.

Violet. That would be the sensible choice. And yet ... unexpected grief tugged at Nora. It was selfish, but she wasn't sure she could bear to use a bowdlerised version of her name.

As she finally crawled into bed, switching out the light without reading her book as usual, Nora was still mulling over Violette's name. As she drifted off to sleep, the impressions of the day floated before her eyes. She was back in St Mabon's with the sea glittering in the harbour, and on the rumbling bus with the chatter of passengers. And the garden, the wild and rampant beauty of the garden at Hope Cottage.

Her final vision as she drifted towards unconsciousness was

crystal clear. Nora shot up in bed, wide awake, the luminous purple of irises against the brilliant yellow of rose petals before her eyes.

'Iris,' she said aloud. 'That's the name. That's what we'll call you while you're here with me in St Mabon's. Iris.'

TWENTY-NINE

SABINE

France, 1940

Sabine pulled herself unwillingly to her feet, fastening on her threadbare boots to help her grandmother hitch up the cart once more. All around them groups of refugees huddled in the faded grandeur of the abandoned *manoir* where they'd found refuge from the night air were stirring, coughing, ready for the day ahead.

Leaving Valérie with her mother, Sabine followed Mémé outside amongst the ripening grapes where many more refugees had camped out in the open, too terrified to shelter inside walls that might collapse should bombs fall from the sky during the night. They hitched the horses in silence, manoeuvring the cart onto the driveway of the manor house, where wheelbarrows and perambulators were already making their slow journey towards the road.

Sabine returned inside, with its remnants of once-elegant Louis XIV chairs and tables, where Maman was feeding Valérie with the last of the bread and milk they'd been given at the last farmhouse, while Poupée lapped up the scraps. As Sabine watched, her mother eyed the final piece of crust longingly before placing it on the floor for the puppy to finish.

'Poor thing, she's only a baby. She has to eat too,' she said defensively, seeing Sabine. 'We're bound to find something later, little ones like that don't understand. She's nothing more than skin and bones, poor creature, and Valérie has been so much calmer since she joined us.'

'We'll find something better for us all tonight,' said Sabine. 'The woman from the American Red Cross said the border into the part of France the Germans don't control is just up ahead. They've set up camps to house refugees: there'll be food and a place for us to sleep. We just have to keep going.'

They placed Valérie in the cart on the blankets, now filthy with being placed so often on the ground and with no means for anyone to have even the most cursory of washes. She was joined by an elderly woman, too weary and footsore to continue, and as many children who could fit. There was more space for such passengers now the last of their stored food had gone.

Sabine walked alongside the cart, as she had done despite Maman's protests for the past week. She was young and strong, and her boots were less worn than those who'd been forced to walk hundreds of kilometres from Orléans down the Loire valley, where the routes to the south converged, before the journey towards Limoges and their final destination of Corrèze in the Massif Central. Thank goodness for the Red Cross, whose members from various countries had been there at intervals along the way, doing their best to help the local population which, despite their generosity and eagerness to help, threatened to deplete all their resources.

At least they knew there was another American Red Cross station further along towards Limoges, on the border between what had now been agreed was the occupied zone, under German control and the *Zone Libre*, the free zone, the so-called État Français, with its new headquarters in Vichy.

Sabine chatted as cheerfully as she could to Valérie, staying close to the side of the cart, ready to sweep her up and away to whatever cover she could find at the first hint of an approaching engine. Poupée trotted at her heels, pausing now and again to sniff the roadside, scampering to catch up if they got too far ahead, determined not to let her new family too far out of sight.

They were all on high alert for the sound of a plane. Sabine wasn't the only one whose eyes automatically sought out the nearest place to hide up ahead. Even the smallest of the children knew to run at the first signal, to throw themselves flat in the ditches at the side of the road if no other cover could be found. Poupée had learnt too, hurtling in amongst them, pressing in amongst the bodies. Sabine had lost count of the times she'd huddled in a ditch with the puppy pressed against her, feeling the little creature trembling violently at the roar of engines and the rain of bullets above their heads.

Like all those around them, she was weary to the bone, her clothes hung off her and every last nerve was shredded. The villages and the farms they passed along the way had been as generous as they could be, but with so many on the move overwhelming any organisation that had been put in place, every day had become a matter of trudging slowly, preserving as much energy as possible and finding enough food and water to continue. At least the horses had grass most of the time, allowing them to preserve the hay as much as they could for when none was available, and to soften the rocking of the cart.

And all along the way they passed the debris of the refugees who'd gone before them, abandoned prams with broken wheels, boots so worn there was nothing left of the soles. A toy left stranded in the middle of the road. And then there was the stink of human waste, and the now familiar stench of death warning them not to look too closely at the huddled shapes half hidden in the grassy verge.

The heat was growing unbearable. Everyone was tired and thirsty, the little group slowing to a crawl.

'Looks like that might be it,' said Mémé at last from her vantage point at the front of the cart, as the roofs of a village began to appear amongst the trees, a somewhat tattered Red Cross flag strung along the railings. As she drew closer she slowed. 'Those are German soldiers.'

'Must mean we're near the border to the *Zone Libre*,' said M. Rubin who was walking alongside the cart. He drew painfully on what remained of the spittle in his dry mouth and spat into the dust next to him. 'No doubt they'll take the opportunity to lord it over us.'

'At least those damned planes won't bomb us,' remarked his wife, plodding along next to him. 'For fear of hitting their own.'

'Yes, that's true enough.' He grunted. 'They can hardly claim we're cover for the retreating French army if the village has got that damned swastika of theirs all over the place.'

At the first house they were greeted by several women, some from the Red Cross, others from the village, who'd set up a large urn of boiling water flavoured with mint from a nearby garden, alongside bread and a pan of vegetable soup. With the children happily clutching chunks of bread, Sabine left Valérie in the care of her mother and made her way to a trestle table set up as a makeshift office outside a barn. It was unnerving seeing the German uniforms, but the young men were polite, unable to hide their shock at the tide of humanity making its way past, and the impossibility of how to even begin to address the most basic of needs.

At the table, tempers were beginning to fray. A German officer, hopelessly young and clearly out of his depth, snapped at a lanky man in round glasses wearing the badge of the American Red Cross on his shoulder.

'*Français?*' suggested the Red Cross man, who'd obviously been through this conversation dozens of times already that day.

'*Parlez vous Français?* Okay, English, then. *Sprechen sie Englisch?* I don't speak German, I'm afraid. *Kein deutsch.* Well, at least not enough to have any idea what you're trying to tell me.'

The young soldier's face turned puce, followed by a barrage of exasperation barked out in rapid German.

'Well, I'm sorry you feel like that,' said the American without batting an eyelid. 'But you really are going to have to find someone to translate or we're not going to get anywhere. Stalemate, my friend.'

The officer glared, frustration rising. 'Papers. *Dokumente.*'

'Yes, I've got that, Hauptmann. But whose? And which ones?' The man's lips tightened. 'And for what purpose? I'm not having anyone signalled out on my watch.' This being beyond the linguistic skills of either, the exchange ground to a halt. The queue of exhausted men and women shuffled uneasily; safety, once so near, suddenly so far.

'He's checking if anyone's Jewish,' hissed a woman with a small child next to Sabine, her voice shaking. 'I'm sure he is. Even now, they can't let it go.'

'Hopefully not,' replied Sabine. 'It looks like that's why the Red Cross official's standing his ground, to make sure.'

The woman sank to the ground, gathering her little boy into her arms, spent with exhaustion and despair.

Sabine hesitated. She'd been careful not to admit she spoke German for fear of being suspected as a spy or a Nazi sympathiser by her companions. But now they'd reached an impasse. She scrutinised the face of the Red Cross man. He was still courteous and patient with the young soldier, confident enough in himself not to need a show of heavy-handed masculinity, but instead trying to diffuse the situation. Sabine drew on every instinct, honed over the past weeks of vulnerability, as to who could be trusted or not. She saw an open face with no obvious desire to wield power over his fellow human beings, and the

thin band of a wedding ring on the hand holding down the
papers on his desk against the hot breeze.

Taking a deep breath, she pushed herself forward through
the queue until she reached the desk.

'I speak a little German,' she said. '*Nur ein bisschen,*' she
added hastily, as both men turned eagerly towards her.

'Thank goodness for that.' The Red Cross man beamed. 'If
you wouldn't mind, *Madame.*'

The young officer clicked his heels. '*Entschuldigen,
Madame.* I have no wish to trouble you.'

'It's no trouble,' replied Sabine.

The officer relaxed, relief spreading over his face. The
tension eased a little from Sabine's body. Now she could see
him close to, he didn't have the look of a fanatic, the schoolboy
who'd followed his classmates into the *Hitlerjugend,* his head
filled with the exhilaration of being the superior race, on the
brink of defeating evil forever and ruling the world with the
heroism and justice of the old myths.

Unlike some of the conscripts she'd seen on the road he'd
probably been eager to join the army, to do his bit for his country, to build a bright future for his children. What he shared
with the conscripts was the deep shock at the back of his eyes,
the sense that this had not been what he'd been sent to do.
Dying a glorious death for the *Vaterland* was one thing,
corralling desperate civilians, passing the bodies of old men
lying crumpled where they'd fallen and watching babies die in
front of his eyes from a simple lack of water, was another.
Maybe not enough for him to question the Führer, at least not
yet, but something that would stay with him for as long as he
lived.

A few casual-sounding questions allowed her to gauge that
Hauptmann Ziegler had little interest in identifying Jews or

Gypsies, or even communists. Whatever his original orders, he'd clearly realised that the chaos of so many civilians needing to be housed and fed and filtered across the border left little time for rigorous efficiency.

As Ziegler was briefly called away by one of his men, Sabine met the eyes of the American Red Cross man, his relief they didn't have to deal with some officious fanatic reflected in his face.

'The ones we've dealt with have been okay so far,' he remarked. 'But there's always a first. And it makes it so much easier when you have someone who can speak the language.' He held out his hand. 'Howard Jackson.'

'Sabine ...' Just for a second, she hesitated. 'Bourret,' she added, using Mémé's maiden name, as she had done on the road. It was unlikely anyone had heard of Emil Schongauer or knew that he produced equipment for the Third Reich, but she wasn't taking any chances. She was all too aware that a war zone was a brutal, unforgiving place, where any suspicion she was associated with the enemy regime could put herself, and her family, in danger.

'Pleased to meet you, Mme Bourret.' He gestured to a chair at one side of the table. 'Won't you join me.' He gave a wry grin as Hauptmann Ziegler strode back towards them, irritation in his every step. 'I'm sure Thelma can find you a cup of tea, I rather feel you might need one.'

'With pleasure,' said one of the women handing out cups of tea and tumblers of water to a weary line of refugees waiting to be found a bed for the night. 'No milk, I'm afraid,' she said, filling a teacup to the brim. 'We ran out of the powdered stuff last night. But at least it's real tea.'

'Thank you,' Sabine replied gratefully. Thelma was a tall woman in her late thirties wearing the grey uniform of the American Red Cross, her red hair tucked neatly into her cap.

'That's okay,' said Thelma, placing the cup and saucer next

to Sabine, returning shortly with another for Jackson. 'The least we can do is supply you with tea. It's about time the professor had backup.'

'Professor?' said Sabine, wondering if she'd misheard as her ears adjusted to the unfamiliar American pronunciation.

'For my sins,' said Howard Jackson. 'I was supposed to be heading for the ivory tower of university life in Europe before all this kicked off. Not much point now, with so many of my students having signed up or about to be conscripted. Besides ...' His eyes travelled over the wretched tide of humanity heading towards them. 'Not sure I could just go home and leave all this.'

All that afternoon Thelma regularly supplied Sabine with tea as she sat at the side of the table, translating Ziegler's demands when necessary. By the time they'd got through half the queue, even the legendary German efficiency had abandoned Ziegler, who waved increasing numbers through with barely a glance. In those short hours she could see he'd already begun to conclude that spies, agitators and soldiers from what remained of the French army were unlikely to be hiding amongst this wretched trickle. Eventually he left the Red Cross to deal with the final group of women and children.

'Now we can all breathe,' said Howard Jackson as the officer disappeared into the village, no doubt to requisition himself a beer from the local tavern. 'I'm afraid everyone left will need to be accommodated in the church, there's no place else.'

Sabine explained in French to the weary mothers, who were beyond caring where they went so long as it was out of the dusty heat, and allowed themselves to be led away by the priest.

It was getting late. Sabine rose stiffly, hoping that Maman and the others had been given something to eat and drink and a place for the night.

Jackson stood up. 'Thank you, Mme Bourret. That was a great help. Perhaps we can call on your services again tomorrow?'

'I need to get back to my family.' She squared her shoulders. Desperation had also made her brave. 'But I also need to find work to support them.'

'Of course,' said Thelma, as she helped Jackson clear away the papers. 'We have funds to pay a translator, Professor. It's not a lot, mind. Just a few francs a day if you're interested, Mme Bourret?'

'Yes,' said Sabine before she could think better of it. 'Thank you.'

'Excellent.' Thelma smiled. 'We'll find somewhere more permanent for you and your children.'

'Child. My mother is looking after her,' she said, as Jackson began to look a little guilty.

'I should have asked.'

'I would have had to stay anyway.'

He grinned. 'And a lot longer if it had just been up to me and Thelma to keep our German friends at bay. See you tomorrow then.'

'Tomorrow,' replied Sabine. The last thing she wanted was to stay this side of the border, but the money they'd managed to bring with them was running low, and she had little idea how long it would take to reach the refugee camps. She was lucky to have secured some employment.

Sabine went with Thelma to find Maman and Valérie who were still in the village hall with Mémé, before heading to a large house at the edge of the little settlement. It was in a somewhat shabby state and had clearly been abandoned by its owners.

'You're welcome to join us here,' said Thelma. 'It's for the women of the Red Cross, the men are next door. There's enough room for you all. At least you'll get a room of your own, better than a mattress in the village hall.'

'Thank you,' said Maman. 'We're eternally grateful.'

'And the little dog,' said Thelma, smiling a little wistfully at

Valérie. 'We'll give you the room at the back, opening out onto the garden. That's best for a puppy and a child, and I can see how attached they are.'

'You've very kind,' said Sabine, fighting back an overwhelming urge to break down into uncontrollable tears. Once she started she'd never stop.

'It's the least we can do.' Thelma sighed. 'Back home, it felt like the right thing to do, coming here to help with the civilians. I had no idea. I'm not sure Professor Jackson had either. None of us were sure he'd stick it at first. He found the children hard to deal with. His wife died in childbirth you see, just before the war, and their baby too. He's not the kind to get over such a thing. That what's makes him so good at this work, of course. He really cares. From the heart, you know?'

'Yes,' said Sabine, quietly. 'He said he was supposed to be teaching at a university.'

'That's right. The University of London, it was supposed to be.'

'He was going to England?' exclaimed Sabine eagerly. London. That was where Violette must be at this very moment. 'But not anymore?'

'I'm sure he will once this is over. He's quite well known as a history professor you know. He's written several books on Anglo-Saxon England.' Thelma grimaced. 'Bit different from what we're facing out here.'

'Very,' murmured Sabine, only half listening. If Howard Jackson took up his post in London, she might be able to ask him to find Violette at Nora's address in Turnham Green. Perhaps there might even be a way for the Red Cross to reunite her with her child.

'Mind you, I suppose it's just as well,' added Thelma. 'He's a good man. Compassionate, you know? I'm sure he'd be out in the thick of it otherwise.'

Thelma's tone jolted Sabine back to the present. 'The thick of it?'

'The bombing. Of course, you won't have heard. The Luftwaffe are bombing London every night now, most likely in preparation for an invasion. It must be terrible for the civilians being under such constant shelling. I've heard they're using Underground stations as refuges, and huge numbers have been killed already. It must be terrible out there, like it is here.'

Sabine followed her in silence, fear clawing at her insides. They'd managed to keep Valérie safe all this time and were within a few metres of safety from the Germans. Had she hurried Violette away to save her, only to send her to her death?

'Of course I'll look after Valérie while you're working,' said Maman, relief on her face. 'No one's going to employ me, not at my age, but you have the right skills. I'm just grateful for a roof over our heads and the chance to support ourselves.'

'It'll mean staying in the occupied zone for a bit longer.'

'It'll be worth it. We have to be realistic. If you work with the Red Cross here, you've more chance of finding a job with them somewhere else. A proper job.' She sighed. 'You shouldn't have to work like this. That's a husband's role.'

'Women always work, Joelle, and twice as hard, too,' said Mémé, joining them. 'It's just that no one takes any notice.'

'Well then, you can find work too,' said Maman tartly.

Sabine smiled. Her mother was painfully thin, wrinkled like a woman twice her age, but at least her spirit was back. Mémé's solid frame had shrunk just as much and her hair was now almost completely white.

Then she saw a familiar determination on her grandmother's face, and her belly tightened. 'You're not staying, Mémé?'

'What would I do here? I'd just be in your way. Besides, I can't abandon the families we've been travelling with. I've promised I'll take them to the first resettlement camp in the *Zone Libre*, where they'll be looked after. With a bit of rest the horses will be able to take more across, and bring supplies back.' She gave a wry chuckle. 'You should have seen the eyes light up at the sight of a cart. Besides, the Rubins didn't even want to stay one night. It was only when I promised to take them over first thing tomorrow that they decided to stay at all. They're terrified the Germans will round them up in the night. The rumours they've told me are almost beyond belief.'

'But you will be back?' said Sabine anxiously. She hadn't realised how much they'd relied on Mémé, with her will and her determination.

'Of course, my dear. And if I'm prevented from getting back across, I'll make sure I get a message to you so you can meet me. They're disorganised at the moment and just want to get rid of us, but I can't see that lasting for long. I'll try and get as many across as I can before they become organised enough to check everyone's papers. And don't worry, I'll make sure I won't be travelling alone. We've got this far, we've nothing to lose. Besides, this will give me an opportunity to see what the accommodation is like there, if we can get a private house, or at least a part of a house, to ourselves. From what I've heard, the resettlement camps aren't really suitable for babies, and I'm fairly sure they don't allow dogs, even small puppies.'

'I hadn't thought of that.' Sabine glanced down at Poupée who was stretched out on the warm grass at their feet, stomach positively bulging with scraps, the remains of a cow's knuckle clutched protectively between her front paws. 'Valérie has been so much more settled since she's had Poupée to cuddle up to. I know she's only a dog, but I can't bear the thought of the two of them being separated.'

'There's no such thing as *just* an animal,' said Mémé. 'They have their joys and their fears too, and a right to live their lives. And there aren't many that slaughter each other just for pleasure, or turn the world that feeds and protects them into a barren wilderness. Poupée is the heartbeat Valérie will miss until she's reunited with her sister. That makes her a member of the family.' She squared her shoulders determinedly. 'And none of our family will ever be left behind.'

Mémé left just after dawn the next morning. The cart, now divested of all but the most essential supplies, was crammed full to bursting with the weakest and the smallest, M. and Mme Rubin sitting up front with her, clutching each other tightly as they headed off towards the tracks and back roads that would allow them to cross the border without having to show their papers.

Sabine couldn't help wondering if she'd ever see her grandmother again.

THIRTY

NORA

September 1940

Mrs Dawson's mother returned to Hope Cottage in June 1940, with the papers full of news about the retreat to Dunkirk and the heroic efforts to rescue the trapped soldiers there.

Nora was glad for the elderly lady's sake that she hadn't been forced to leave her beloved home, and did her best to accept that the cottage might not come up for rent again for several years. Perhaps it was just not meant to be. Although her sister remained adamant in her letters that she was staying with Mum and Dad in London, Nora's search became increasingly urgent over the summer. As they'd all feared, the deceptive calm of the first months of the war had been shattered, with reports of supply convoys being attacked, and airfields and factories being bombed.

Then, one afternoon in late August, Nora was called into Miss Maltby's office, tucked behind the kitchens in what had once been the dining room for the household servants.

'I take it you still have an interest in renting Hope Cottage,' remarked Miss Maltby.

'Yes, I do,' replied Nora, heart beginning to race.

'I'm afraid the tenant, Mrs Teal, has had a fall, not her first. She's not badly hurt, but it's clear she can no longer live on her own. She's moving in with her daughter. Since you expressed an interest, I thought I'd mention it to you first. It was something to do with your sister, wasn't it?'

'Yes, I'm trying to persuade her to leave London and come to the countryside. She has a small child of her own.'

'Ah, I see. So, company for you, and she'll be able to help you with Iris?'

'Yes,' replied Nora. She still had to think twice when she heard the name Iris rather than Violette, but her supposed daughter's transformation into a little English girl had been so gradual that over the months her old name (her middle name, Nora explained to anyone who asked) had already faded from view. Thankfully, Iris herself had rapidly got used to the sound, accepting it as part of the learning process of the world around her.

'A family environment would be better for a child,' agreed Miss Maltby. 'I'm not entirely unaware of what takes place under the eaves when I'm out of sight,' she added dryly. 'I've made my own way out of a few windows in my time when the moon was full and love was in the air. And I don't regret a minute of it.' She sighed, then shook herself. 'Very well. That will suit. The furniture goes with the house of course, and Mrs Dawson has offered to leave some of the bedding and linen; her mother has collected so much over the years. So you should have something to get on with, especially as I imagine your sister will be coming by train.'

'I've promised I'll go and fetch her,' confessed Nora. 'She's nervous about travelling on her own, especially with so much talk of bombing; she's afraid they'll target the railways next.'

'Or London,' said Miss Maltby. 'I was on leave from the field hospital in France and visiting, well, a friend, in London, when it happened in the last war.' She shuddered. 'The things we saw – I wouldn't wish that on anyone. So I take it you're asking for time off?'

'It'll be just there and back. I'll leave everything prepared so it just needs heating up. Alice has enjoyed helping me in the kitchen over the past few weeks; she's more than capable of taking over while I'm gone.'

Miss Maltby nodded. 'And Iris?'

'I'm not sure.' Nora hesitated. She hated the thought of leaving her, even for one night. But on the other hand, a lengthy train journey and then the Tube and bus across London would be no fun for a child.

'Better to leave her here,' said Miss Maltby decisively. 'It's familiar, she has her routine and I'm sure Milly will be more than happy to look after her for the night. She's become very attached to her.'

'Thank you,' said Nora, relieved. For all her misgivings, she knew it was the sensible thing to do. 'I'll talk to Milly,' she said, 'and see what she says.'

'And the sooner the better,' said Miss Maltby. 'I've agreed the tenancy will end the first week in September. That'll give the Dawsons time to clear Mrs Teal's personal belongings. If I were you, I'd start making arrangements now.'

Nora wrote that night to Pearl, painting as warm a picture as she could of the cottage. She reassured her sister how peaceful and secluded it was and told her of Milly's kindness and of the other young nursery nurses looking after the children at Maltby Abbey. Pearl was finally persuaded to make the journey.

I'll come with her if I have to, wrote Mum in a separate letter. *The main thing is to get them out of harm's way.*

Aware there was no time to lose, Nora spent her first evening at the cottage with Alice and Milly giving the place a hasty clean, strewing quilts and blankets out on shrubs and hanging sheets on the washing line to freshen up in the late sun.

'It feels like home already,' she said as she wiped down the iron bedsteads in the two tiny bedrooms, and made up the beds, along with a cot for Jonny hastily located by the members of the local WI.

The cottage, like the rest of those in St Mabon's, had no gas or electricity, relying for warmth and cooking on an ancient range at one end of the main room. A wooden rack hung from the beams to dry clothes in the heat from the range. The only light came from candles or oil lamps, brass bases neatly polished, their wicks trimmed and bulbous glass covers carefully cleaned.

As daylight began to fade, Nora quickly mopped the floor after all the toing and froing, while Alice beat the rug which was to go under the armchairs either side of the range. Nora paused to look around. She could still scarcely believe that in a few days' time Pearl would be with her, and this would be their home. There was even a tiny attic where she and Iris could sleep if they managed to persuade Mum to come with them, or at least visit.

The thought of them all – maybe one day even Dad – gathered round the large wooden table to eat just like when she was little made Nora's heart squeeze with anticipation. She'd been trying not to miss them, but despite the good life she'd built for herself and Iris in St Mabon's, she couldn't wait to be part of a family again.

The next day, as Nora prepared pies and a large gooseberry tart to keep the inhabitants of Maltby Abbey fed while she was away, the news came that London had been bombed.

Annabel shot down to the telephone box in St Mabon's to phone her sister, returning pale-faced and clearly shaken.

'Susanna said it was vile,' she told them over a more than usually subdued lunch. 'The noise was terrible and they had to spend the night in a Tube station. Susanna said it sounded as if the bombers were heading for the docks, but now they're saying homes were hit instead, and there was a huge fire. She thinks hundreds, even thousands, may have been killed. I told her to get out and come and join us here, but she works with Churchill in the War Office and she's adamant she's not leaving.' She burst into tears. 'Supposing the Luftwaffe attack Buckingham Palace next, and the Houses of Parliament? Her house is only a mile away in Mayfair, and I can't bear the thought of Susanna in the middle of all that.'

'They must have a shelter,' said Alice, hugging her. 'Besides, if she's working with the Prime Minister I'm sure they'll have the safest shelter possible there.'

'That's true.' Annabel blew her nose. 'It's Mummy I'm really worried about; she's hopelessly stubborn and she's quite determined she won't go anywhere near a Tube station. With the "hoi polloi,"' she explained apologetically.

'If it happens again she might change her mind,' said Linda.

'Yes, I suppose so.' Annabel gave a watery smile. 'And Susanna promised she'd drag her there herself if she has to.'

Nora found several pairs of eyes turned towards her.

'You'd better return here safe and sound,' said Alice firmly. 'There's no way we're going back to boiled cabbage.'

'And I'm sure your sister will be much better off here,' said Linda.

'I've worked it so I'll get there well before dark,' Nora reassured them. 'I'd have thought it's pretty safe during the day, and I'll have time to get away from the centre. Pearl's staying with Mum and Dad so we can get off as early as possible the next day, and they've got an Anderson shelter if we need it.'

'Oh my goodness,' said Alice, turning slightly green around

the gills. 'Are you sure, Nora? I can't imagine going anywhere near a place where there might be bombing.'

'I'd go like a shot if I thought it'd make any difference,' said Annabel. 'I'd even live with Mummy again if I thought I could persuade her to leave Mayfair. She is rather impossible though.' She sighed. 'Nora, you're so lucky your sister's finally seeing sense.'

'I hope so,' said Nora. A twinge of worry went through her that Pearl might change her mind again at the last moment. But she at least had to try. The thought of heading to a place where enemy bombers were intent on obliterating everything they could terrified her. What would happen to Iris if she didn't return?

Nora pushed the thought from her mind. It was only one day, one night. Iris had people around her who loved her. It was just a few hours in London, where she could see Mum and Dad, and then bring her sister and Jonny to the safety and peace of Hope Cottage. She had to hope, as everyone hoped, that it wasn't her time just yet and she'd return unscathed to St Mabon's, and to Iris.

THIRTY-ONE

SABINE

France, 1940

Over the long, hot weeks of that summer, Sabine waited for Mémé to return to fetch them, or at least send news of a place she had rented so they could join her. But with no sign, anxiety began to turn to despair. She'd seen all too clearly how vulnerable refugees could be on the open road. Her grandmother might have escaped the Luftwaffe, but who knew what other perils might arise en route to the refugee camps?

Meanwhile, all she could do was be thankful she had the means to support her family, and that the village was at least a place of relative security. After a few weeks, Thelma found a small house for them with a patch of garden where they could sit in the cool of the evening and where Valérie and Poupée could run around together, as if there was no such thing as a war.

Sabine enjoyed being at the Red Cross station, translating and helping with paperwork and the smooth running of the place. The work was relentless, but at least it gave them a roof over their heads, and she found it helped to ease her own bewilderment and the ever-present memories of the journey.

Not that there was ever any real respite from anxiety. As the Red Cross had feared, after the armistice between France and Germany was signed, the border between the two zones rapidly became more formalised. Getting across the border without papers was becoming impossible. Within days, Hauptmann Ziegler and his men were replaced by a more experienced unit under a battle-hardened officer, who was still shocked by what he saw, but knew what was expected of him.

The new officers seemed even less familiar with French or English, meaning her translation skills were required more than ever. Despite the heartbreak and the chaos, she enjoyed the feeling of being at work. She missed Valérie, but at least she knew she was safe with Maman, who was already making friends amongst the other women in charge of young children.

It was good to have a purpose again. She wouldn't have given up a moment of when the twins were small, but even in the midst of tragedy and fear she needed something else. *Especially* in the midst of tragedy and fear. Working out people's problems, trying to find ways of securing papers, or finding billets for those without the right papers to cross into safety really taxed her brain. Having to deal with German soldiers, some sympathetic to the civilians' plight, others impatient, sharpened her mind. Despite weeks of exhaustion and semi-starvation, of acute terror waiting for the next bombs to fall, the roar of an engine heralding the arrival of another plane with its scattering of death and agony if the pilot chose to strafe the road with bullets, she was more alert than ever. Or at least since the day she'd arrived in Colmar, to find herself with no other role than as a dutiful wife and mother.

'That is something I can never be,' she acknowledged to herself. 'It's not in my nature. I'd go mad.' Deep in her heart, she wondered if she'd ever see Emil again.

Her mind strayed back towards Violette. She hadn't had time to send a letter before they left to tell Nora where they were heading. She had to hope Nora would find out from the English newspapers what was happening in France, and that she'd write again as soon as she could. Sabine had no paper or envelopes, or even a pencil, and amidst the chaos and destruction of the roads she doubted the postal service had survived.

The worst thing was not knowing. That night she woke in the pitch black, bolt upright, trying to calm her breathing so as not to disturb Valérie and Maman. This time it hadn't been the scream of a plane or the thud of bombs, or even the crackling of undergrowth, with the ever-present fear of enemy soldiers coming across them on the road, just a group of the old, of women and children unable to put up any resistance to men with guns and a mission to do as they pleased. This time the panic came from her last sight of Nora, holding Violette in her arms as the train wound its way from the Gare du Nord, taking them towards the only hope Sabine could offer her child.

Maman turned, her breathing shallowing towards waking. Sabine forced herself to lie down again. Looking after a small child was tiring, and the last thing Maman needed was disturbed sleep.

As Sabine pulled the blanket over her, something warm licked her hand. 'Back on the floor, Poupée,' she whispered. 'Down.' There was a moment of hesitation, followed by the feel of a small body ingratiating itself next to her, enthusiastically licking her face, and the salt left by her drying tears.

With children and animals, Maman would often tell her, discipline must always be maintained. But sometimes discipline went out of the window. She found the rough little head in the dark and stroked it as Poupée curled up against her, until they both relaxed into sleep.

Surely the Red Cross could get a letter to England? Or perhaps Howard Jackson would agree to take a letter with him and send it to Nora's address in London once he arrived to take up his post. After all, they'd be in the same city. Thank goodness she still had her little notebook, carefully preserved with her letters and postcards in the bag she carried with her everywhere and which now formed her pillow, as it had done every night of their journey. She would write first thing in the morning, so it was ready for when the opportunity arose. And once Mémé took them to their new home, she could let Nora know where she could find her. There had to be a way she could reassure herself that Nora and Violette were safe. There had to be.

'You do shorthand,' said Howard one day, looking up from her notes.

'I trained as a journalist.'

'Now, why am I not surprised? If you're interested in doing a few more hours, I'm working with an organisation attached to the University of London trying to note down the testimonies of the civilians who pass through our hands. I suppose it's the historian in me. There are too few records of ordinary people, and as we've all seen too well, they're the ones who suffer. It may be foolish of me, but perhaps one day they can be used as evidence if any of these monsters ever come to trial. I can't offer much more money, I'm afraid.'

But it was a way in, Sabine saw immediately. Even more than her translation work. Working for an English university might give her an even better chance than the Red Cross to travel there and find Violette.

'Yes,' she said quickly. 'The answer is yes. I need to talk to my mother, but if she agrees to look after Valérie, I'll start as soon as you want.'

'Tomorrow then,' he said with a smile.

Maman saw the advantages just as clearly. 'Didn't you and Emil always want to be journalists in London?'

'That was his idea, not mine,' said Sabine. 'He was going to write his great novel there, the one that was going to dazzle the world.'

'He's made his bed,' said Maman tartly. 'That's no reason for you to give up your dream of being a journalist. This could be a way in. And with an English university as well.'

'Maman! Are you trying to marry me off?!'

'Doesn't have to be a husband,' said Maman. 'This professor seems a responsible man, the sort who'd welcome a family. Things are different in wartime. It might be a way for you to take Valérie away from all this, to safety with Nora and Violette.'

'I'd never leave you.' Still bemused at her mother's resignation at the prospect of her child descending into sin, Sabine smiled down at the small creature sitting neatly on her haunches, feathery tale vigorously sweeping the floor. 'Or Poupée. We'll stick together.'

'We'll see,' said Maman quietly.

Sabine started the following morning. Once she'd finished helping with translating and paperwork, she chatted to the refugees over cups of tea as they waited for their paperwork to be processed, finding anyone willing to tell their stories. The tales she heard were heart-breaking. Of elderly relatives refusing to leave or unable to make the journey; of children lost in the chaos and terror of an plane attack, some never to be found again. Some of the younger women separated from friends and family in the panic began speaking hesitatingly at first, before the words poured out of them, as if they couldn't stop.

'They were soldiers,' said a young girl, one of several to come in together, none of them more than fourteen. Their eyes, dark in the hollowed sockets of their sunken faces, were blank, which Sabine found even more unnerving than more obvious expressions of grief.

'French soldiers,' the girl added, barely more than a whisper. 'We expected it of the enemy, we'd have run and hid rather than accompany them. They gave us food and water and said they'd protect us from any Germans. That's all we asked for. They knew we were schoolgirls. But that didn't matter. They took what they wanted, then they left us. They didn't care what happened to us afterwards.'

'I'm sorry,' said Sabine. 'You don't have to go on.'

The girl fought back her tears. 'I want to. I want people to know what happened. It wasn't just us. And at least we're alive, we were lucky. At least, *I'm* lucky. I started my monthly bleeding as soon as we stopped walking.' She gave a harsh laugh. 'I never thought I'd see stomach cramps as a life saver. Marie's too young, she hasn't even started yet, but Annalise ...' She shook her head. 'God help her. They blame the woman, you know. It doesn't matter if it's rape. They always blame the woman. Maman used to tell me what happened to the women who had babies after being raped by German soldiers in the last war. I thought she was silly, telling me stories like that. I never dreamed they were true. Now I'll probably never see her again.'

'The Red Cross will help you, and your friends,' said Sabine gently as the girl broke down into a rigid silence, as if frozen by the horror of those days and nights. 'They'll look after you, make sure you're safe.'

At times, over those summer months, Sabine staggered back to the little house drained of emotion. She learnt to contain her feelings while she was taking down the stories. She had to be the listener, the truthful recorder, she couldn't allow her emotions to get in the way. It was exhausting and painful, but satisfying. She had no idea if the charity would be pleased with her work, or if it was what they wanted, or even if, given the vagaries of war, it would ever reach them. But she was doing her best, and she could hope.

Even more than that, she could feel her old passion stirring again, but not for the glamour of being a female journalist. Her dreaming student days were gone. Not to win prizes or see her name in *Le Figaro*, but to be the quiet listener, the *confidante*, the conduit for all the untold stories of the routine, casual horrors of war. Not the glories of the battlefield, but the struggles of the ordinary civilians, who never asked for their families and hard-won dreams to be torn apart. Forget riches and conquest: these were the things that truly made a life.

She swore she'd never be irritated again by a quiet existence, the scent of washing on the line, the clear half-light of a spring dawn. Summer afternoons under the apple orchard with platters of meat and salads they'd once taken for granted, when hunger was merely the augur of enhanced pleasure, not a dull ache, a constant reminder of the uncertainty of the next meal, of their very survival.

She reached the house, deep in thought. She'd found her purpose, and this time she was not about to be deflected. For now, her care was for her family and children, but she had found her life's work, her meaning, her place in the world. She had faced horrors herself, and heard of far worse from the many refugees she interviewed. She'd find a way to carry on, and nothing was going to stop her.

The door was open. She came back to the present with a jolt. She could feel the silence in the cool interior, no Valérie chuckling delightedly at her approach, no bounding of a scruffy bundle of puppy, dashing towards her, legs akimbo, yapping in excitement. She calmed her instinctive sense of alarm. They must have gone for a walk. That must be it. The day had been particularly hot, the evening breeze rustling through the trees, bringing with it the scent of thyme and rosemary, had begun to cool the air, making it pleasant. They never went far, staying within the bounds of the village, despite the temptation of the river.

They'd be back soon. That was the thing about living in fear for months, it never left you: the slightest hint of anything out of the ordinary and the mind was filled with the worst possibilities, all rationality gone. She'd start preparing the evening meal with the tomatoes and onions she'd bought from the small stall in the market square, along with *haricots verts*. She'd even found peaches, too ripe to last another day, their aroma a delicious anticipation.

'So it is you.' Sabine froze, eyes blinded by sunlight. The room was a dark shadow, but she'd know that voice anywhere. The last voice on earth she ever wanted to hear again.

She blinked, hoping against hope it was an illusion, a nightmare. But the man in a German officer's uniform sitting at the table, turning one of Valérie's toys over in his hands, was all too real. 'When they talked of the woman with the white-haired child,' he continued, 'who was working for those busy-body Americans at the Red Cross, I knew it had to be you.'

'Karl,' she managed, throat constricting. He was watching her, as he'd always watched her in Colmar, with a mixture of contempt and a far too intimate awareness of her body. Except now he was no longer simply her husband's friend, she no longer had that protection. This was war, with all rules gone.

Sabine could see in his eyes the enjoyment Karl Bernheim was experiencing in finally finding himself in a position of power. Where he could do as he pleased with her. Where there could only be one end.

In the street outside, coming ever closer, she could hear the excited yapping of a puppy.

THIRTY-TWO

NORA

London, 1940

Nora arrived in London far later than she'd expected. The train had been delayed for hours by debris from a stray bomb damaging the line, leaving her despairing of ever reaching Paddington Station.

Far from arriving in time to see Mum and Dad and helping Pearl take Jonny to the station for the return to St Mabon's, she emerged into the streets as dusk fell.

Around her, the few Londoners still out began to head for the nearest Tube station. Men and women, some with children clutching their hands, quickened their pace, but with the air of putting up with a habitual nuisance rather than genuine panic.

'Better hurry, love,' said a woman as Nora hesitated.

'I'm trying to get to Hammersmith.'

'Left it a bit late, ain't ya? No chance of getting there tonight. Not with Jerry on the way. You'll have to wait till morning.'

The sirens wailed again, the movement towards the shelters quickened in pace, the conversations now terse and to the point.

A small girl waddling in a coat too large for her, gas mask swaying as she clutched the hand of an elderly woman, began to cry. A white-haired man swept her up, vanishing amongst the sway of bodies.

But there was nothing for it. She had no wish to be caught out in the open when the bombers arrived. Following the crowd of Londoners, Nora clattered down the steps into the crammed space below.

'People are living down here!' she exclaimed.

'Not all of us have bomb shelters, dearie,' replied an elderly woman, 'and it's safer down here in the Tube.'

Nora had only just found a place to settle when the first thud set the ground trembling.

All through that night Nora crouched, bracing herself against the next thud, against a direct hit and the roof caving in. She tried to take comfort from the calm around her as people settled down for the night. Those further along the platform were more organised, the stragglers like herself finding places where they could, curling up amidst the smog of bodies, sleeping in any space they were able to find.

Thank goodness she had left Iris back in Cornwall. Her arms instinctively reached out to hold her little charge, as if they were back on the boat and the journey from France, in the terror of waiting for the submarine to strike. Only that had been in a deathly silence, this was punctuated by the pounding of explosives.

The ground shook.

'That was close,' said the woman next to her.

What would happen to Iris if the roof caved in? She had no idea if Sabine was even still alive. How could she have left Iris alone?

Nora tried to calm herself, focusing on the task ahead. Mum and Dad must be worried by now. If she'd arrived earlier, they could at least have sat this out in the Anderson shelter together.

Nora stopped herself from crying out as yet another explosion rocked the ground above them. Those around her barely winced. How could you live like that, night after night? And then go to work the next day, as Mum had described in her most recent letter, as if nothing had happened?

Nora shut her eyes, willing the night to end, willing herself to survive and for there still to be a train to take Pearl and Jonny to safety. With no other recourse, she prayed as she'd never prayed before, prayed that she'd live to see St Mabon's, and to hold Iris once again, safe in her arms.

THIRTY-THREE

SABINE

France, 1940

'Stupid dog.' Karl aimed a kick at Poupée as she rushed in ahead of Maman to greet Sabine with her usual tail-wagging hysteria. The puppy yelped in fright and scurried under the table.

'There's no need for that,' exclaimed Sabine.

'Dirty things. Shouldn't be in the house.' Maman came to an abrupt halt in the doorway, Valérie in her arms. Sabine saw her daughter's contented smile die at his harsh tones, the threat of casual violence. The half-eaten peach in her fist dropped, forgotten, sending up a brief swirl of dust into the heat.

Somewhere inside, her heart broke. Her arms ached to hold Valérie, to comfort her, but that would bring her inside the house, closer to Karl. She shook her head quickly at Maman, desperately hoping she'd understand, and what she must do. Her mother held Valérie's sobbing body against her, the baby's face against her shoulder, holding her tight. If she could distract Karl, at least Maman would stand a chance of getting Valérie away.

But where to? Despair seized her. Why had she stayed, why

hadn't she insisted they all go with Mémé? They could have been safely under French jurisdiction in the *Zone Libre* where Karl had no right to be, where he would never have stumbled on their presence. She'd been stupid. Selfish. She was no better than Emil, putting her own ambition before her child's safety. Here, Karl was in control, holding all the cards. The German soldiers would obey his orders, and what power did the villagers or the Red Cross have against guns? She had seen too many ordinary citizens being treated as nothing, mere wooden pins to be knocked down in a game, not living, breathing creatures, each with a life to lead, networks of love surrounding them.

Fury replaced fear. Sabine refused to be cast aside as if she were nothing. Maman had moved inside the house, a stubborn look on her face that said she was not leaving Sabine to her fate. Whatever happened, they were going to face this together.

'The child is tired,' Sabine said, as calm as she could manage. 'She needs food and sleep. And her napkin changing,' she added impatiently. 'There are several soaking in the bucket ready to be washed, and I expect this one's filthy. She's had an upset stomach these past few days.'

As Maman drew closer, Sabine reached out for the baby's outstretched arms, holding Valérie tight as she turned to the softness of her breasts, her body shaken by frightened sobs.

She had a moment of hope as Karl made his way to the door, but it was only to speak to several soldiers in the street outside. He returned within minutes with a dusty bottle of cognac that from the look of its label had been stolen from a restaurant or a cellar in one of the abandoned mansions.

'*Verre*,' he barked at Maman, who quietly reached for a small glass, placing it on the table without glancing in his direction.

Sabine tried to ignore him as she changed her daughter. With Valérie clean and reassured by her presence, she held her on her hip while she cooked one-handed as her mother prepared vegetables. She could feel Karl watching her every move, every stretch of her dress tight across her body as she reached for a pan, every brush of her skirts against her thighs.

'Won't you join me.'

'I have work to do.'

'Pour.'

'Excuse me?'

'Like you did when we were in Colmar. When you measured out the wine for both of us.' He laughed. 'Always too little. Claudette always was mean with her spirits. Hated Emil to have a good time. Didn't think much of his friends, either. Didn't think they were good enough for her precious son.'

'I'm sure she didn't. Claudette respects you as Emil's friend.'

'Useful, but not good enough,' he retorted. He banged the table with his fist. 'Pour.'

He drank steadily as the meal cooked, wolfing down the stew put in front of him without tasting it while Sabine concentrated on feeding Valérie, who was growing fractious with the tension. She felt Poupée lean against her leg and placed her own meal on the floor. The little dog ate quietly, delicately, sensing the need not to draw attention to herself. The oppressive warmth of the day was cooling, the light beginning to fade. Every sense was alert. She was aware of the shuffle of feet outside the door, the occasional exchange of the soldiers, the faint scent of cigarettes.

She had to get them away. But the soldiers stationed outside would prevent them leaving. And where would they go? She almost prayed for a raid that night, but the Luftwaffe must know this was the occupied zone, that the French army was defeated and incapable of resistance. She smiled and chatted to Valérie, trying to calm her, willing the warm food to do its work and lull her into sleep. Valérie responded to her smiles, but even when her eyes drooped she jerked them awake, watching the

interloper at the table, as if, like Poupée, instinctively understanding he intended no good to any of them.

'That's enough,' said Karl irritably. 'I can see you spoil the
child. Your mother can take care of her.'

'She's nearly asleep.'

'Then it doesn't matter where she is.'

Don't antagonise him. Bide your time. Wait. Sabine silently
rose and placed Valérie in Maman's arms, meeting her eyes.
They'd get only one chance, said the glance between them.
They were going to survive this, for Valérie's sake and for
Violette, so far away. Whatever happened, they would survive.

Maman shushed Valérie who was too exhausted to resist
being overcome by sleep, while Sabine poured a *tisane* for
herself and Maman before returning to her seat, as far away
from Karl as possible.

'Pour,' he said, banging the table next to his empty glass.

How many women were facing this tonight in the chaos of
war, where the tight social structure that had kept them all safe
had been swept away? When the Karls of this world could do
exactly as they pleased. Sabine steeled herself.

She quietly filled up Karl's glass again in the vain hope he
might succumb to the cognac, ignoring the brush of his hand
against her breasts as she bent over.

Don't react, don't react. That's what he wants. It's the
excitement he craves. Fear and humiliation. That's what he
needs to feel any sensation at all. Keep calm, keep quiet. She
fixed her gaze on the ancient knots and swirls of the table to
hide the loathing in her eyes.

She couldn't help glancing at his face. It was even more
fleshless than she remembered, with the unhealthy pallor of a
man with no interest in the riches of the palate. He even
knocked the cognac back – a vintage beyond the reach of any
but the most wealthy – rather than savouring its time-enhanced
flavours.

She'd made a mistake. She saw it in the tilting of his head, the narrowing of his bloodshot eyes, before she lowered her eyes to the table.

'That's what he taught you to do, was it? Look down your nose at me?'

'No of course not. You're Emil's friend.'

'Friend.' He spat into the fire. 'Not after he found his fancy Paris *intellectuels*. Degenerates every last one of them. And his fancy Paris bit of skirt. The one from a castle.' His hand closed over her arm, drawing her closer towards him. 'I hope you know that's what really impressed him. He always dreamt of being some aristo.'

'We're not aristocrats. Just an ordinary family.'

'No matter. That's what he wanted. That's what got him going. You don't think it was really about you, do you?' His voice turned to mockery. 'Poor girl, didn't realise it was always the chateau he was screwing.'

In the silence, she heard the crackle as a log fell in the dying fire and Maman's sharp intake of breath. Valérie began to whimper.

'Shut that child up,' he snapped irritably, downing the last of the brandy and rising unsteadily to his feet, his grip tightening on Sabine's arm. 'Get a move on.'

'It's all right Maman,' said Sabine, keeping her voice as even as she could as she was propelled towards the bedroom at the back of the house. 'Look after Valérie. Take her somewhere safe. Remember I love you both. That's what matters. Nothing else. Nothing else at all.'

'I said get a move on,' said Karl, giving her a violent push. Sabine stumbled, her head smashing against the doorframe. Dazed, she struggled desperately to remain upright. As if from a distance she heard a loud crash. His grip on her arm was instantly released; there was the thud of a body falling to the floor. In the deathly silence, Valérie began to scream.

'Darling ...' To her relief it was Maman's voice that reached her in the dizziness as she struggled to maintain consciousness. 'Thank the Lord. I thought he'd killed you. He can't hurt you now, not ever again.'

'Valérie ...' she muttered.

Maman helped her to the nearest chair. 'She's safe, don't worry, I'll bring her to you.'

As Valérie's sobs began to calm, the silence unnerved Sabine. As her eyes began to focus, she could make out Karl's body, uniform awry, sprawled out on the floor, a long gash on his forehead oozing red onto the tiles.

Valérie was placed in her arms, her face, hot with sweat and damp with tears, pressed against her neck.

'Ssssh,' she whispered, cradling her. 'It'll be all right, it'll be all right.'

'He cracked his head on the fireplace as he went down,' said Maman, grabbing a sturdy poker from where it had landed next to him. 'I couldn't see that happen again. Not again. Not to my child.'

Sabine's relief turned to fear. 'Is he dead?'

'Stunned. Maybe I should finish the job.'

'The village ...'

'Yes, I know. I wouldn't do that to them. They'd pay the price if a German officer was killed. But we can't stay here.' Maman pulled open the kitchen drawer where they kept their papers. 'Damn.' She jumped away as the front door opened and a strong smell of cigarettes wafted in.

'Hauptmann?' The German soldier was tall, well built, somewhere in his early thirties. 'Hauptmann, there is a message—' He came to a halt as his eyes fell on the figure on the hearth.

'It was me,' said Maman in German. 'I was the one. Let the mother and child go. It was me. Not anyone else. It was me.'

'I'm sure it was, *Madame*.' He made a comment to the men

outside which drew several guffaws, then turned back, shutting the door behind him.

Sabine gazed up as he approached, trying to sooth Valérie, trying to glean any hint of whether it was the gun that would finish it, or if it was to be other payment first. The soldier's skin was browned from years of working in the wind and rain. She could imagine him managing a vineyard, overseeing workers, serving on the local council, a respectable upstanding man of the community. Was this really the end of all things?

'Your daughter?' He'd stopped in front of her and was gazing down at them.

'Yes.'

'What is her name?'

'Valérie.'

They killed children in front of their mothers for the pleasure of seeing their anguish. She knew that from the refugees on the road. The last thing you saw before the bullet hit your brain.

'Valérie,' he repeated.

Desperation shot through Sabine. 'Don't hurt her. Please. Anything. Just don't hurt her.'

At the sound of her name Valérie had turned towards the soldier, and was now eyeing him curiously.

'A pretty girl,' he said in halting French. His hand reached out. Sabine died inside. But the fingers that touched the damp little cheek were brief in their caress. 'I have daughters. Two. One this age. I don't think I'll ever see them again,' he added in German.

'I hope you will,' responded Sabine, in the same language. At the hearth, Karl began to stir.

'Perhaps it's better if I don't,' said the soldier, eyes on Karl. 'I joined to give them a better life, a better future. Now I fear one day they'll despise me.'

'I'm sure they could never do that.'

He grunted. 'I hope you're right.' He lifted the bottle of

cognac and took an appreciative swig. 'Bloody drunks,' he remarked, calmly pouring the remains over Karl. 'And this one's hardly ever sober. Can't stand Nazis,' he added quietly. 'Not many of us can. They had me when I was in the *Hitlerjugend*, but never again. I've seen too much of what they do.'

On the hearth, Karl began to snore. The soldier called in the rest of the men, who lifted Karl unceremoniously and carted him out.

'He won't come to until tomorrow, never does,' the soldier said as he followed them. 'Perhaps not until we're on our way.' He glanced back to reassure himself that the men were in the street and out of earshot. 'Hopefully he'll think he tripped. All the same, I'd get out of here.' He hesitated. 'I'm sorry I can't do more. If I did ...' He smiled wistfully towards Valérie. 'The Nazis hurt their own countrymen just as much as foreigners. I must protect my family too.'

'I understand,' said Sabine. 'And thank you, from the bottom of my heart. I hope your daughters stay safe and one day you'll be with them again, when this is over.'

He nodded briefly, and was gone.

There was a moment's silence. Then Maman returned to the drawer, hastily retrieving their documents. It took only a few minutes to throw their few belongings into a shoulder bag and grab their threadbare coats.

'Supposing we can't get over the border?' said Maman.

'We'll find a way,' said Sabine firmly. She pushed the terror of the past hours deep within her mind. One day there'd be time to let the emotions flood through her. They'd been lucky, incredibly lucky. So many women never lived to tell of such an experience, or never felt able to reveal what had happened to them. Sabine's determination to tell their stories was back, fiercer than ever.

She pushed that aside too, for now. The first thing, the only thing, was to find a way to cross the border before Karl recovered, and to somehow find Mémé.

Sabine swung Valérie into her arms while her mother retrieved Poupée from under the table. As she opened the door, Sabine could see the street outside was dark and silent with not a soldier to be seen. Maman was right. It was their only chance to reach safety.

Taking a deep breath, Sabine stepped out into the deserted street, as they headed out once more into the unknown.

THIRTY-FOUR

NORA

London, 1940

She had survived.

By the end of hours of relentless thuds and explosions, Nora's nerves were shredded to pieces as calm finally returned to the Underground station.

Once the all-clear sounded, she emerged with the others into a misty dawn, pulling her coat about her, picking her way through rubble as the destruction of the night before was revealed.

She was pointed towards a café opening amidst the destruction, front window blown out but the glass already swept up, and offering a welcoming cup of hot tea. Around her, the city was returning to a kind of normality, buses and Underground trains running, people heading off to their offices and places of work.

How on earth could they go through that time and time again, never knowing when it might end, or whether their house or flat might be the one that bought it in the night? Just one night in the shelter had left her drained. She had no idea how people did it night after night, then picked themselves up and went off to work.

Tea finished, Nora headed for the nearest bus stop. She hoped her parents had guessed the train had been delayed and she'd been forced to take shelter. At least she knew her way around London, it wasn't like being stranded in a strange city. As the bus rumbled through the streets and she looked down from the top deck at the ruins of bombed-out buildings, sadness overwhelmed her at the destruction of the city she loved, part of her childhood and her memories gone forever. It no longer felt like home. At least Pearl had said there was less likelihood of raids during the day. With any luck, they'd be safely out of the city before the next siren sounded.

At last the streets became more familiar. Away from the centre there were less signs of damage. Some areas even seemed little different from how she remembered them. At least she'd have a family again. She'd finally be back with Mum and Dad, as well as Pearl and Jonny.

The bus turned a corner and came to an abrupt halt.

'Bloody hell,' muttered the man next to her. 'Someone got it last night.'

Down below, the bus driver was calling to men in the road attempting to remove the rubble of a collapsed house.

'Can't go no further,' he called. 'Next street has been hit bad. No way through.'

Nora was already on her feet, heading down the spiral of stairs to the open door.

'Oh my Lord,' said a woman clambering down behind her.

In front of them, rubble lay scattered everywhere, smoke hung in the air, obscuring all but the gap-toothed façades of the streets, the shadows of firefighters attempting to douse the last flames, families trying to retrieve what possessions they could.

'Can't go there, miss.' A policeman blocked her way. 'Them houses on Walford Row took a direct hit. It's too dangerous.'

Nora ducked under his outstretched arm and ran towards what was left of her home.

She reached the familiar hedge, broken and blackened, to the edges of a crater that had obliterated the garden.

'You'd best not go any further, miss.' The firefighter emerging from the destruction was kind, but there was nothing he could do, nothing he could say. 'Family is it?'

'Yes,' she whispered.

'Do you have friends? Place to stay?'

She shook her head. 'I was just here to fetch them, to take them to the countryside where they'd be safe.'

'I'm so very sorry.' He must see this every night, she realised, a terrible numbness creeping over her. Houses consumed in flames, the remains of lives scattered around. The front of the house had partially fallen away, revealing a still neatly made bed, Pearl's suitcase on top next to the blackened shell of a cot. 'You're all right miss.' The man caught her arm as she stumbled. From the twisted remains of the Anderson shelter a sad procession appeared through the smoke, bodies completely covered between the stretcher bearers. 'It was a direct hit,' he added gently. 'They would have all died instantly.'

Was that true? She didn't dare glance at his face, to recognise the kindness of a lie. Had Jonny's tiny form been the first she had seen them bring out? Had he still been alive when the roof caved in, shielded by the bodies of the adults? She could hear Iris's desperate screams when she was late feeding her, or when she woke up in the dark, always grasping for something that wasn't there, until Nora took her into the bed next to her or pressed her toy lion into her arms. The screams filled her head, threatening to overwhelm her.

'I hope so,' she murmured.

'I'm afraid there's nothing left in the house, smoke or water got everything that was left. But there was this, looked as if it had been thrown clear.' He held out a photograph in a cracked frame. It was the one of her parents on the day they'd moved into the house, just months after their wedding. They'd just learnt they were expecting Pearl, Mum had told her. Their faces looked out, beaming and happy, looking forward to the new life they'd worked so hard to achieve, finally leaving the back bedroom of Granny's house and renting a place of their own. They hadn't even had a bed for the first year, just an old mattress on the bare floorboards along with a sideboard and the kitchen table.

Deep inside, her heart began to break. It was all gone now. Just so much ash and ruin. All that was left of the safe little world that had enfolded her with love from the day she was born. All gone.

Nora steadied herself. All she could do was get back to St Mabon's and to Iris, who was now the only family she had left in the world. As she turned to make her way towards the nearest bus stop, Nora had never felt so alone.

THIRTY-FIVE

SABINE

France, 1940

As she led Maman through the silent streets, Sabine knew the only place she could go to for help was the Red Cross house. She daren't ring the bell, knocking instead on the side door, hidden from the road by the wall of a small courtyard.

Howard let them in, ushering them into a sparse kitchen where the volunteers were sitting round a large table planning the next day's work.

'Bernheim?' he said as Sabine tried to explain, stumbling over her words as her numbed mind attempted to convey the urgency of the situation. 'Are you certain?'

She froze. Karl was in a position of authority. Perhaps Howard didn't believe her story. It might be easier for him to assume she was overreacting rather than jeopardising his negotiations at the border.

'You know him?' she asked warily.

'I know of him. He has a particularly unsavoury reputation. The kind of man who could only progress in a regime like the Nazis. I had no idea he was here.'

'I think he may have been seeking me out,' said Sabine. 'He was a friend of my husband.' It was Howard's turn to be wary. She had never disclosed anything about Emil to any of the Red Cross workers. You learned not to ask in the ever-shifting circumstances of war, and she'd no wish for it to be known she was married to the enemy, however broken that marriage might be. 'I was always a little afraid of him. He was so obsessed with Nazi ideology. And I suppose with me. I don't think women liked him much. I always had a feeling I represented everything he lacked, and he resented me for it.'

'Then we need to get you away immediately,' said Howard, reaching for his jacket. 'I only know of him through his reputation. Most of the Germans we deal with are reasonable men, just doing their jobs, but even his fellow officers don't want Bernheim anywhere near them. He's a nasty piece of work, the kind that likes to throw his weight around, and he has a particularly bad reputation when it comes to his treatment of women.' He took a bunch of car keys from a hook by the door. 'And he holds grudges. The last officer I dealt with said he was quite unhinged, the sort who'd go to the ends of the earth to pay someone back for even an imagined slight.'

'Then you can't risk it,' said Sabine, glancing in despair at the pale faces around the table. 'You still have to work here.'

'We'll take our chances.'

'We have to go, Sabine,' said Maman. At her feet, Poupée began to whimper. 'We've come this far, we can make it to the border without the Red Cross.'

'We're involved whether you like it or not,' said Howard firmly. 'You're lucky it's only a crescent moon, there's less chance of being seen. I'll take you through the back roads to avoid any border guards. It's what we do with any Jewish refugees who don't have the right paperwork. There are safe houses on the other side; the people there will help you get to the refugee camps. The sooner we go the better.'

They slipped out into the streets again, following Howard to a barn on the outskirts of the village where the Red Cross car was kept. Sabine crouched low on the back seat with Maman holding Valérie between them and Poupée pressed against their legs for reassurance. She held her breath as the engine stuttered into life, waiting for shouts and the sound of gunfire. There was nothing.

Slowly, warily, with no lights to betray them, Howard urged the vehicle onto the narrow road. Within minutes he veered off onto a rough track, leading between fields and past the silhouettes of farms looming darkly against the faint light of the stars.

It felt like hours as they bumped over grass and the ruts made by tractors, until Howard pulled the car into a yard in front of a small farmhouse, a shadow amongst surrounding trees.

'Wait here,' he said as he swung himself out of the driver's seat. 'I just need to check with the family that they're happy to take you in. If not, there's another in the village. Don't worry, we crossed the border a couple of miles back. You're in the free zone.'

He returned within minutes with a boy of no more than twelve who took hold of Sabine's bag, carrying it proudly in front of them as they were led into the house.

As the door was shut and the lamp turned up, Sabine blinked in the light at an elderly couple watching them from the fireplace. A large sheepdog sitting alert on the rug between them gave a low growl.

'Quiet, César,' said the man, 'these are friends.' The growl subsided and César settled down on the rug, chin on his front paws, eyes still observing them carefully, paying particular attention to Poupée, who took refuge behind Maman.

'Good boy, Alfonse,' said a fair-haired young woman, not much older than Sabine, who emerged from a side room and took charge of the bag. 'Come on in, come on in. You're most welcome. I've put the kettle on.'

'I need to get back,' said Howard. 'Mme Thierry will look after you. You'll be safe now.'

Sabine accompanied him to the car. 'I can never thank you enough,' she said.

'There's no need,' he replied, a little gruffly. 'Just keep that family of yours in one piece, and I hope you find your grandmother again.' He cleared his throat. 'You're a good journalist, Sabine. Don't give that up. I understand how difficult it is.'

'Because of my husband, you mean.' His silence told its own story. 'You're right, of course. If he's a friend of Karl Bernheim, he must be profiting from all of this.'

'But not you,' he said. 'Or you wouldn't be where you are now. Besides, I doubt a bully like Bernheim would have dared to harm you if he thought it was against his own best interests.'

'That's true,' she said, wincing. She had tried to keep the thought at bay, but she could no longer avoid the fact that, whatever happened from now on, she and Emil were worlds apart. He was still the father of her children, but apart from that there was nothing left. Not even love.

'Then be a journalist,' he said. 'You can always contact me through the Red Cross. I'll help you any way I can. The stories of the people on the road need to be told, the real stories of war. One day this'll be over, and we'll need journalists to record exactly what happened, so we never forget.'

'Yes.' She took a deep breath. 'There is one thing you could do for me.'

'Anything.'

'If you ever get to England, I have a daughter there, Violette, Valérie's twin sister. My friend Nora took her there for an operation on the day war broke out, when we thought the Nazis were about to invade Paris.' She pulled out the crumpled envelope containing her letter to Nora. 'This is her address. She lives in London, in Turnham Green. If you can, will you find out what happened to them? It's the only place I know where to look.'

'Of course,' he said. 'That can't have been an easy thing to do, Sabine.'

'There was no other choice,' she replied. 'At least Nora gave Violette a chance. I'm more certain than ever that if she'd stayed with me she wouldn't have survived.'

'I'll find them,' he said firmly. 'Whatever happens, I'll find them. You stay in touch with the Red Cross, and I'll get a message to you as soon as I have news.'

'Thank you,' she said, overcome by tears.

'And don't forget what I said about being a journalist. You understand the true realities of war more than most.' A brief press of her hand and he was gone. She watched as his car made its slow way back towards the border, and the endless tide of desperate humanity, until it finally vanished into the dark.

Over the next few days, the little family were back on the road again amongst the slow trail of families who'd made it this far, heading towards the refugee camps. On the first morning, Mme Thierry drove them in an ancient cart, Alfonse beside her, to the next village, where another safe house took them in. Then, armed with a list of addresses of those who'd help, they followed the main road towards the Massif Central, sometimes walking, occasionally being given a lift in a car, or more often a rickety wagon piled high with bits of furniture.

Early one morning, as they wearily emerged from a little camp by the roadside they'd shared with others too tired to reach the next town, Poupée, who'd been trotting happily in front, suddenly began to bark hysterically.

'What can she have seen?' said Maman, sounding nervous.

'It wouldn't be German soldiers, surely they can't have tried to take the *Zone Libre*?'

'I don't think so,' said Sabine, blinking in the slanting light, not quite daring to trust her eyes as a cart came lumbering towards them out of the sun, a single figure holding the reins.

The cart pulled up next to them, an excited Poupée jumping up at the driver.

'I see you still can't control that hound,' said a familiar voice. 'I might have known she'd be running rings around you the moment I left.'

'Mémé!' exclaimed Sabine, hugging her grandmother as she swung to the ground.

'Thank goodness,' said Mémé, embracing them all, tears in her eyes. She looked older, face gaunt, her clothes hanging off her more than ever. 'I was afraid I'd never see you again. I should never have left you behind. This damned chest of mine had me laid up for months, not a thing I could do about it.' She kissed Valérie and bent to fuss Poupée's ears, who immediately rolled over for a belly rub.

'We thought we'd lost you,' said Maman, blowing her nose.

'You should know better than that, Joelle. Tough as old boots.' Practical again, Mémé turned her attention to the horses, turning the cart round so that it faced the opposite direction. 'I've found a house for us near the camp where we can sit it out until the war's over. I could do with a bit of peace and quiet, I tell you.'

Sabine had never been so glad to see Maman take her customary place next to Mémé. She lifted Valérie up amongst the familiar piles of coats and belongings and Poupée jumped up and settled down next to them. Then Mémé set the cart once more into motion, heading south towards the safety of the mountains.

THIRTY-SIX

NORA

Cornwall, 1940

Nora returned to St Mabon's racked with grief.

'Take your time, my dear,' said Miss Maltby when she reached her office, swollen-eyed and dishevelled. 'We've managed while you've been away, we can manage for a few days more.'

Nora shook her head. 'I'd rather keep busy,' she said. 'Less time to think.' She took a deep breath. All the way back, one thought had constantly been in her head. 'I'd still like to take over Hope Cottage. I can manage the rent the same as if it were the two of us. Iris is all I have left now. I want more than anything to be able to give her a home.'

'We'll come to some arrangement,' said Miss Maltby gruffly. 'Don't you worry about that. You just settle in there and take care of your child.'

That night was the first Nora spent with Iris at Hope Cottage. Despite waves of grief, she felt calmer in the peace of the rooms and the tangled beauty of the garden. After Iris had gone to sleep in the cot once meant for Jonny, Nora sat out in the darkness wrapped in a blanket, drinking tea to keep warm.

She had never loved the stillness more. A breeze caught the leaves now and again but apart from that the only sound was the sea and the distant call of an owl. At that very moment families were huddling in the Underground and the Anderson shelters in London and other major cities. On the continent families were living amongst piles of rubble, or trailing down endless roads away from the fighting and destruction towards some kind of safety.

She hoped Sabine was amongst the survivors, but she'd learnt all too brutally how life could be taken away in an instant, even without an invading army bulldozing across the land obliterating everything in its path. She had a nagging feeling she'd never see her, or Valérie, again.

Back inside, she lit a table lamp and picked up an ornate biscuit tin she'd found at the back of the larder, which must once have been used to store lavender bags. Removing the lid she carefully placed the photograph of Mum and Dad inside, along with her letters from Sabine.

'One day, that will be for you, Iris,' she said aloud. 'One day, when you're ready, I promise I'll tell you the truth about who you are and where you came from. I'll tell you that your mother loved you more than life itself, and did everything she could to make sure you were safe and would grow up free and happy. Until then, it's just you and me, my darling. Just you and me.'

THIRTY-SEVEN

SABINE

France, 1945

For the rest of the war Sabine stayed in a small village just outside the resettlement camps near Corrèze in the Massif Central.

With the help of the American Red Cross she was able to let Howard know they were safe, and in return received reassurances that no one had commented (in public, at least) on the fact that a translator and her family had vanished overnight. It was such a common occurrence in war; they could have gone anywhere, even back towards Paris. She was glad to know that the Red Cross station could still do its work relatively unhindered.

Through Howard's glowing recommendations, she was soon able to resume her work translating documents and collecting testimony from refugees in the overcrowded resettlement camps. She continued to use Mémé's maiden name as her professional name, feeling that the fewer connections that could be traced to Emil, the safer they'd be.

She heard many things in the course of her work that were

too shocking to tell Maman or Mémé, and left her drained and hopeless at the end of the day. She played with Valérie in the evenings trying her best to hide her despair at the cruelty human beings were capable of, and her fear at what the future might hold for her daughter.

The stories she heard from refugees who'd made it from Germany itself were the worst. At first her brain refused to take in the litany of extermination camps where thousands of men, women and children were put to death in gas chambers, while those capable were made to work until they died from exhaustion, starvation or disease.

'I never thought about it, when they started with the disabled,' said Ruth, a painfully thin young woman of no more than nineteen who'd made her way from a village near Frankfurt. She'd been visiting a cousin the day her family and neighbours had been rounded up and sent on trains, like cattle, to a camp called Auschwitz somewhere in Poland. She could only bear to tell her tale in brief snatches: hiding in forests, riding in goods trains, not knowing where she was heading but desperate to get as far away as possible from her homeland. Sabine could see from the blankness in Ruth's eyes how much she left untold.

'None of us saw it coming,' replied Sabine, a twist in her heart as she remembered Violette's train disappearing into the distance, to what, at the time, she had presumed was safety.

'It wasn't just that, Mme Bourret. We all tried to ignore it when the Nazis started on their political opponents, and then the Jews and the Romanies and anyone they said wasn't "pure". Most people in the village didn't agree with them, but how do you fight a whole state? My family was just like the rest, we tried to lie low and not draw attention to ourselves. I don't even know why they picked on my father, except he had a disagreement with a Nazi official over the ownership of a piece of land. That's all it took.'

'Do you know what happened to them?' asked Sabine

gently. Ruth shook her head. 'My mother walked with a limp and my grandmother was too old to work. My sister had two small children. From what I've been told by people who escaped, they would all have been gassed as soon as they arrived. I'm certain I'll never see any of them again.'

It was the calm of her voice, the matter-of-fact manner of telling, devoid of all emotion, that haunted Sabine afterwards. Ruth's experiences, like so many of those who'd made it to the relative safety of the refugee camp, were too terrible for the mind to take in and for the heart to understand. All through the war, she was never able to escape that look in the survivors' eyes. It was something that would haunt her for the rest of her life.

With her knowledge of German and her fluency in English and French, Sabine was in increasing demand as a translator. Occasionally she was asked to translate articles in newspapers some of the refugees from Germany had used to wrap precious items, in order to obtain some idea what the state-controlled media was feeding the German population.

One day in early 1942, as she smoothed out a sheet of newspaper from the first year of the war, her eye was caught by a photograph of Nazi Party officials. Her heart stopped at the face of the man at the centre, a smiling young blonde woman on his arm, a champagne flute in his hand. For a moment she was sure she was imagining things, but the caption, although partially torn, confirmed it was Emil Schongauer, a leading businessman and producer of miracles who would help ensure the eventual victory of the Third Reich. She'd never felt so glad she'd ceased using her married name.

Despite the elegant cut of his suit, she could see Emil had filled out, his face rounded towards portliness, his once thick hair thinning. His expression was one of triumph; a man who'd achieved the recognition he'd always craved.

A second photograph showed him inspecting machinery his

company had recently installed. Another tear in the paper had almost obliterated the name of the location. Not that it mattered. The piece by some acolyte of the German propaganda minister Joseph Goebbels looked as if it contained the usual rant against degeneracy. She hesitated: it was too painful to see him again, both familiar and yet changed. On the other hand, the article might include something of interest. She filed the paper at the back of the little cabinet, putting it out of her mind for now.

Despite the increasing feeling that now America had entered the war Hitler must eventually be defeated, she dreaded coming across any mention of Karl. Just the thought of him was enough to turn her stomach. However irrational, she still lived in fear that he might appear again, intruding on their new-found security, determined not to let her escape this time. But he was a soldier, not an official, and therefore unlikely to be mentioned in newspapers. She couldn't help but hope he was no longer alive.

As 1945 approached, and it became clear it was now only a matter of time before the Allies prevailed, Sabine found herself more in demand as a freelance journalist. As occupied regions were liberated, so many atrocities came to light and were described to her by the refugees, some so terrible as to be beyond imagination.

All the same, when Marie, one of the young journalists on the local newspaper, asked her to accompany her to a camp in Alsace, in the mountains not far from Colmar, she couldn't refuse.

'But darling, that must be a thousand kilometres away, maybe more,' exclaimed Maman. 'And some of the stories you hear. Are you quite sure about this?'

'It was liberated some time ago, Maman. There are no

prisoners left. They won't let Marie go on her own with two men, and I'm the only one who knows German.' She hesitated. With the war coming to an end, their minds were turning to the future. 'I want to see if I can do it, Maman. Be a journalist, I mean. If I'm serious about earning a living covering stories after the war I need to know I can face places like that. I don't want to cover tea parties or village fairs. I want my work to be serious. Besides, we've all suffered enough, I don't want it all to just be forgotten.'

'Don't worry, we'll look after Valérie,' said Mémé, coming in from working in their tiny vegetable patch. 'You go. We'll be returning to the chateau before long to see if there's anything left. This might be your last opportunity to do some serious journalist work before we go back to Paris. You go.'

Sabine left a few days later, sharing the driving with M. Perrot, an elderly journalist, while Marie and Jean, a young photographer, did their best to follow the map. They headed through the *Zone Libre* towards areas liberated from the Nazis, stopping to record the destruction on their way. The camp itself was in a remote valley reached by a road winding amongst dark pillars of woodland on either side, allowing only a flicker of light to come through.

The little group were silent as they entered the iron gates between fences of rusting wire, the remains of watchtowers positioned at regular intervals. The camp had been partially destroyed amidst the chaos of liberation, but some parts still remained.

The door of the nearest accommodation hut was wide open, hanging from its hinges. Sabine peered inside at trestle beds stacked row upon row above each other in the gloom. A rusting bucket lay just inside the door, next to it an abandoned lump of material that looked as if it might once have been clothing, congealed with damp and rot.

There was nothing there. Nothing terrible or frightening. Just the stark timbers of beds, crammed so close it was almost impossible to move between them. Silence hung there, permeating the shadows, broken now and again by a shaft of faint light stretching down from a hole in the roof, amongst a faint smell of decay. Sabine scarcely breathed, unable to break the stillness. It was as if every emotion, every fear, every despair, every act of kindness between those who'd spent their last hours there still hung in the atmosphere, deep and profound.

They were just normal people, all of them, stripped to their barest humanity, while those who lorded it over them had abandoned theirs. Pity shot through her, along with a cold, hard fury, too profound to be expressed. She was aware of it becoming part of her, part of her lifeblood.

Once, as an idealistic young student, she'd headed for Paris with a headful of dreams of writing about social justice and making the world a better place. The Sabine of those days, talking revolution over coffee and wine in the pavement cafés beneath the Eiffel Tower, would never have believed she'd one day come face to face with evil itself in the shadows of a long-abandoned building. But that old Sabine, despite being nearly broken by years as a rootless refugee, was still there.

She could feel the fire returning, this time tempered by reality. She was no longer a fighter for abstract concepts like beauty and justice. Her fight was real. It had begun amongst the women and children, the unconsidered victims of any conflict, and the stories she'd been told. It was here, now, in the silent testimony to suffering. There was no doubt left. She would fight to tell their stories for as long as she could draw breath. This was no longer simply a way to earn money, or even, as Emil had once dreamed, to be heralded as a Pulitzer prize-winner. This was becoming more and more a vocation.

'It's horrible, isn't it,' said Marie, joining her. 'I wish I'd never come, but I'm glad as well, if that makes sense.'

'Completely,' replied Sabine, turning to smile at her reassuringly.

'M. Perrot and Jean have gone to see the crematorium and what they think is a gas chamber,' said Marie, shuddering. 'I can't bear to. I can't bear to stand where those people stood, just before they died. It's like looking through their eyes. I'm too much of a coward.'

'That's not cowardice,' said Sabine firmly, steering her away from the doorway and its darkness. 'We've all seen so much and been through so much, none of us have many defences left. I think maybe we all know when we come to a point where we need to protect our own hearts.'

'Yes. I suppose so.' Marie brightened. 'I came to say there are still some papers left in one of the offices. Most of the files are empty, I expect taken away, but a couple look as if they were missed. It's all in German. I can't understand a word. You never know, there might be something important, something we can use for a story.'

'I'll come and have a look,' said Sabine, grateful for the distraction.

The files were in a large building which looked as if it had been the main office. Sabine sorted through a small pile of papers that had been stuffed into a cardboard box and abandoned, either by those fleeing the scene of their crimes, or missed in the chaos of the liberators trying to gain as much evidence as possible for any future trial. There was nothing about the life in the camp, not even the names of any inmates. Most were invoices for supplies, wood, timber, lengths of piping. One was for a domestic oven, another for a table and chairs. It sent prickles up her spine to see tokens of everyday life amidst the bleakness of death and deprivation.

She was glad when she reached the final few papers. Again, only invoices, delivery notes ...

She paused, retrieving a piece of paper, holding it in her hand.

'Anything?' said Marie at the door. 'M. Perrot says he's seen enough, he wants to go before anyone reports us as being here.'

'Nothing,' said Sabine. 'I'll put these back, then I'm ready.' Marie vanished. Sabine could hear her chatting to Jean as they got ready to leave. She looked down at the paper in her hands. It was confirmation of delivery of a piece of equipment, signed by the camp commander and the representative of the company, Emil Schongauer. Even if she hadn't recognised the flourish of the signature, his name was there, neatly typed. It referred to equipment for the more efficient conversion of gases ...

She could read no further. She wavered. Emil could have signed the paper at the factory; he might never have been here, never known what it was for ...

'Anything worth photographing?' said Jean, putting his head round the door.

'I don't think so,' said Sabine, looking up. She gasped. The angle was different, the desk had been moved slightly and the swastika torn down from the walls, but surely it wasn't just her imagination.

'You okay?'

'Yes, nothing, just pins and needles.'

'All right then. If there's nothing of interest I'll put these in the car.'

Sabine scarcely heard him, the paper with Emil's signature still in her hand. He'd been here. If she was right, if this was the office in that photograph in the old newspaper, still stashed away at the back of the filing cabinet, then it was proof Emil had been here. He had seen what this place was. He must have known what his new and improved equipment was designed to do. Even with a bottle of wine inside him, Emil couldn't be so blind.

Out in the daylight she could hear the voices of her colleagues, subdued, haunted, but already lightening at the relief of leaving this place behind.

What good would it do? Emil could be dead, or have fled. What good would it do to hand over evidence that he'd been complicit? His was such a small contribution. A mere cog in a machine. She could easily destroy the invoice, and burn the newspaper cutting as soon as she got back.

There might be other evidence of course, but not so immediate, and likely to be overlooked amongst the overwhelming number of cases. Emil wasn't a high-ranking Nazi official, or one of Hitler's inner circle. What good would it do? If she destroyed it, Valérie – and Violette if she were still alive – need never know. Wasn't that what a mother did? Protect her daughters at all cost?

She stood up, crumpling the paper in her hand. Then stopped. She was back in the barracks with its heavy atmosphere of suffering, stifling the light out of the day, cloying with its memories of horror. A cog in a machine. Cogs upon cogs, each one ignoring the rest, each one going home to the warm of family dinners, good wine and the rosy cheeks of children, shutting out what they had done.

Smoothing out the paper again, she called to Jean, who was still loading his equipment into the car. 'There is something after all, Jean. Would you mind taking a photograph of the office? There's something I want to check when we get back.'

'Of course,' he replied, returning. 'Now, which angle would you like, *Madame*?'

PART 4

THIRTY-EIGHT

IRIS

Cornwall, 1964

There was a long silence after Mum had finished speaking.

'People really didn't know?' asked Iris, 'about the concentra-tion camps and the genocide and what happened to the refugees during the war?'

'Only if you came across people who'd experienced it directly. And even then it was hard to believe. There were a few refugees here in St Mabon's as the war went on,' her mother replied. 'And we saw some things in the newspapers and heard about them on the radio. Hardly anyone had a television in those days, remember, and I suspect the government wanted to keep up morale. Besides ...' She hesitated, as if trying to find a way of explaining something so that Iris would understand. 'The thing is, when something like that's happening, something you couldn't have imagined only months before, the only way to keep your sanity is to focus on what's happening around you and what you have to do to keep life going. You don't dwell on the bigger picture. You can't. Especially during that early part of the war, when we knew we could have been invaded at any moment. Sometimes it's best not to know what's going to happen to you just around the corner. It's not cowardice, or avoiding the truth. It's knowing the truth all too well in your heart. The only thing left is to survive.'

'We that are young,' said Iris.

Her mother gave a sad smile. 'Quite.'

'But the war was over,' said Iris. 'You must have been glad it was all behind you.'

'It was strange, when the war was over,' said Mum, sounding wistful. 'We thought that was the end of it, that we'd survived. But things are never that simple. So much had changed. In one way, war makes things simple; you just do what you need to survive. It's afterwards the complexities come in. How to live, how to live well, and not to harm others. And of course, evil's never defeated that easily. I'm afraid, my darling that for all of us, it had only just begun.'

THIRTY-NINE

NORA

Cornwall, 1945

Nora spent the rest of the war at Hope Cottage with Violette, now generally accepted as Iris. She had little time to dwell on her grief as there was too much work to be done at Maltby Abbey, and too many others quietly absorbing their own losses.

As more young woman came to work in the grounds there were never enough beds to accommodate them all, so the second bedroom that had been intended for Pearl was never empty.

By May 1945 the end of the war was finally in sight, with even St Mabon's celebrating Victory in Europe with bonfires.

'Look, the dolphins are back,' said Nora a few mornings after VE day, as she walked back over the cliffs with Iris.

'Dolphins,' said Iris, smiling as the dark shapes slid through the waves.

'It's a whole school.'

'Do dolphins go to school?'

Nora laughed. 'I suppose they must do, darling. That's what

they're called when they're in a group like that. I've no idea why. Maybe Miss Philipson will know. You could always ask.'

Violette nodded, absorbed in following the leaping shapes.

She was a bright little thing. Confident, full of boundless curiosity, already doing well. Nora had found Maltby Abbey strangely empty during Iris's first weeks at the local school. She'd planned to do so much with her precious hours of freedom, but she'd ended up missed her presence.

The school was only a few minutes' walk away, but it was still an absence. She was getting used to the idea, and she knew this was the start of regaining her own freedom and her ability to do so much more, but she missed Iris. This was the very beginning of Iris moving away from her into her own life, becoming the child who would then become the adult; who, one day would take her own path, moving beyond her, into her own future. She might not even stay in Cornwall; so many young people moved away to the towns and cities to find work that was less harsh and better paid than fishing. She wanted with all her heart for Iris to do as well as she could and to follow her dreams.

She breathed in the sea air. It was good to be reminded there were no more submarines lurking around the coast threatening the fishing boats, or an invasion force, poised to destroy their lives forever. She shuddered. The war might be over in Europe but news was emerging of the terrible things that had happened there under Nazi occupation, stories of death camps and whole populations eliminated. No wonder Sabine had been so afraid.

There had been no word from Sabine, no reply to the letter Nora had sent to the chateau telling her they were in Cornwall. There was still a chance the family had survived, but the photographs of ruined towns and lines of refugees brought home the dangers they must have faced.

'Ouch, Mummy. You're squishing me.'

'Sorry, darling.' She eased the tightness of her grip. 'Is that better?'

'Much better,' said Iris solemnly. She turned to watch the dolphins as they vanished out of sight around the bay. 'Do they breathe in water, like fish?'

'I don't think so. I think that's why they come to the surface, to breathe air, like we do.'

'What do they do when they sleep?'

'I don't know.' She smiled down at Iris's expectant face. 'But I think we should find out. Let's ask Miss Maltby if we can borrow her encyclopaedia. That might be able to tell us.'

'Yes please,' said Iris, eagerly.

'And how about if we go to the library on Saturday and see if we can find a book all about dolphins?'

'And whales?'

'And whales. And sharks, and sea urchins and octopuses. Everything.'

'And crocodiles?'

'And crocodiles.' Nora smiled. She still couldn't get over the darting of a child's mind, unbounded by rules and the assumption that was how the world was, and that's how it always would be. It was bringing back her own earliest memories, both sad and happy, of her parents; their presence, for all its annoyances and constraints, so secure and eternal, and Pearl, her constant companion.

She suppressed a shudder. Thank goodness you had no idea of the future, or of what it might bring. Better to live in the moment, like a child. She tried to shut out the images in her mind of refugees, of the women and children trudging the roads of Europe, of the millions of displaced and dead. And the haunted skeletal faces of the survivors in extermination camps. Of the piles of the dead. One day Iris would need to learn about it all, and all she'd lost. But not now. Not yet.

'How about we make pancakes?' she said hastily to distract

herself. 'The hens are laying and we've still got some of last year's honey.'

'Mmmm,' grinned Iris, who had a sweet tooth that could never quite be satisfied by their sugar ration. She raced on ahead as they reached the gate into Maltby Abbey, Nora following with her bag and cardigan.

She would miss this, she thought, as she halted in front of the Abbey while Iris joined a gaggle of children at the little pond, fishing for minnows with their nets and jam jars. She would miss this community, this life she'd built for herself that allowed her to take care of Iris. She couldn't imagine a world without either of them.

But they would survive, she told herself firmly. Wherever they might find themselves next, as the world changed again with the coming of peace, they would survive.

FORTY

SABINE

France, 1945

Sabine saw Emil for the last time in a *commissariat* in a small, dusty town near Limoges, where he'd been taken for trial.

It was a journey she knew she had to make the moment she heard he'd been arrested on a small private airfield nearby. One of her journalist friends told her that, along with several others fleeing the collapse of the Third Reich, he'd chartered a plane and pilot to take him to Spain, then onto South America. Where, exactly, none of them seemed to know. Yet another kingdom of grandiose dreams, no doubt built on the back of those they saw as inferior to themselves.

'Mme Schongauer?' said the *gendarme* who greeted her.

'Yes,' she murmured. Already the name did not feel hers. From this day forward, she'd promised herself, she would never use it again.

She found Emil sitting at a table in a small, airless room, devoid of pictures or any other furniture. Her stomach contracted at the sight of him, head bent over, staring intently at a postcard in his hands. She was glad he wasn't handcuffed and was wearing his ordinary clothes. He was far too lowly a culprit amongst the chaos and overwhelming numbers of those who had been part of the Nazi regime to be considered dangerous. He would most probably not warrant more than a few years behind bars, with the prisons already overflowing with the guilty to be processed.

'Sabine,' he said, looking up with a smile as she approached. 'I hoped you'd come to see me.' His face fell slightly. 'No Valérie?'

'This is no place for a child,' she replied. His eyes slid away from hers. So he hadn't forgotten that time he'd tried to snatch their daughter away. She wondered if he saw this as her way of punishing him for so nearly depriving her of Valérie. She couldn't tell him that she was beyond punishment, she had shut it from her mind, unable to even consider what might have happened to Valérie had he succeeded.

There had been no young woman with him when he had been detained, and she had a terrible suspicion that, heading to his new life, he might not have wished to burden himself with the demands of a small girl. If she thought about it too closely in his presence, she could never keep the cool head she needed to face him.

'Next time then,' he said. She didn't reply. What was there to say? His mouth tightened. He'd lost the comfortable portliness of the photographs, his face now gaunt and lined, the scalp showing clearly through the greying remnants of his hair. She could no longer see the handsome, passionate young man she'd fallen in love with, so full of eager ambition. That was a lifetime ago. A lifetime upon lifetimes ago.

'They won't keep me inside for long,' he said. 'Just a formality. It's what the winners do. There're so many of us they can't deal with us all, there's no place to house us, they're already turning a blind eye out of necessity and letting some go free. A few years, maybe even months, and I'll be out, you'll see. I'm a businessman doing my job, we're not the kind they want, even to make an example of.' His eyes returned to the postcard. 'Still, I'd like to see Valérie. She must have forgotten what I look like. It's not fair on the child to keep her from me until we become a family again.'

She'd been expecting raving and ranting, but not this calm assumption that nothing had changed. 'A family?'

'I still have contacts, we can start again.' A sly look came over his face. 'I may even have some things stashed away where no one can find them, just in case. Maman will look after you until I get out. You and Valérie and Violette. We'll be a family again.'

That was a jolt, hearing her name on his lips. 'Violette?'

'The operation in Paris,' he said impatiently, in the manner of a man unaccustomed to such stupidity amongst his acquaintances. 'Maman said you took her there to be healed, just like you said. So she could be just like Valérie.'

'The operation was cancelled, Emil. I sent Violette to England for safety. We talked about this when we were last at Chateau Saint-Céré. Surely you remember?'

He returned to the postcard, frowning. 'But the operation can be done now. We can find a hospital. Like I said, I have the money, I can afford to pay for any amount of surgery. Maman said the doctors told you there was no sign of mental impairment. That's the main thing.'

He seemed to have blanked from his mind everything that had taken place during the long years of the war. When she'd telephoned to make the appointment she'd been warned he was sometimes confused, as if he didn't know quite where he was, or even why he was being detained. Is that how you live with yourself? With being a monster? With the evil you have done?

But she couldn't be kind, whatever his state of mind. Not now. Not ever. She hardened her heart against the memory of the man he used to be, the warmth of the body entwined so intimately with hers, and the new life they'd brought into this uncertain world. Her heart was stretched too thin.

'I don't know where Violette is, Emil,' she said. 'I haven't seen her since the first day of the war.'

'But she's safe?'

'I don't know. I hope so. But we may never know. I sent her away with a woman I barely knew, like I told you. At the time it seemed the only way she could survive.'

'Sent her away?' He was indignant. 'You sent our daughter amongst strangers?'

'I wasn't the only one,' retorted Sabine, fighting down a sudden wall of anger that threatened to overwhelm her. 'Remember the *Kindertransport*, the children put onto trains by parents certain they would never know their fate? I met more than one young boy on the road who'd been told by their families to simply go. I met mothers who'd been separated from their children in the chaos, and children who'd been left to fend for themselves. And I saw what happened to them.'

'But I'd have looked after you,' he said, as if he hadn't heard her. 'I had a position, money, influence. I'd have made sure you were safe.'

'That's not the point, is it?' she replied angrily. She would give anything to get through to him just once. To reach the Emil who'd once been there, just to know she hadn't been mistaken in loving him all those years ago. 'You knew what was happening, Emil. I know you saw it with your own eyes.'

He looked up. 'So it was you.'

'I beg your pardon?'

'Who handed over the newspaper photographs and the paperwork. No one would tell me, but Karl was certain it was you. The final revenge, he called it.'

She felt a stab of fear. 'Is Karl here?'

'Of course. They're trying to charge him with all sorts of ridiculous things. We were so close to getting on that plane.

Some busybody had circulated that photograph you must have given them. Someone tipped them off. The police were waiting for us at the airport. That's how they got Karl as well. He said he came across you when you were at the border and tried to help you, but you refused. You might at least have let him help you, for the girls' sake.'

'Help me? Emil, the last thing he wanted was to help me.'

He frowned impatiently. 'You never did like him. You never gave him a chance.'

'What?' The tight knot inside her belly abruptly burst, evaporated into nothing, leaving her in a state of detached calm. There was no point trying to explain, he believed what he wanted to believe. There was indeed a kind of madness inside him that would never let her through. Just being next to him was stifling the life out of her. She took a deep breath. 'I'm sorry, Emil, there's no easy way to say this, but I came to tell you that I'm divorcing you. I thought it better it came from me.'

'You've met someone else,' he said with no sign of emotion, face towards the window. 'Karl said you would.'

'No, Emil. This is nothing to do with anyone else. That would be the easy way out. This is between you and me. Our lives will always be separate from now on. Surely it's better for both of us if we're free.'

'But you'll bring Valérie to see me. You've no right to deprive a daughter of her father.'

'I've thought long and hard about this. I'm sorry, but the answer is no. Valérie, and Violette if she's still alive and I can find her, are the ones I want to protect now. All I want is for them to be able to live their lives unburdened by the past. I'll tell them one day, when they're ready, but I'm not having the knowledge of what they've come from darkening their child-hood. I want them to live free.'

'Karl said you'd punish me,' he said, turning to watch her, eyes narrowed. 'He told me you'd tell lies and find ways to make me pay for not taking you with me to Freiburg and for having Helga by my side instead.'

'Oh for goodness' sake, Emil.' Exasperation finally overcame her determination to be civilised. 'Can't you just, for once in your life, consider someone other than yourself? They are children. *Our* children. They'll live for years after we're gone. Don't you want the best for them?'

She expected an explosion of rage, but instead he was silent, face turned away. The postcard dropped from his hand, sailing gently to the floor where it lay face up to reveal a picture of Paris, their favourite pavement café in the shadow of the Eiffel Tower where they'd spent so much of their courtship and those brief first months of their marriage.

Grief made her ruthless. Grief for the past, for the Emil she'd lost, for the life together they'd once dreamed of. For their children. For the things that might have been.

'Didn't you ever think that one of those children your efficient machinery was designed to suffocate might have been Violette? Or that you and I, in a different world, might have been the ones to be shoved inside gas chambers, to be annihilated, or shot, or starved, simply because somebody could. Because they no longer saw us as human?' He bent to retrieve the postcard, muttering something under his breath, but she was beyond listening. 'If there's one thing I learnt along the road, with all those refugees, it's that no one in this world is worth nothing. When it comes down to it, we're all the same. Every single child you caused to die of poisoning, violence or neglect were Valérie and Violette. And for me, that will never change.'

He looked up, eyes dark, brows drawn together in the manner she knew so well. Somewhere inside the shell he'd become, she knew she'd finally reached him. The glance that met hers was briefly from the Emil she'd once known. Then it was gone.

He reached for her hand. Whatever her harsh words, she

could read his thought processes, a woman always forgives, always understands. It's what women are.

'Sabine ...' he pleaded.

She shook her head. 'I'm sorry. I've seen too much, you'll never make me change my mind. This is for me, as well as for our daughters. So we can live our lives as they should be. Goodbye, Emil.'

With that she shot out into the corridor, tears flooding down her face.

'Sabine!' A woman sitting on a bench a little way down jumped to her feet. 'Emil said you were coming to see him. I knew it'd be all right.'

Sabine hastily blinked away her tears, her eyes focusing on her mother-in-law. She could easily have passed by without recognising her. Claudette had shrunk from being in the prime of life to a sliver of a woman, the bones of her face jutting out beneath the flesh, eyes unnaturally large.

'It's good to see you,' she said awkwardly, for a lack of anything else to say.

'Of course, it's terrible what they're telling people about him. Terrible. Awful. I knew you wouldn't believe it, my dear. You know him too well. He was just doing the best to support his family, to give us a good life. No one knew those dreadful things were happening. No one. And I'm sure half of them aren't true, it's the British and the Americans determined to punish us now they've won.'

'I have to go,' muttered Sabine.

'And the girls?' Claudette grasped her arm, her face hungry. 'You kept them safe, my little Valérie and Violette? I still think of them as babies, they must be little girls by now.'

'Valérie is safe,' said Sabine. 'She's with my mother.'

'And Violette?'

'I don't know.' Pity went through Sabine. Claudette would hear it from Emil, if not from her. 'I sent her away,' she said gently. 'With a friend. Someone I was sure I could trust, even though I hadn't known her for long. I hope they got through the war, I hope they're safe. As soon as I can, I'm going to London to find her.'

Claudette was horrified. 'You sent our baby all the way to London? To live amongst strangers?'

Sabine bit her lip. She hadn't meant to say so much. But for all her faults, Claudette loved her grandchildren, both of them. She couldn't be circumspect with the truth as she'd been with Emil. Faced with another woman's love for two small children, she was unable to lie.

'Believe me, I wouldn't have done it if I hadn't been so desperate. I still don't know whether it was the right thing to do. But at the time, it was the only thing I could do.'

Claudette embraced her, Sabine could feel her frail body racked with suppressed sobs.

'I know you'd do your best, my dear. I know you'd do anything for those girls. One day you'll find Violette, you'll be together. I can feel it in my bones. Then you'll bring them to me.'

Sabine kissed her. She might not be able to see Claudette ever again, for fear of what her loyalty to Emil might cause her to do once the raw emotion had passed. But she would do her best to let her know if she found Violette. It was the least she could do.

A sudden uneasy sense of being watched made her turn abruptly. A prisoner was being brought in from outside. It was Karl, in civilian clothes, eyes bloodshot, face gaunt, yet at the same time puffy with an unnatural pallor. He didn't say a word, but stood there, eyes on her face, boring into her. As he was shuffled along towards the cells his eyes never left her, fixed on hers with an expression of such intensity, such loathing, she would never forget.

Emil had told her Karl suspected she'd given the information that had prevented their escape to South America. Emil would find a way of letting him know that he was right, and that, in doing so, she'd ensured Karl himself would face justice.

He would find her, those silent eyes told her. He wouldn't be held in that overcrowded police station, or in the equally overcrowded prisons, forever. One day, perhaps soon, he'd be released and then, however long it took, he would find her, and those she loved, and this time he would appease the darkest recesses of his twisted soul by watching their slow destruction.

Sabine kissed Claudette, who'd barely noticed Karl, and shot out into the blazing heat of the day, blinded by sunlight and the brilliance of roses winding themselves around the water fountain at the centre of the square. She splashed her hands and face with cold water to wash off as best she could the last remnants of encounters with her past.

There was nothing she could do about Karl, a true madman, whose cruelty and thirst for power over others had been fed by the war. But she'd do everything in her power to keep her children safe. Squaring her shoulders, she strode to the little side street where her battered Citroën was parked, and set off as fast as she dared to rejoin Mémé and Maman, already on the way in their trusty cart towards the Chateau Saint-Céré, to finally take Valérie home.

FORTY-ONE

NORA

Cornwall, 1945

'They sound happy,' said Miss Maltby one afternoon as Nora sat in the sun with a cup of tea before starting on the evening meal.

'So they are,' replied Nora, watching Iris playing with several other children on the rope swings hanging from a sturdy branch of one of the large ornamental pines, their excited chatter spilling into the still air.

Miss Maltby sighed. 'I'll be sorry to see them go. Odd, isn't it? We've been such a tight little community here during the war. I shall miss it. And I hate the thought of this old fossil being returned to mothballs, like it was between the wars, all purpose gone, just a monument to my ancestors. But life must go on. And you, my dear?'

'I'm not sure.' A terrible emptiness gaped inside her. Was this a hint? Was this Miss Maltby's way of telling her she'd no longer be needed now the volunteers were gradually drifting back to their old lives, or at least a new version of their lives?

There was a flutter of panic in her belly. She'd always known she'd have to find another position at some point, that their lives here would only be for as long as the war lasted. She knew all too well how few jobs were available in Cornwall, but she had to find something that would allow her to support the two of them.

She'd come round to the possibility of having to move back to the capital, but it would mean disruption for Iris just as she'd settled into a routine at school and was starting to make more friends. And Nora would miss it here. There was nothing for her in London. Even the thought of being in those familiar streets was painful. Her life was here, in Cornwall, with the hint of fish in the air and the wide-open skies. Perhaps she could find something in Exeter?

'I see.' Miss Maltby was staring up at the house. 'The thing is, my dear, I'm going to have to do something with this monstrosity. Ironic, isn't it, that one war almost destroyed it by killing the heir, only for another war to preserve it, for a while at least, for its ability to produce food. Now that's all gone. Imports will start again before long, and rationing can't last forever. The sensible thing would be to sell, of course.'

Nora had been expecting it, but it was still a blow to the stomach, the future suddenly terrifying. 'I understand.'

'I've made enquiries. There's a businessman from London prepared to snap it up.'

'That's good, isn't it?'

Miss Maltby snorted. 'He won't pay me half what it's worth due to the state of the building and believing I must be desperate. And dealing with a woman, of course. It's quite clear what he'd do with the place. He made a fortune creating a chain of hotels before the war. It's clear he's buying cheap while he still can. He's taking a risk assuming people will want to come on holiday again. Which got me thinking. This place is the only asset I have. If I sell off some of the land instead, I can invest in turning it into a hotel myself. In which case, I shall be looking for a cook.'

'A cook.' Nora's heart began to race.

'A chef, in fact. It struck me that if I made Maltby Abbey famous for its food as well as its surroundings, that would make it stand out amongst the rest. I was hoping you'd consider staying on. You're an excellent chef and you know how to make the most of the rations and what we can produce here. The gardens will give us an advantage, being able to produce our own food. It might fail, I'm prepared for that. But on the other hand, it might prove a success. I understand it's not exactly the bright lights for a young woman, so I'll understand if you say no. Just something for you to think about.'

'I don't need to think about it!' She wasn't letting this chance slip through her fingers. 'I don't need bright lights, especially not with a child to think about. The answer is yes. Thank you. You've no idea how much this means to me. Thank you.'

A look of anxiety passed over Miss Maltby's face. 'I should warn you that it might not survive, with times being so hard for everyone. I might yet have to sell.'

Nora smiled at her, warmth rushing through every part of her body. 'I'll take that chance. And besides, between us, I'm sure we can make it a success.'

At last, she had a place to call home and work that she loved. Over the next weeks Nora cooked for the few remaining volunteers and helped Miss Maltby clean the Abbey from top to bottom while Iris was at school. She compiled lists of repairs for the local carpenter, decided the threadbare curtains in the dining room needed replacing and began planning menus for their prospective guests.

It was like the day the blackout curtains came down. A reassurance that the war really was over, that life could resume, and that there was a future. This was only the beginning. If visitors did return to Cornwall, there would be a renewed need for cafés and restaurants. She might finally be able to use her training with Mme Godeaux from those weeks in Paris, a lifetime ago. But this time not for anyone else. This time it would be for her. For her and Iris.

It didn't even mean they'd necessarily stay in Cornwall forever. Iris already showed an intelligence and curiosity that might require them to find a larger school offering broader opportunities than those offered locally. But even if they did eventually move to London, it would be on their terms, and Nora swore to herself she would one day return to Cornwall.

Finally, Nora began to relax and feel more optimistic about the future.

FORTY-TWO

SABINE

France, 1945

Sabine had never thought she'd see the Chateau Saint-Céré again. She could scarcely believe it when she finally paused, hand on the twisted and rusted gate, gazing up at the familiar walls.

Among the overgrown and neglected grounds, the chateau rose up much as it had always done. But even from here she could see several of the shutters were missing, others hanging precariously from their hinges. She could make out broken panes and detritus accumulating amongst the fading autumn leaves.

'Well, at least it's still standing,' said Maman.

'I suppose that's something,' rejoined Mémé as Sabine pulled back the gates, which moved unwillingly, allowing the cart to creak and rumble its way through, followed by the Citroën. Safely on the other side, Sabine jumped out again to pull the gates back into place, before urging the little van in Mémé's dusty wake. As they reached the house Poupée slid past her through the opening door of the Citroën, nose to the ground as she raced gleefully in search of rabbits.

'We're home,' said Sabine, lifting Valérie down from her seat.

'Home,' said Valérie, holding her hand tightly.

'This is where I lived when I was a little girl,' she said, smiling reassuringly. 'Look, Poupée is happy. She knows we're safe here, this is where we will live for as long as we like.'

'Poupée.' Valérie's solemn little face broke into a smile as the rough-coated little dog arrived with a stick in her mouth and settled down at their feet to chew contentedly.

'Such a mess,' said Maman, clambering down stiffly from the cart, her voice breaking a little. 'Heaven knows how much of it is left inside. I swear this is even worse than the last war. I can't believe we're going to have to start all over again.'

'At least it's still here,' said Sabine.

'And let's face it, the place was in need of improvement,' added her grandmother, swinging down to join them. 'Sometimes it's hard to sweep away the past unless someone else does the job for you.'

Sabine laughed. 'Trust you to look on the bright side, Mémé.'

'Yes, well, someone has to round here. And once Guillaume is back on his feet, we'll be able to get started. But that's for us. You have your career to consider.'

'I can't leave you to deal with this!' exclaimed Sabine. It felt a miracle that Guillaume had survived the war, and had finally tracked them down to the refugee camp to let them know he'd been injured in the last weeks of the fighting and was being treated in a hospital in Paris. They still had little idea whether her brother would ever recover enough to take on the physical demands of restoring the land to its former productivity.

Sabine sighed. 'I'm not sure I even want to live in Paris

again. The most important thing is for us all to have a home and for Valérie to be settled.'

'But you also have to earn an income,' said Mémé, 'now you have no husband to support you.' She gazed around at the ruined fields, the shell of a house that had once been a home. 'It could take us years to make this place provide for all our needs once more. We will all need to work. At least you have a chance to make a proper living. You never were a farm girl at heart.'

'Maybe,' said Sabine, an unexpected emptiness opening up inside. Returning to the chateau was not the triumph of good over evil she had clung to through the dark years of the war.

They had survived. Amidst such suffering, and death on an industrial scale, they had survived. Even Guillaume would soon be released from hospital to recuperate at the chateau.

'Come on,' she said, taking Valérie's hand. 'Let's see what the soldiers have left.' With Poupée trotting along behind, they followed Mémé inside.

'Oh my Lord,' said Maman as they pushed aside the broken remains of the door. They'd been warned as they passed through the shattered remains of the village that soldiers had been stationed there for several months. The table was still there, covered in empty tins and bottles of wine, but most of the chairs had been broken and the sideboard had been smashed for firewood, its charred remains now cold in the fireplace, Maman's prized plates and dishes were scattered on the floor.

'Bastards,' she exclaimed. 'After we'd managed to keep that crockery in one piece last time. It's been passed down through the family for generations.'

'As long as enough has remained for us to eat from,' said Mémé philosophically. 'Besides, tastes change. With all that destruction we passed on the way back, and the things Sabine has reported on, things we could never have imagined, it seems the world needs to be built again. Now might be as good a time as any to start.'

Change had come to stay whether they wished it or not, Sabine acknowledged as they inspected the rubbish-strewn remains of their home. All that mattered was that Valérie was safe and happy, could grow up with a bright future and be whoever she wanted to be. To do that, to secure the future of the chateau, one of them had to earn enough to support them, at least until they could get the routine of crops and animals in full swing again, and Guillaume was strong enough to take over.

Sabine paused at the door of her bedroom. The bed she'd slept in as a child and had later shared with Emil on their brief visits to her family was still there, but the rest had been ransacked. One of her shoes lay abandoned on the floor and the wardrobe door was half off, revealing that all her clothes had gone.

Well, at least we still have our winter coats, she told herself wryly. That was the important thing, to be able to keep warm. Like everyone else, they had lived with so little over the past years, they were all accustomed to being stripped down to the bare essentials. They could live that way for a bit longer while they got back on their feet.

Sabine sighed. She hated the thought of being away from them, and most of all from Valérie. Yet at the same time she couldn't imagine living without the adrenalin of a deadline, or hearing stories that women would only tell to other women; many never made it into print but were stored in her tape recorder, her photographs and notebook upon notebook of shorthand. She'd applied to join several newspapers and magazines as a journalist but even if she was unsuccessful, she could still continue her work as a freelancer until she found something more permanent.

'There's a letter for you,' called Mémé from the kitchen. 'Must be recent, the mice haven't got to it. Looks like it's from England.'

'England?' Sabine raced downstairs, heart in her mouth,

and took the envelope. 'It's from Howard. He said he'd find out what he could about Nora once he got to London; the Red Cross must have told him we were on our way home.'

She tore it open, reading eagerly.

'Well?' demanded Maman, appearing at the door of the kitchen, Valérie on one hip. 'What does he say?'

'He found the address,' said Sabine, sitting down on the nearest chair as the room around her began to sway. 'But there was nothing there.'

'What do you mean by nothing?' demanded Mémé.

'It was just waste ground. A bomb site.' She swallowed, trying to take in Howard's words. He was trying to be kind, but there was no glossing over the destruction he'd found, and they'd worked together too long dealing with loss and grief, and respected each other too much, for him to hide anything from her. 'He says the people he spoke to told him the Anderson shelter had a direct hit. No one survived.' Her voice wavered. 'One woman told him there was a disabled child in there.'

'Oh my Lord,' said Mémé, taking the one unbroken chair at the other side of the table.

'It still might not be them,' said Maman. 'Until you have absolute proof, there's still hope. Surely Professor Jackson isn't going to leave it there?'

Sabine returned to the letter, fighting to take in the information. 'You're right, Maman. He says he's going to try and track down any surviving records, or anyone who knew them. He's found the address of a neighbour who's now living in Hammersmith who might know more. But he says the records are difficult to find. So many have been destroyed.'

'Then there's still hope,' said Mémé firmly. 'It's bound to take time, my dear, and the professor must only have limited time because of his own work, but he struck me as the sort never to leave a stone unturned. If Nora and Violette are still alive, he'll find them.'

'Let's hope so,' said Sabine. Across the room she met her mother's eyes, glossy with tears, but trying to remain cheerful for Valérie's sake. The waiting, the not knowing, was the worst bit. But there was nothing else they could do. If anyone could find out what had really happened to Nora and Violette, it was Howard Jackson, who'd spent the war standing up to authority on behalf of those whose lives hung in the balance. All they could do, torn between hope and dread, was wait.

Despite their exhaustion, the family started the next morning, clearing away the bottles, the remains of meals that had attracted a veritable plague of rats and mice, and worn-out boots and equipment. Over the next few days they heaped everything they could burn into a large pile; the rest they buried as far away from the house as possible. At last the rooms were clear enough to be able to start removing the years of ingrained filth. The kitchen was scrubbed from top to bottom, the grime removed from the tiles of the kitchen stove and the table, and all the unbroken crockery they could find was returned to the cupboards.

'Well, at least now we can cook without poisoning ourselves,' said Maman dryly as Valérie helped her clean carrots and potatoes for that night's stew, and Sabine cleared the last piles of papers and old shirts from the small room at the top of the chateau, lugging them down to feed into the bonfire.

As she pulled away a particularly vile-smelling pair of army trousers, along with bandages stained with congealed blood heaped next to the fireplace, she found a stack of German newspapers scattered amongst the remains of floorboards to be used as kindling. The first few toppled over. As she reached for them, her eye fell on the last pages, open at a photograph of a group of party officials collected around Hitler, all eyes turned to a newly unveiled statue.

Sabine tore the page to pieces, shoving it with the rest of the detritus into the large bag she used to cart her next load of offerings for the bonfire. She could smell the smoke in the evening air, the crackle as Mémé threw on the remains of a broken wardrobe, sending flames shooting up in an orange glow.

Now all that was left was a collection of envelopes and old letters, scrumpled up, ready for the fire. She paused. Perhaps she should keep them? But they were in a vile state, half eaten by mice, most of them water-damaged and unreadable. She began shoving them into the bag with the rest.

It was the stamp that caught her eye. An English stamp. She dragged out the envelope. There'd been no post since the occupation, but surely that was Nora's handwriting? Someone had opened it. A shiver went down her spine. If they'd stayed, could that have been used against them? Would that innocent contact with an Englishwoman have been enough to send them all to the nearest concentration camp? It had arrived the very day they'd left. To her frustration, the envelope was empty. She searched hastily through, but there was nothing. She looked again, more closely. At least she could try and make out the postmark. This time she could feel something caught inside. Something that must have been missed.

She pulled out a black and white postcard of a grand mansion, a stretch of sea in the background. She turned it over. There was Nora's familiar writing. This was where she was working, it said, where they would be safe.

Scarcely daring to breathe, Sabine turned the photograph to face her. There it was, clearly printed in one corner. Maltby Abbey, St Mabon's, Cornwall.

Cornwall.

'Maman!' Sabine raced down the stairs.

'What is it?'

'They weren't in London.' At least not unless by some terrible twist of fate they had returned. The suspense, now she had renewed hope, was unbearable. 'Nora and Violette. They weren't in London. They were in Cornwall. Far away from the city. By the sea.' She held out the postcard. 'Nora sent us this to let us know where they were. Thank heaven the soldiers left before they could use it to light the fire.'

'It doesn't mean they're still there, darling. It was years ago. So much could have happened.'

'I understand that.' Sabine's heart was racing, caught between joy and fear. 'But at least this gives us a chance to find out if they've survived. It's such a grand house, Howard must be able to find the address. I'll write to him straight away. Maman, just think, there's still hope we can bring Violette home.'

FORTY-THREE

NORA

Cornwall, 1945

On a sunny afternoon a few weeks later, Nora returned with Iris on the coastal path to Maltby Abbey to find a stranger walking towards them. He was tall and fair haired, wearing a brown corduroy jacket, worn thin with use, with a canvas ruck-sack slung over one shoulder, an Ordnance Survey map in his hand.

'Excuse me,' he said in an accent she couldn't quite place. 'I seem to have missed the way. Could you possibly direct me to Maltby Abbey?'

'You're nearly there. If you go through the kissing gate it'll take you straight to the front of the house.'

'Good grief!' Kissing gate forgotten, Nora found the stranger gazing down at Iris, who was looking up at him with her usual open curiosity.

'We're late,' she muttered, grasping the little girl's hand.

'I'm sorry, I didn't mean to startle you. It wasn't what I expected, that's all. She is the very image—' At the look on Nora's face he came to a halt. 'Of a little girl I knew in France.'

'Knew?'

'I met Sabine and her family during the war, when I was working for the American Red Cross. You must be Nora Herridge?'

'Maybe,' she replied warily.

'I'm sorry, I should have sent a letter to warn you first, but when Sabine wrote me—'

'Sabine? You mean she's alive?'

'Sure. She found your postcard of Maltby Abbey when they returned to the Chateau Saint-Céré.'

'Oh my goodness.' It was like a blow to the stomach, relief that the family had survived, but at the same time a terrible sense of impending loss. 'And you came all the way to Cornwall to find us?'

'It seemed only fair. I was the one who told her you'd most likely been killed with your family in London. You and the child.'

A jolt went through her, like a knife. 'Poor Sabine! That must have broken her heart.'

'It felt only right to come here myself to see if I could find you, and reassure myself with my own eyes before I raised her hopes again.' He cleared his throat. 'I didn't intend to spring this on you. I'm Professor Jackson, I've booked a room at the Abbey for the night.'

'Oh,' said Nora. She'd seen the name that morning among the guests who'd booked for dinner. Professor Howard Jackson, Department of History, University of London. Strange how a meaningless name on a hotel register could change your life.

Professor Jackson was gazing at Iris again, this time with more than a tinge of sadness. 'And I suppose I thought it might be less of a shock if I was able to break it to you gently, not all at once. If you see what I mean? I had a daughter once,' he added. 'Cora. She only survived her mother for a few hours ...' He was silent for a moment. 'If she'd lived, she wouldn't have been that much older than this little one. Even now, after all these years, I still think of her every day.'

'I see,' said Nora, feeling his kindness, his understanding of her imminent loss, like a stab to the heart, telling her of the future. She had a wild urge to grab Iris and run, head for the Outer Hebrides or some such remote place. If only she'd never sent that postcard! If only Professor Jackson had never existed. If only they'd never been found.

She pulled herself together. This wasn't about her, it was about Iris and the family she might have lost forever. Her real family. The one she had no right in the world to keep her from a moment longer than was necessary. And it was about Sabine, who'd handed over her baby when there was no other choice, and must have lived the long years of the war not knowing if she'd ever see her again.

'You have no real claim,' she told herself silently. 'You never did. None at all.'

Professor Jackson's eyes were still resting on her face. 'I saw what had happened to the house in London.'

She couldn't quite repress the grief, even now. 'I'm not the only one to lose a family during the war.'

'But it doesn't make it any easier.'

'No.'

'Mummy?' Iris had lost interest in the conversation and was tugging at her hand. 'Mummy, can we go home now, please? I'm hungry.'

'Yes of course, darling. Professor Jackson is coming with is. He's staying in one of the guest rooms at Maltby Abbey.'

'The one we picked flowers for this morning?'

'That's the one. They looked lovely.'

Iris's attention was back fully on the visitor. 'What are you a professor of?'

'Shhhh, don't be nosy,' said Nora.

'That's okay.' Howard was smiling down at her inquisitive face. 'History. I teach and I write books about history.'

'Story books?'

'Not exactly. Although they do have stories in them,' he added hastily as her face fell.

'Kings and queens and princesses?'

'Sometimes. And ordinary folk, too.'

Iris pulled a face. 'Ordinary.'

'Ah, now that's the thing. If you look, really look, no life is ordinary. Far from it. We all have stories to tell. Happy ones, sad ones and some in between. Those are the ones I find really fascinating.' He shook his head. 'I can't get over it. They're so completely alike. If it wasn't for the language ...' He met Nora's eyes again. 'Well, that's for another day.' He fell into step beside them. 'Now, young lady, how about I tell you some of the stories I'm researching just now, from a long time ago before people even had houses ...'

Once the evening meal was over in the little restaurant and the diners were settled into comfortable armchairs to chat with Miss Maltby over their coffees and brandies, Nora finally removed her apron and took her own coffee out onto the terrace.

'Okay if I join you?' said Professor Jackson, hesitating at the open door.

'Yes, of course, Professor. Please do.'

'Howard, please. My title makes me sound like a stuffed windbag, which I promise you I'm not. Or at least I try not to be.'

'Howard,' said Nora, returning his smile.

He disappeared, returning a few minutes later with a bottle of wine and two glasses. 'I don't mean to presume, but if you've spent time in France, I'm pretty sure you drink wine, and your red wine sauce was delicious, so I hope ...'

'Thank you.'

He squinted at the bottle. 'I can't vouch for its quality, but at least it's French. I'll brave it if you will?'

Nora laughed. 'I think it's better than most you'll find in English hotels. Miss Maltby has contacts in Bordeaux and she knows her wine. She isn't one to be fobbed off with any old rubbish.'

'Perfect.' He uncorked the bottle with ease, splashing the dark liquid into the glasses.

This was no time to be ladylike. Nora downed her wine, feeling the alcohol hit her brain like a wave. Howard quietly refilled her glass and sat back, gazing out over the broad sweep of the bay where pleasure boats had returned, their sails catching the fiery glow of the sun, reflected in the clouds strung out across the horizon.

'Beautiful,' he said at last. 'I promised myself I'd make it to Cornwall one day. My grandmother came from just outside St Ives. I promised Mom I'd find the family farm and the church where the Kelynacks are buried. Generations of them, so she said. Strange feeling to know that a place like this, one you've never seen before, is part of you.'

'I'm sure it is.'

'Walking through the village, I couldn't help wondering if I shared blood with anyone I passed. It's just as strange to think my grandmother's eyes would have seen all this once. She wanted to come back for one last time, but then the war came and she never got the chance. She always told me to grab life and run with it while you can.'

'She was right,' said Nora. 'I didn't think about it until I was on that train from Paris the day war broke out. I never thought the world could change so suddenly, or that my life could end at any time. Gives you a different perspective.'

'You can say that again.'

She eyed him. 'I see from the register you're booked in for

several weeks. I don't expect you'll need that now you've found us.'

'On the contrary.' He gave a wry smile. 'I'm afraid this wasn't simply to find you and Iris, although I did hope I'd be able to track you down. When I found out Maltby Abbey was just outside St Ives it gave me the push I needed.' He took a thoughtful sip of wine. 'To be honest, I've been wanting to take time away. I'm not settling back into university life the way I imagined. I worked with the Red Cross out in France for most of the war. That's how I met Sabine, she was my translator for a while.' He was silent for a moment, eyes gazing out to sea. 'I suppose it all catches up with you, in the end. All the things you've seen, the lives that have been destroyed.'

'I'm sure it does,' said Nora. 'I think we've all been changed, living through something like that. It must have been far worse when you were dealing with it every day.'

'I hate what human beings can do to each other,' he said vehemently. 'And at the same time, I love their kindness, their compassion, and the way they look after each other under the very worst of circumstances. That's the part I want to remember out of all this, not the rest.'

'Then hopefully you will,' she replied.

'Maybe. I just need to find a way to do it.'

'So you'll go back to America?'

'That was my first thought. But I feel at home in England. Must be my good Cornish blood coming out,' he added wryly. 'I suppose you can't ever truly run away, however far you travel, not in the end.' There was a moment's silence. 'Did you always want to be a chef?'

'From the moment I started the course in Paris,' she replied. 'That's when I really got to know Sabine. I had no idea then how much those few months would change my life.'

'I suppose you could go and work wherever you like, now that ...' He came to a halt.

'Maybe.' Pain shot through her, along with a touch of panic. Iris had been the centre of her life, and everything she did, for the past six years. She couldn't imagine existing without her. What was she going to do? She felt hollow inside. Returning to a career in London would at least fill the empty days, bring noise to the silent evenings. Or maybe not. 'I've been happy here, despite everything. I'm not sure what ambition is any more, apart from living a good life. I have a feeling I wouldn't fit in anymore in a London kitchen.'

'Ah.' He cleared his throat. 'I see.'

'And anyhow, not many kitchens would ever allow a woman to be a chef. I'd be stuck prepping vegetables and offal for the rest of my life. Miss Maltby's got far more vision. I love it here. I even love working my way round rationing and finding solutions that don't always involve turnips or cabbage. I have to confess I like being in control of what I do.'

'That sounds excellent to me. In fact, the best choice.'

She put down her barely touched glass. 'I'm sorry, but I need to go. Morwenna, the girl who looks after Iris – I mean Violette – when I'm working late will need to get home soon.'

'I should go up to my room, too.'

He was too tactful to remind her that he had a letter to write. The unspoken truth hung in the air between them. She paused. He was a good man. And besides, she'd barely asked him how he knew Sabine, or what had happened to her and her family during the war. It had felt too real, too close to the reality of her losing Iris, who was already becoming Violette again, bit by bit. But she longed to know. If neither of them made the first move, they'd most likely never come across each other once his letter was written and Sabine was on her way. It struck Nora that she'd very much like to see Professor Jackson again.

'It doesn't look as if either of us are big drinkers,' she said. 'Look, if you like, I'll ask them to put the bottle behind the bar. I'm working tomorrow evening. Perhaps you'd like to join me afterwards? Morwenna won't mind staying an extra half hour or so if I let her mum know in advance.' She'd never thought she could be so bold. Forward, that's what Mum would have called her, she thought with a sad smile. 'Of course, I'll understand if you prefer to stay in St Ives a bit later.'

He smiled. 'And miss the best restaurant in town? Not to mention the clearest view of the sunset. Thank you, I'd like that. I'd like that very much.'

'Good. I'll see you here, then.'

'Until tomorrow.' His hand touched hers briefly. 'It'll work out. Just you see, Nora. As bad as things feel, you'll find a way through.'

'I hope so,' she murmured, fleeing before tears overcame her.

Later that night with Morwenna safely home, Nora quietly made her way upstairs. She was tired, bone tired, the adrenalin of service rapidly fading, but sleep was impossible.

As she reached the little bed, Iris turned in her sleep, snuffling slightly as she settled back into the pillows. Nora adjusted the eiderdown, pulling it gently back over the blankets, picking up the fallen copy of *Swallows and Amazons* Morwenna had been reading to her at bedtime, carefully replacing the bookmark.

'Mummy?' In the light from the landing she could see that Iris's eyes were wide open.

'Yes, darling. I'm back.'

'Did you save me some mess?'

Nora smiled. Iris had only recently discovered the delights of Eton Mess, which, with the help of the Abbey's hens and some judicious hoarding of sugar, was always a favourite with the guests. 'It's in the larder, all ready for tomorrow.'

'Mmmm,' said Iris contentedly. 'Did Professor Jackson like it?'

'I think so.'

'Good.' Iris's eyes drifted shut, then flew open again. 'Can he come for tea?'

'I don't see why not. Perhaps you'd like to ask him tomorrow.'

'Yes,' murmured Iris, drifting back into sleep. 'He's nice.'

'So he is. Very nice.' *And kind, and easy to talk to, and understands about loss.* After all these years with no time to consider anything so personal, she found herself wishing he'd stay in Cornwall. She was being foolish. Selfish. It was just her aching heart seeking something to fill its looming emptiness when Iris was no longer the centre of her existence.

Nora sat by the bedside in the half light, listening to Iris's regular breathing. At the open window the curtains stirred against the blackness of the night, billowing like ghosts amongst the distant shimmer of stars. Silence hung in the air, broken only by the drag of pebbles as waves surged onto St Mabon's beach.

Even as she grew cramped and cold, she wished she could stay there forever, listening to Iris's gentle breathing, and never let her go.

FORTY-FOUR

SABINE

France, 1945

They were alive.

Sabine reread Howard's hastily scribbled letter yet again, terrified she'd misunderstood the English, that he was trying to be kind and break the truth to her gently. But it was no mistake. He *had* found them. He had spoken to them. He was staying in the hotel where Nora was working as head chef. He'd walked through the village and seen where Violette went to school.

She owed Howard more than she could ever repay. Bless him for taking the time to travel all the way to Maltby Abbey to find them. He'd have known them anywhere, he wrote. Violette was the perfect image of Valérie, the same white-blonde hair, the same features. Finally, she dared to believe it was true. Nora and Violette were safe and thriving in Cornwall. They were safe.

Sabine blinked away the tears. All the years of the war she'd tried to envisage her daughter as completely healed, but despite the photograph Nora had sent her after the operation, all she could ever see was that final glimpse at the Gare du Nord of the scrap of a child with a gash in her lip, so utterly perfect in her imperfection. Through Howard's descriptions she had a vision of her as she really was now. A little girl who'd grown, just as Valérie had grown. She couldn't wait to hold her.

'If we hurry I can catch the train for the night ferry,' she said to Maman. 'I could see her tomorrow. At last I'll be able to bring her home.'

'Maybe not so soon,' said Mémé, pausing from gluing together one of the dining chairs that was not entirely beyond repair. 'It will be a shock for the child. And what about Nora? At least allow them a few days to get used to the idea. A few days longer can't hurt.'

Sabine's joy wavered. She'd been trying to shut out from her mind that Howard had been describing a family, a mother and daughter living happily together. Was that a subtle warning? Was Howard, who understood loss more than most, cautioning that her happiness might come at the cost of Nora's broken heart? Two broken hearts. Lives torn apart forever. Sabine pushed the thoughts away. All she could think of for now was that Violette was safe.

'Very well, but only a couple of days,' she said. 'I have to see her.' Her heart was racing. Less than a week from now there could be two fair-haired children racing round the courtyard and playing in the river. All the sorrow, all the suffering of the past years would be wiped away. They would be together once more. They could start afresh.

Again that nagging sensation at the back of her mind. But she couldn't bear to allow it into her heart. Once again she pushed it firmly away.

A few days later, Sabine emerged onto the landing of the Chateau Saint-Céré, overnight bag packed, her stomach twisted into a tight knot of excitement mingled with anxiety.

Throughout the restless nights since she'd found out they were alive, she'd been unable to ignore the understanding dawning in her heart. Violette would have no memory of her. All the life her daughter had ever known was with Nora in Cornwall. Valérie was just starting to make the first overtures of friendship in the village but was still lost without the friends she'd made while they'd been away during the war. Howard had said Violette was a bright student who'd settled well at school, building a network of friendships with other children who were similarly curious and eager to learn.

And Nora ... She couldn't afford to think too deeply about Nora's feelings. And yet she couldn't avoid them completely. Nora had saved Violette's life. She had put her own future to one side to look after the little girl. Sabine winced. It had come to her in the darkness of the night that even at the worst of times she'd always been able to count on the support of her mother and grandmother. Nora had left her family to travel to an unfamiliar place to keep Violette safe from the bombings in London, and now she had no family of her own left. Sabine had seen how unmarried mothers were often viewed in France and feared it might be similar in England.

Sabine felt stretched too thin to have any emotions left. It was impossible! She owed everything to Nora. Was she really going to tear her away from the child she'd raised over the past six years? A lifetime. Was she really going to snatch that away and leave her with nothing?

'But I can't be apart from my child,' she said aloud, feeling her heart break.

The sound of childish laughter reached her through the open window. She peered down into the courtyard where Valérie was throwing sticks for Poupée, who was barking hysterically. This was for Valérie and for Violette. They were twins. They had grown together inside her, been born together. They belonged together. With her. Valérie still curled up with

Poupée whenever she could, calmed by the dog's rapid heart-beat next to hers. Howard had said they were so alike he was pretty sure that if he saw them together he'd be unable to tell them apart. Surely it would be doubly cruel to *keep* them apart?

She caught sight of a car heading up the track towards the chateau, stirring up clouds of dust.

'Maman!' she called. 'Guillaume is here.'

'I thought he wasn't arriving until this evening?'

'He must have been released from the hospital early. I'll be able to see him before I go after all. He'll be so excited to hear that Violette's been found.'

She raced down into the courtyard, reaching Valérie and Poupée who'd paused in their game, curious at the approaching engine.

'Maman?' Valérie's face turned towards her for reassurance. She might be too young to remember much, but it was still there, deep in her memory, the scream of the aeroplane bearing down towards them on the road, the passing of ambulances and trucks, the lumbering of the occasional tank. It would be there, somewhere, all her life.

'It's all right, chérie. It's Uncle Guillaume.'

'The one who was hurt in the war?'

'That's him. Remember, you helped me make the room ready for him downstairs, next to the kitchen, until his leg's better? A friend promised to drive him home from the hospital. Uncle Guillaume is going to get strong and help us repair the chateau and get the orchards and the vineyard working again.' She kissed Valérie. 'So we can all stay here forever.'

The battered Fiat made its way gingerly up the driveway, dodging the potholes.

'Guillaume!' Maman reached the car as it came to a halt, reaching in through the open window on the passenger side.

'It's all right, it's all right,' came Guillaume's familiar voice. 'No need to strangle me.'

'What have they been feeding you?' his mother demanded, releasing him just enough to open the door. 'You're nothing but skin and bone.'

'But at least in one piece,' he replied good-humouredly, reaching for his stick and struggling out. 'This is Jacob, Maman,' he said, gesturing to the driver who was looking a little awkward amidst this family reunion. 'He was in the hospital with me. I promised you'd offer him a bed for the night if he drove me here.'

'Of course,' said Maman. 'You're very welcome.'

'If you are certain, Madame? I can easily catch the train.'

'Where to?' demanded Guillaume. 'Jacob's village was destroyed during the war. There's no guarantee it'll ever be rebuilt.'

'And your family—' Maman halted in response to Guillaume's warning shake of the head.

'My sister's family emigrated to America while they still could,' Jacob replied quietly. 'The rest were taken to the death camps. Most ended up in Auschwitz. I was the one in danger in the army; they were supposed to have been safe. But here I am and none of them survived. Not even the babies.'

'I'll make up a bed in the bedroom at the side,' said Mémé who'd come out to join them. 'You're welcome to stay as long as you wish.'

Jacob coloured. 'Thank you. But I've no wish to intrude.'

'We have need of workers,' said Mémé firmly. 'We can't pay, but we can offer bed and board. That is no intrusion.'

'There, what did I tell you? No escape,' said Guillaume drily. 'Mémé's no fool. Jacob is a carpenter by trade, and good at all kinds of repairs. The hospital was very unwilling to let him go. Come on man, it'll give you time to get back on your feet and you'll be doing us a good turn at the same time. I'm not going to be much good for a few months yet, and the house and the ground can't wait.'

Slowly Jacob nodded. 'Very well. Thank you.'

'Good,' said Maman, undisguised relief suffusing her face. 'Come on in. Mémé managed to get hold of some real coffee. Time for a celebration, I think.'

The next morning Jacob drove Sabine to the station, Guillaume perched in the back seat giving him directions.

'Good luck,' Jacob said as he unloaded Sabine's overnight bag from the boot.

'Thank you.'

'I'm glad you were able to find your daughter. Some hope at last amid so much uncertainty.'

'So it is,' she replied. She looked at the little station, battered but defiantly struggling on, the village gradually starting to put itself back together and return to life. Panic began to surge up inside her.

'It'll be fine,' said Guillaume, hobbling round to join her.

'She won't remember me. I'll be a stranger, come to take her away from everything she knows. That feels a little cruel.'

'You're her mother. She has a sister and a loving family here,' he replied. 'I took you to the station in Paris, remember. I know how it broke your heart making that decision. You did it to keep her safe.'

'Yes,' said Sabine. She turned to watch Jacob, who was perched on the bonnet of the Fiat, tactfully leaving them to make the final few steps to the station. She couldn't help but notice the yearning in his eyes as he watched the morning shoppers hoping to glean something from the few shops that had reopened on the main street, and the small café defiantly setting out tables and chairs beneath a torn and half-scorched awning.

What must it be like to lose everyone you know? For your entire family to be brutally torn away, leaving only haunted imaginings of the cruelty of their last moments? They had survived. Despite everything, they had each other. Even their home, though damaged, was still standing. They still had a roof over their heads, and there were still familiar faces in the village as it returned to a semblance of life.

She hugged Guillaume tightly. 'I'll be back before long,' she said, as she hurried to join the train from Paris heading towards the coast, eyes blinded by tears, her heart torn in two.

PART 5

FORTY-FIVE

IRIS

Cornwall, 1964

'So I'm Violette,' said Iris when her mother finished speaking. 'And I have a twin.'

'Valérie,' said Mum a little sadly. 'Believe me, my darling, we never intended to keep you apart. We agreed that as you were settled here it wouldn't be in your best interests to take you away to a strange country that had suffered much more destruction than Cornwall. But the plan was that when you were old enough you'd be able to visit her, and we'd become one family. It seemed so simple. But in the end it didn't work out that way.'

Iris frowned at her. 'Why not?' She saw the answer in her mum's face. 'The man Jeanie Dixon the journalist wanted to know about. Karl Bernheim.'

'Yes.'

'She said he killed a woman. Not in the war, recently. That's why he's on trial.'

'She wouldn't have been interested if it had been years ago, when he was complicit in the death of thousands,' said Mum.

'She had no right to bring us into it.' She glanced at her watch. 'I promise I'll tell you the rest in a little while. I'm going to change. I'm tired of wearing my invalid's clothes. Even the NHS have agreed I'm recovered enough from the hysterectomy to start doing more than lift a kettle. It's time I looked like myself again.'

She headed off upstairs leaving Iris alone at the kitchen table, trying to absorb all she'd been told.

France, 1939.

She'd known she might have a family out there somewhere and that they might even be looking for her amongst the chaos left by the war. It had never crossed her mind until she'd seen those words on her certificate of adoption that they'd be in France, close to Paris, a place Mum and Dad had always promised to take her. And that her parents knew about her family – her birth family – all this time.

She took refuge in the only way she knew how, heading through the garden and the little gate onto the cliffs. She breathed in the sea air, drawing it deep into her lungs. St Mabon's with its little harbour, the curve of the bay, were just as they had always been, her world, her childhood horizon, the place that would never change. St Mabon's had remained a constant, but she had changed. She clenched her fists tightly together, feeling pieces of her spiralling out into the breeze, until there was nothing of her left. She was a different person, with a different name, a different past, different blood. A different language even.

Why hadn't Mum and Dad told her this before? Why had they hidden the truth from her? Why hadn't they let her decide how much she wanted to know? Because there was no other choice, came the answer, deep in her heart.

She opened her eyes, the parts of her falling back into place. She was still herself. She was still Iris, who'd grown up loved, secure and happy in St Mabon's. Whatever her past, this was the place, and the community, that had made her. A wave of love rushed over her for Mum and Dad. She'd always under-stood that while they weren't related to her by blood, they had loved her and always wanted the best for her. They, too, had made her. They had given her the love that had allowed her to turn and face whatever awaited her. The part of the story Mum couldn't bear to tell. The part about Karl Bernheim and the woman who'd died.

Slowly, Iris returned through the gate towards Hope Cottage. Lost in thought and the sound of the sea, she hadn't heard the car arrive in the driveway. She'd never been so glad to find a second car parked next to her Mini. Dad was back. Dad, who was kind and gentle, and not afraid of anything. Dad was home.

She was about to run to meet him when she saw him emerge with a woman she'd never seen before, small, compactly built, in an elegant trouser suit, hair greying slightly at the temples. As they retrieved a couple of suitcases from the boot, Iris hesitated, unseen, suddenly unwilling to call out and attract attention. She was certain she'd never seen the woman before, and yet ...

'It's okay,' said Dad, shutting the boot. 'She won't have gone far. I'll make us all a cup of tea, she'll be back in a bit.'

'Ah, the cup of tea,' said the woman, speaking fluent English with only the faintest hint of an accent. 'You have become so very English, my friend.'

He chuckled at that. 'I expect I have.' He smiled at her, the smile of people who know each other well. Not the smile of love and trust Iris sometimes caught passing between her parents, but an expression she'd seen before with those who'd shared an experience, an accident or some traumatic incident that drew strangers together in a bond that could never be broken.

'I sure didn't plan to,' he was saying. 'Funny how things turn out, eh? Don't worry, it'll all be fine.' He took the suitcase into the cottage. The woman turned to gaze at the whitewashed walls, the front garden with its path winding between the brightness of spring flowers, as if she were fixing the memory in her mind.

There was something familiar about her, about her voice. Something with the quality of a dream. It was the suggestion of a scent that reached Iris, soft, with a hint of roses, that stirred a memory, the one gathering at the edges of her mind. She was in her bedroom at home, the distant sound of the sea drifting in through the open window along with the mellowness of newly mown lawns. Caught deep in sleep, she could sense someone sitting next to the bed, looking down on her with a gaze so intense she could feel it weaving through her dreams. Her ears were filled with the sound of weeping.

When she looked again, the woman had disappeared, but the faint scent of roses lingered.

This was the point, Iris understood in a flash. The point of her spending this time with Mum, and why Dad, who'd refused to leave her side when she'd been ill, had been away. Even why Jeanie Dixon had pursued a story she'd hoped would prove the scoop of a lifetime, setting her on her way to a sparkling career, heedless of the pain and chaos she might leave behind.

Somewhere deep inside, amongst the swirl of emotions and her own shifting identity, she understood. And that this was something she could put off no longer. Taking a deep breath, Iris made her way towards the cottage.

FORTY-SIX

NORA

Cornwall, 1945

Howard accepted Iris's invitation to join them for afternoon tea with undisguised pleasure. Over the next days, Nora found herself falling into the habit of meeting him for a glass of wine when she was working late, or bumping into him when she was picking up Iris from school in St Mabon's and walking back with him to Hope Cottage.

He was such a gentle, reassuring presence it sometimes felt as if he'd always been part of their lives. He had a natural way with children too, chatting to Iris with ease and showing her books with photographs of the discoveries in Egypt and the more recent finds at Sutton Hoo in Suffolk that fired her curiosity. At times, Nora glimpsed a look of pain cross his features as he showed Iris the treasures from the tomb of Tutankhamun, perhaps stirring a memory of the family he'd lost, along with all the child refugees wandering the roads of France during the war, who still had nowhere to go.

Before the war, before Iris, Nora had dreamt of love and

romance, despite spending her time at *La Belle Époque* batting away hands constantly pawing at her blouse and her skirt. *That* Nora would never have believed that one day all she'd ache for would-be companionship, and the sharing of joys and troubles at the end of the day. She felt old, as if life had already passed her by. Her days and nights had, over the past six years, been filled with Iris, absorbed in far too rich an existence to long for anything more.

What a fool I've been she told herself one evening as she joined Howard at the little table by the window overlooking the bay that was now, by some kind of silent agreement, reserved for them. *Placing my everything into another woman's child.*

'How did you find St Ives?' she asked, rousing herself into cheerfulness.

'Busy. I see the artists and the tourists are already returning. It's very beautiful and it was good to see my family's headstones in the graveyard. Although I have to confess I prefer St Mabon's.' He took the empty seat as Nora poured them each a glass of wine. 'I think I've had enough excitement over the past few years.' He gave a wry smile. 'Or maybe not.'

'You could always do both,' she said.

'That's what struck me,' he replied. 'The work during the war was relentless, it got into your soul and left you in a very dark place that seemed impossible to escape. I should have known a return to dry academia wasn't the answer. But a return to Cornwall – well, maybe. I can see that being a way of keeping the soul alive, if you know what I mean.'

'Hope and beauty and the milk of human kindness,' she said.

'Something like that.' He lifted his glass in a half salute. 'And you? What will you do?'

'What's best for Iris,' she said. 'It's the only thing I can do. That was always the pact between Sabine and me: that we'd do the best for the twins, whatever it might cost us. I've no right to keep Iris here, away from her real family.'

He cleared his throat, eyes resting on the distant sea. 'And your husband?'

'My husband?'

'I was told by some of the staff here that he's in the army. I take it he'll be demobbed soon.'

He'd asked. He'd tried to find out whether her title meant she was married, divorced or a widow. Her heart gave an unexpected leap. She squashed the feeling firmly back down. He was most likely reassuring himself that she wasn't recently bereaved, she told herself, having to contend with that grief as well as the loss of Iris. The dignified course of action would be to go along with this fiction that had kept her safe from unwanted male attention for so long. It would be the kind thing to do, letting Howard believe there was a life awaiting her, with a husband and future children of her own.

But that would be shutting a door. One, she knew in her heart, she had no wish to close, however small the chance it would ever be opened.

'He's made up,' she confessed. 'Because of Iris. He doesn't exist.' She caught his eye and saw the funny side. 'I haven't quite worked out yet how on earth I'm going to get rid of him.'

Howard laughed. She caught a gleam in his gaze that had nothing to do with quietness and understanding, and fought down a blush.

'I'll help you work out a suitable fate, if you like,' he said with a grin. It was a glimpse of the other side of Howard; the Red Cross man who'd remained at his post doing everything in his power to help refugees, facing down officials from an evil regime, smuggling refugees like Sabine and her family across borders at his own risk, his fury at all the horrors he'd witnesses still deep inside him needing some kind of outlet.

'Didn't you say you have friends working with the United

Nations Refugee Council?' she said. 'I'm sure there's still plenty of work to be done.'

'More than ever,' he returned. 'The war may be over, but it feels as if half of Europe is still on the move with nowhere to go. I'm not sure I can abandon them entirely for ancient warriors, laid to rest in splendour. Although I may need to return to them every now and then, if only to keep sane.' He was gazing over the sea once more. 'I've found there's nothing quite like the kind of work that really absorbs you, to bring solace, even in the most difficult of times.'

'I'm sure that's true,' replied Nora sadly.

A few days later Nora removed her chef's whites and walked through a day of sunshine and rain towards the little school at the heart of St Mabon's. It was a journey she'd made so many times, but now she feared each one might be her last.

Although it was too early to expect a reply from Howard's letter, she knew deep in her heart that if she was Sabine she wouldn't have waited; she would have caught the first train to be reunited with the child she'd lost.

How many times had she rushed down from the kitchens at Maltby Abbey, her mind still on her work? Still mulling over the need to adjust the evening's recipes to take account of the unexpected unavailability of yet another ingredient, or a new under-chef who was failing to fit in with the rest of her tight-knit little team, or the need to find a replacement for a waitress down with chickenpox. Every single one of those minutes should have been filled with the anticipation of meeting Iris and hearing her chatter happily about her day.

How many times had she been dead on her feet after a particularly stressful day, and longed for the hour or so of peace when Iris had gone to bed, when she could sit with a book, or sometimes just a cup of tea in the garden, being herself again for a few hours? How she wished she could take that time back and read her a bedtime story for a little longer, or just sit watching Iris sleep, absorbing everything about her. Iris had become so entwined in her life she'd forgotten that one day she would have to let her go.

'Let's hope the rain keeps off,' called Glenis from the next cottage as Nora reached the small group clustered around the school gates.

'I hope so,' Nora replied with a smile.

'And that it's fine for the weekend,' added Glenis as a stir at the door announced the imminent emergence of the children. 'Demelza's so looking forward to her birthday party, she'll be disappointed if it rains all day.'

'I'm sure it won't,' replied Nora, her mind automatically checking whether Iris's new party frock was clean and pressed, and the matching ribbons for her plaits were ready.

Now the frock might never be worn. Or at least not here in Cornwall. It hadn't crossed Nora's mind that this would be the last time, as she carefully followed the Simplicity pattern using a bolt of white cotton covered in tiny scarlet polka dots that Miss Maltby had rescued from her attic, and which now appeared as skirts and dresses for half the girls in the village. She would never be able to face polka dots again.

It was for the best. She had to hold on to that. She had done what needed to be done to keep Iris safe. Now that time was over, and a new life for both of them was about to begin.

Once back amongst her real family, would Iris remember her? Nora tried to grasp at her own childhood memories. Disconnected images came to her, sounds and tastes accompanied by vague impressions of people she knew were her mum and dad. If she'd left London as a child, would she have remembered them at all, or would they have been overlaid by other memories? Once back with her mother and sister, and the richness of life at the chateau and its proximity to Paris, Iris's time in Cornwall might quickly fade away.

'I'll no longer be part of her life,' she acknowledged to herself sadly as the children began to emerge. 'Not even in memory.'

FORTY-SEVEN

SABINE

Cornwall, 1945

Sabine emerged from the station at St Mabon's, blinking into the afternoon light. A flurry of rain dashed itself against her face, bringing with it the saltiness of the rollers crashing against the long line of cliffs, and the lingering aroma of seaweed.

'Maltby Abbey?' she enquired of the station master.

'The hotel, you mean madam? Up there on the cliffside, that's the one. There's a bus in half an hour, or you can take the path.' He pointed. 'It's not far. Follow the road through the village, and take that gate, see, right next to the church. That'll take you straight there.'

'Thank you.' She needed to clear her head and, slinging her overnight bag over one shoulder, she began to make her way through the village. Even a cursory glance told her it was a bustling, close-knit little place, not so very different, despite the style of houses and the lack of pavement cafés, from the villages at home. It had the secure feeling of a location where everyone knew everyone else, and apart from a few curious glances, a lone woman could walk through and be left alone to continue with her business. Looking back, she could see the curve of the beach within the shelter of the cove, the clear turquoise water turning to a deeper green beyond the rocks where the wildness of the open sea began.

A group of middle-aged women were walking their dogs along the edges of the water, deep in conversation while their four-legged charges dashed in and out of the waves. A fair-haired child in a blue romper suit broke free from his mother's hands to join the race, landing on his bottom as an excited spaniel rushed past, but up again in an instant and waddling cheerfully in the dog's wake.

Pain stabbed through Sabine. That could have been Valérie and Poupée tumbling together, fearless in their pursuit of the novelty of water. Already, after just a few hours, she missed them both horribly, leaving an emptiness next to her heart. It was the same every time she went away with work, even though it was only ever for two or three nights at the most. She knew her daughter was safe with Maman, while Mémé would fight wolves with her bare fists to protect her great-granddaughter. Today she was feeling more torn around the edges. How could she ever bear to leave them at all?

As if to torment her further, the sound of children's laugher rang in the air. She'd reached the centre of the village with its little church and the adjacent school, where a small flood of children were being set free for the day, some joining their waiting mothers and grandmothers, others already setting off between the houses, shrieking and giggling as they made their way home.

She found the familiar face almost immediately. Nora looked older, less rounded, flesh sculpted more closely around her cheekbones, hair cut short and curled neatly out of the way, her expression pensive. The next moment it lit up with a glow as one of the last girls to emerge ran towards her. Sabine drew in her breath sharply. It was a miracle. She'd known from

Howard's description, but it was still a miracle. It could have been Valérie. From this distance there was no sign of a scar on her mouth, while the expression on her face was animated, the chatter reaching her ears that of a lively little girl.

Sabine stood there, unable to move, overcome by a desire to put her head in her hands and weep. The relief of finally seeing her daughter again overwhelmed her. Violette left Nora, racing to whisper something to two girls of her own age. The three of them burst into irrepressible giggling, before she returned to take Nora's hand, looking up at her as they turned to take the path up towards Maltby Abbey.

That smile! All through the years of war and uncertainty, Sabine had longed for that look. How could she bear to see such love and trust being directed at another? Just as painful was the smile on Nora's face, the warmth of a mother greeting her child after a few hours apart.

'Are you quite well, madam?' She hadn't seen the middle-aged woman passing with a small child, a look of concern on her face.

'Yes. Yes, thank you.'

'If you're sure.'

'Yes, thank you so much.' Sabine escaped the woman's kindness and fled to the sanctuary of the little churchyard. She sat for a while on a bench under the mosaic of sunlight filtering in through the trees as the racing of her heart slowly eased. It was peaceful and strangely reassuring among the generations of villagers, 'dearly beloved' carved on their headstones along with names and dates, the majority neatly tended, the ancestors still keeping this little community safe.

As her breathing settled, she wended her way between the flowers and the cropped grass. Lives gained, lives gone. Marriages lasting decades. Men lost at sea, women lost in childbirth, and between them lives lived into ripe old age. She paused in front of a Victorian angel, crumbling but clear of moss and ivy, guarding the remains of Mary Kellin, who'd lived for just one day.

Taking a deep breath, the turmoil inside rising again, Sabine turned and made her way through the gate and onto the path leading up towards Maltby Abbey.

FORTY-EIGHT

NORA

Cornwall, 1945

Nora opened the door to Hope Cottage, wiping the flour from her hands.

'Oh my Lord,' she exclaimed, joy and grief wrestling together in her heart as she saw Sabine standing there.

'Hello Nora.' The mix of expressions crossing Sabine's face reflected Nora's own. 'I didn't wish to intrude.'

'Dearest Sabine,' replied Nora, her eyes swimming with tears. 'How could you ever intrude? It's so good to see you. I was expecting you, just not so soon.'

'We're making biscuits, Professor,' called a child's voice from the kitchen. 'Oat and honey. And raisins.'

'It's not the professor, sweetheart,' returned Nora. 'Not yet. And remember I counted those raisins.'

'I only ate one,' said Iris, sounding suitably guilty. 'The littlest one.'

'Then make sure it's just the one, or there won't be any left.'

'Yes, Mummy.'

Nora turned back to Sabine. 'You'd better come in. '

Iris looked up from her careful cutting of biscuit dough, rolled out ready on the table. There was a smear of flour on her nose, another on her chin.

'Hello,' said Iris, eyeing the newcomer with interest. 'Do you like honey biscuits?'

'Sweetheart, this is ...' Nora came to a halt. This was too soon, too abrupt. How do you start to tear a life apart? Why had she not put her own feelings aside and begun to prepare Iris for the transformation from the moment Howard had first found them? She'd thought they'd have a few more days, or weeks even, until they could make proper arrangements for Sabine's arrival.

'A friend,' put in Sabine hastily. Nora sent her a grateful smile.

'Mummy's friend?'

'Yes,' said Sabine. 'And Professor Jackson's.'

'Oh,' said Iris eagerly. 'I like Professor Jackson. He's nice. He tells stories. Not scary ones,' she reassured her.

'I'm sure. I knew you too, a long time ago, when you were a baby. I live in France, so I haven't been able to visit before.'

'Because of the war?'

'Because of the war.'

Iris considered this. 'So, are you French?'

'*Oui*. Yes.'

'I haven't met anyone French before. Mummy teaches me French. I'm not very good.'

'I'm sure you are,' said Sabine. 'And it takes a long time to learn to speak a language.'

Iris nodded vigorously. 'Mummy says that, too.'

'I'll put the kettle on,' said Nora. Iris caught the slight crack in her voice. Her hands paused on the round metal cutter. 'They're nearly all done,' Nora continued, voice steady once more. 'If you arrange them on the baking tray, I'll put them in the oven, then they'll be ready by the time Professor Jackson arrives.'

Iris nodded, reassured that all was well, and began to lift each biscuit carefully, spacing them out on the tray with a practised hand.

'Can I help you?' said Sabine, joining her at the table. Iris nodded, absorbed in her task. 'Do you like making biscuits?'

'Sometimes. When Mummy has sugar.'

'Yes, we sometimes don't have sugar either.'

'Aunt Winifred has bees.'

'Miss Maltby,' explained Nora, lifting down teacups from the dresser. 'My employer at the hotel.'

'Mummy's a chef,' said Iris. 'A proper chef. Girls can be chefs,' she added, with the air of having had to defend her corner against scepticism at any female holding a position of such skill and responsibility.

'I know how good she is,' said Sabine. 'I met her in Paris when she was training to become a chef.'

'Paris?' Iris's eyes widened. 'Where the Eiffel Tower is?'

'*Bien sûr.*'

'Bi-an sure,' repeated Iris, as English as could be.

Nora caught the pain on Sabine's face, almost, but not quite, hidden behind the smile.

'Sweetheart, why don't you go and collect those flowers from the garden and get them ready for the table when Professor Jackson arrives? Here, take the scissors, and be careful when you cut the roses.'

'No prickles.'

'Definitely no prickles.'

Iris disappeared into the garden, holding the scissors carefully, points away from her body as she'd been taught.

There was a moment's silence.

'She speaks very well,' said Sabine at last. 'No impediment.'

'None,' replied Nora. Everyone agrees she's very bright,' she added, placing the teapot between them along with a small jug of milk retrieved from the larder. 'And advanced for her age. She's getting on well at school. She has an enquiring mind.'

'So much for mental incapacity.'

'She certainly has none of that,' said Nora, her anger reflecting Sabine's. 'And to think what they might have done—'

'If you hadn't taken her,' finished Sabine.

Nora's hand shook slightly as she poured the tea. 'I'm afraid that's why Iris doesn't speak much French. She's starting to pick it up now, but I didn't encourage her during the war while there was still the danger of an invasion, so people in St Mabon's assumed she was English.'

'The only way you could keep her safe.'

'So many records were lost it was easy to register her at school under an English name. No one would have ever known. Now they've started to show pictures of the camps and describe what happened there, I dread to think what might have happened.'

Sabine shuddered. 'I can't bear to think about it either.'

Nora eyed her. So much about Sabine was familiar, but so much had changed from the young woman she'd known in Paris. Sabine was painfully thin and there were lines on her face that belonged to a much older woman. Nora's heart went out to her for all she'd been through, for the things she must have seen.

'Howard said you're a journalist, just as you always wished.'

'Yes.'

'And that you've seen them. The extermination camps.'

'Yes. I will never forget. And my husband ...' Her voice broke. 'How do I tell them?'

Nora put her hand over hers. 'What you tell them is for the future, dear Sabine. For now, they have survived. At least we were safe here in Cornwall. You had to fight every day to keep

Valérie alive. Now, I've made you tea with milk, the English way.'

'I like the English way,' returned Sabine.

'Mummy ...' Iris returned, hands overflowing with late flowering roses. 'Why is the lady crying?'

'Sssh, darling. She's a bit sad, that's all.'

'Because of the war?'

'Because of the war. But it's all right now. Let's find a vase and you can arrange the flowers properly before we put them on the table. If we hurry they'll be ready for when the professor arrives, then he might have time to tell you one of his stories before the pie's cooked.'

Sabine blew her nose. 'I'd better—'

'You're staying here,' said Nora firmly. 'With us. There's plenty of dinner. Besides, Howard won't want to miss you. He'll be here soon, he's been joining us the evenings I'm not working at the hotel. It's mostly vegetables and not a lot else, but I think that's the same in France too. And there's a spare room. It won't take a minute to make up the bed. You can stay for a long as you wish. Until ...' Her voice drifted into silence.

The heavy scent of tea roses filled the room, with their hint of summer, their hint of autumn. What was there to say?

They both looked up at a knock on the front door. 'I'll go and get it, Mummy,' said Iris, abandoning the flowers in her enthusiasm.

'Bring the professor in here,' replied Nora. 'I think it's warm enough for us to sit in the garden until dinner's ready.'

FORTY-NINE

SABINE

Cornwall, 1945

Sabine smiled as Howard's familiar tones mingled with Violette's, who immediately launched into telling him of the novelty of the French lady who'd come to visit. 'He's a good man,' she said.

'So he is,' said Nora, just the faintest touch of colour brushing her cheeks. 'I'm glad he came to find us. He has a good way with children. It seems so cruel that he lost his own; he would have made a wonderful father.'

'I owe him my life, more than once,' said Sabine, watching her closely. 'And Valérie's too. I trust him more than any man I've ever known.' Something, perhaps a dream, an impossible fairy tale of what might have been had the world turned differently, faded into the distance. 'He of all people deserves to be happy,' she added, so quietly the words were barely there. 'As do you.'

In the hallway Howard was still chatting to Violette as he hung up his hat and coat. He'd already deflected any further questions about the French lady by telling Violette about the photographs he'd brought of richly decorated clasps and brooches recently found in the ancient burial mound in Sutton Hoo, proof that people from the distant past were far cleverer than anyone could have imagined.

'We'll work things out,' said Nora quickly. 'Between us, we kept them safe against all odds during the war. That's what matters. That they're safe and thriving, and will help build the future we all fought for.'

'I agree,' said Sabine, smiling between her tears. 'They're both where they belong. That's what matters now.'

She turned as Howard appeared at the door, Violette still chatting away confidently at his side. He looked older, lined, as they all were from their experiences, yet at the same time there was an air of contentment she hadn't felt in him before. A man finally making his peace with the world.

'Sabine,' he said, grasping her hands. 'Dear Sabine. It's good to see you.'

'And you,' she replied. 'The last time I saw Howard,' she explained to Nora, 'he'd just saved our lives, all our lives.'

He looked faintly embarrassed. 'I think it was a lot of people who did that, Sabine.'

'But you were the one who risked your own life getting us over the border. I'll never forget that.'

'Then I'm glad you've used it wisely and become a journalist,' he said, appearing awkward at receiving such praise.

'And I'm glad you were able to return to the academic world after all.'

'Maybe, maybe not.' She saw him exchange a glance with Nora. 'That's what I've been mulling over while I've been down here. I suppose the truth is you can't ever go back to the way you were, not after something like that. I'm not sure straight academia is the way forward for me anymore. Nora suggested I should talk to my friends working with the UN Refugee Council. The war might have ended, but there are so many still displaced and in dire need, especially children. I'm going to think it over. It makes a lot of sense.'

Sabine smiled. 'I agree with Nora. I can see you making that your life's work.'

'We'll see,' he replied, turning his attention back to Violette, who was clearly itching to ask him more questions.

The warmth of the little kitchen embraced them all as they ate their meal. After Violette had gone to bed, the three of them talked together long into the night, exchanging stories of the war and their ambitions for the future, by silent agreement avoiding the one subject at the forefront of all their minds.

As Howard finally made his way across the fields to Maltby Abbey and Nora ironed clothes for the following day, Sabine made her way to Violette's little room.

Curtains stirred briefly at the open window, bringing in the distant rumble of waves on pebbles to mingle with the steady rhythm of the child's breathing. In the light from the hallway Sabine could make out her rounded cheeks half hidden against the pillow, surrounded by her fine white-blonde hair, now beginning to darken towards brown. It was a sight so familiar it tugged at her heart with an urge to hold her body close to her own, to feel her warmth and the steadiness of her heartbeat and never let go. Yet at the same time the sight was so unfamiliar it broke her apart.

She picked up the cloth lion, worn and threadbare with love, that had tumbled from Violette's arms, and placed it next to the sleeping child. On the bedside table she could make out an illustrated book of fairy tales, along with Howard's pictures of the Anglo-Saxon treasures found at Sutton Hoo. As her eyes adjusted further, the shadows of the room emerged, the safe place Violette called home, with its scent of an unfamiliar soap mingled with a hint of salt from the sea. This was

Violette's world. The only world she knew. Where she belonged.

Violette turned in her sleep, arms instinctively tightening around her toy as she settled once more.

Sabine crouched down, as close as she dared without disturbing the sleeping child, resisting the temptation to brush stray strands of hair away from her face. There was no other choice. She had known it, deep in her heart, the moment she'd seen Violette racing towards Nora waiting at the school gates, surrounded by her friends. To tear her away would be unbearably cruel, she acknowledged, as the tears came.

Sabine could feel the shock and bewilderment of a child snatched from everything that made her, to be thrust into an unfamiliar world of new rules, new adults she would now have to depend on for everything, bringing with it the knowledge that the foundation of her existence could be ripped away at any moment. She had seen it in Valérie's unease at any hint of change, stirring up impressions, if not distinct memories, of their time as refugees, shaking the foundations of the earth beneath her feet. If it had happened once, she could see the child's mind questioning, why shouldn't it happen again? All the more terrifying for those too young to fend for themselves, should the worst happen.

'I would be no better than Emil,' she acknowledged to herself.

This was not about her, but about Violette. What was best for Violette. Her own feelings she could deal with. She was an adult, that's what adults do. But she had no right to rip apart a life that was just starting to find its feet in the world. That was the pact, even though you didn't know it at the time, when you brought new life into the world. Not ownership. But to nurture an existence that would one day move apart and beyond you, into a new life, a new world, one you knew nothing about. Love was always an act of keeping safe and letting go.

Sabine remained there for a while, listening to Violette's contented breathing, still torn by the agony of a part of her being ripped away. She would never see those blue eyes, so like Valérie's, gaze at her with the love and trust of a child for her mother. She would never hear her call her '*maman*'. She would miss those subtle changes, day by day, week by week, of a small child slowly growing into her own skin.

She couldn't bear it. Grief and loss overwhelmed her. After everything they'd been through. She would sweep Violette up and run, and no one could stop her.

But this was about Violette, she reminded herself again. This was about Violette. To rip her away from her secure existence, where she was flourishing, would be a betrayal of trust, one that Violette would surely never forget.

'I would lose her for sure,' she told herself sadly.

With a final glance at her sleeping daughter she made her way quietly downstairs where she found Nora sitting in an armchair in a warm pool of light from the standard lamp.

'Sabine, are you sure about this?'

'Yes. It's the right thing to do. But I don't want to give you such a burden unless you're sure too.'

'I am, and I always will be,' said Nora quietly. 'Believe me, dearest Sabine, I only want what's best for Iris.'

'I want only the best, too.' Sabine's eyes filled with tears. 'I fear so much I couldn't have kept her alive when we had to flee, and I would never have been able to make sure she had her operation. You have given us both so much.'

'I have no regrets, and never will,' said Nora, rising and putting her arms around Sabine. 'I wish I could make this easy, but it was never going to be, for either of us.'

'No,' said Sabine, holding her tight as the tears began to flow. 'There is no answer. Only what is best for Iris. That's all that matters now.'

FIFTY

IRIS

Cornwall, 1964

As Iris hesitated at the door of Hope Cottage, Dad came out.

'There you are,' he said, enveloping her in his familiar bear hug. 'I knew you wouldn't have gone far.' He released her, scrutinising her expression. 'You always went to the cliffs when you wanted time by yourself to think.'

'Mum's better,' she said, aware of voices coming from the kitchen, unable to face them, not yet.

'So much better. She's going to be fine. I can see you've done her a power of good.'

She looked up into his face, noticing for the first time the deep lines on his forehead beneath the greying fair hair, lines of anxiety and grief. Families never told each other their very deepest thoughts, even Dad, who was more willing to express himself than most of the men in the village. It was hard to start now.

'It's all right Dad,' she said, to reassure him. 'Mum's told me. At least, most of it.' She glanced instinctively towards the sound of female voices deep in conversation, speaking rapidly in what sounded like an interflowing mixture of French and English, as if trying to catch up for years of lost time. 'There are still some things I don't understand.'

He pushed the hair from her face with the affectionate gesture she'd known since childhood. 'That's all right, darling. That part's not for your mum to tell.' He kissed her gently where her hairline met her forehead. 'All you need to remember is that we love you and we always will. We might not always have got everything right, but we did what we could, and what we thought was for the best, to keep you safe and secure. All we ever wanted was for you to be able to live your own life.'

Iris smiled through her tears. 'I think I understand.'

'Come on,' he said, tucking her arm into his. 'There's someone I'd like you to meet.'

Iris stepped through the door, holding on tightly to his arm for reassurance. Mum and the new arrival were standing in a pool of sunlight close to each other. She could see the glossiness of unshed tears in their eyes.

'Here she is,' said Dad, gently releasing her arm. 'I said she wouldn't be far.'

Iris couldn't take her eyes from the woman's face, so unknown, yet so familiar. She could see the shape of the nose, the curve of the brows that echoed the face she saw in the mirror every morning. The reflection of herself she'd always longed for with an instinct so strong it was deep pain in her heart; the reflection she had never, until this moment, found.

Mum took her hand. 'Darling, this is the journalist Sabine Bourret. Sabine is your mother, my dear.'

After a while Iris led Sabine out into the garden, to the bench under the apple tree.

'I think I've heard your voice,' she said. 'When I've listened to French radio, and sometimes on the BBC.'

'That's possible,' replied Sabine.

'And I never knew.'

Sabine winced. 'I'm so sorry. This is not what we planned. But in the end there was no other choice.'

'Because of Karl Bernheim.'

'Yes. He was – is – a vile man.' She paused for a moment, as if pulling her thoughts together before she tried to explain. 'He was always so angry and bitter, thinking the world owed him something. I know from rumours when we lived in Colmar that he was brutalised by his father when he was a child. But he's not the only one, and some turn that experience into helping others and making the world a better place. Karl turned it to evil. He was just the kind of man to thrive when the war came. It fed his cruelty and his need to dominate. And to win. He always had to win.'

'So is that what you were afraid of?'

Sabine nodded. 'He always hated me. It wasn't just me, I think he bore a resentment against all women. But I was the one he blamed for his capture and imprisonment at the end of the war. I gave information to the police, you see. If it hadn't been for me, he'd have been living a life of luxury in South America. One of the German soldiers imprisoned with him came to the newspaper where I was working, to warn me of the things he boasted he'd do to me once he was released, and that he'd make sure I'd know what he'd done to my children first. I knew he was capable. Like so many of the more minor officials, he was released a few years after the war. After that, none of us ever felt completely safe.'

'Which is why you left me here.'

'It seemed the only way. I couldn't risk him finding either of you. He knew I had twins, you see. It seemed safer for you to stay apart.'

There was a moment's silence. Iris grappled with the question she had to ask next, the one they'd all been avoiding, all the time she'd been sitting next to Sabine on the squashy old sofa in the living room, not quite able to stop her eyes from straying to the stranger who was so much a part of her, feeling Mum and Dad's grief, mingled with joy at them being together again.

'Didn't my father want to see me?'

She knew the answer from Sabine's face, before she'd even finished speaking.

'Your father is dead, my dear. He died a long time ago, when you were still a small child. I promise I'll tell you the truth about him, but not here, and not now. For now all you need to know is that, even if he manages to avoid the guillotine, Karl Bernheim will never be released from prison.' Her eyes filled with tears. 'I wish there'd been another way, but we're safe from him now.'

'A journalist was here asking Mum about him. She said he'd killed a woman.'

'So he did. Heaven knowns why, and why now. He refused to say at his trial. To be honest with you, he looked to me like a man finally driven insane by the bitterness inside.' She took Iris's hands. 'This is never going to be easy. The woman he murdered was your grandmother. Not my mother, but your father's mother, Grandmother Claudette. He went to Colmar, convinced she knew where you and Valérie were living. Claudette loved you, with all her heart. She died protecting you, and she managed to alert the police. They might have been too late to save her, but they got there before Karl could escape. Your Grandmother Claudette protected you to the very end, and I hope that somehow she knows she's made it possible for all of us to be together again.'

As the blazing summer drew to a close, Iris travelled with Nora to finally meet her birth family and to be reunited with Valérie. Dad drove them to Dover to catch the ferry to Calais, followed by the train to Paris.

They were met at the little village station near the chateau by Sabine, who embraced them both tightly.

'Nora, you look so well,' she exclaimed in English. 'I swear you look twenty years younger.'

'I doubt it,' replied Nora. 'But it certainly feels good to have my energy back again. I'll be glad to get back to work at the Abbey. Idleness has never suited me.'

Sabine turned with a smile to a big bear of a man with a shock of brown hair, his skin deeply tanned by the sun, who was watching them with curiosity.

'This is my husband,' she said in French. 'I'm afraid Jacob doesn't speak much English, although it is improving.'

'Pleased,' he said in English, nodding to them both. 'I try,' he added. 'Very hard.' He gave an infectious grin, relapsing into French. 'Valérie tells me I have to learn to speak English because the English are so terrible at French.'

'Well, I know Nora is fluent,' said Sabine, laughing. 'And she's told me Iris is nearly as good.'

'If not better,' added Nora. She gave Iris's hand a reassuring squeeze as they headed towards the car.

It was only a few minutes' drive to the metal gates of the driveway, where Iris was finally able to look up at the painted shutters and tiled roof of the Chateau Saint-Céré. It was strange to think that this place had always been a part of her. That she belonged here, in a country whose language and history she'd learned so much about.

'Are you all right, darling?'

'Yes of course, Mum.' She smiled at her mother, who was looking anxious. 'It's just a bit overwhelming. In a good way,' she added, kissing her. She turned her smile to Sabine, who had paused to make a fuss of a rough-haired puppy, barking hysterically at her return.

'Ready?' said Sabine. Iris nodded. 'Just don't let them over-whelm you. Especially Mémé. She might be over ninety, but she's still a force to be reckoned with.'

'Violette!' An older version of Sabine, hair almost completely grey, and with well-worn hands, ran towards them, tears streaming down her face. '*Ma petite* Violette.' Iris was embraced so tightly the breath was knocked out of her. 'Let me look at you. You are so pretty, so – my goodness Mémé, can you see? She is the spitting image ...'

'Well I can't if you monopolise her like that,' retorted a bent, wrinkled little woman installed in a large armchair, eyes bright and blue in her hawk-like face. 'Bring her here will you, Joelle. My eyes are not as good as they were.' She waited until Iris was close to her. 'Well, well, well... Who would have thought? I hear your French is good. I can't be bothered to speak English anymore. It's all those dratted Americans nowadays, anyhow. Can't understand a word they say in the movies.'

'I hope it's good enough,' said Iris, slightly dazed by this onslaught. 'Mémé,' she added hastily.

'Good for you. Definitely no mental impairment there,' her great-grandmother remarked with a sniff. 'Cursed fascists and their ilk. Looks like you brought her up well.'

'I hope so Mémé,' said Nora, kissing her. 'It's good to see you again.'

'And at least I get to see Violette as a grown young woman before I go.'

'You're not going anywhere, Mémé,' said Sabine, smiling. 'You're as strong as an ox and will most probably outlive us all. Besides, how would Guillaume and Jacob manage if you weren't there to keep them in order and tell them what to do? Remember, I told you Iris is studying French, and she's looking into doing part of her degree in Paris. In that case, you'll see her all the time.'

'Good, good,' Mémé grunted. 'I suppose we should be

calling you *Eeris* now. I can't get used to all these name changes.'

'I like being called Violette as well,' said Iris quickly. 'It'll always be a part of me.'

Her great-grandmother beamed. 'A girl of sense, I see.' She bent forward, blue eyes sharp. 'That father of yours was a fool, you know. Two bright, beautiful daughters to cherish. What more could a man desire? A future to be proud of. Not some empire-building nonsense built on despicable cruelty. He deserved to lose it all.'

'You're quite right, Mémé,' said a new voice, stepping out of the shadows. Iris blinked. She'd been forewarned. She'd seen photographs. They'd spoken several times on the telephone. But nothing could have prepared her for the mirror version of herself appearing in the rays of sunlight crossing the room. It was like looking at herself, and yet not herself. She felt a strange tugging inside, something that was memory, and yet not memory. The heartbeat next to hers she'd been seeking all her life.

'Hello,' she said shyly.

'Hello,' replied Valérie.

'My goodness,' said Maman. '*C'est incroyable!* You were right Sabine, it really is almost impossible to tell them apart.'

Except one was so very English, the other so very French, thought Iris, a little sadly. A wry grin appeared on Valérie's face. She was thinking exactly the same. It was the oddest feeling, meeting the eyes of the other half of her she'd never known, and yet who was as familiar as the rise and fall of her own breathing.

'Come on,' said Valérie. 'I'll show you the chateau. It's not really a castle, not like a princess in a tower kind of castle. But it's still home.'

They didn't of course, instead escaping upstairs to Valérie's room. 'They've put you next door,' she said as they reached the landing. 'It was the old nursery where we stayed when we were babies. We can put a bed in my room, but Jacob thought you might need time on your own. He's thoughtful like that. He's good for Maman, he calms her down when the stories she's researching get to her, or bring up memories of the war. Horrible things happened to him too, but it's made him kind. It's all a bit overwhelming, *n'est-ce pas*? So you might want somewhere to escape.'

'That's very kind of him, thank you.'

'Can I call you Iris?'

'Yes, of course, that's been my name since I was a little girl. But I'll keep Violette as my middle name, so it's always part of me, Valérie.' They smiled at each other, both as shy as strangers but with that strange recognition of having known each other all their lives.

The rough-haired puppy shot onto the bed next to them.

'It's all right, Mirabelle,' said Valérie as the dog launched itself at her, licking her face in a comforting sort of a way. 'I'm not so very sad, not really.' She ruffled the silky brown of the little spaniel's head. 'I still miss Poupée. My dog when I was little, during the war,' she explained. 'Poupée was the best dog I'll ever have. I don't know what I would have done without her. When we came back here, she'd wait outside the school until it was time to come home and she loved lying in the sun in the courtyard, even when she was very old and could barely walk. I still miss her, but we always keep one of the puppies, we always will. There'll always be a part of Poupée at the Chateau Saint-Céré.'

FIFTY-ONE

IRIS

Paris, 1964

On their last day in France, for now at least, Nora and Iris took the short train ride to Paris with Sabine and Valérie.

'There's a place I want to show you,' said Sabine later that afternoon as they all began to tire after seeing the sights. 'Just you and me.' They left Nora and Valérie at the *Musée de l'Or-angerie* and headed back along the banks of the Seine. When they reached the Eiffel Tower, Sabine directed them to a little pavement café beneath its shadow.

As Sabine ordered, Iris gazed up at the huge steel structure that, like St Paul's in London, had miraculously survived the devastation of war.

It felt odd to think, as it had at Chateau Saint-Céré, that Paris was just as much a part of her as London and St Mabon's. It made her even more determined to study here. She even had an aunt who'd spent most of the war in Biarritz but had returned once Paris was liberated. Valérie stayed with Marie-Thérèse while she was studying to be a journalist and Iris was welcome to stay there too. Or the two of them could find an apartment of their own and really get to know each other at last.

There were so many things she needed to sort out in her mind. Some of them on her own, some with Valérie. It was a new life, stretching out ahead of her. She took a last look at the metal struts rising up as far as she could see. A new life. A new certainty of where she was going. And time to let go of the past.

'The next time we come here it'll be you and me and Valérie,' said Sabine as the waiter put down their coffees and left. 'But this one time I wanted it to be just you and me.' She looked around at the checked table cloths, the little groups of friends deep in earnest discussion, the couples absorbed in each other, the occasional man or woman sitting on their own reading the paper. The smoke from Gitanes spiralled peacefully into the air to join the traffic fumes, the garlic and the sweetness of peaches.

'You asked me about a postcard,' said Sabine. 'You wanted to know what it meant.'

'This one,' said Iris, reaching into her shoulder bag, taking out the postcard of the Eiffel Tower. 'It's this café,' she exclaimed, finding herself sitting in the same chairs as in the photograph.

'This was where it all began,' said Sabine. 'It was our favourite café when I first knew your father. It was always special to us. It was where we came when we could afford it, if only to absorb the atmosphere for the price of a coffee.'

'Before the war,' said Iris.

'When we couldn't imagine the world would go mad, even though, if you really looked, the signs were there. This would have been the last thing your father saw. The postcard was in his hands when he was found. He must have been looking at it as he died.'

Iris stifled a gasp, as something that had remained unspoken, even with Valérie, fell into place. 'You mean, he took his own life.'

'Yes.' Sabine looked up with tears in her eyes. 'I knew I had to tell you some time, just as I'll tell Valérie. No one else knows, although they may have guessed. I thought for a while maybe neither of you need know. But it was always a secret I couldn't keep for the rest of my life. Emil had a cyanide pill. Heaven knows how he managed to conceal it. He was found dead a few hours after I last saw him.' She turned the postcard over to gaze at the faint handwriting. 'This was the only thing he left. "Forgive".'

'Do you know what he meant?'

Sabine sighed. 'Emil wasn't always the man he became. The seeds were there, but he was a grown man. He made choices. They weren't written in the stars. It didn't have to end this way. I think that, deep inside, he never really changed. Karl was always consumed by his demons, he'll never face the truth. But I think there was still enough of the old Emil left, the one I fell in love with, the man he was when you and Valérie were born, to finally understand the reality of what he'd done, the unspeakable inhuman cruelty his ambition had led him to be a part of. I have a feeling that's when he could no longer live with himself. It was his humanity that destroyed him in the end.'

'I understand. At least, I hope I do.'

'You are not him,' said Sabine with sudden fierceness. 'I want you to remember that. Not you, not Valérie. You both have your own lives to live, you must never allow them to be over-shadowed by his.'

'I'll make sure they're not,' said Iris.

Sabine smiled, tears filling her eyes. 'You were always close to my heart, chérie,' she said, her voice breaking.

It was strange, thought Iris, being so close, seeing the ghost of her own features in Sabine's face. She could feel the warmth of the body that had once held her safely inside next to her beating heart, that had given her life.

'Life is not enough,' said Sabine gently, as if reading her thoughts. 'It's raising you, looking after you, that's the hard part. That's what truly makes a life, not breath alone. I will always love you, you will forever be my child, but Nora is your mum, just as Howard is your dad. You must always remember that, as well.'

'I will,' said Iris, hugging her tight. 'I'll never forget. But you will also always be a part of me, and I'll always remember that, too. And I'm so glad to have found you, all of you.'

Sabine kissed her, the tears running unchecked down her face. 'And I'm glad that you found me, too, and I can hold you once more, as I used to, so long ago, before the world fell apart. I hope now we can finally find a way to heal.'

A few days later Nora and Iris took the train from Paris to Calais and the ferry across the Channel, heading towards home.

'What was it like?' asked Iris as they stood on deck watching as the long, flat coast of France was left behind and the white cliffs rose up in front of them. 'What was it like, when you came over that time, when I was a baby?'

'Terrifying,' replied Nora. 'I was so young, younger than you are now. I didn't have much confidence in myself, and I'd just watched a country prepare for war, and families parting forever. Something I'd never imagined I'd ever see. I wasn't even sure if we'd get safely across to Dover, and I knew next to nothing about babies. I think it was the thought of being responsible for you that scared me most of all.'

'But you didn't leave me in France, or send me to an orphanage.'

'Of course not! How could I?'

'What would you have done if Sabine had insisted on taking me back to the chateau after the war ended?'

'I would have done what was best for you, my darling. For both of you. I would have let you go.'

'But you and Dad kept me safe.'

'Just as Sabine and her family kept Valérie safe. Such terrible things happened in the war, that fear never goes away. We kept you both safe, the only way we knew how. It's what families do for each other, however they're made. It's what your Grandmother Claudette did when Karl Bernheim came looking for us. She died to protect us. To protect you and Valérie. In the face of such evil, it was her final gift. The gift of love.'

'I understand,' said Iris. She stood for a while watching the swell of the waves lapping against the hull, as the white cliffs rose up ever higher and the wall of the harbour at Dover became ever clearer. 'Mum?'

'Yes, darling?'

'Are you sure you don't mind if I do part of my degree in Paris? My tutors in London have suggested trying for the Sorbonne.'

'Of course you should, sweetheart. It's time you and your sister got to know each other.'

'And Valérie can't wait to come and see St Mabon's, she's always wanted to visit Cornwall. And I can show her round London, too.' She slipped her arm through Nora's. 'You know, I'm sure that's Dad waiting for us. That looks like his car.'

'I think you're right. There was really no need, I told him we'd be fine taking the train.'

'I think he knows this will have been hard for both of us,' said Iris, kissing her. 'He likes to take care of us.'

'So he does,' said Nora. 'Do you know, darling, apart from you, Howard was the best thing that ever happened to me. And the funny thing is, if I hadn't taken you when Sabine handed you to me in desperation, when I was waiting on that train to leave Paris the day war broke out, I would never have met him. And our lives, my life, would have been so much poorer.'

'He'll always be my dad,' said Iris, hugging her tightly. 'And you'll always be my mum. I want to learn about the other side of me, but that won't ever change.'

'We won't feel any different about you either sweetheart, I hope you know that.'

'I do. It made me think about Sabine too when I was walking through Paris. I can see she's always put what was best for me above her own feelings, letting me stay where she knew I'd be safe and looked after and grow to be the best I could be. Between the three of you, you were the best parents I could have ever had.'

'Thank you, darling.' Nora kissed her. 'And I hope you'll always know that it was no sacrifice, not for any of us. We had to be apart to keep you safe, but you and your sister have enriched all our lives. You always will.'

And they stood arm in arm, holding each other close, as the protective wall of the harbour closed around them, and the sea finally calmed, taking them home.

A LETTER FROM THE AUTHOR

Dear reader,

Huge thanks for reading *The Last Train from Paris*. I hope you were swept along with the journeys of Nora and Sabine, Valérie and Violette – and little Poupée, of course! If you would like to join other readers in hearing all about my new releases and bonus content, you can sign up here:

www.stormpublishing.co/juliet-greenwood

If you enjoyed this book and could spare a few moments to leave a review that would be hugely appreciated. Even a short review can make all the difference in encouraging a reader to discover my books for the first time. Thank you so much!

I so hope you enjoyed *The Last Train from Paris*. It's a story I've been longing to write, ever since I was a little girl and my mum first told me about studying French near Paris on the day war broke out in 1939. I couldn't imagine then what it must have been like to have been a 17-year-old English girl, on her own, catching the train to Calais through a country preparing for war and, like Nora, finding herself on a ferry in the middle of the Channel, being stalked by a German submarine. It's a story that's haunted me, especially since we found the letters Mum exchanged with my dad in London, and the scribbled note she sent him when she finally arrived in Dover. I also remember visiting her French friends and relatives, some of whom were forced to flee like Sabine, heading from Paris towards safety with nothing more than they could carry.

All the characters in *The Last Train from Paris* are imaginary, as are their stories, but they are woven from my research and things my mum told me, along with memories of my teachers at school, several of whom were refugees from France and Germany, along with Holocaust survivors. These were people I viewed simply old at the time, but I hope can now see more clearly as the young girl who survived a concentration camp, the German teenager fleeing alone through war-torn Europe as his only chance of survival. All survivors of human cruelty, saved by human kindness, who lived their lives forever touched by what they had experienced.

When I started writing this story, I had no way of knowing that I would be following Sabine along the perilous roads of WW2 France just as pictures started appearing on our TVs showing families fleeing Ukraine. For weeks I stopped, unable to carry on. But then I remembered my mum, and how she never forgot the families she saw on French stations saying goodbye forever, or how she waited in the darkness and the silence of the ferry for the torpedo to strike. That made me even more passionate about writing this story. I have tried to tell it with truth, and to the best of my ability. And in the hope that it's something we never have to face again – and that we never forget.

Thanks again for being part of this amazing journey with me and I hope you'll stay in touch – I have so many more stories and ideas to entertain you with!

Juliet

www.julietgreenwood.co.uk

facebook.com/juliet.greenwood

twitter.com/julietgreenwood

instagram.com/julietgreenwood

ACKNOWLEDGEMENTS

First of all, I would like to thank Kathryn Taussig for being such an insightful and enthusiastic editor, and for taking on this story and allowing it to flourish. I'm loving working with you! I also owe a huge debt of gratitude to my structural editor, Emma Beswetherick, for cutting through the impossible knots I'd tied myself into, setting me on the path to making this book the best it can be. And many thanks to everyone at Storm – your energy and enthusiasm is inspiring!

I would also like to thank my amazing agent, Judith Murdoch, without whom this book would never have seen the light of day.

Many, many thanks to everyone, from all sides, too many to mention, who shared their stories. You will always be with me. I would also like to give special thanks to Sally for the expertise and the insights into the impact of trauma. And merci and thank you to Fran, Gael, Jess and Tilly.

Thank you, as ever, to my friends and family for their patience and understanding, and my fellow dogwalkers for helping ensure there is a happy, muddy and dishevelled dog snoozing at my feet while I work. A big thank you also Trisha Ashley and Louise Marley for keeping me going with support and constant exchanges of ideas, as well as the members of Novelistas Ink, for inspiration, coffee and writerly conversations. And thanks once more to fellow author, the inimitable Carol Lovekin, for never allowing the passion for the craft of writing to fade, or creative despair to take hold – with (mostly) virtual chocolate and (definitely) real laughter along the way. And finally, as ever, diolch/thank you to Dave and Nerys, Catrin and Delyth, for being the best of neighbours – writing this story has confirmed to me more than ever that a strong community remains the greatest gift of all.

Made in the USA
Las Vegas, NV
06 May 2024

89618928R00225